THE LOSER TAKES ALL

JOSEPH AMAEZE

DARUDAN PUBLISHING

First Published 2023
By Darudan Publishing

Milton Keynes, Buckinghamshire, U.K

www.darudanpublishing.com

ISBN: 978-0-9935860-5-7

Printed in Great Britain by Lightning Source UK Ltd

Cover design: Rebecacovers

Image used with kind permission of © Pexels

To those who have learnt in every situation
to be content
Philippians 4:11-13

PROLOGUE

Hertfordshire, England – Autumn 2008

It was the sort of day that started off dry and bright then unexpectedly turned cloudy.

'It looks like rain,' muttered Sue, the middle-aged, white sandwich van proprietor to the tall, dark-skinned police officer standing beside her mobile sandwich van.

Sergeant Roger Downey glanced up at the greying sky and nodded. The forecast had promised clear skies.

'Doesn't seem to be harming business though,' he observed, glancing at the drivers munching her sandwiches in the warm cabins of their large haulage trucks.

'But your presence is,' said Sue grumpily.

For Downey and his partner, Joe Baker, visiting Sue's van in the lay-by along a quiet dual-carriageway was a weekly ritual.

As well as being a useful source of information about local criminal activities, Sue also prepared arguably the best snacks of any mobile catering service in the region. Being regulars, Sue knew that Downey always had a large ham, cheese and tomato packaged in a mini baguette, whilst Joe was partial to a malted bread BLT.

'Maybe you should stop calling by so early in the day,' she mumbled, as she wrapped up their meals. 'You know how uneasy this lot get when they spot you lads.'

Downey grinned grimly. Her apprehension was not misplaced. Long distance drivers hated pulling into lay-bys where there was a police presence, because of the potential impromptu inspection of their cargo. It was highly likely that they had radioed to alert others.

'So, what's hot right now?' asked Downey.

Sue glanced around her casually. 'There's a foreign crew targeting late model Bentleys.'

'We know about the thefts. There's been three in the past month. What do you know about the crew?'

'They're Eastern European and very high-tech.'

'Come on Sue, I need specifics.'

Sue surveyed the lay-by again. 'They have links to a Luton-based logistics business exporting out of Tilbury.'

'A logistics business?' he mused.

His thoughts were punctuated by the roar of a powerful engine, and as he swung towards the road, a large blue Bentley whipped past, doing well in excess of the 70 mph speed limit.

'Someone's obviously running late,' drawled Sue, handing Downey the two large sandwiches in a brown paper bag.

Downey snatched the sandwiches unceremoniously and hurried over to his patrol car, a Volvo station wagon. He dived into the passenger seat next to Joe Baker, who was already speaking over the radio, and buckled up.

'Let's go!' barked Downey, slamming the door shut.

The Volvo leapt off in pursuit, spitting loose gravel behind it, and Baker switched on the siren. As the flashing blue lights came on, traffic ahead compliantly scrambled out of the way. Baker was one of the most proficient drivers in the Hertfordshire Constabulary Road Police Unit. A veteran of almost twenty-five years, he still did amazing things behind the wheel of any car on any terrain.

'He's headed east!' said Baker urgently, as they dominated the fast lane, 'but we need aerial cover.'

Downey activated the console mounted VASCAR unit, identified himself, then listened attentively as the chopper pilot overhead relayed the vehicle's registration and its present location. The vehicle was a late model Bentley Continental, and it was wearing a private licence plate. Using the information obtained, Downey quickly ran a DVLA search, supplying the registration and vehicle make to the licensing

—

authority. Roughly one minute later, the computer was reeling out the vehicle owner's personal data.

His name was Gordon Pinsent, aged thirty-seven, and he resided in the affluent suburb of Radlett. Though it wore a private licence plate, the Bentley was registered to his private company, hinting that he was a well-heeled company director. The vehicle hadn't been reported stolen, at least not yet, but it was certainly being driven as if it had been, by a wheelman who was giving Joe Baker a run for his money.

Several miles later, guided by navigation from the chopper above and propelled by Joe's ferocious driving skills, they found themselves sitting on the tail of their quarry, weaving in and out of traffic along the A5183 road to Radlett. At this point, Downey activated the digital video recording system.

'Is he lost?' asked Joe, braking hard to avoid a school-run SUV that blundered into their path.

'Why do you say that?' asked Downey, bracing himself against his seat for support.

'Because he's heading back to the very suburb where the motor's registered. What sort of thief does that?'

'Maybe he's a joyrider.'

Joyriders stole fast cars to drive recklessly for pleasure, wrecking them in the process, and then dumping them.

The radio suddenly went erratic with static crackling as confirmation was received that the road ahead and several side roads had been sealed off by local mobile patrols. Downey sighed with relief at the impending conclusion to the breathless roller coaster. This was the wrong time of day for a high-speed pursuit through a small town. It was the busiest hour of the morning when parents did the school run increasing the risk of collateral damage.

Looking ahead, Downey noted the roadblock created by half a dozen patrol vehicles and braced himself. Baker slowed down, but the Bentley sped up and they watched in disbelief, as it skidded onto the pavement sending pedestrians scattering in all directions. The driver shoved the car through a narrow gap between a parade of shops and a bus stop, sped around the roadblock and re-joined the road at the other end. Unable to emulate his quarry, Joe braked hard, using the handbrake to intensify the process.

'What now?' asked Downey, glancing sideways at his red-faced partner whose chest was heaving from the exertion.

'It's up to them,' muttered Joe, gazing skyward as the police helicopter above maintained the pursuit.

Downey didn't respond as his brain furiously tried to figure out their next move. He was still pondering, when the video display from the helicopter revealed their target racing through the streets of Radlett.

'I know that location,' said Downey pensively. 'He's definitely heading back to the registered address.'

'Yeah?' asked Joe, looking at him quizzically.

'Yeah,' confirmed Downey. 'I don't think we're dealing with a theft here.'

Joe shrugged and quickly backed-up the vehicle, using the handbrake to execute a neat U-turn. Driving at a more casual pace without siren, but keeping the blue lights flashing, they headed in the direction of the Bentley's registered address. As they drove up the short, gravelled driveway of a Mediterranean-styled villa, in the heart of Radlett, Downey's heart sank. The only vehicle parked outside the house was a black Range Rover.

'Are you sure about this?' asked Joe, pulling up behind it.

Downey didn't respond but considered the possibility that he'd got it wrong.

The radio suddenly crackled into life, and the chopper provided an update on the vehicle's location and direction. Downey's countenance brightened and he punched one fist lightly into the palm of his other hand. His theory had been right. Both men alighted from the vehicle and stretched their limbs in anticipation. Seconds later, the battle-scarred Bentley crunched its way onto the driveway and abruptly pulled up.

Downey strutted towards the driver's door like a cowboy in a Western, and his grim stare met the buoyant grin of the dishevelled white male driver, clad in rumpled pyjamas. The

—

8

man's face sported two-day old stubble and his spiky brown hair was unkempt. From the crazed glint in his eyes, he looked like a kid who'd just survived his first bungee jump.

'Step out of the vehicle, please,' said Downey, stopping beside the vehicle's open door.

'With pleasure!' said the driver, getting out jauntily. His grin broadened as he surveyed the damage he'd inflicted on the expensive vehicle's coach line. 'What a rush!'

'I hope you still feel that way twelve months from now,' said Downey, relaxing his limbs, realising that he was unlikely to be dealing with an offence of resisting arrest.

'You know something about my future officer?'

Downey was about to respond but was interrupted by the arrival of several patrol vehicles pulling up on the road. Half a dozen flustered police officers alighted, but remained on the pavement, assessing the situation dispassionately.

'Gordon Pinsent?' asked Downey taking a step closer.

'In the flesh, my good man, in the flesh.'

'Have you been drinking, sir?' asked Downey, sniffing the air around Gordon Pinsent.

'I believe I had a large tequila for breakfast.'

Downey took a deep breath, knowing that he would have to breathalyse him, but wondering whether he ought to summon his colleagues over to assist. As he considered his next move, a flatbed truck pulled up outside, and its befuddled driver was immediately swamped by several police officers.

'Before I book you for dangerous driving,' said Downey, turning back to Gordon Pinsent, 'I need to breathalyse you.'

'Why?'

'Because I can't book you for driving under the influence without it. But believe me mate, whichever way you look at it, you're getting a custodial for this morning's little stunt.'

'Now, that's where you're wrong, officer,' said Gordon Pinsent, laughing maniacally. 'You see, I've got this whole thing figured out.'

'What are you on about?'

'This,' said Pinsent, fishing one hand into his breast pocket and producing what looked like a business card. 'It all begins with this,' he muttered with momentary sobriety, 'but it was never supposed to end this way.'

He shook his head slowly and with a careless flick of the wrist, he let the thin card flutter from his fingers and float downwards to rest on the ground between them.

Downey involuntarily glanced down at the card, his eyes registering the details.

M. Ammon

Venture Capitalist

Cell Phone: 01-666-666

Downey's gaze lifted just in time to see Pinsent draw a small black revolver from beneath his pyjamas. Downey froze, realising that the rules of engagement had just changed. For a nanosecond, their eyes locked in a gaze that seemed to transcend time. Downey's startled eyes confronted Gordon's frenzied ones and then, in the furthest recesses of his mind, he heard the loud report of the revolver unloading a bullet. He watched, frame by frame, as Gordon's eyes glazed over, and his body jolted before flopping forward with blood spurting forth from his skull.

Oblivious to the hysterical voices in the background, Downey stepped backwards mechanically, creating room for Gordon Pinsent's dead weight to crash unhindered onto the gravelled driveway.

Downey felt half a dozen arms gripping him almost at the same time and heard the same number of concerned voices enquiring if he was okay. As he was steered back to his patrol car, he singled out Joe Baker's voice above the noise. After he had been carefully arranged on the front passenger seat, he stared numbly through the windscreen at the death scene. In a daze, he observed Joe heading towards the front door of the Pinsent residence, and in the back of his mind heard the cacophony of urgent voices speaking over the car's radio, updating each other on the incident in Radlett. Despite the frenetic activity, the image of Gordon Pinsent's demonised gaze colonised his thoughts and the maniacal laugh of the tormented soul echoed in his ears.

*　*　*　*　*　*　*

Downey vaguely recollected the short journey from the death scene to the local police station at St Albans. He was met on arrival by a cute looking Asian lady with an empathetic smile, who gave him a cup of tea and some digestive biscuits.

The woman introduced herself as a counsellor, and gently pumped him for information about his wellbeing, eventually giving up when he wasn't forthcoming. In the background, he overheard her conversation with the station superintendent, as she recommended that he be given at least a month's leave to recuperate from the trauma.

After what seemed like an eternity, Joe Baker showed up and, in complete disregard for the counsellor's instruction to leave his partner alone, began to update Downey about the events that had unfolded after he'd left.

According to Joe, after Gordon's suicide, he had gone to see if anyone was in the deceased's house. However, when he received no response to his repeated ringing of the front doorbell, he'd arranged for a search warrant and then invaded the property. Inside the house, they'd found three bodies belonging to a young woman in her thirties and twin girls aged about five. Forensics' initial assessment indicated that all three had died less than four hours before, but more tests were being carried out. All three had died from single gunshot wounds to the back of the head, and ballistics indicated that they'd been killed with the same gun that Gordon Pinsent had eventually turned on himself.

The driver of the flatbed truck was an agent for a company

specialising in the repossession of vehicles with outstanding finance. It transpired that Gordon Pinsent was bankrupt following the winding–up, four months before, of his medical supply business, resulting in the redundancies of twenty staff.

Pinsent was obviously aware that the Bentley was due for repossession that morning which probably explained his bizarre last-minute joyride after murdering his family. The house itself had already been repossessed by the mortgage providers and sold at auction. All Gordon owned in the world were the clothes on his back. The motive for the multiple homicides was inevitably down to the stress resulting from the downturn in his financial affairs.

Downey absorbed the information in silence. He suddenly recalled the business card Pinsent had been brandishing before he died and spoke for the first time since the incident.

'Who is M. Ammon?'

Joe Shrugged. 'Pinsent's financial adviser perhaps.'

'We need to find him.'

'I'm on it.'

Downey heaved a sigh. 'Surely there was another way out.'

'Another way out of what?'

'The mess he was in.'

'Perhaps,' said Joe, 'but when you invest in a snake pit, you should expect to get bitten.'

Downey looked up at his partner's impassive face and wondered how anyone could be so insensitive.

DOWNEY'S DILEMMA

1

Downey struggled to avert his eyes from the portrait of Mother Teresa on the wall of Kirsten Thorpe's modestly furnished office. The expression of serenity on her face was having a more positive effect on him than Kirsten's carefully choreographed smiles and inflections. A short middle-aged woman with fiery-red hair and prominent freckles, she reminded him of the strict headteacher at the comprehensive he'd attended about two decades ago.

In her quest for familiarity, Kirsten had insisted on calling him 'Roger,' ignoring his discomfort. He hated it because the maths teacher who once assured him that he would amount to nothing was named Roger. He'd considered changing it by deed poll, but never got around to it. Anyway, all his mates called him *Downey,* so his first name was redundant by default. Only anticipating a couple of sessions with Kirsten before being pronounced fit for duty, he'd played along. But when she revealed that she would be seeing him at fortnightly intervals over the next six months, he'd regretted his acquiescence.

It had been over two months since the incident in Radlett, but frequent nightmares and a nervous disposition frustrated his efforts to resume patrol duties. To aid his recovery, the occupational health team had referred him to Kirsten, a contracted trauma therapist. This was their second session, but despite her best efforts to engage, Downey found it uncomfortable looking into her probative green eyes.

The first session had been taken up with discussing the rules of engagement as well as the clinical approach for the duration of their time together. At that session, the portrait of Mother Teresa had provided a sporadic source of great comfort. But it looked like Kirsten had noted his diversion.

'She was a remarkable woman, wasn't she?' remarked Kirsten, glancing behind her at the object of his attention.

'Yes, she was,' agreed Downey. 'Did you know her?'

Kirsten shook her head. 'I wish I did, though,' she mused. 'I'm told we have a lot in common.'

Downey kept a straight face.

'So, are you still having the palpitations?' she asked, peering at him through the frameless spectacles perched at the tip of her nose.

Downey nodded even though Kirsten already had that information in her notes. At the first session she'd suggested hypnosis as a means of probing his mind, but he'd declined for fear of spending the rest of his life braying like a mule because of some failed experiment. There had to be a simpler way of neutralising the recurrent flashbacks.

'And this nervous disposition only began after you witnessed the suicide?'

'That's correct,' answered Downey, stopping short of reminding her that she'd asked precisely the same question at the start of the session.

'And are you on any sort of medication for this condition?'

Downey shook his head sullenly.

He had a sneaking feeling that she was just trying to make up her contracted hours.

'It must be terrible for you having to cope with the trauma without any medication. She tried to convey empathy but fell far short. 'I can't imagine how it must feel having a broken sleep pattern.'

Downey shrugged, unwilling to give anything away.

'Does the erratic sleep pattern have an adverse effect on your concentration?'

Downey shook his head slowly, maintaining indifference

in the hope that she would get the message. But she merely smiled warmly in response, infuriating him. In her eyes he was probably a repressed client who needed to unburden himself.

'Tell me about yourself.'

The question was out of the blue.

'You've got my file.'

'Yes, but I want to hear about you from you.'

'What do you need to know?'

'You decide.'

'Well, I'm originally from Barbados. I've been in the Police Force coming up to twenty years, I'm married with two teenage daughters, and I'm a practising Christian.'

'How's your marriage?'

The question threw him momentarily. He shrugged and briefly averted his gaze. 'Like all marriages it takes work, but its strong.'

'Are you close?'

'Me and my wife? Of course.'

'What about your mother-in-law?'

Downey frowned. 'We get along – why?'

'Interracial marriages have their challenges.'

'Like any other. How is this relevant?'

She'd clearly done her homework on him, so he couldn't understand her inquisition.

'I'm just trying to build up a picture,' she replied. 'What about your daughters?'

'We're close.'

'Still living at home?'

'One's away at university and the other is in secondary school – so still living at home.'

'And how are your finances?'

It was another question that threw him.

'In good shape – I pay all my bills on time and have no credit cards.'

'Loans? Mortgage?'

'Car loan, mortgage – I thought this was a counselling session.'

16

'I'm still trying to build up a picture.'

'What do my finances have to do with my health?'

'Potentially everything, as you discovered the other day.'

'I'm not suicidal.'

Her patronising smile upset him. 'Does your wife work?'

He paused before answering. He hated the intrusion, but his Superintendent had advised him to cooperate, as Kirsten's report mattered. It was a choice between a return to active duty, a desk job, or medical retirement.

'She got laid off three months ago.'

'What was her job?'

'She was the Chief Planning Officer at Waldon Town Borough Council.'

'So, you're the sole income earner?'

'For the time being. She's got a severance package, so we're all right. She's also actively looking for a new role.'

'And how will you cope if she doesn't find another job before her package runs out?'

'We'll survive – we've been through tough times before and God saw us through.'

'God?'

Downey nodded slowly, steeling himself for the expected scepticism.

'Your faith is admirable,' she said stroking her chin, 'we've all got to believe in something…'

'In someone,' he interjected.

'Yes, in your case – someone. But I guess I'm trying to establish in a practical sense how you would manage a downturn in your finances or say in the event of a recession.'

'We've got savings and we're pretty sensible.'

'Ah, that's better,' she said scribbling in her notebook.

'But we'll still trust God to bring us through.'

She stopped writing and her flustered face met his calm stare, betraying the first sign of vulnerability. She quickly regained her composure.

'Is it all right if we explore your childhood at our next session?' she asked, hinting that the session was about to finish. 'I'm keen to hear about any early experiences which might possibly shed some more light on the situation.'

'Is it relevant?' asked Downey, cringing at the thought of having to travel back down memory lane.

'It could help you identify the root of the problem.'

Downey sucked in his breath to emit a groan but caught himself in time. She had probably already diagnosed him as passive-aggressive and any display of exasperation might see him referred for anger-management therapy.

'If we must. I'll give it some thought.'

He faltered as soon as the words escaped his lips, realising that he had unwittingly betrayed his unease. Kirsten would conclude that he had some great childhood secret buried away in the depths of his mind requiring mental excavation. Her thin-lipped smile confirmed his worst fears and he rose with the weight of the world on his shoulders.

'Till the next time,' he muttered.

'Don't worry Roger,' said Kirsten, with an exuberant grin that did nothing to put him at ease. 'With your co-operation and my skills, I'm confident we'll have you back in uniform in no time at all.'

Downey nodded dejectedly and trudged toward the door.

*　*　*　*　*　*　*

'I guess she's only trying to help,' said Sally-Ann, handing him a mug of aromatic Jamaican coffee.

Downey sipped the brew, assimilating its rich flavour for a moment, before lowering the cup and shaking his head.

'She's doing her job,' he said hoarsely, 'but making a right pig's ear out of it; she's an incompetent...' His voice faltered before the expletive escaped his lips.

'That's a bit strong,' observed Sally-Ann, seating herself on the cosy Chesterfield, cup of tea in hand.

Downey stared across his living room at an old photo of his daughters, before taking a ponderous sip from his cup.

'I'm nothing more than a statistic to her,' he said firmly,

'someone she can add to her tally of professional conquests. That one-size-fits-all approach just doesn't cut it with me.'

There was silence as they sipped their beverages, avoiding eye contact, each reluctant to restart the conversation.

Sally-Ann understood her husband's difficulty with having to attend counselling sessions. She however saw it as her duty to encourage him not to give in to depression. Having herself been a victim of post-natal depression after the birth of Emily, her second daughter, she knew first-hand the mental complications that could form a cell within a person's mind.

In her case, it had been six months of psychological hell and recovery had been jerky. During that season, Downey had taken time off work to care for Naomi their first daughter and baby Emily, ensuring that neither child was left alone with their mother for any length of time. Now, in his hour of need, she was struggling to repay the favour.

This was the *'for better or worse'* that she had recited so eloquently when they'd exchanged marital vows twenty years ago in a registry office, in the presence of six friends and the registry official. The tall, dark, bright-eyed young Sidney Poitier look-alike, who'd swept her off her feet at the tender age of nineteen, was now reduced to a hollow shell, who woke up most nights shivering and perspiring. He still professed a strong faith in God and read his bible every day, but night after night he relived the nightmare that had imprisoned him.

She'd allowed him space to indulge in his favourite pastime of sketching, uninterrupted, but he had lost interest even in that. She'd taken over the chores he normally helped with like mowing the lawn and taking out the garbage, as he was neglecting to do them. Fortunately, Emily, their last born was on hand to assist most evenings when she came back from school. With her older sister away at university, Emily had grown into a mature young thirteen-year-old who enjoyed cooking healthy gourmet meals for her father.

'I can't take this anymore!' said Downey suddenly. 'God, why me? Why do I still feel like this? What have I done to deserve this? How long am I to suffer?'

These were questions she'd heard before but learnt never to intervene as it only increased his agitation. As was her custom, she excused herself, leaving him immersed in tormented monologue.

Out of boredom, rather than necessity, Sally-Ann busied herself cleaning-up the kitchen. Sporadically, her mind roved over life before the incident that had bestowed on her a quasi-widow status.

She missed her job as chief planning officer at Waldon Town Borough Council. Her profession had kept her meaningfully engaged and provided a different frame of reference. Being apart from her husband most of the day had enriched their relationship, enhancing the value of any shared time. Unfortunately, she'd lost her job several months ago, in circumstances that still left a bad taste in her mouth. Following an unsuccessful internal appeal, she was considering an appeal to the employment tribunal, but the most challenging aspect was not being able to discuss her claim with Downey.

Whenever she moaned to her mum, she was reminded that it was less strenuous nursing a psychologically damaged man than a physically disabled one, like her father.

Her father had served as a pilot in the RAF and survived active service in enemy territory. He retired early to indulge in his hobby of restoring old light aircraft, only to crash-land the first plane he'd worked on, sustaining a spinal injury that rendered him wheelchair-bound for the rest of his life. The burden of caring for a paralysed man with an active mind fell to herself and her mum, but not even their combined efforts could lift his spirits or quell his belligerent self-pity. To make matters worse, her job in the council provided no respite from the constant demands of the grumpy Falklands War veteran.

Two years later, Downey walked into her life, in the most unromantic of circumstances. He was a newly qualified constable who had pulled her over for speeding but let her off with a caution in exchange for her phone number. Seeing an escape route from the drudgery of home life, she had seized the opportunity with open arms. He called her that evening,

20

and they met up. It helped that he was charming and looked extremely appealing in uniform. Her mum adored him, even though the same couldn't be said of her dad.

Her father's objection was simple. Downey was black and she was a fair-skinned, blue-eyed, straw-haired romantic novice who'd lived a sheltered life. In dad's eyes they were racially incompatible. Dad was always cordial to Downey but never warmed to him.

Ignoring her father's objections, she'd married her Romeo five months after their first date and quickly moved into his studio flat, carefully omitting to mention that she was four months pregnant. Their honeymoon had been a formality, but her first real holiday abroad, away from dreary Waldon Town. They'd flown out to Australia to see his cousin, a chef, who'd emigrated there, and her mind still retained a vivid slideshow of that subliminal experience. Waking up to blue sky, sunshine, humid climate, and the lithe, dark skinned hunk named Roger Downey was the highlight of that moment.

Her dad had passed away over a decade ago and, Elsie – her mum – had remarried, getting hitched to the local vicar, who looked like a younger version of her dad. All had been uneventful for a while, until that afternoon when Downey arrived home early and headed straight to bed, without bothering to explain why.

The ringing of the doorbell jolted her out of her reverie, and she went to answer the door.

'If it's for me, I'm not in!' called out Downey.

She desperately hoped that it was Sharon, their next-door neighbour, or at the very worst her mum, come to check up on her. Downey's reclusive behaviour meant that well-wishers who called to see him often departed in frustration, as she had to explain that he was either sleeping or out walking the dog. On several occasions, she'd blushed with embarrassment as the callers heard his voice in the background, reiterating his instruction for her to tell them that he wasn't in. She hated lying, especially to close family friends. Lying undermined her faith but it was a conundrum. Right now, she needed alternative company and a possible shopping companion to provide respite.

She composed herself before opening the door, and her heart sank as she saw Joe Baker standing there, grinning toothily. In the background, she could see his classic Ford Capri, with a flame-haired beauty in the front passenger seat. The girl looked young enough to be his daughter, and Sally-Ann suppressed a frown. She knew Joe and his wife Gillian were going through marital problems but had been led to believe that they were on the path to reconciliation.

'Sally!' exclaimed Joe boisterously, approaching her with open arms and pecking her on both cheeks. 'Is he sleeping or out walking the dog?'

She knew Joe could see through her excuses but was determined not to betray her husband.

'Eh, he's not in,' she said awkwardly.

'Hmm,' said Joe, with a crafty smirk on his chubby face. 'Now, that's a new one.'

She pretended not to have heard, but instead looked past him at the girl in his sports car.

'Your daughter?' she asked innocently.

'My niece,' replied Joe, with a knowing wink. 'She's visiting from Ireland.'

'Was she stranded by any chance?'

Joe ditched the crafty grin. 'Look, Sally,' he said, altering his tone, 'we both know your husband's at home. Now, I realise how awkward it is for you because he doesn't want to see anyone, but I'm not leaving here till I see him.'

Sally-Ann sucked in her breath and averted her eyes from Joe's placid but enquiring stare. She hated being put in these sorts of situations and her thoughts became mangled as she mentally scurried around, looking for a way out.

In her apprehension, she frantically tried to adjust her countenance, fearing that it had exposed her. Without a mirror for feedback, she could only grin and pray that her crimson complexion didn't betray her depth of unease.

In the living room, a sense of guilt and shame began to

rack Downey's mind. Lying didn't come easily to him either and he realised that it was unfair to expect a greater degree of impropriety from her than he did of himself. His instincts for self-preservation had blinded him to the effect the endless deception was having on Sally-Ann.

With a muffled groan, he rose and trudged to the door like a man walking through freshly mixed cement. He paused at the doorway that led from the hallway to the living room, and strained his ears, till he recognised Joe Baker's voice.

Sally-Ann was on the verge of reiterating her lie about Downey's absence, when she sensed his presence behind her and turned to confront him. Neither of them spoke as Downey telepathically apologised. She simply nodded in the direction of Joe and silently headed back to the kitchen. Downey waited till she had departed.

'She was acting on my instructions,' he said quietly as Joe's eyes met his.

'I know,' said Joe. 'She's an honourable lady.'

There was momentary awkward silence.

'Look,' said Joe, pitching in first, 'I don't think it's right for me to come in after what's just happened. I reckon she'll need some space for a bit. Why don't we head out to the Horse and Canary and catch up?'

Downey considered the proposal. Despite his reticence, he knew it was the most sensible thing to do.

'I'll just grab my wallet,' he said, turning to go inside.

'Just grab your jacket,' said Joe. 'The drinks are on me.'

'Who's that?' asked Downey, eyeing the young lady in Joe's car, as he reached for his leather jacket on a cloak rack.

'My niece,' answered Joe simply.

∗　∗　∗　∗　∗　∗　∗

The Horse and Canary pub was sparsely populated when they arrived, but Downey was surprised to find two of his colleagues from Hertfordshire Constabulary glued by their lips to large pints of lager.

Barry and Martin greeted him heartily each fussing over getting him a drink and poking fun at his choice of pineapple juice. Despite their jocularity, however, he detected slight hesitancy in their laughter.

Joe had probably briefed them because they studiously avoided the usual spate of vulgar jokes. Everyone in his team knew Downey was outspoken about his faith and many poked fun at him because of it. Today the mood was more respectful, but when his pineapple juice arrived and he tasted the alcohol in it, he couldn't resist a quivering chuckle. It wasn't clear who was behind the prank, but he appreciated the gesture.

Whilst Joe's 'niece' went to play on the pinball machine, Joe explained how, amid his impending divorce, he was discovering relatives he never knew he had and how they all appeared to be pretty, and young enough to do all the things his wife was no longer interested in. Downey listened but unlike the others he could detect the hint of despondency in his partner's voice. Joe was clearly putting on a front. He wasn't as happy as he wanted them to believe he was.

'Aren't you afraid of Gillian wiping out your savings?' asked Barry, starting to unwind.

'That's always a risk,' agreed Joe, with a nervous guffaw.

'Unfortunately, it's an uninsurable one,' said Downey, relishing the taste of alcohol after two months of abstinence.

'Yeah, and worst of all, she could raid your pension,' added Martin, 'frustrating your plans for all those newly discovered young, attractive relatives.'

All four erupted with laughter, and Downey felt himself losing some of the tension. He hadn't laughed in a long while, and he'd forgotten how good it made him feel.

'So, Downey, when are you coming back or are you planning to quit on medical grounds?' asked Martin.

Downey noticed Joe flashing warning signals via squinted eye to the tipsy police constable, but Martin pressed on.

'What was it about the shooting that messed up your mind anyway?' he asked, leaning forward.

'If he knew that, he'd be back at work, wouldn't he?' cut in

Joe vehemently. 'Now quit playing psychologist and talk about the weather or something.'

Downey was taken aback by the thrust of Martin's questions and stared at him blankly unsure whether to say something or just hide behind Joe's timely intervention.

He was still struggling with indecision when the sound of raised voices provided reprieve. They turned toward the pub's counter where a handsome young Asian man in a handmade suit was ordering drinks for a group of admiring punters.

'Vijay Pandya,' said Barry distastefully, 'he wins the lottery and now he thinks he's a Bollywood star.'

'That's Zula's brother isn't it?' asked Downey.

'Yeah.'

Zula Pandya was a well-liked constable in Hertfordshire Constabulary who was in an interracial marriage but had retained her maiden name.

'I hear that he was selected to join the Apple Seed Project,' said Joe, 'and since then he's moved up in the world.'

'Apple Seed Project?' asked Downey.

'It's a community development scheme run by Eden Fruit Foundation,' answered Martin. 'It invests in young entrepreneurs from disadvantaged backgrounds, developing them into community leaders to drive regional growth.'

'They call it economic empowerment,' added Joe.

''They invest something like £700,000 in those they call Gold Seed partners,' said Barry, sipping his drink morosely.

'That's a lot of money,' said Downey.

'Yeah, it's like winning the lottery,' said Barry.

'And how are they selected?'

'They apply, stating what they propose to use the funds for. Their objectives have to be entrepreneurial and include some social value initiative.'

'Sounds laudable.'

'You mean laughable,' muttered Joe. 'It's a gimmick by big business to be seen to have a conscience.'

'But there have been a couple of success stories,' said Martin. 'I hear that Amy McBride the hairdresser is also an

Apple Seed Project partner.'

'Yeah, and Nicole Matisse that Art college student who used to pull pints here is another,' said Barry. 'The Landlord confirmed that she moved out six months ago.'

'She was gorgeous,' said Joe smirking, 'and I loved her accent – French wasn't it.'

'Calm down boy,' chuckled Martin.

'You should apply, Downey,' said Barry. 'I hear the Project is strong on diversity.'

'That's right,' said Martin, 'and they'll probably give you enough dosh to hire a really good shrink…'

Martin's voice faltered as Joe shook his head slowly. 'I didn't mean it like that…,' he began.

'I know,' said Downey, playing it down resiliently. 'It's awkward. Until you experience something like that you don't know how it's going to affect you.'

'But don't you ever wonder why he did it?' asked Barry.

'Why who did what?'

'Why the Pinsent guy killed himself and his family,' said Barry. 'I mean let's face it, he had other options.'

'Such as?' invited Joe.

'He could have liquidated his assets and then legged it with his family,' answered Barry, 'or he could have hidden his assets offshore and then faced his creditors. What's the worst that could have happened to him?'

'Bankruptcy?' offered Joe.

'Precisely,' said Barry. 'These aren't the Victorian times where you get sent to debtor's prison.'

'But think about the stigma,' said Joe.

'Suicide carries a stigma too.'

'Yes, but what about his state of mind at the time?' Joe countered.

'Yeah, that might be,' said Martin, 'but what kind of pressure would make a perfectly normal bloke lose his marbles and go on a massacre? My Uncle Ned was forced to close his furniture business in Leeds last year because it was on the verge of insolvency. He lost his house and his life savings, but he's rebuilding his life, and working on a new business plan.'

'People handle pressure differently,' pointed out Joe, pausing to sip his pint. 'Your uncle was probably one of those strong, silent types brought up in an era where real men didn't show weakness or buckle under pressure.'

Downey stayed outside the conversation, choosing instead to soak up the unconvincing viewpoints. He'd read in the newspapers how an army private, returned from a tour of duty in the Middle East to face home repossession due to outstanding mortgage arrears. He'd tried to make a stand against the bailiffs who'd turned up to evict him, but when that failed, he'd set fire to the property and taken his own life. The private had grown up in a rough part of East London and prior to the army had been in the most ruthless gang in his neighbourhood. So, why had *he* folded like a pack of cards?

'What's on your mind, mate?' asked Joe, leaning sideways.

'Nothing,' replied Downey.

'You sure?'

Downey nodded and then something occurred to him.

'Have you tracked down the guy on the business card?'

'M. Ammon?'

'Yes. Do we know anything about him?'

Joe shook his head. 'The number was disconnected and he's not in the Yellow Pages or the electoral register.'

Joe's 'niece' returned, causing all eyes around the table to momentarily swing in her direction.

'You want to know the worst thing about that Pinsent guy?' asked Barry tipsily. 'He shot himself on his birthday. Now how sick is that?'

Downey reckoned that he'd heard enough and rose to his feet. 'Take me home, Joe,' he said softly.

* * * * * * *

That night Downey laid awake in bed dwelling on the latter part of the uncomfortable discussion with his mates. In fact, he'd thought of nothing else all evening.

Noting his demeanour, Sally-Ann had given him space. Dinner was eaten in silence, and they'd sat watching a gameshow on TV without any exchange. They'd gone to bed together but as had become customary, she had rolled over to her side and faced the other way. He sensed she wasn't sleeping and half an hour into their bedtime, she spoke.

'Emily asked me if you were having an affair.'

Downey froze and turned to her in the gloom, noting that she was still backing him. It was an odd sort of question and he wondered whether it had indeed come from Emily.

'Why?' he managed to ask.

'Because you haven't told her about the suicide you witnessed – she's old enough to know.'

He didn't respond. Emily was only thirteen and he had no intention of letting her know. He however began to think about Sally-Ann – something he hadn't done in a while. He hoped she was confident enough in their relationship to trust that he would never have an affair. But, after the strain of the past two months, he wondered whether she still felt secure in the marriage. He hadn't made love to her since his breakdown, though she'd never been the demanding type. He could also sense her frustration whenever she tried to curl up next to him and he flinched or rolled away.

'She's got an inquisitive mind.'

'Perhaps,' answered Sally-Ann gently.

Sally-Ann's laconic answers were often quite deep.

A part of him wanted to reach out to her, to reassure her, and make love to her till she was convinced beyond all reasonable doubt that he still cared for her. But the more dispassionate part of him couldn't be bothered. She hadn't become less attractive; he'd just become less interested.

2

As the choir struck up for what he hoped was the final hymn, Simon Fay saw Roger and Sally-Ann rising from their pew and followed suit. It had been over two months since he'd last seen Roger. Although he'd occasionally bumped into Sally-Ann in Waldon Town's shopping mall, she never had any useful update on her husband.

Today was his chance to confront his closest mate, and the best man at his wedding. He needed to get to the bottom of why Downey had become so reclusive.

'Shouldn't we wait till the vicar leaves?' asked Diane, making no effort to copy his example. 'It's simple courtesy.'

'I've got to get to Downey before he sees me and makes a run for it,' said Simon urgently, edging his way towards the nearest aisle. 'I'll see you outside.'

'But what if he doesn't want to see you?'

'He'll see me all right,' grunted Simon.

Diane clicked her tongue irritably as her husband hurried out of the church and wondered at the idiocy of one-sided friendships.

From the outset, she'd never liked Roger. Yes, he was pleasant enough and strikingly good looking, for a black person, but they'd never hit it off. She still recalled his underwhelming response when Simon first introduced her to him as his fiancée. Having got over the shock of discovering that her blond-haired, blue-eyed fiancé's best friend was black, she was livid when Simon informed her that Roger felt their marital plans were too hasty. Fortunately, she'd been able to persuade Simon that six weeks wasn't too short for a courtship, citing her mother who'd married her father a fortnight after they'd first met. At the time, she'd omitted to mention that her relationship with the man she called 'father' wasn't biological. Her biological father had walked out on her mum the day he discovered she was pregnant.

Simon only found out the truth a year later when he'd stumbled upon her birth certificate. At the time, he'd muttered something about wishing he'd listened to Roger's advice. For that, she hated Roger Downey and delighted in calling him 'Roger' even though Simon had made it clear that Roger preferred to be addressed by his surname. When she heard about his breakdown, she'd secretly hoped it would fragment his relationship with her husband.

Simon sighted his friend getting into the front passenger side of a BMW SUV and hurried over, obstructing the closing door with his shoulder.

'Hello, Downey,' said Simon, 'long time no see.'

'It's good to see you, Simon,' said Downey awkwardly, realising he'd been cornered. 'How's Diane?'

Simon shrugged. 'The same,' he answered.

Downey nodded. He knew Diane hated his guts.

From the corner of his eye, Simon noticed Sally-Ann's reddening complexion and sensed from her body language that she didn't approve of her husband's behaviour.

'Sorry, I've not been in touch,' mumbled Downey, struggling to make conversation.

'Sorry doesn't cut it,' fired back Simon. 'I've been worried sick about you!'

Downey knew his friend was upset. Simon had been to the house dozens of times over the past two months and bombarded the phone line, but Downey hadn't been motivated enough to either see him or take his calls. A part of him wanted to reconnect socially but another part couldn't be bothered to make the effort.

'Ah, Roger!' said the vicar, appearing out of nowhere and

standing beside Simon. 'I thought I saw you at the back of the church during the service.'

He was a jovial, barrel-chested man with fluffy grey hair that extended down to his massive sideburns. His twinkling eyes, reddish complexion and bulbous nose conveyed a reassuring bonhomie that reminded his parishioners of Father Christmas, a role which he frequently performed for local schools each festive season.

'Good morning, Vicar,' said Sally-Ann, sounding relieved for the intervention. 'That was a really inspiring sermon.'

'I'm glad you liked it,' said the vicar, beaming proudly. 'I've long advocated that the love of money is the root of all evil.' His countenance dipped slightly, as he searched both Downey's and Simon's faces for concurrence.

'I hope everyone else received it in good faith,' he went on. 'After all, it is a rather sensitive topic.'

'Your message was spot on,' said Simon, smiling awkwardly. 'There's far too much avarice about these days.'

'Yes, quite so,' said the vicar ponderously. 'Don't you agree Downey?'

The query startled Downey who had been studiously avoiding eye contact with the spiritual leader of St Joseph's Anglican Church. How was he supposed to answer?

John Asker, the vicar of St Joseph's, also happened to be Sally-Ann's stepfather and Downey's father-in-law. John was a poignant fellow with a proclivity for putting people on the spot, subjecting them to his brand of evangelical inquisition. Downey felt guilty, because he'd also been avoiding the vicar who had called by the house on a number of occasions.

'Yes, I agree,' mumbled Downey, struggling to inject some enthusiasm into his tone; 'money is the root of all evil.'

'I believe you mean the *love* of money,' said John softly.

'Yes, that's right,' said Downey, through gritted teeth.

'Too much greed,' said John, clasping both large hands together loudly. 'So, how's your recovery coming along?'

'I'm on the mend,' answered Downey shiftily.

The vicar nodded to himself but looked like he was

expecting a lengthier response. 'I would love to stay and chat,' he said after a brief lull, 'but I just came over to suggest that we catch up. How about lunch at the Horse and Canary?'

'Today?'

'Why not. It's been a while since we met up for our traditional Sunday pub-lunch date.'

'Well, I don't know,' said Downey, battling to think of a plausible excuse. 'It is a bit sudden…'

'Nonsense!' said John, 'the weather's great and we can sit in the pub's grounds soaking up the sun and stuffing ourselves with ale and roast. What do you say?'

'Great I'm up for it,' said Sally-Ann to Downey's dismay.

'Excellent,' said John, 'Shall we say twelve thirty? You should come along too Simon and bring Diane.'

'Thank you, Vicar, we'd be delighted to.'

Downey's heart sank but he had no strength to protest.

'Good, I'll see you all later,' said John, turning on his heel and striding back towards the church.

'I'm expecting to receive the full low-down Downey,' said Simon quietly before heading towards his car.

Downey groaned.

'Here's your chance at redemption,' said Sally-Ann, starting the vehicle's engine.

'What's that supposed to mean?' asked Downey bitterly.

'You're the cop in the house,' she replied coolly, 'so you figure it out.'

*　*　*　*　*　*　*

The Horse and Canary was Waldon Town's busiest pub and as always it was heaving. John and Elsie Asker, Downey and Sally-Ann, and Simon and Diane were seated in the large grounds doing what so many families in the community did on a Sunday afternoon. The British pub lunch was a tradition. As was their pattern, they split into two groups after demolishing their Sunday roast, with the women drifting to another table to catch-up and the men availing themselves of the opportunity for frank discussion. It was a watershed moment for Downey and against the dictates of his discomfort he unburdened himself.

At the end of his tale which started with Gordon Pinsent's suicide and ended with his referral for counselling, he was surprised by the wealth of empathy he received. The vicar was particularly tearful whilst Simon was intensely subdued. Their reactions were unexpected, and this made him reflective and a tad remorseful. He'd blocked them out, preferring to suffer in silence, but looking back now it was crazy.

'I had no idea mate,' mumbled Simon, patting him across the shoulder. 'Here I was thinking it was a mid-life crisis.'

'Sadly, I knew him,' said John Asker, dabbing at the corners of his eyes with a handkerchief.

'Gordon Pinsent?' asked Downey, perking up.

'Yes, he used to be one of my parishioners.'

'Did you realise he was battling those demons?'

John shook his head slowly. 'I had no idea you were battling yours. When people stop showing up on a Sunday and start avoiding your calls and visits, all you can do is pray for them. Sometimes God reveals what's going on and other times you have to find out through the media.'

'So, what do you think happened to him?'

'The Apple Seed Project.'

'He was one of their partners?'

'Yes.' The vicar's voice was grave.

'Surely that's a good thing,' interjected Simon.

John Asker shrugged. 'It depends on your definition.'

'Well, I've heard some partners are doing really well,' said Simon, reaching for his pint of bitter and taking a deep sip.

'Such as Vijay Pandya and Amy McBride?' asked Downey, recalling information gleaned from his colleagues.

'Yes, absolutely!' said Simon lowering his pint. 'I think the project is a great example of corporate social responsibility.'

'It's exploitative,' grunted the vicar.

'Look John,' said Simon. 'It's a shame about Gordon, but there's got to be another reason for his suicide.'

'I hear that the project is all about creating and empowering regional leaders to promote economic growth within their communities,' said Downey.

'And who will those leaders be more loyal to? Their communities or Apple Seed?' asked John.

Downey shrugged.

'He who pays the piper dictates the tune,' said John ponderously. 'I last spoke with Gordon about three years ago, at the peak of his success. We met at the Town Hall where he was applying for planning permission for an extension to his business premises. It was a brief but poignant chat.'

'What did you talk about?' asked Downey.

The vicar shook his head, as if realising that he had said too much. 'He'd changed. His views on life were troubling.'

'Maybe you never really knew him.'

'I buried Gordon Pinsent and his family eight weeks ago — four coffins containing the bodies of people I knew intimately well. I married the couple; I christened their daughters and now — I've presided over their funerals.'

Downey's curiosity was stirred. 'So, what had changed?'

'He wanted me to speak with his wife. They were having marital problems because he was away from home a lot. He wanted me to make her see reason — help her to see that everything he was doing was because of her. He said she was small-minded and too easily content. He claimed she didn't share his vision for financial empowerment and that that was putting a strain on their relationship.'

'Well, that's a surprise,' said Downey. 'Lots of couples break up due to the lack of money rather than an excess of it.'

'Hmm,' murmured John. 'I told him to try listening to her, as having more money wasn't the route to fulfilment. But he didn't take that too well and said it was why the church had ceased to be relevant. He said a lot of other unprintable stuff and walked away in a huff.'

'Sounds like he was under a lot of stress,' said Simon, 'maybe there was an underlying psychological challenge.'

'More like a need for anger management,' said Downey.

'When I first met him, he was the complete opposite,' said the vicar quietly. 'He was happy with his career as a technician and his part-time role as youth counsellor in church. He lived modestly and gave generously. I never saw him flare-up or give in to stress or mood swings.'

Simon shook his head vigorously. 'And so, you're saying that his wealth produced an emotion that wasn't already buried deep within him? I don't buy that.'

There was a pause.

'I suppose you heard what happened to poor Paul Munnelly,' said the vicar, clasping his hands beneath his chin.

'The garage owner?' asked Simon. 'Yeah, that was terrible.'

Downey, who had boycotted all forms of media since the start of his sick leave, sat up.

'Who's he and what happened to him?' he asked.

'Ghastly episode,' said John, oblivious to Downey's query. 'They say the bank manager is still pretty shaken-up about it.'

'Who's Paul Munnelly?' asked Downey wearily.

'…and I knew him quite well, too,' went on Simon, now deeply engrossed in the topic. 'He serviced my car some months ago, and we were talking about his expansion plans within Waldon Valley.'

'It's an indictment against the entire banking system!' boomed the vicar, shaking his head emphatically. 'Mercy is an alien word to those brood of vipers.'

'Will someone please tell me who he is and what happened to him?' asked Downey frustratedly.

They turned towards him, stunned by his raised tone. The vicar cleared his throat.

'Paul Munnelly was a young mechanic who jumped out of the third-floor window of his local bank last Friday,' said John. 'It was in all the local papers and has caused quite a stir all over Waldon Town.'

Downey wanted to know whether Paul had died but was unsure how the others would react.

'Was it a suicide?' he asked jerkily.

'Attempted,' said Simon, shaking his head sadly, 'though

I'm sure after the prognosis, he'll wish he'd been successful.'

'Thank God he survived,' said the vicar with a gentle sigh.

'That's one sentiment I'm not sure he shares,' said Simon morosely. 'When he landed on the pavement, he damaged his spine. They say he's in a critical condition and that he may never walk again.'

'Oh no!' said Downey with a hollow gasp. 'How ghastly!'

'Yes, quite so,' agreed the vicar. 'It's why I based my sermon on the love of money.'

'Was he wealthy?'

'He used to be, but it seems he'd fallen on hard times and had gone to the bank to arrange a loan. Oh, by the way, he happened to be an Apple Seed partner – chew on that.'

The rest of the discussion revolved around society's obsession with wealth and the various get rich scams which were ensnaring the greedy and the gullible. Downey listened and chipped in every now and then, but his thoughts were centred on Paul Munnelly.

* * * * * * *

The first thing Downey did when he got home that evening was head to his study, boot his dusty desktop computer and surf the internet. He scrolled through a popular news website until he arrived at the headlines for Hertfordshire and then started to search for all news items relating to Paul Munnelly. A couple of clicks later, he was reading about the twenty-five-year-old mechanic's suicide attempt.

According to the latest news report, Munnelly had broken both legs in the fall and damaged his spine. He'd been moved to a hospital in Stanmore that specialised in spinal injuries, but the physicians weren't optimistic about his chances of making a full recovery.

The news report detailed how Munnelly had gone to the local bank to finalise arrangements for a business loan, which got turned down at the last minute. In despair, Munnelly had hurled himself through a window after telling the female banker who'd been attending to him that his life was over anyway. She'd watched in a daze, too stunned to raise an alarm until she heard the sound of his body hit the pavement.

The police were still investigating and the detective in charge of the investigation, Inspector Wajid Hussain, assured the news reporter that early enquiries ruled out any suspicious circumstances surrounding the incident.

Downey knew Inspector Hussain. They'd joined the force at the same time, but Hussain had shown great skill and aptitude very early on in his career and been fast-tracked to Inspector. Joe Baker had hinted recently that Hussain was in line for another promotion following the successful investigation into the serial murders of some local prostitutes. Downey liked Hussain, and even though it had been a while since they'd been in touch, whenever they did meet up, it was always cordial. Hussain, undoubtedly, knew a lot more about the Munnelly case than he'd divulged to the news reporters and Downey's inquisitive side was beginning to stimulate a line of thought that had to be concluded.

Why would a young mechanic with a promising future jump out of a window just because he'd been refused a business loan? What had driven him to such an act of desperation? There were other lenders who would probably give him the funds at a slightly higher rate of interest, so there was no obvious reason why he'd become so despondent.

Downey recalled his conversation with Joe, Martin, and Barry, a week ago. He also remembered the newspaper article about the soldier who was facing repossession and ended up burning his home and taking his life in the process.

His curiosity was aroused, and he was gripped by deep-rooted desire to unravel the mystery of why some people facing financial difficulties cracked under the pressure of mounting debts. He hoped that in delving beneath the surface of the gruesome phenomenon, he could confront his demons and unravel the mystery of his psychological challenges.

The more he considered his proposal, the more invigorated he felt. For the first time in more than two months, he felt motivated to do something other than lounging about, bemoaning his fate. Suddenly, he could see light at the end of an ominous tunnel.

'Why have you suddenly become so fixated with that young man?' asked Sally-Ann, intruding upon his thoughts.

He turned towards her and grinned, much to her surprise. She couldn't recall when she'd last seen him this amiable. She drew closer, reaching out a furtive hand to touch his shoulder, almost expecting him to recoil. To her pleasant surprise, he tilted the side of his face towards the palm of her hand affectionately sandwiching it between his cheek and shoulder.

The unexpected display of affection from her husband almost knocked her for six. As she struggled to regulate her breathing, she felt heaviness in her bosom, a mixture of fear and expectation that was overwhelming. Was Downey on the path to recovery or was this merely a temporary remission preceding a worse episode?

Whatever it was, she was determined to milk it for all it was worth. She had a pressing need, and tonight looked like the night the drought would be addressed.

She reached out with her other hand, to gently massage his short kinky hair, easing her fingers through his tightly coiled strands till the excitement threatened to choke her.

'Let's go to bed,' she whispered, as he reached backwards with one hand to touch her ear heightening her excitement.

'That's the best idea I've heard all month,' he replied, slowly rising to his feet.

*　*　*　*　*　*　*

Inspector Hussain's office was in a nondescript building located on an unremarkable street in Waldon Town, lined with concrete memorials of drab seventies architecture. By flashing his warrant card around, doors opened before Downey until he arrived in the tight open-plan office space that served as Hussain's operational HQ. Wajid was not expecting him, but his smile was warm and inviting, nevertheless. They shook hands firmly, and after Downey had declined offers of tea and coffee, he was taken into one of the adjoining meeting rooms where Hussain thrust his legs on top of the desk clasping his hands behind the back of his head.

He was a smallish man with premature, male pattern baldness which he compensated for by sporting a shoe brush-like moustache that overlapped his upper lip.

'I'm here about the Paul Munnelly case,' said Downey, getting to the point.

'The attempted suicide,' said Wajid brightly. 'Have you got useful intel for me?'

Downey shook his head. 'I've got a personal interest in this,' he said, lowering his voice. 'I'm sure you've heard about what happened to me a couple of months ago.'

Wajid nodded and his expression became grave. 'Very unfortunate,' he murmured. 'Are you back on duty?'

Downey shook his head again. He knew he was going to have to level with the Inspector if he was going to get his full and continuous cooperation.

'Do you know Munnelly, personally, that is?' asked Wajid.

'No, I only know what I read in the news,' said Downey. 'My interest stems from the incident I witnessed.'

'The Pinsent guy, right?'

Downey nodded slowly.

'Is there a connection with the Pinsent case?'

'Yes, the Apple Seed Project – they were both partners.'

'That hardly counts as suspicious'

'Agreed, but they'd both reached a point where the weight of financial burden drove them to consider suicide.'

'And that interests you?'

'Yes. It might be the key to why I reacted so badly.'

Wajid studied Downey's countenance and his soft brown eyes appraised him, searching for signs of imbalance such as, palpitations, fidgeting, erratic eye movement or other unusual body language, but he found none.

He'd known Downey a long time and knew that he was as straight as an arrow. He recalled how Downey had always intervened in the early days at Police College, when he was subjected to racial abuse, and his respect for the dark giant had appreciated over the years. He knew Downey wouldn't be asking for the information if it wasn't absolutely necessary.

'Look, if it bothers you,' said Downey apprehensively, 'skip the sensitive personal data and just give me a broad outline with sufficient clues for me to figure out the rest.'

'Don't be silly,' said Wajid, looking him straight in the eye. 'I'll tell you what you need to know. Munnelly ran a garage in the industrial park north of Waldon Town. As part of an expansion plan, he approached several banks for a loan but kept getting rejections until he applied to the Sloane Bank who approved his application in principle and asked to see a structured business plan. Munnelly got a firm of management consultants to draw up his business plan for him and forked out a small fortune for their services.

Munnelly turned up for a meeting with the banker to discuss the details of his loan application only to find out that it had been rejected. Apparently, there were inconsistencies in the figures he'd quoted, and to cap it all the bank discovered that the HMRC was investigating him for filing inaccurate tax returns. Munnelly blames his accountant.'

'That's hardly enough for him to want to take his life,' interjected Downey. 'There has to be more.'

'I agree,' said Wajid, 'but Munnelly isn't cooperating. The banker who witnessed his jump, says she hadn't noticed anything unusual about his behaviour up until that point, and had no reason to imagine that he'd do anything so drastic.'

'It doesn't add up,' said Downey, musing over the particulars. 'I take it you've investigated his business dealings and financial affairs.'

'We're running checks on his accounts and speaking to known associates, but nothing unusual has surfaced yet,' answered Wajid. 'His obstinacy just complicates things.'

'He's feeling sorry for himself,' suggested Downey. 'You know what it's like. Once he's adjusted to the fact that he might never walk again, maybe he'll be more cooperative.'

40

'Unfortunately, I don't share your optimism,' said Wajid, with a slight frown. 'I'm facing all sorts of challenges here. To tell the truth, I'd love to wrap this one up and redeploy my resources. I'm under pressure from above to cut costs.'

'Maybe I can help,' said Downey, without thinking. 'I'd like to speak with Paul Munnelly if that's all right with you.'

Wajid turned the request over in his head, weighing all the pros and cons. A decision had already been taken to shut down the Munnelly investigation, because there was no perceived mileage in rummaging through the debris of an attempted suicide.

'All you want to do is to speak with him?' asked Wajid.

'That's all,' answered Downey, 'and, in return, I'll update you on anything of substance.'

Wajid considered the offer briskly and then nodded. He could see the benefits of having someone not on his payroll conducting an investigation and passing the credit to him, if there was any to be had. It was a no-brainer.

'You've got a deal,' said Wajid, swinging his legs off the desk. 'I'll get you the necessary clearance to see Munnelly in the Spinal Injuries Unit and to speak to any of his associates if you feel that'll help, but if there's an angle, I get all the glory.'

'Agreed,' said Downey, 'but does that mean I also get to see his financial accounts?'

Wajid assessed the data protection risk and then nodded. 'I'm sure we can arrange that if it will help.'

'Thanks, Wajid,' said Downey, 'you won't regret it.'

3

Downey alighted from the minicab that had brought him to the Orthopaedic Hospital at Brockley Hill, pondering over the bizarre chain of events that had led him to a patient in the Spinal Injuries Unit. For all he knew, it could be a wild goose chase. On the other hand, there was a slim possibility that it might prove insightful. At the main entrance, he was given directions to the Spinal Injuries Unit which was sited in another building within the complex.

By flashing his warrant card at the hospital staff, he received maximum cooperation and in less than ten minutes, he was standing next to the bed occupied by a docile-looking Paul Munnelly. Staring down at the bedridden young man, Downey immediately recognised the face and racked his brain until it clicked. He'd met the young man at one of Kirsten Thorpe's group therapy sessions. At the time they'd only exchanged first names, but Downey never forgot a face.

The young mechanic on the orthopaedic bed stared up at him blankly, not blinking, and for a moment Downey was tempted to check his pulse. Oddly, there was no facial bruising or upper limb injuries, but his posture told its own story.

Downey put himself in Munnelly's position. Paul had less to live for now than before his suicide attempt, and Downey was convinced that given the chance he might attempt it again.

'Paul, my name's Roger Downey,' said Downey, 'but my

mates just call me *Downey*. If you recall, we met at one of Kirsten Thorpe's group therapy sessions.' He paused to observe Munnelly's countenance but when he didn't register even a flicker of interest, he carried on talking. 'I'm a sergeant with the Road Policing Unit,' he said, 'but I'm currently on extended sick leave, because I reacted quite badly to a suicide that occurred right in front of me.'

He noticed Munnelly's eyelids blink and registered a slight head movement. As Munnelly tried to alter his line of vision, Downey felt rewarded. Having caught the young man's attention, he quickly pressed home his advantage.

'At night, I have recurring nightmares and wake up perspiring,' said Downey opening up. 'Most mornings, I'm too exhausted from my erratic sleep pattern to do anything useful.' As he spoke, he studied Paul's reaction.

'I've been unable to return to active duty,' he continued, 'because of the lasting impression the suicide left on me, and I've become a virtual recluse.'

Paul Munnelly slowly turned towards Downey, and the grimace on his face showed how much discomfort he was in.

'The man who shot himself in front of me was a total stranger,' said Downey, warming to his subject, 'but his facial features are indelibly imprinted in my mind. Now he lives with me, and he isn't a stranger anymore.' He paused for effect.

'Unfortunately, before he killed himself, he also killed his wife and two children. We now know that he'd been going through a rough financial patch. He owed hundreds of thousands to various creditors and was struggling to keep up with repayments. One of his creditors made him bankrupt and set-in motion the fatal chain of events. However, one thing puzzles me, and this is precisely where I need your help.'

He looked carefully at Paul Munnelly whose eyes were now fully on him.

'What was going through that man's mind when he put a gun to his head and decided to end it all?' asked Downey.

'Emptiness,' said Munnelly quietly, in a distinct Irish accent. 'Low self-esteem, fear, shame, anger – take your pick.'

'But couldn't he have exhausted all the other options available to him?'

'Maybe he's already exhausted them,' answered Munnelly.

'So, this is his way out,' said Downey, 'the last stand.'

'Yes,' agreed Munnelly. 'He's had enough. He hates life; it's not worth it.'

'But has he *really* exhausted all his options, or does he just believe he has?'

Munnelly didn't answer, but Downey could see from his furrowed brow that he was thinking furiously.

'He's the best judge of that, after all he's the one in the ring contending,' said Munnelly, after the brief interval.

'That's true,' answered Downey, 'but what if he sincerely believed he'd exhausted all his options when, in actual fact, due to insufficient information, he hadn't?'

Munnelly took longer to respond this time and Downey assessed the situation. He'd succeeded in getting Munnelly talking about himself but recognised the need for sensitivity.

'What other option was there?' asked Munnelly, after three lengthy minutes. From the look on his face, it was clear that he was desperately seeking answers.

Downey was keen not to lose any of the gains he'd worked so hard for. He had to convince Munnelly that he was also on a journey of discovery because men in Munnelly's situation only spoke to fellow travellers.

'But did he have to also kill his wife and children?' asked Downey rhetorically.

'Maybe he felt a sense of responsibility towards them and couldn't bear the thought of leaving them alone.'

'That wasn't his choice to make – it was theirs.'

'So, you're calling him selfish?'

Downey back-pedalled. 'I'm not qualified to judge,' he answered quietly. 'Besides, even if he'd spared his wife and children, they might still label him as selfish.'

'Well, I don't have that problem,' blurted out Munnelly, throwing caution to the wind.

'You don't have any loved ones who would miss you if you

died?' asked Downey, looking pained.

Munnelly stared out into open space and pondered. He recalled Downey's face from one of the group therapy sessions he'd attended, but had no desire to relive the episode, as the sessions had been worthless. Right now, he had bigger problems. The prognosis for his spinal injury was bleak and he wished that he could have a second attempt at ending it all. Sergeant Downey was an all-right guy who said all the right things and appeared genuine. But Munnelly didn't know how to stress that no two suicide-related cases were the same.

'There's often more to suicide than meets the eye,' said Munnelly, blinking back droplets of tears.

'I'm here to learn,' said Downey expectantly.

'What if the man who shot himself in front of you was hearing voices?' asked Munnelly, struggling to control the tear drops, 'and those voices were very persuasive?'

'I hadn't thought of that,' admitted Downey truthfully, 'but even if that were possible, where do those voices come from?'

'Inside his head,' said Munnelly heavily. 'They are constant, always persuasive, always demanding. They urge him to end it all, as there's nothing to live for. The longer they speak, the stronger his conviction, till he twigs that they're right. Life is vanity, breathing is futility, but death brings liberty.'

'Despite their persuasiveness, what if they'd got him believing a lie?'

Munnelly considered the question and found himself entertaining doubts about the veracity of the voices in his head. They told him that he had no close family to mourn him and that if he died, he wouldn't be missed. They told him that to carry on living was to embrace failure, but death held the key to victory.

The voices said that if he couldn't even arrange a little business loan, it was evidence that life had closed the doors of prosperity to him. One voice said life had reserved the wilderness of despair for him because he couldn't get his act together. He'd believed the voices and vowed to take his own life if his loan application was rejected. After seven loan rejections, Munnelly knew that his expansion plans were dangling by the slimmest of threads. He'd already spent all his profit on hiring management consultants to professionally facelift his business, but that had been money down the drain.

Pondering over the decision to share his story with the police officer beside his bed, Munnelly's mind roved over the events preceding his crisis. It wasn't a short tale of woe but a protracted narrative of the migration of wisdom by one who ought to know better. It would take hours if not days to share and he dreaded the prospect of reliving the trauma or hearing his own voice narrating those events. He knew he would have to share the story eventually if only out of a sense of moral obligation. But for now, he felt more comfortable just mentally roving over the events of the cautionary tale.

THE MUNNELLY AFFAIR
(The Bait)

4

At the age of twenty-one, Paul Munnelly became the proprietor of Munnelly and Sons – a vehicle service centre in Waldon Town specialising in Japanese vehicles.

For close to twenty years, Munnelly and Sons had carved out a reputation for punctuality that was the envy of other vehicle service centres in Waldon Town. Not only were their opening and closing hours strictly observed, but the mechanics always managed to finish their allocated jobs in the designated time and to a high standard. The efficiency of the business rivalled that of much larger franchises which had the backing of motoring associations and manufacturers. Over the years, as many of those businesses closed shop, Munnelly and Sons grew from strength to strength.

Built from scratch by Paul's late father – Albert Munnelly, an Irish mechanic from Belfast, Munnelly and Sons opened in a quiet cul-de-sac behind the Munnelly family residence in Waldon Town, much to the irritation of their neighbours.

Following a campaign by neighbours who resented tatty vehicles being repaired in front of their homes, Albert had been forced to fork out the rent on a lock-up in a small industrial estate and move shop.

Business in the early days had been slow and barely brought in enough to justify the effort expended, but Albert plied his trade doggedly, refusing to attend to any other vehicles except Japanese brands. Word soon spread amongst motorists that Albert was the man to see if their Nissans, Toyotas, Hondas and Mazdas needed repairing. Building up a reputation as a specialist in Japanese vehicles at a time when most service centres specialised in more mainstream vehicles of European origin, he was soon receiving more business than he could handle. The growth in business resulted in the need for urgent but, in Albert's eyes, modest expansion.

Munnelly and Sons had moved into new premises, a large workshop in Waldon Town that had once been occupied by a furniture manufacturer and were instantly inundated with service requests. Expanding his workforce from an initial three to fifteen, Albert created an effective delivery schedule with parts suppliers to ensure that jobs could be completed as and when the customer had been promised they would be. At the heart of Albert's business strategy were his three Hs – honesty, humility, and hardiness.

Albert also took a pay cut so he could offer higher wages than his competitors and attract the best technicians and mechanics. At the commencement of trading, Albert traded as Munnelly and Sons, looking forward to the day when his young sons would join the business as apprentices.

Unfortunately for Albert, his older son, Matthew, had zero interest in cars preferring male modelling instead. An Adonis in stature, at age ten, Matthew began to get occasional work, modelling school uniforms for clothing catalogues. Because he was almost six feet tall at age thirteen, and hairy for his age, he secured full-time modelling work for men's magazines.

With one son out of the frame, all eyes turned on Paul who, fortunately loved cars and took a keen interest in his father's trade. Lacking Matthew's imposing athletic stature, Paul had to make do with an average height and build. In all other respects, he was a carbon copy of his father. At sixteen, Paul joined the business full-time, realising quite early on that there was no future for him in higher education.

To Paul's dismay, the business name remained as

'Munnelly and Sons', even though there was no realistic prospect of Matthew having a change of heart.

Paul's love of engines led him to experiment with tuning, and he quickly began to discover solutions to the power deficiency experienced by smaller capacity Japanese engines. Dabbling with superchargers and turbochargers as a means of coaxing more power, he began to attract a new generation of boy racers who desired more spunk from their multi-valve engines. Albert was quick to notice the potential in that line of business and acquired the lease to the adjacent workshop as soon as it became available so that Munnelly and Sons could have an engine-tuning arm to be run by Paul.

Despite the exciting prospect of running his own set-up, Paul resented his father's constant interference, especially with regards to the business accounts. Albert had grown up influenced by a generational work ethic that declared *'all work and no play guarantees steady profits,'* and he lived that maxim to the full. Albert also believed that an Irish pound earned was an Irish pound saved and so practised a fastidious saving culture that thrived on self-denial and delayed gratification.

Unlike Albert, Paul was more charitable, especially with young female customers, offering them large discounts which worried Albert. For this reason, Albert studied the accounts of the tuning side of the business like a hawk, often querying basic expenses for tuning components and then double-checking with the parts suppliers to ensure that the prices hadn't been inflated.

Several times, Paul had threatened to walk out of the business because of the apparent lack of trust, but, on those occasions, Albert's apologies and promises to refrain from micromanagement always won him over. It wasn't all bad though, because Albert always gave him a healthy slice of the profits from the engine tuning business, even though most of it was paid into a trust fund that could only be accessed when Paul turned twenty-one.

For the first five years of his tenure at Munnelly and Sons, working under his father, firstly as an apprentice mechanic and then tuning specialist, Paul had acclimatised to the restrictive regime imposed on him. However, when on the eve of Paul's twenty-first birthday, his father announced, to the dismay of the whole family, that he'd been diagnosed with lung cancer and given less than six months to live, the regime was abruptly dismantled.

In his father's place, Paul was appointed acting general manager and, suddenly, the huge responsibility of running the business fell on his unprepared shoulders. Albert was only forty-two when he was diagnosed. Prior to that bombshell, Paul had lived with the expectation that his dad would be running the show for at least another twenty years.

A lifetime of chain-smoking had taken its toll on Albert's nicotine-laced lungs, and a persistent cough had turned out to be something far worse. Faced with the mountainous responsibility, Paul tried to wear two caps, running both arms of the business, and trying to satisfy both sets of customers.

When his mum quit her receptionist role in the business to care for Albert, Paul hastily recruited an attractive, blonde-haired replacement, named Cindy, who spent more time on the phone to her girlfriends than she did answering customers' calls. At his mum's behest, Cindy was replaced, much to the chagrin of the male mechanics, with a less glamorous middle-aged woman named Violet, a widow who swore like a sailor, but was ruthlessly efficient at her job. With Violet in place, things gradually began to assume a semblance of normality.

Albert defied the medical experts and struggled on for nine months, three months longer than predicted. Realising that he was losing the fight for life, he hastily drafted his will, something he'd never seen fit to do before. A customer who also happened to be a solicitor, witnessed the will in exchange for a free oil change and, two days later, Albert breathed his last. His burial attracted a hundred close relatives, friends, and customers in a small crematorium that could only seat fifty.

Matthew had been unable to attend the funeral due to a fashion shoot in Monaco, so Paul was left to read the tribute. With Albert's ashes scattered over the Irish Sea, the Munnelly clan all converged at the solicitor's office in Waldon Town for the reading of the will. Unsurprisingly, Matthew had managed to rearrange his schedule and shown up.

After a long preamble, the solicitor got around to the sharing of the estate and to Paul's surprise, Albert had left the entire assets and business of Munnelly and Sons solely to him. Albert had given the solicitor a power of attorney to cash in his insurance policies and use the proceeds to pay off the lease on the business premises occupied by Munnelly and Sons and then to buy the freehold to the site. In a gesture that had brought a lump to Paul's throat, Albert had instructed the solicitor to change the business name to 'Munnelly and Son'.

The residue of his estate was given to his wife Irene and included a generous cash lump sum and the family home, which was mortgage free. Matthew walked away, dejected at having been passed over in the will, but for Paul, however, it was the start of better things to come.

*   *   *   *   *   *   *

'Mr Munnelly, phone call!' called out Violet from the cubicle that served as reception.

Paul, who was working on the gearbox of a first-generation Lexus, sighed with despair. He was at a critical stage of the task, and he'd promised the customer that the vehicle would be ready for pick-up by five pm.

A quick glance at his timepiece indicated that the time was racing towards the four pm mark, and he wasn't amused. Munnelly and Sons had a reputation for delivering on time. Against his father's instructions, he'd reverted back to the original business name and kept the pluralized 'Sons' because it sounded better. Besides, he looked forward to the day when his own sons, if he had any, would join the family business.

'I'll be right over!' he called back.

Violet had been told to never disrupt him when he was in the middle of a job. But since she'd already given the caller the impression that he was available to take the call, it would be

———

discourteous not to take it. He turned to the apprentice mechanic who was standing next to him under the chassis of the jacked-up vehicle and shrugged.

'I'll be back,' he said apologetically.

He strolled towards the reception trying hard not to frown. From the moment Irene announced that she was returning to Belfast to live out the rest of her days, Violet had become a law unto herself. For Paul, it meant having to put up with her bizarre behaviour and abuse of protocol. Around her, he never felt like the boss.

He would've got rid of her, but for the fact that Violet had been indispensable to his mum both during Albert's illness and after his demise. Being a widow herself, she had moved into the family home to be with his mum. Before Irene returned to Belfast, she'd made him promise to keep Violet on. Unfortunately for him, Violet had been present when he'd made the promise.

He found Violet applying lipstick as he walked into the reception but pretended not to notice. An elderly Italian electrician named Giovanni, who worked three evenings a week with Munnelly and Sons, had taken a shine to her and Paul noticed that Violet always made an extra effort with her appearance on those days.

He took the cordless handset and left the reception, moving out of Violet's earshot, before answering the call. It was from a property developer named Vijay Pandya, who'd been pestering him for a fortnight to inspect a new industrial site in Waldon Town. Paul kept fobbing him off, unsure of how to convey that he couldn't afford the investment. He was, however, flattered that Vijay considered Munnelly and Sons to be the sort of business worthy of occupying premises in the ultra-modern business park which was still under construction. It was no secret that all the big hitters from the motor industry were eyeing the new site, drawn by all the extra parking space available at less cost than their existing sites. To be counted among the commercial heavyweights was intoxicating and Paul was in danger of becoming addicted.

'Mr M,' said Vijay, as Paul answered the call. 'I've sent you an invite for the open day this Friday, and I have to tell you I fought like a dog to get it. There's just so much interest, but very few spaces. So, tell me, are you up for it or what?'

Vijay was a smooth-talking, sharp-dressing, property guru who never lost his cool no matter what was said to him. Paul didn't know what impressed him more about the man, his lifestyle, or his vibes.

'I don't know, Vijay,' said Paul, trying to psyche himself up to drop the bombshell. 'I'm really kind of busy right now.'

'Mr M don't miss this,' said Vijay, cutting in edgily. 'Believe me, Sir, this is the big one and the first to get in will buy off-plan and then clean up with all the extra business that the area is billed to attract. Did you know they're planning to build the largest shopping mall in Europe, just a stone's throw from the Waldon Valley business park?'

'A shopping mall?'

'The biggest in Europe, Mr M.'

'I didn't know that. Have you mentioned this before?'

'You must've forgotten,' said Vijay, breezily. 'Anyway, if you can't make it this Friday, I'll understand; after all, you're a busy man…'

Paul swallowed the hook. 'What time is the programme?'

'Seven pm start, but I'll be there for six.'

'I'll be there for six-thirty.'

'Awesome. I'll see you then. By the way, my old man's Honda needs a service, can you fit him in tomorrow?'

'I'll see what I can do.'

'Nice one, Mr M,' replied Vijay. 'I'll be seeing you.'

After he'd hung up, Paul mused over the whole tone of the conversation and smiled wryly to himself. Vijay was more of a PR man than a property developer and his specialty was networking and deal-fixing. The programme on Friday was nothing more than a PR event, but for Paul it was important to be seen in the right company.

He'd recently acquired a couple of designer suits that *fell off the back of a truck* but had nowhere to wear them to. In the old days, Albert would've laughed at him if he'd turned up to work all dressed-up for some corporate event. The first suit Albert ever wore was at his wedding and the second was the one the undertakers dressed him in for his funeral.

Albert had hated PR events. Rubbing shoulders with car dealers and motor industry reps, whom he labelled 'synthetic rip-offs', was not his thing. But Paul was determined to transcend that mindset. This was a new era.

*   *   *   *   *   *   *

Paul knew he was looking good. Even Violet had paid him a compliment, telling him he scrubbed-up well. He had had a manicure to remove grease from his fingernails, and a fresh haircut to complete the transformation from grease monkey to city slicker. As he alighted from his car and strolled towards the main entrance of the office complex where the event was being held, he felt like a model out of a men's fashion magazine. His thoughts inevitably drifted to Matthew, his older brother, who was always well groomed and seemed to spend a fortune on his appearance. Matthew would have no problem mixing with the crowd at this evening's event.

Vijay was waiting at the entrance, looking as sharp as always. Although he was deep in conversation with several business-suited individuals, as soon as he sighted Paul, he broke away from the group, grinning brightly.

'Looking good, Mr M,' said Vijay, shaking his hand firmly. 'I'm glad you could make it.'

'I'm glad to be here,' said Paul, looking around the ground floor hall where a catering company was serving cocktails and *hors d'oeuvres* to the smattering of smartly dressed guests. People were standing around in small pockets, engaging in chit chat and as they walked in a couple of the younger women sized them up, making lingering eye contact. Paul was tempted but Vijay tugged gently at his sleeve, steering him away.

Vijay procured two crystal flutes of champagne and Paul sipped the bubbly, trying not to grimace as the sour flavour coated his tongue. He wished they'd served Guinness. He was still deciding what to do with his half full glass when Vijay drew him to one side and lowered his voice.

'Now here's the game plan, Mr M,' said Vijay, looking around him furtively. 'Just tell anyone who asks that you're the proprietor of *Munnelly's*, an exclusive automotive business outfit based in Waldon Town.'

Paul squinted at him, trying to make sense of what he was saying. 'What's wrong with Munnelly and Sons?' he asked.

'It makes you sound like a trading outfit.'

'But that's what we are,' said Paul, still trying to figure out where Vijay was going. 'How am I going to attract any new business if I don't give them the right name?'

'It doesn't matter,' said Vijay hurriedly. 'As long as you give them the correct address, they'll find you; besides most of these people drive company cars which are serviced by their fleet managers at main dealers. Tonight, all that matters is that you project yourself in a way that ensures that the property developers fall all over you and offer you a huge discount to attract you to this site.'

'What have you told them?' asked Paul uncomfortably.

'I've said you're looking at a number of other sites, as part of your expansion plan,' said Vijay, 'and told them to do all within their power to attract you to this one.'

'Why?'

'Because I know if the price is right, you'll be interested,' explained Vijay, 'which in turn means more commission for me. The developers pay me a fee for every new customer I bring them, whether or not it ends in a sale. I just get paid more if they seal the deal.'

'So, I don't even have to put down a deposit before you get your commission.'

'That's the beautiful thing about this deal, Mr M,' said Vijay, leaning closer. 'These mugs pay for the publicity, so who am I to refuse, eh?'

Paul nodded, even though he didn't understand how a person could get paid for merely facilitating an introduction.

In his line of work, anyone trying to attract new business under that arrangement would most likely go out of business in next to no time. Albert had always had a ruthless disregard for middlemen, brokers, and agents of any sort. He would never have approved of Vijay.

'So, what's in it for me?' asked Paul, drawing back slightly so that he could study Vijay's face.

'You get exposure,' answered Vijay laconically, 'and a marvellous opportunity to invest in a platinum-plated, money-spinning venture.'

'You've lost me,' confessed Paul, who could only foresee expenses with no benefits.

'It's elementary, Mr M,' said Vijay, with the laugh of one who knew more than he was letting on about. 'You lease new premises, upscale your business, attract new clientele and start to clean up big time.'

'But what if I'm happy where I am?' asked Paul cautiously.

'Then, my friend,' said Vijay sadly, 'you'll never be bigger than Albert Munnelly and, with the sort of growth potential you've got, that would be a crying shame.'

Paul soaked up the analysis and a part of him wanted to flare up and demand an apology from Vijay for the snide remark about his father. However, a part of him began to see some truth in Vijay's remark and concede that maybe Munnelly and Sons was stuck in a time warp. Sure, the business was turning over a tidy profit from the service centre and engine-tuning arms, but they weren't breaking any new ground. The competition was using Munnelly and Sons as a template for efficiency and were gradually catching up.

The reassuring thing was that the business had a loyal customer base, and repeat business accounted for almost sixty percent of turnover, which was quite a feat in a community where there was increasing choice. In justifying his decision to remain where he was, Albert Munnelly had always said, '*Know your game and stick with it.*'

'My dad was a civil servant,' said Vijay. 'He worked with the Inland Revenue for thirty years, relishing his pension and the amount of annual leave available to him each year. Then, one day, my uncle came over from India and opened an estate agent's in North London. He offered dad a partnership in the business, but my dad turned it down, saying he was happy paddling his own canoe. Within two years, my uncle owned twenty properties all over the capital, but all my dad had to show for his career was our family home, which wasn't even mortgage-free at the time. Today, dad's retired, but he looks back at his decision not to accept the partnership with regret.'

Paul knew Vijay's dad, Mr Pandya, who was one of Munnelly and Sons' oldest and most valued customers, a decent, hardworking man whose family had been thrown out of Uganda, with nothing but the clothes on their backs by Idi Amin in the 1970s. According to Albert, Mr Pandya had run a very successful textile business in Kampala and had made valuable contributions to many community-based projects.

The loss of earnings meant having to start life from scratch in the U.K, but not even the financial assistance offered by the government could persuade Mr Pandya to get involved in business again.

Paul was sure that Vijay knew the background but chose to ignore it, because it didn't gel with his philosophy.

'Here comes Mr Truman,' said Vijay in a hushed tone. 'He's the chief executive of the company developing the business park. He's an American with solid connections in Wall Street, so he's a man you need to meet.'

Paul's eyes followed the direction of Vijay's stare and sighted the powerfully built, balding, white guy in a dark double-breasted suit who was striding towards them, as if he owned the earth. As Truman came within hearing range, Vijay spun around with a look of surprise as if he were just noticing the new arrival.

'*Mr Truman,*' he said exaggeratedly, 'good to see you.'

'Looking good, Vijay,' said Truman, with a slight drawl, as he thrust one hand forward at the fascinated young Asian man. They shook hands briefly and then Vijay turned towards Paul, who felt his heartbeat accelerate slightly.

'Mr Truman,' said Vijay, gesturing towards Paul with a broad grin, 'this is one of my clients, Paul Munnelly, and he runs one of the oldest and most prestigious motoring outfits in this part of the country. He's quite graciously cancelled another event just so that he could be here, and I know you'll definitely make it worth his while.'

'Pleased to meet you, Mr Truman,' said Paul, wavering slightly as his hand met Truman's chunky sun-tanned one.

'Call me Sam,' said Truman, pumping his hand till Paul's shoulder almost popped out of its socket, 'and is it all right if I call you Paul?'

Paul nodded weakly as the imposter syndrome kicked in, wondering how on earth he'd allowed Vijay to steer him into such a nerve-racking situation. This man was a power broker, used to hanging out with captains of industry, and he'd suss out in a second that Paul wasn't a person of substance.

Paul remembered Albert's advice given during a visit to the prestigious Ascot racecourse to collect a customer's Lexus – *'When in Ascot, keep shut.'*

'Let me get you a refill,' said Sam Truman, beckoning to a passing waiter, 'and then let's talk about the future.'

'Good,' said Vijay, bowing slightly, 'I'll leave you both to it then.'

Paul watched Vijay drifting away to join a company of attractive looking females and sighed within, feeling like an abandoned child.

'So, you're looking to open a new site,' said Sam, handing him a fresh glass of champagne and relieving him of the half full glass.

'Uh-huh,' said Paul distantly.

'So, is it part of an expansion plan or are you closing down one site and looking to relocate it elsewhere?'

'Well, to be honest,' said Paul uneasily, 'I haven't really given it much thought.'

'Ah, so your business plan hasn't been finalised yet,' said Truman, gulping down a quarter of his glass's contents in one mouthful. 'It's always a difficult decision when you're looking at new sites. On the one hand, you'd like to move your HQ somewhere with a better profile, while on the other you're wondering whether to stick it out with a weak performer and watch the market.'

'Yeah, tough decision,' agreed Paul, sipping the champagne whilst trying to conceal his disgust, 'but it really depends on what's on offer.'

'The deal of your life, boy,' said Sam affably, slapping him across the back, almost knocking the wind out of him. 'I flew in all the way from Michigan to close this deal and I'm prepared to be generous. I'm offering the first ten clients who buy off-plan the chance to move into this site for thirty per cent less than the cost of their existing leases.'

Paul did the math and was impressed at the amount of potential saving for anyone moving from a less prestigious but more expensive part of town. However, he knew there had to be a catch and he hadn't heard it yet. How was Truman able to bear the loss associated with such generosity?

'I know what you're thinking, son,' said Sam Truman, downing the rest of his drink. 'How do I cover the losses I make on this deal?'

'You pass the losses on to future buyers, who'll pay the full asking price to relocate here once you've roped in all the big players,' suggested Paul, who'd spent enough time with his dad to understand how retail outlets could afford to host half price sales or the popular buy-one-get-one-free schemes.

'Precisely,' said Sam Truman grinning effusively. 'That's why this presentation isn't for everyone, except those businesses who have the kudos to attract smaller players into the vicinity. It's like fleas on a cow.'

Paul had heard that expression before. Albert had often used it when describing how retail outlets sold quality stuff to full-price-paying customers and then cleared their warehouses of slow-moving merchandise to gullible punters who paid half price for stuff that cost pennies to produce in the Far East and was probably going to be off-loaded anyway. The manufacturers and retail outlets always made a profit, as long as the bargain hunter was convinced he was getting a deal. Albert's advice was to always shop around.

'And how long do I have to make up my mind?' asked Paul, unwilling to rush in.

'Till next Wednesday,' answered Truman. 'That's when I fly back to the States.'

Paul sipped the rest of his drink unhurriedly and was grateful when a shapely brunette pulled Sam Truman to one side for a private chat. Right now, he needed space to think.

5

Paul stood, lost in thought, patiently tightening the bolts on the sump guard of the Mitsubishi rally car that was resting on the ramp above him. He didn't usually turn up for work early on Saturdays, but today he'd been in since six-thirty am. He found that he thought better when he was working.

The previous night's presentation had been an eye- opener. As the evening progressed, the hall became full of business-suited men and women who guzzled their way through gallons of champagne and spoke at the top of their voices on their blackberries and smart-phones. At one point, a large-scale model of the proposed development was rolled out for viewing and Paul, who'd been more interested in the attention to detail that had gone into the model itself, overheard some of the other invited guests discussing the buzz that it was attracting on the street and how the site was billed to become a showcase for the retail arm of the motor industry in the U.K.

There was a subsequent half hour multimedia presentation by Truman in which he painted a vision of the future of automobile retail and the role that the site would play in manifesting that vision in Britain. He stressed the importance of jumping on-board early to take advantage of the unbeatable offer, as well as the prestige of belonging to an elite community that would have first call for occupancy of future sites to be planned in other parts of the country. In addition to state-of-the-art workshops, modern showrooms and generous office space, the site would boast leisure facilities unrivalled anywhere in the country to create an experience for the whole family.

As impressed as he'd been with the quality of the presentation and the proposals for the site, Paul was hesitant to commit. Albert had passed on a debt-free business for him to manage and there was an expectation that he would keep it so. He owned the freehold to his existing site, and there was no shortage of business from customers who often booked at least a week in advance to have their vehicle attended to. Even their most visually impaired customers knew where Munnelly and Sons was located, so advertisement was restricted to a weekly entry in the local newspapers and flyers that were left at various public places.

Paul's biggest fear, however, was the challenge involved with managing a larger business. Sure, he wanted to take Munnelly and Sons to the next level and attract lucrative new business so that he could build on his father's legacy, but that was a move he wasn't ready for right now. With less than a year's managerial experience under his belt and no professional qualifications, he felt vulnerable.

On arriving home the previous night, he'd emptied his pockets of all the business cards he'd received from other invitees and noted that more than two-thirds of them bore the professional qualifications of the person named on them. Not one single one of them was a mechanic and that worried him. At his present location, his neighbours were small industrial firms and workshops run by people who'd progressed from apprenticeship to management, so he was in good company.

It had been a good night out, but this was one offer he was going to have to pass up. He resolved to phone Vijay later that afternoon to break the news to him. He didn't think the Asian deal broker would be too broken up about it, especially with all the commission Truman's corporation was paying him for the relatively painless task of introducing potential customers. It was best to back away early rather than lingering on and risk being sucked in. Albert hated procrastination in such matters.

His thoughts were intruded upon by the sound of tyres crunching to a halt at the entrance to the workshop and he diverted his gaze from the oil sump guard to a shiny black Porsche 911 Turbo that had pulled up outside. The vehicle didn't look like it could've been more than a few months old, and a quick glance at the registration plate confirmed this.

The vehicle's driver took a while to alight, and Paul remained where he was, wondering who'd bring a brand-new vehicle to his establishment. All Munnelly and Sons' customers drove older Japanese cars that no longer qualified for the manufacturer's standard three-year warranty.

The man who alighted from the Porsche was a fair-haired Caucasian clad in a sports jacket over a dark turtleneck, khakis, and expensive looking suede loafers. Though large sunglasses screened his eyes, he didn't look more than thirty years old, and he walked with a gentle swagger that projected a degree of cockiness. The wall clock near the entrance recorded the time as a few minutes past seven am, and none of his staff had turned up for work yet.

'Paul Munnelly?' asked the man, pausing beside the car that Paul was servicing, with his hands buried in his jacket pockets.

'Who wants to know?' asked Paul cautiously.

'I'm told you specialise in performance vehicles,' said the man softly, 'and I'd like you to have a look at my vehicle.' His accent was posh but difficult to place.

Paul stepped out from beneath the rally car to confront his prestigious new customer, wondering who'd done the publicity work. Face to face, the man was at least two inches taller than Paul and broader shouldered. Glancing at the man's wristwatch, Paul noted the classic looking Rolex submariner attached to his wrist, which had to be worth a small fortune.

'What seems to be the problem with it?' asked Paul, looking past him at the menacing black sports car.

'I don't know,' said the man, in the same soft tone, 'but I was hoping you could tell me.'

'What symptoms are you noticing?' asked Paul, walking towards the vehicle, 'mechanical or electrical?'

'Well, you're the expert,' said the man, 'so you tell me. It just doesn't feel right.'

Rather than pointing out that he wasn't being helpful, Paul opened the driver's door, noting the contrasting blood red leather interior and savouring its rich aroma. Reaching for the key in the ignition, he started the vehicle, triggering a powerful roar from its rear-mounted engine.

Seeing nothing unusual, he went around to the rear and popped the bonnet to inspect the engine, listening for any alien noise and studying the visible moving parts for signs of abnormality, but again he neither heard nor saw anything.

'Seems fine to me,' he said, stepping back from the vehicle. 'Besides, it's a brand-new car, so you shouldn't be having any problems with it.'

'I didn't say there was a problem with it,' said the man calmly. 'I asked you to have a look because it didn't feel right.'

'Well, I can't find any problem with it,' said Paul, getting slightly irritated, 'and my job is to locate and rectify problems.' He stopped short of saying that he wasn't a vehicle quality control inspector for Porsche. He'd inherited Albert's temperament, which was characterised by an extremely short fuse that often detonated without warning.

'Well, maybe you should test-drive it,' suggested the man, walking around to the passenger side with a thin-lipped smile.

'I'm afraid I won't be able to do that right now,' said Paul, eyeing the thoroughbred machine covetously. 'I'm the only one in the workshop, and my staff don't arrive for another hour. I could try running a diagnostic check to detect fault codes if you want.'

'Doesn't that man work for you?'

'What man?' asked Paul, looking around him quizzically, until he sighted old Giovanni, strolling towards them, puffing on a fat cigar. Giovanni never worked Saturdays because that was the day he helped his brother out at the family restaurant. Paul was surprised to see him but more curious to know how the customer had made the association between Giovanni and the workshop.

'Yes, but he doesn't work Saturdays,' said Paul remaining where he was. 'I suspect he's just here to pick up something.'

'Good morning, Mr Munnelly,' said Giovanni cheerfully. 'I didn't think I would find you here so early.'

'Hi, Giovanni,' answered Paul. 'Did you forget something?'

'No,' said Giovanni, 'the restaurant is closed for renovation, so I decided to see if there was any work for me to do over here.' He glanced at the Porsche and grinned. 'Is it an electrical problem?' he asked.

Paul shrugged. 'I'm just going out on a test drive to find out,' he said gently, shutting the hood, 'so it's a good thing you turned up. Don't answer any calls. Let them go straight to voicemail. I'm just taking it around the block.'

He got behind the wheel, and pulled away, instantly impressed with the sharp acceleration. He'd always dreamt of driving one of these vehicles and even had a large poster of one in his office. But buying one was completely out of the question, at least for the present.

'I can tell you like it,' said the man, as they glided around a gyratory at twice the speed of other traffic. 'You seem to have a keen eye for technical excellence.'

Paul glanced at his passenger with a grin but said nothing. He was too busy relishing the sensation of speed and balance.

'There's nothing wrong with this car as far as I can tell,' said Paul, setting course for the workshop, 'but if you want, I can run a diagnostic check when we go back...'

'A diagnostic check won't find anything,' said the man, reclining back in the heavily bolstered seat. 'I guess I was just expecting it to be... a little faster, perhaps.'

'How much faster do you want it to be?' asked Paul, slowing down rapidly, as he sighted a patrol car. 'There's a speed limit in this country in case you've forgotten.'

The man chuckled to himself and ran his fingers slowly through his hair, massaging his scalp.

'You're an interesting young man,' said the man, after an interval, 'almost the complete opposite of your father.'

'You knew him?' asked Paul, negotiating the turn for the industrial estate, and then accelerating all the way up to the workshop's entrance just for the thrill of it.

'Not as well as I would've liked to,' said the man as they pulled up at the workshop. 'He was quite a hard nut to crack, very set in his ways, but good company all the same.'

'I don't recall ever seeing you around here,' said Paul, switching off the ignition. 'Were you one of his customers?'

'Yes, I was,' said the man quietly, as he gazed through the windscreen, 'but that was a long time ago, long before you joined the business.'

Paul stared at him through a squint. He'd called Paul an *interesting young man*, as if he were in a different age bracket, yet at the very most he couldn't be older than thirty.

'How old do you think I am?' asked the man, taking off his sunglasses, so that his dark brown eyes framed by long lashes were unveiled; he looked almost pretty.

Paul stuck to his gut guesstimate. 'Thirty something.'

'You flatter me,' said the man, with a short laugh, 'but I'm addicted to flattery so that's okay. Actually, to put things into perspective, I was your father's customer long before Matthew took up male modelling.'

Paul wanted to burst out laughing, but something in the man's countenance arrested him. It was clear from the calm, but straight-faced expression that he wasn't making it up. He was either one of those men with exceptional genes or he'd done a nip and tuck to hold back the years; either way he looked good for a man Paul now estimated to be in his forties, about the same age as Albert when he'd died.

'You look good for your age, Mr…'

'I haven't revealed my age,' laughed the man, 'but nice try anyway. You can call me Mr Ammon, spelt with a double m.' Mr Ammon slipped his fingers beneath his jacket and drew out a business card printed on the highest quality stationery.

Paul glanced at the card and his lips curled in a smile.

‘Venture Capitalist?’ he noted out loud with inquisitively raised eyebrows.

‘I fund growth.’

Paul’s bemused stare made Mr Ammon chuckle.

‘I fund start-ups, helping them to maximise profit for the sake of profit,’ explained Mr Ammon.

‘And your mobile phone number seems kind of weird,’ observed Paul, still staring at the thin piece of pasteboard balancing between his fingertips.

‘It’s on a private access network,’ said Mr Ammon, ‘but I can assure you it works. It’s an access number only. The network will only permit calls from authorised numbers.’

Paul had never heard of a private access network, but he was intrigued. It sounded like the sort of facility reserved for the wealthy and privileged.

‘And what’s the initial for?’ asked Paul, switching topic ‘Mike? Martin? Moses?’

‘Now, that’s *not* for public consumption,’ answered Mr Ammon, stroking his chin. ‘Just call me Mr Ammon and we’ll get along fine.’

‘Okay, Mr Ammon,’ said Paul, starting to feel slightly uncomfortable in the man’s presence. ‘There’s nothing wrong with your car. Most new cars need to be fully run-in before the engines loosen-up and deliver their best. I’m sure in another five to ten thousand miles you’ll notice an increase in performance, but if not, then maybe you should head to NASA and buy a space shuttle for ultimate thrills.’

‘Now there’s a problem with that,’ said Mr Ammon slipping his sunglasses back on. ‘You see, I travel quite a lot and don’t get to use my cars very often. You won’t believe that I've got a two-year-old Ferrari in my garage that I've owned from new, but it's still got less than five hundred miles on the clock. So, you see, Mr Munnelly, I still need your help.'

'You're losing me,' said Paul truthfully.

'I need you to help me run-in this car,' answered Mr Ammon simply.

Paul jolted, as if he'd been struck by lightning. He'd received a number of weird requests in his time, but none topped this. He could understand a customer asking him to road-test a faulty vehicle as a prelude to fixing it, but no one had ever handed him a brand new hundred grand sports car and asked him to drive it till it was fully run-in before.

'I'm not going deaf, am I?' he asked, fearing that it would be confirmed.

'No, you're not,' said Mr Ammon. 'I understand that it's not the sort of work you would normally undertake, especially seeing that you're the manager of this establishment, but I would be grateful if you could do it for me as a favour.'

'But I'm not insured to drive it,' began Paul, realising that the premiums for someone his age would be sky high.

'Don't worry; I can afford to insure you,' answered Mr Ammon, obviously recognising the reason for the remark, 'and don't think I'm expecting you to do this for free. I'll cover your petrol expenses for as long as it takes till the car is run-in and, in addition, I'll pay you a thousand pounds a week for your trouble.'

Paul suddenly felt slightly light-headed. The man had to be either very generous or absolute bonkers and if he was the latter, Paul didn't want to be driving his car.

'I'm not crazy, Mr Munnelly,' said Mr Ammon, 'It's just that I trust you with my property and know that you'll look after it as if it were yours.'

Paul nodded gently, but he was still not convinced. A thousand pounds a week in addition to picking up the fuel bills for a seriously cool supercar was like winning the lottery. He was effectively being given free transport for the next five thousand miles at least and if he broke the car-in gradually, not driving it every day, he stood to gain one grand a week for the next one year. Then an alarm bell went off in his mind as he remembered income tax and VAT. He would have to record the income for tax purposes.

'If I pay you cash in hand, they'll never know,' said Mr Ammon, reading his mind, 'and why should anyone at Her Majesty's Revenue and Customs be any the wiser?'

Paul gripped the chunky steering wheel in both hands and tried to consider what Albert would do in the same situation. Knowing his dad, the allure of so much money would be too strong to pass up and he would've probably caved-in and accepted. Besides, there was a bonus.

Driving a Porsche 911 Turbo was a track-day enthusiast's dream come true. He began to imagine himself drifting in power slides around Silverstone in Northampton, relying on the huge dollops of torque to glide him around the track. Better still, he thought of all the girls he could pull on a night on the town and began to salivate internally. Only a mad man would turn down such an offer, and fortunately insanity didn't run in his family.

'Good,' said Mr Ammon, with a satisfied grin. 'That's settled. Now, I would appreciate it if you drove me home. It'll save me the hassle of calling a taxi.'

'It'll be my pleasure,' said Paul, unable to erase the boyish grin plastered across his face.

*　*　*　*　*　*　*

They drove up to a pair of huge wrought-iron gates at the end of a private road in a rural part of Buckingham, and as they drew within ten metres of them, the gates swung open of their own accord. The copper-plated plaque on the righthand gate's pillar gave the address as *Paradise Villa* and beyond the gates was a lavish white art deco style mansion. Rolling down the gravel driveway, Paul's eyes widened involuntarily at the sight of the black late model Rolls Royce Phantom parked there. Paul's heartbeat increased as he realised that he wasn't in some elaborate trance. Reality was gradually beginning to set in, and it was scary. What was happening? How had he landed in such a surreal world? And just who was this enigmatic character?

'Drive up to the front entrance, and come in, so I can get you some cash,' said Mr Ammon casually.

Paul pulled up under the porch overshadowing the front door and then hesitated as a trio of dark Dobermans emerged from nowhere and began to silently prowl around the vehicle. Though they looked trained, Paul wasn't taking any chances.

'They're harmless unless provoked,' said Mr Ammon, opening his door, 'and they're not provoked unless I require them to be.'

'I'll take your word for it,' said Paul, eyeing the hounds with trepidation.

'Come on Paul,' invited Mr Ammon, as the dogs gathered around him in the doorway, affectionately sniffing his hands. 'They won't harm you as long as I'm here.'

Paul nodded but made no move to alight from the safety of the driver's seat. Mr Ammon stepped out of the car with a brief chuckle and then emitted a low whistle which sent the dogs scurrying away in terror. Paul, however, waited for a further half minute just in case they were lurking about, before mustering enough courage to open his door and briskly alight.

Mr Ammon walked up the few steps leading to the front door and then looked back at Paul in amusement as the latter walked almost on tip toe, looking around him cautiously.

'I used to keep a couple of Pit Bulls,' said Mr Ammon, 'but I found them too frisky.'

'Hmm, that's interesting,' murmured Paul, who was still maintaining vigilance as he crept forward. 'I don't suppose you've got any Rottweilers lurking about.'

'As it so happens, I've got two on order,' said Mr Ammon, opening the front door and leading the way into the house. 'I tend to bond quite well with Rottweilers.'

Paul followed Mr Ammon into the wide hallway and paused there on the marble flooring, looking around him in fascination at the grand décor, marble columns and large paintings bordered by heavy frames, wondering how much the house was worth.

The hallway led into a vast living room that appeared to have adopted a Roman-themed design, and dead centre in the middle of the hallway was a winding marble staircase that led all the way upstairs. Mr Ammon mounted the staircase, and as he walked upstairs, he waved towards the living room.

'Make yourself comfortable in the mini bar,' he said charitably, 'and help yourself to the drinks. I'll be right back.'

Paul found the *mini* bar adjoining the living room and smirked, as he realised that it was closer in size to a small English pub. The bar was well-stocked, and he grinned with satisfaction as he opened the taps to a vat and pulled himself a foamy pint of Guinness. Finding a comfortable armchair, he stretched out and imbibed his drink as if it was the first stout he'd ever tasted. This was breakfast just the way he liked it.

'Hello,' purred a softly accented female voice, 'have you seen Mr Ammon?'

Startled by the suddenness of the intrusion, Paul almost let go of his glass and, as he struggled to retain his grip on the handle, he spilt some of the precious dark liquid on the intricately woven Persian rug beneath him. Turning in the direction of the voice, Paul literally froze.

She was about six feet tall in her knee-length riding boots into which were tucked riding breeches, and her brunette hair flowed over the shoulders of her polo shirt. Intelligent green eyes appraised him, whilst her partially parted lips offered a glimpse of even rows of perfectly formed teeth. Devoid of makeup, she was still a vision of loveliness and Paul stood rooted to the spot unsure of how to react in the presence of such unadorned beauty.

'I'm sorry I startled you,' she said, in an alluring accent that sounded French, 'but I was looking for Mr Ammon.'

Paul stared at her as if he was hard of hearing, his eyes more concerned with studying the corners of her mouth and the slight dimple in her chin.

'You *are* Mr Ammon's guest, aren't you?' she asked,

drawing closer with a slight frown, presumably unaware of the effect her appearance was having on him.

'Yes, yes,' answered Paul, snapping out of his reverie. 'Sorry, I wasn't paying attention.'

'So, where is he?'

'Who?'

'*Mr Ammon?*'

Her mouth curled slowly into a smile, and he found himself drifting off course again.

'Oh, he's upstairs,' he said quickly, resisting the temptation to fall prey to his misguided desires again.

'Ah good,' she said. 'When he comes down, could you tell him that breakfast is served on the patio…please?'

'Yes…no problem,' said Paul, discovering a rapidly diminishing coherence.

'Thank you,' she answered sweetly, before turning around and heading out of the bar, leaving him mesmerised by the elegance of her gait.

Paul watched her until she'd vanished out of sight, feeling like the poorest man on earth. Beauty, class, and charisma were lacking in all the women he'd dated, but Mr Ammon's friend had all three in spades.

'Is something wrong with the Guinness?' asked Mr Ammon, returning to the room unobtrusively with a brown envelope in his hand. 'Would you prefer some tea instead?'

'The Guinness is fine,' said Paul, reaching for his glass. 'By the way, a lady came in here looking for you.'

'Ah! Nicole,' said Mr Ammon, with a wink, as he handed the brown envelope to Paul. 'But trust me, she's no lady.'

The suggestive remark rattled Paul slightly, but he refused to allow it to pollute his mind. In his opinion, Nicole was still a goddess and worthy of his worship.

'I suppose breakfast is ready,' said Mr Ammon, leading the way out of the bar. 'I know you haven't eaten yet, so I presume that you're joining me.'

Paul nodded dumbly and followed him like a lap dog. He desperately wanted to know how Mr Ammon knew all these things. Mr Ammon led the way to the large patio at the rear, where breakfast was laid out overlooking an Olympic-size pool. A large, glass-topped breakfast table had been laid for two with a full assortment of kippers, scrambled eggs, sausages, bacon, tomatoes, and muffins, and as they sat down at opposite sides, Nicole returned with a tray laden with strawberries and peach slices. As she turned to go, she held Paul's eye for a fraction longer than a glance.

'She's my chef,' said Mr Ammon, reaching for the bowl of strawberries, 'but she also has other hidden assets and less obvious talents.'

Paul didn't say anything, but his mind was active. For the next five minutes, they ate in near silence, and it wasn't until Paul was sipping his coffee that Mr Ammon spoke again.

'What is your vision?'

'My vision?' Paul understood the question but didn't have a ready answer.

'Yes – you do have one I hope.'

Paul took a deep breath. 'I want Munnelly and Sons to be the most successful garage in Waldon Town.'

Mr Ammon studied Paul's face for a few seconds before erupting with laughter.

'Sadly, you can see no further than your father,' he said as his mirth subsided.

Paul flinched but wisely restrained himself.

'If your father had listened to me,' said Mr Ammon softly, 'he could've had the most successful group of service centres in the UK. But he was set in his ways. Your brother, Matthew, recognised this flaw and decided early on to pursue his dream and see where it's landed him. He probably rakes in more in a day than you earn all month.'

'Money isn't everything,' said Paul uncomfortably.

'That's what your father used to say. But he toiled all his life to earn it.'

'What's your obsession with my family anyway?' asked Paul staring at him in consternation.

'Don't misjudge me Paul,' said Mr Ammon caressingly.

'I'm just trying to open your eyes to another world – one that Albert knew nothing about.'

Paul wrestled with guilt-ridden thoughts of betraying his father's memory for the sake of financial gain.

'And what world is that?' asked Paul amid the turmoil.

'One whose citizens have discovered and perfected the art of maximising wealth with other people's money.'

Paul frowned. 'Isn't that dishonest.'

Mr Ammon chuckled and shook his head gently. 'I'm talking about a good line of credit.'

Paul had credit facilities with all his parts suppliers, but he always settled the accounts within thirty days of receipt, in accordance with the memorandum of understanding drawn up by Albert Munnelly. Outside this business facility, he had no personal credit arrangements.

'You will never become wealthy by tying-up funds in your business premises,' said Mr Ammon. 'You need to be more adventurous. You should be leveraging your assets to enhance your investment pot and then diversifying.'

'I'm not following you.'

'Use your property as collateral to borrow funds and then invest the money in different sectors.'

'Isn't that risky?'

'Not if you want to be wealthy,' purred Mr Ammon. 'In your father's era, people held on to property for sentimental reasons regardless of market conditions. However, today's smart investor spots lucrative investment opportunities and releases his equity in real estate to yield capital.'

Paul didn't respond, but deep within he was reminiscing about the times when Albert would sit him down and lecture him about money management. Albert used to say that it was better to be a debt-free pauper than a debt-ridden millionaire, because the pauper always slept better at night. Albert's wisdom had influenced his approach to financial matters, but today, it was losing its credibility in the face of Mr Ammon's subtle reasoning.

'Your father's generation was motivated by fear of failure,' said Mr Ammon, pausing to sip his cup of tea, 'and so they sat on their hands and failed to grow their potential.'

'But dad built up a successful business,' said Paul weakly, as loyalty to blood kicked in.

'It all depends on your definition of success,' answered Mr Ammon dryly. 'Albert played it safe and stayed small, but in today's business environment that's suicide. The marketplace has evolved, and you have to evolve with it.'

Paul started to ponder over Mr Ammon's analysis but was disrupted by the return of Nicole. She briefly leant over Mr Ammon to whisper in his ear and then departed again, pausing to treat Paul to her enchanting grin.

'Nicole has just hinted me of another appointment,' said Mr Ammon, rising to his feet unceremoniously, 'so I'll have to defer our discussion to some other time.'

Paul sprang to his feet for fear of being labelled a free-loader and stretched out a hand to his host, which was ignored, so he hastily withdrew it. Mr Ammon's message was clear – he'd outstayed his welcome.

'Thanks for breakfast and everything else,' said Paul, feeling he had to say something in parting, 'and I promise to think about everything you've said.'

'You'll need to do more than think,' said Mr Ammon, coldly. 'You'll need to act and fast. Remember, a woman without a womb can receive seed, but she'll never be able to multiply it into a harvest. You, however, have a womb, so use it before you hit menopause. Goodbye, Mr Munnelly.'

Paul found Nicole waiting in the main house to escort him to the front door. They walked side by side in silence, but as they arrived at the hallway preceding the front door, Nicole cleared her throat and turned to face him.

'He likes you,' she said quietly, 'and believe me that's a good thing. An invitation to have breakfast with him is an endorsement, so he definitely believes you have potential.'

'Potential for what?'

'Have you heard of the Apple Seed Project?'

Paul nodded slowly. He had considered applying but after

discussing it with his accountant Basil Mead had discarded it.

'I never applied,' he answered.

'That doesn't matter,' she said. 'Many apply but some are chosen – I was chosen.'

Paul chewed on her words and his heart raced faster.

'So, have I been chosen?'

'It depends.'

'It depends on what?'

'On whether you realise your potential.'

'I hope I'll be able to deliver,' said Paul, summoning up the courage to maintain eye contact.

'*Hope* is not a word we use around here,' said Nicole, opening the front door. 'We believe in making things happen by being spontaneous and proactive, and Mr Ammon expects all his protégés to be the same. He often says that *hope is the product of a lazy mind.*'

'So, I'm his protégé now, eh?'

'Everyone he takes under his wing is his protégé,' replied Nicole, looking him straight in the eye, 'including me.'

Paul didn't say anything, but his eyes flitted about, searching for the ferocious guard dogs. Finding the coast clear, he awkwardly stretched out a hand to Nicole, expecting to be rebuffed, but was relieved when she shook the proffered hand and let her fingers remain enclosed in his for a couple of seconds longer than necessary.

As he drove away from the porch, he glanced in the rear-view mirror and was surprised to find her still standing there, watching his departure. He didn't know what to make of it, but he hoped it was a positive sign.

6

Paul's eyes trailed Basil Mead's emphatically ponderous strides around the room, whilst his brain tried to compute what was going on in the elderly accountant's mind. Like a Victorian schoolteacher, Basil Mead paced around with his arms behind his back and a grave expression on his face that was accentuated by his frameless glasses.

He was a little man, about five foot four inches tall, and well under the eight stone mark in weight, but what he lacked in vertical grandeur and body mass was compensated for by his large head crowned by curly grey hair.

Basil had been the family accountant for the past two decades and had guided Albert Munnelly along the path of prudent, risk-averse financial planning. Basil came from an era when accountants were viewed as dream killers by anyone who was blessed with unbridled imagination but cursed with a shortage of funds.

A stickler with an eye for detail and a nose for a con, Basil had saved Albert on more than one occasion from handing over his hard-earned cash in exchange for a money pit. Basil belonged to the exclusive club of old school accountants who hated credit and the hidden charges that often accompanied it. Basil was the reason why Paul's books were in order and in Paul's eyes he could do no wrong.

Resting on Basil's desk was the glossy brochure for the new business park that Paul was considering investing in. Alongside it was an innocuous folder containing Munnelly and Sons' up-to-date profit and loss accounts. Beneath the folder, scribbled on two sides of A4, were Paul's sketchy financial plans, awaiting Basil's approval.

Paul had never consulted Basil with an investment proposal of this magnitude before. Even though he didn't require permission from anyone to spend his own money, he still felt a degree of apprehension. It was a measure of the degree of influence that Basil wielded over him.

'Have you thought this through?' asked Basil predictably.

'Eh, sort of,' confessed Paul, fidgeting on his seat, 'but I was hoping you could dot my 'I's' and cross my 'T's'.'

Basil's bespectacled eyes latched onto Paul's furtive stare and his expression acquired a new depth of gravity.

'It's unworkable,' said Basil bluntly. 'It's simply unfeasible.'

'I don't follow you,' admitted Paul demurely.

'Expansion must always bow to the law of sustainability,' said Basil, pausing by one of the windows overlooking the high street, with his back to his wet-eared client.

'Now, you've *really* lost me,' said Paul, raising his hands in mock surrender.

Basil turned around. 'For any expansion plan to be viable,' he explained, 'it must first of all be sustainable and by that, I mean it must be a justifiable reaction to a pre-existing state of affairs. Do you follow me so far?'

Paul nodded enthusiastically, even though it was all Greek.

'I'll illustrate,' said Basil patiently. 'Let's assume you suddenly have a massive influx of new customers and gradually find your current premises too restrictive for the new business. In that case, your expansion plans would be a justifiable reaction to the state of affairs which pre-existed your plans.'

'I see,' murmured Paul, masking his ignorance with a series of brief nods.

'Your existing business needs have to drive the expansion and not the other way round,' said Basil slowly. 'In other words, the acquisition of larger business premises becomes justifiable because of the real risk of losing not only the new customers, but some of the old ones as well, due to your inability to handle the increased volume.'

'*Now*, I get you,' said Paul brightly. 'You're saying that if I get too many new customers, I might lose them if I don't move to a larger site, right?'

Basil nodded curtly though his flustered face betrayed his dismay at his client's lack of comprehension.

'Now, I've been studying your books, particularly your profit and loss accounts,' said Basil, digging his hands deeply into his pockets, 'and, to be honest, I'm struggling to see how you can justify the need for expansion on the basis of your current business levels. It just doesn't add up.'

'You mean I don't earn enough?'

'Oh, you're certainly profitable,' said Basil. 'In fact, you're very profitable indeed, but that's not the point Paul.'

'Then help me out here,' said Paul, on the verge of frustration. 'You're the man who understands financial matters. I'm just a mechanic.'

'Why do you need to move from your existing site?'

The question threw Paul.

He thought it would be fairly obvious from the glossy brochure why he needed to move. After all, the business park was more upmarket and all the big players in the motoring industry were looking to move their operations there. Munnelly and Sons would be right in the hub of Hertfordshire and Bedfordshire's motor city, attracting new business from all the major retailers.

Vijay had indicated that in light of the recent recession all the major motor retailers were looking to reduce overheads by outsourcing their motor servicing needs to reputable independents like Munnelly and Sons.

In the past, the motor retailers had all maintained an in-house vehicle servicing arrangement but changing times and the need to remain profitable had meant that downsizing was the name of the game. Coupled with European legislation, that permitted independents like Munnelly and Sons to carry out vehicle repairs under the manufacturer's warranty, it meant that the in-house arrangement was on its last legs.

More importantly, many cash-strapped customers would be driving their new motors to cheaper reputable independent garages for work not covered under warranty. By sub-contracting out their repair work, the retail outlets were ensuring that they retained a piece of the action. Paul had scribbled it all down for Basil, and he was dismayed that the man hadn't read it.

'I don't see the problem,' said Paul. 'You've read my proposal, haven't you?'

Basil nodded, but his face still looked unsettled.

'It's based on speculation,' he said, 'and accountants do not – rather *should* not – base our advice on speculation and dubious financial projections.'

'I still don't see the problem,' muttered Paul obstinately.

'Ahhhh!' sighed Basil. 'Let me put it this way. Your current business levels enable you to comfortably break even and retain a healthy profit at the end of every financial year. Even during the lean years of the recession, you are managing to remain profitable, because the risk in your portfolio is minimal. You own your own debt-free premises, so there's no business rent. You own your own machinery and equipment, so you're protected from the vagaries of fluctuating interest rates on leasing arrangements. You employ very few staff, so your wage bill is relatively low and more importantly, you stick to Japanese brands, which is your unique selling point, so your customer base remains loyal. As long as you stick with your existing business plan, you will increase at a modest rate and always remain profitable. That's not speculation, my boy; that's fact.'

'Meaning, I don't rock the boat.'

'In a word – yes.'

'So, I remain where I am.'

'You remain profitable.'

'Just like my dad, right?'

'Your father left you a debt-free estate,' said Basil, stepping forward, 'and it's my job to see that it remains that way.'

Paul didn't answer, but his nerves were in shreds. He'd never fought Basil and never thought he'd have to, but today he was determined not to give in without a fight. His parents had always adhered to Basil's advice and paid the man an annual retainer to ensure that they never encountered poverty again. Their objective was simple, and Basil had fulfilled his brief. However, Paul was convinced that the man hadn't given the business proposal the attention it deserved and had shot it down without even reading it.

'I have the chance to upgrade the business from a local mechanics workshop to a really modern upmarket business capable of attracting new customers,' said Paul, injecting as much passion as he could into his pitch. 'I now have a terrific opportunity to stamp my mark on Munnelly and Sons and take it places it's never been before.'

'Like into administration,' grunted Basil, under his breath.

'What was that?' asked Paul who'd heard him but wanted to be sure that his ears weren't deceiving him. Basil wasn't known for his sarcasm.

'Look, just step back and look at the facts,' said Basil, sidestepping the invitation to repeat himself. 'Statistics show that many small businesses that fold-up usually hit rock bottom when they over-reach themselves. Spurred on by a grand vision, sold to them by business consultants with ulterior motives, they leave their traditional areas of operation and invest in unsustainable expansion plans that involve instant cost increase, but delayed profitability. A win-win would be instant cost increase with a guarantee of instant profitability, but sadly the reality is that the increased costs have to be recouped first before the business can return to profitability, and there are no guarantees that it'll happen within the projected timetable.'

'More business equals more profits,' said Paul stubbornly.

'Sadly not,' said Basil, shaking his head emphatically. 'The size and timing of the profits are dictated by forces outside your control.'

'Such as?'

—

'Interest rates, tax increases, local authority rates just to name a few.'

'Aren't you being just a little bit pessimistic?'

'Pessimism has saved me more money than all my other attributes put together.'

'Well, at least just read through my proposals again,' said Paul, weakly, 'and see if you can improve upon them.'

'You're not listening, Paul,' said Basil, strolling over to where his young client was seated with a compassionate smile on his face. 'Reading through your proposal again will not change my position. Have you given any thought to how you'll deal with unexpected events such as a further downturn in the economy? Change of circumstance such as ill health? Or even aggressive competition that dramatically reduces your customer base? How will your business react to and survive these changes? If all you end up doing is breakeven, would you still consider yourself viable?'

'At least I can try,' said Paul tenaciously. 'I've already given Mr Truman my word and, even though I've got a twenty-one day opt-out option, he's expecting me to invest.'

'You don't owe Truman, or his ilk tuppence!' said Basil, turbulently. 'But you owe Albert everything.'

Paul absorbed the statement with a heavy heart. He couldn't escape the old man's shadow.

'Your proposal is to buy two business units by raising a loan for the deposit and taking out a mortgage on the balance,' said Basil, calming down slightly. 'According to your notes, your agent Vijay Pandya's finance company will loan you sufficient funds to cover the deposit and he has promised to recommend you to a reputable lender for the mortgage with a guarantee that you'll get the money because you're credit-worthy.'

'And what's wrong with that?'

'Debt affects your risk profile,' answered Basil. 'There's too much risk in the portfolio and you haven't done a risk assessment to show how you intend to manage or mitigate it. Only a loan shark or disreputable lender will loan you money without a sound business case that identifies all the core risks and incorporates a viable strategy for containing them.'

'I'll repay the debt by letting out one of the business units and my existing business premises,' answered Paul. 'Vijay reckons that the rental income from both should be enough to cover all the loan repayments and still leave me with a healthy profit.'

'That's because he wants you to take out a loan with him and a mortgage from the lender of his choice, who'll also give him a tidy commission for attracting new business for them,' said Basil exasperatedly. 'What you need is a comprehensive risk assessment that reveals your areas of vulnerability and then based on that, you need a business plan that charts the realistic way forward for you in growth terms.'

Paul nodded and sighed heavily. 'Will you do that for me then?' he asked wearily.

'I've already started work on it,' answered Basil, 'but it'll take at least another fortnight.'

'But I need it in the next seven days,' said Paul desperately, 'because my opt-out period expires then.'

'You can negotiate an extension,' suggested Basil, 'and if they're keen to attract your business they'll grant it to you.'

'I doubt that very much,' said Paul, ponderously. 'After all, they're doing me a favour.'

'You've got a lot of growing up to do,' said Basil, shaking his head disapprovingly. 'You need to realise that in business nobody does favours for anyone. There's no such thing as a free lunch. Every gesture comes weighted with conditions attached.'

* * * * * * *

'Hmm, nice wheels, Mr M,' said Vijay, drooling over the Porsche. 'Is this all part of the image makeover?'

'Actually, it's a client's car,' answered Paul, locking the car from the key fob, 'and I'm just running it in for him.'

'Well, it suits you sir,' said Vijay, still eyeing the aggressively styled vehicle like a hyena circling a carcass, 'and I'm sure you must be pulling a different babe every other night.'

Paul grinned awkwardly and shrugged to spare himself the embarrassment of revealing his shortcomings in that department. In the fortnight that he'd had the vehicle, he hadn't even been able to woo back Patsy, the cute shop assistant, who'd dumped him for Bradley, the local butcher's son. On the pretext of accepting his offer of a date, Patsy had made him drive her to the bowling alley where she was meeting Bradley and then made it clear that she'd moved on. It would take more than a top of the range Porsche to improve his prospects in the dating arena.

'So, what brings you to this part of town?' asked Vijay, leading the way into the sales office on the site of the business park. 'Are you finally ready to part with all that cash you've been making?'

'Actually, I've come to negotiate an extension on the twenty-one day opt-out period,' said Paul, once they were inside the warm reception area.

'Are we getting cold feet?' asked Vijay, masking his apprehension with a nervous grin.

'No, nothing like that,' said Paul, avoiding eye contact. 'I'm just waiting on my accountant to finalise the paperwork, and he says he needs another fortnight.'

'He can't sort out your accounts in seven days?' asked Vijay, looking bemused. 'It's not as if you're buying Big Ben or the Tower of London, is it?'

Paul shrugged. 'Well, he says he needs the time and I promised to renegotiate,' he murmured. 'Unfortunately, he's a cautious kind of guy and he probably wants to be sure that the deal is viable.'

'He's trying to slow you down,' said Vijay, plunging backwards on to one of the plush sofas, clasping his hands behind the back of his head, 'and in a deal like this, you can't afford to be slack.'

Even though Vijay's comments resonated with him, Paul became defensive. 'I think he genuinely wants to go over the whole proposal just to make sure,' he said.

'All he's required to do is make sure that you're credit-worthy,' said Vijay, shaking his head incredulously, 'and how difficult can that be for a man like you who owns a mortgage-free property in a sought-after industrial estate?'

'I need an extra seven days,' said Paul, sighing heavily. 'Do you think you could have a word with Truman for me? Tell him I'll be ready to go in a fortnight.'

'That might not be so easy,' sighed Vijay, shaking his head again. 'Since the launch event we've been inundated with enquiries by retailers wanting to cash in on the unbeatable sale price for early birds and we're literally sold out. We even have a waiting list of businesses ready to put down deposits on any surplus business units within the next seven days. That means we can sell your reserved units in less than twenty-four hours and still make the deadline set by Truman.'

Paul looked around him furtively and his eyes met those of the middle-aged brunette seated in a small cubicle at the other side of the reception area with a mobile handset glued to her ear. The plaque on her desk indicated that she was the sales manager, so Paul headed in her direction determined to get an extension.

'What's up, Mr M?' asked Vijay, springing up from the sofa. 'Where are you going?'

'To see the sales manager,' answered Paul, striding towards the cubicle without looking back at his frantic agent.

'But she can't help you' said Vijay, walking briskly after him. 'She'll only deal with me because I'm your agent.'

Paul froze at the doorway of the cubicle and slowly turned around in exasperation. Vijay was right. Property developers would never bypass a customer's agent to deal directly with the customer. He heaved a dejected sigh and headed back to the reception area. He wasn't about to lose out on the deal of a lifetime and right now he found Vijay extremely unhelpful.

'Look, Mr M,' said Vijay, placing a gentle hand on Paul's shoulder, 'I know how you feel and everything, but it's a rather awkward situation and I'm stuck in the middle. If you pulled out of the deal now, I could find new buyers just like that.' He snapped his fingers for emphasis. 'So, I'm not at risk of losing any sales commission, but that's the problem, Mr M. Because you're a good friend and a valuable client, I won't feel right about doing that. If, on the other hand, you could sort out your accounts in the next seven days…'

'I thought you were a mate,' muttered Paul.

'Now you're blackmailing me, Mr M,' said Vijay sadly. 'As you know, Truman's gone back to the States and he's looking to close the offer in seven days. I could try talking to him, but I know what he's going to say, so don't get your hopes up.'

'Well, at least try,' implored Paul, sensing a lucrative opportunity slipping through his fingers because of an old accountant who was hell-bent on frustrating him.

Vijay was silent for a while and his expression conveyed inner turmoil. After five minutes, he shrugged and whipped out his mobile phone with the sigh of a man carrying the weight of the world on his slender shoulders.

'You're blackmailing me, Mr M,' he reiterated as he speed dialled a number on his phone.

Paul sat down whilst Vijay made his phone call picking up snippets of information from Vijay's body language, as well as his long pauses. At the end of the call, Vijay looked like a man who'd just run the London Marathon.

'Well?' asked Paul, rising expectantly.

Vijay nodded, as he flopped down on the nearest sofa. 'He'll extend the deadline for you,' he said, 'but only on the condition that you can provide documentary evidence from a chartered accountant within the next five days that you have the deposit, and he wants the deposit lodged in my business account within seven days.'

'I don't understand,' said Paul, mulling over the bizarre pre-condition.

'He wants a guarantee that you're a serious buyer,' said Vijay, slipping his phone back into his pocket, 'and he needs the funds paid in my account so that if after the seven-day period you pull out of the sale he can deduct ten percent as penalty. If you agree to those terms, then I'll get the sales manager to issue you with a copy of their special terms and conditions which you need to sign and return.'

Paul pondered over the conditions and nodded. The penalty was only ten percent of the deposit, but it was still a reasonable sum. He knew that Basil would blow a fuse, but that was a risk worth taking as he had absolutely no intention of pulling out of the deal.

'I can live with that,' he said. 'I'll get Basil to get the documentary evidence over to you ASAP and then we can meet up to sort out the loan you promised to arrange for me.'

'Good stuff,' said Vijay, brightening up. 'By the way, who's Basil?'

'He's my accountant.'

'Basil,' said Vijay, almost to himself. He mentioned the name quietly to himself a few more times. 'What's his last name?'

'Mead, why?'

'Basil Mead of *Mead and Sykes LLP*?'

'Yes, do you know him?'

Vijay chuckled to himself. 'Yeah, I know him,' he said, buoyantly. 'Wasn't he the accountant who was sued by Titan National Bank last year for professional negligence?'

'What?' asked Paul, looking aghast. 'Professional negligence?'

'Yeah,' said Vijay, obviously loving every minute of it. 'It was a big case that was eventually settled out of court by Mead's insurers from his professional indemnity cover.'

'I don't believe it,' said Paul, convinced that Vijay was up to his usual mischief.

'Go online and check the net,' said Vijay. 'I'm sure you'll be able to pick up more details on the case. Apparently, Mead was having some personal difficulties at the time, that affected his judgement and his mistakes cost Titan National almost a million pounds. They withdrew their retainer from his partnership and then sued him for the money.'

Paul absorbed the news in silence, but voices inside his

head had become a cacophony.

* * * * * * *

Paul pulled up outside his workshop in a daze and remained seated at the wheel of the car. On his way back from the business park he'd taken a detour via his home where he was able to surf the net in privacy. He rarely visited online news sites and never read newspapers, but this was an emergency. To his dismay Vijay's claims were confirmed. Basil had been embroiled in a High Court claim filed by Titan National who accused him of professional negligence with respect to some business advice he'd provided. Acting on the advice had cost the bank almost a million pounds in lost revenue and they'd promptly sued. Basil had eventually admitted liability and his insurers had paid up opting to settle out of court for a sum allegedly in excess of one million pounds.

The newspaper reports had turned the spotlight on Basil's private life, suggesting that he was having marital problems and that these in turn had affected his professional competence. According to some of the reports, Basil had subsequently lost several other lucrative business accounts for large multinational PLCs, and a number of professional staff, including a junior partner had also jumped ship.

Though the events had happened over a year ago, the internet had a habit of bringing archived news to life, making the facts as fresh as if they'd just happened the previous day. For Paul, the news was the most damning he'd received since his dad passed away. He'd always held Basil in high esteem but was now struggling to reinstate him to that pedestal. Suddenly, Basil's professional advice seemed flawed.

The difficulty now was deciding whether to confront Basil with the news or whether to transfer Munnelly and Sons' business elsewhere, and then drop him via letter or e-mail. How would Basil react? Would he remain aloof, or would he beg for the business not to be taken away? If he remained aloof, the situation was easy, but if he begged, what then?

Irene Munnelly still held the man in high regard and Paul didn't put it past Basil to contact her to intervene if his firm lost the business. To keep the business with Basil was the last thing he wanted, but it meant having to find another accountant and then build-up trust in someone who was to all intents and purposes a stranger. It was a tough call.

The rapping of knuckles against his window startled him out of his ruminations, and he stared up at Violet's bemused face. Ever since her first date with Giovanni, her clothing had become trendier, and her make-up applied more meticulously.

'Phone call,' she mouthed, making comical gestures with her hands to mimic the act of making a phone call with a cordless handset.

Paul nodded but made no effort to get out of the car. Realising that he wasn't budging, Violet opened the door and leant inside the cabin much to his discomfort.

'Phone call,' she said unnecessarily.

'I heard you the first time,' he said, pulling back from her and turning away. 'Take a message and I'll call them back.'

'It's Irene,' said Violet flatly, as her oppressive perfume pulverised the aroma of the vehicle's leather interior.

Paul groaned inwardly. What did mum want? Had Basil contacted her to discuss the business park proposal?

'I'll call her back,' he said irritably.

'She says it's urgent,' persisted Violet. 'She was about to leave a message when I saw you drive up, so she knows you're not working on any customer's car yet.'

'Right,' said Paul, nursing a vehement agenda for the disloyal woman. 'You can tell her I'm coming.'

'That's more like it,' said Violet, withdrawing from the vehicle's cabin much to his relief.

'You haven't heard the last of this,' he growled, as he emerged from the car and followed her into the workshop. She didn't respond, but as she handed the handset to him, she winked, delighting in his angry reaction.

'Hi Mum,' he said quickly, 'is everything okay?'

'Hi Paul,' she said in a wavering voice that instantly put

him on alert. 'No, everything isn't all right. I've just received some disturbing news.'

'Look Mum, I can explain,' said Paul, determined to defend himself before she weighed in with any accusation of financial mismanagement. 'It's not as bad as it sounds.'

'What can be worse than your brother lying in a coma?' she asked, in a voice that verged on the hysterical.

'Matthew?' asked Paul carefully.

'Yes!' she wailed, in a shrilly voice that threatened to pierce his ear drums. 'He's in a coma at a hospital in London!'

'What happened?' he asked, heaving a quiet sigh of relief.

'I'm told he fell off the catwalk during an exhibition for the London Fashion Week,' she went on, agitatedly, 'but I'm not well enough to travel.'

Irene was well known for her various allergies, and whenever she had a particularly severe bout, she was unable to leave her bed for at least three days.

'Are you all right, Mum?'

'Forget about me,' she shrieked, 'and get down to London to find out how your brother is! I've just lost my husband and I'm not ready for anymore tragedies, you hear me?'

'What hospital's he in?' asked Paul calmly.

*   *   *   *   *   *   *

Albert Munnelly always said, '*Expect the worst and prepare for it,*' but on this occasion that maxim was rendered redundant, because Paul walked into the private ward at Charing Cross Hospital to find his brother sitting up in bed chatting merrily to two very impressionable black female nurses. To Paul's relief, as their eyes met, there was no trace of the age-old hostility in Matt's. Instead, Paul was welcomed with a warm grin. Paul hadn't relished the prospects of visiting his elder brother in the aftermath of all the nastiness surrounding their father's will. Throughout the intervening year, Paul's attempts to contact his brother had been rebuffed to the extent that Matt had even changed his phone number.

All the way on the train to London, Paul had prepared himself for the worst. The fact that Irene had been contacted hundreds of miles away in Northern Ireland confirmed that she was the only person Matt identified with as next of kin.

The two nurses reluctantly exited the ward leaving the brothers alone in awkward momentary silence, which Paul hurriedly fractured.

'So, you cheated death,' said Paul, placing a bag of grapes on the bedside drawer then perching on the edge of the bed.

'It was a close call,' said Matt, leaning backwards.

Paul glanced at the bandage wrapped securely around his brother's head and at the plaster cast encasing his right leg and realised that his injuries weren't life threatening.

'Fractured ankle and mild concussion,' confirmed Matt. 'I was probably out cold for the ambulance ride and woke up hours later with a severe headache.'

'Mum said you were in a coma,' murmured Paul. 'I wonder who told her that.'

'Most likely Amy – my employer,' said Matt, with a heavy sigh. 'I guess she just wanted to make sure that my family visited me. Because I'm so private, she probably doesn't believe that I have a family that cares.'

'Well, we do care,' said Paul quietly.

'Do you – really?' Matt studied Paul's countenance.

'Yes,' replied Paul, 'we do – I care.'

'It's good to see you,' said Matt, stretching out a hand in fellowship which Paul clasped in his, gripping it tightly.

'So, it looks like you'll be out of action for a bit,' observed Paul, glancing at the leg in plaster. 'Maybe you could hang out with mum till the leg heals, what do you think?'

'Tempting offer,' chuckled Matt, 'but I'm not sure Amy would approve.'

'There's no sick leave in the fashion industry?'

'Of course there is,' said Matt, grinning at Paul's ignorance, 'but Amy's no ordinary employer and this job pays in all sorts of different ways.'

'You're going out with her?'

'That's the polite term for it,' said Matt smugly.

'She's obviously older,' observed Paul, 'but is she married?'

'What do you think?'

Paul recalled Matt's early escapades in Waldon Town when he became the scourge of the neighbourhood because of his preference for older women. Paul suspected the reason behind Matt's preference was a need for the motherly affection he lacked growing up.

'So, how's business at Munnelly and Sons?' asked Matt, turning the spotlight.

'Steady,' said Paul, choosing his words carefully; 'same old customers, same old cars.'

'Same old profits?'

Paul was quiet, as he considered the most appropriate response. He'd hoped the conversation wouldn't touch on the family business or the subject of money.

'Have I made you uncomfortable?' He appeared to be relishing the effect his words were having on Paul.

'Business is steady,' repeated Paul, staring past Matt at the skyline visible from the window beside him, the grey skies outside seeming to mirror the mood inside the ward.

'Don't be uncomfortable,' said Matt, with a smile flitting around his lips; 'I'm not bitter about what Albert did – at least not anymore. After all, what's that favourite saying of his, *'The lad who carries the barrel of ale …'*

'Has every right to get drunk,' completed Paul soberly.

'So, I'm not bitter,' said Matt.

'And I'm not drunk either,' said Paul, studying the walls. 'In fact, you could say I'm still carrying the barrel.'

'Struggling to blend into dad's shadow?'

'Struggling - period.'

'Is mum still active behind the scenes?'

'No, but Basil Mead's convinced that Albert Munnelly's soul lives on in him.'

Matt chuckled knowingly. 'I forgot all about him,' he said gently. 'Did dad bequeath him to you as part of the estate?'

'It sure feels that way sometimes,' muttered Paul bitterly.

'It's almost as if Albert lives on, except this time around I'm the one paying him for the aggravation.'

'So why don't you fire him then?'

'Because mum would intervene and get him reinstated.'

'Does mum run Munnelly and Sons or do you?'

Paul considered the question. If he fired Basil Mead, all Irene could do would be raise a passionate plea or try some new brand of emotional blackmail. Ultimately it would be his sole decision, whether Basil ever handled the business accounts again.

The belated realisation gave him an adrenaline boost and his mind drifted to Violet and her irritating habits. Why did he have to put up with her anymore?

'I see you're getting the message,' said Matt, with a wry grin, 'so I'll leave you to sort it out. If you believe you're the boss, then do what all bosses do – take charge. After all, it's not as if Albert's going to resurrect and issue you a reprimand for running the business your way.'

'Thanks,' said Paul pensively. 'I'm glad I came.'

'So am I,' said Matt quietly.

The ward door opened before Paul could respond and a gorgeous looking, red-haired woman in her thirties clad in a shapely cashmere dress and six-inch heels strolled in. There was something familiar about her, but he couldn't immediately place her face. He knew her from somewhere but where?

'How's my baby doing?' she asked.

'Missing you,' Matt answered elegantly.

Gushing effusively, she hurried over to the bed with two designer shopping bags dangling from her arms and planted a kiss on Matt's cheek, before turning to his guest with a smile accentuated by her blood red lipstick.

'Let me guess,' said Paul, 'you must be Amy.'

'Amy McBride,' she said curtly.

She held out one expensively manicured hand, letting it dangle limply in front of him, as if she were expecting him to honour it with his lips. Instead, he reached across to shake it noting the residue of grease under his fingernails.

She seemed to have noticed it too, and abruptly withdrew her hand. 'And you are?' she asked disdainfully.

'Paul. I'm…'

'He's an old mate,' cut in Matt. 'We were at Business College together. Paul's got a really urgent appointment and needs to dash, don't you Paul?'

Paul nodded, but as his eyes met Matt's intense stare, he realised that his brother was still trying to distance himself from his roots. In an industry renowned for its snobbery, having a brother who was a mechanic wasn't a virtue.

As he headed out of the ward, he suddenly recalled who she was. Amy McBride used to be his mum's hairdresser back in Waldon Town. He'd heard that she'd moved on but had no idea it was into the fashion industry. Given Matt's preference for older women, Paul sensed that this wasn't a recent affair. Matt and Amy were like peas in a pod; they were two pretentious people trying to reinvent themselves.

7

Paul reached for the torque wrench in the nearby toolbox and returned to the undercarriage of the Mazda MX5 he was working on. As he tightened the bolts that secured the transmission to the engine, his mind drifted back to his trip to the hospital to see Matt and what he'd learnt since then about Amy McBride courtesy of Violet.

Amy McBride had become an Apple Seed partner about four years ago and quit hairdressing to move into the fashion industry. She'd quickly built up a brand simply known as '*Amy*' specialising in designer bags and unisex clothing. Her product range was reputedly one of the fastest selling new clothing brands in Europe, outselling many more established brands.

Paul recalled dropping off and picking up his mum from Amy's hairdressers on Waldon Town High Street, soon after passing his driving test. Amy looked a lot plainer then and whilst not unattractive, she was easily forgettable. He didn't know much about her but remembered seeing her about town especially at the Horse and Canary Pub on Sundays with a man and two young sons whom he reckoned were her family. She always looked subdued. However, the transformation he'd seen the other day at the hospital lingered in his mind.

Matt had been modelling her new winter product range for men, when he'd twisted his ankle and toppled from the catwalk, knocking himself out cold. Fortunately, he was well insured against that particular risk and was receiving the very best medical care.

Violet had read somewhere that after the London Fashion Week, Matt had been due to strut his stuff at another exhibition in Melbourne, Australia, but Amy had graciously offered to cover his lost income as her contribution to his recovery. Apparently, Matt earned something like ten thousand pounds a day for photo shoots and had been billed to model the designs of a well-known Turin-based fashion house at various locations in Australia.

Paul hadn't realised how much in demand his older brother was and just seeing Matt's face on the cover of a men's fashion magazine on the way home had increased his thirst for fame and recognition.

He was reminded of the early days when Albert had boasted that Matt would one day be running the family business. Well, the family business didn't extend to clothing, and contrary to Albert's prophecy, the mantle had now fallen to the one considered least likely to succeed.

Against all odds, Paul Munnelly was running things now and he was determined to become the most popular mechanic in Hertfordshire.

The ringing of his mobile phone distracted him, and he reached for the handset in his back pocket where he always left it. He didn't recognise the number on the caller ID screen, but answered the call, nonetheless. It was Mr Ammon.

'How's the car running?' asked Mr Ammon, dispensing with pleasantries.

'Like a dream,' answered Paul. 'I reckon she's fully run-in now.'

'Good,' said Mr Ammon. 'I want you to drive the car down to Silverstone this Saturday. I've hired the track for the whole afternoon for me and a couple of friends to race their Bentleys and Ferraris, and thought you'd like to come down. We've hired some racing instructors to put us through our paces and improve our lap times, so you'll be in good company. You can put in a couple of miles around the track in the Porsche and blow away the last of the cobwebs.'

'Terrific,' said Paul, wiping the perspiration off his brow

with one of his sleeves.

'Good,' said Mr Ammon. 'So, I'll see you there then.'

'Eh, before you go,' said Paul quickly, recognising the opportunity to resolve his personal issues, 'I was wondering if I could get some advice on a personal matter.'

'Always,' said Mr Ammon, accommodatingly. 'How can I be of help?'

'Can you recommend a good accountant,' said Paul hesitantly. 'You know, someone reliable – with a good reputation.'

There was silence at the other end and Paul wondered if he'd been too forward. After all, Mr Ammon was in a different social class and was obviously used to dealing with things on a larger and more sophisticated scale.

'You need your books audited?' asked Mr Ammon at last.

'Actually, I need a second opinion about a business proposal,' replied Paul.

'Financial advice?'

'Yes.'

'You may either need a financial adviser or a business analyst,' said Mr Ammon, 'but I can't say which without knowing a bit more about the business proposal. Has it got anything to do with the business park you're thinking of investing in?'

'Yes.'

'Leave it with me,' said Mr Ammon, in a reassuring voice. 'I'll get my PA to invite my personal financial adviser to come along to Silverstone this Saturday, so you might be able to kill two birds with one stone. How does that sound?'

'Fantastic,' said Paul jubilantly. 'Thanks very much, Mr Ammon.'

'Forget it,' said Mr Ammon. 'That's what mentors are for.'

∗ ∗ ∗ ∗ ∗ ∗ ∗

The light drizzle left a sheen of fine mist along the circuitous tarmac that made up the Silverstone racetrack. As Paul drove around it towards the works area, as directed by the security personnel at the entrance, he was stunned to see dozens of high-end sports cars racing around it at breakneck pace.

Paul had always desired to come to Silverstone to participate in track day events which were open to the paying public, but had never really got around to it, even though he had a competition licence. Today was a dream fulfilled. Steering his way towards the paddock area and hospitality suites via the grid, he sighted the breath-taking spectacle of two dozen supercars all lined up outside a pit garage.

Paul gawped at the Lamborghinis, Ferraris, Maseratis, Porsches, Astons, Bugattis and McLarens with googly eyed enthusiasm and wondered what right he had to be here. A couple of eyes turned in his direction as he pulled up, but then they quickly swung the other way as he emerged from behind the wheel in his cleanest pair of workshop overalls, reinforcing his conviction that he was a poor fit. Working class didn't belong with upper middle class.

The men all looked middle aged and wealthy, but their female companions looked several decades younger and trendier. Paul recognised most of the men as celebrities, sports personalities and local politicians, all power brokers who were obviously not used to rubbing shoulders with commoners.

'Ah, Paul!' said Mr Ammon breaking away from the small crowd around him and making his way towards Paul, much to the bewilderment of his other guests. 'It's so good of you to come, despite your busy schedule!'

Paul cracked a grin, masking his confusion. Why had Mr Ammon given him such an inordinately grand welcome?

'How was the drive down?' asked Mr Ammon, pulling him aside, aware that all eyes were on them. 'Are you ready to show us what stuff you're really made of?'

Paul shrugged uncomfortably and allowed himself to be steered away to a secluded area of the VIP paddock, where Mr Ammon paused and chuckled out loud to himself, slapping Paul hard across the shoulders.

'Did you see their faces?' asked Mr Ammon, with tears of

mirth streaking down his cheeks. 'Right now, I bet you they're enquiring amongst themselves trying to unravel your identity, convinced that you must be some major celebrity they've never heard about. I tell you it's a joke! They're all a joke.'

'But I thought they were your friends,' said Paul softly.

'Friends?' asked Mr Ammon, looking bemused. 'No way,' he said waving his hand dismissively. 'They're the Chipping Norton set; all pretentious. I've helped them make shedloads of money by giving them investment tips that have doubled their wealth. Many of them were on the brink of financial ruin when I met them. But for the Apple Seed Project, they would've been more wretched than you. They all revere me as a miracle maker and jump whenever I snap my fingers but are unrelenting in their quest to discover what makes me tick. No, they're not my friends, Paul – they're my pawns.'

Paul absorbed the information silently, his face twisted in a grim stare, as he surveyed the giggling couples standing next to their shiny, expensive metal and wondered where he fit in. If they were Mr Ammon's pawns, then what was he? Mr Ammon's toe rag?

'You're my friend, Paul,' said Mr Ammon, wrapping a lean muscular arm around Paul's shoulder, 'and that's why I propose to do more for you than just make you rich.'

'I don't understand,' said Paul uneasily.

'Merely introducing you to my financial adviser and you getting sound advice from him, which you subsequently act on will earn you a profit,' explained Mr Ammon, steering Paul towards the Paddock's upper deck. 'But helping you to change your outlook in life will make you wealthy.'

Paul's face scrunched up in bewilderment. What was Mr Ammon going on about?

'Did you know that a wealthy person can always become rich and stay rich, but a rich person has no guarantee of ever being wealthy?'

Paul shook his head. Was there any distinction between being wealthy and being rich?

'Wealth is much more than just being rich,' said Mr

Ammon, waving a hand in the direction of his invited guests.

'But aren't they the same thing?'

'Many of those characters are rich, but hardly any of them are truly wealthy. All it takes to burst their bubble is one financial downturn. A wealthy person survives downturns; you know why?'

Paul shook his head.

'Because wealthy people are people of influence,' said Mr Ammon, smiling smugly to himself. 'They influence in every area of life. Anyone who plays the lottery can become rich, but how many lottery winners become truly influential?'

Paul shrugged. All the lottery winners he knew hadn't won more than a thousand pounds between them, and he was yet to meet anyone who had won the big prize.

'Paul, if you let me, I can free you from the regressive mindset that you inherited from your father, and when I do, you'll never have to walk in his shadow again.'

'Regressive mindset?' asked Paul, slightly offended.

'The mindset of mediocrity,' clarified Mr Ammon. 'It's the mindset that chains men to a life of insignificance.'

'Albert wasn't insignificant,' said Paul, flinching as he struggled to control his tone.

'He was a good family man,' said Mr Ammon unremorsefully, 'even I'll concede that much, but what were his accomplishments beyond the Munnelly clan?'

Paul, who was on the verge of retorting, paused to contemplate the issue, battling to keep an open mind as he rewound the video of Albert's life in his head, searching for any scrap of evidence that hinted at greatness.

'What awards did he ever win during his lifetime?' asked Mr Ammon soothingly. 'What community benefits did he provide? Think about it, he spent the whole of his life fleeing poverty, but never escaping mediocrity.'

Paul stared out across the circuit beneath them, and his silence betrayed his impotency. Albert was his hero even though they'd not always seen eye to eye on the business front. He'd respected the man's tenacity and integrity, but that image of success was being stripped away and he had little evidence to form a robust defence of the Irish bulldog whose shadow still loomed large over Munnelly and Sons.

'Like all skilled labourers, Albert solved problems for a price,' said Mr Ammon, 'but he never changed his world and if you continue in his footsteps, you'll be no greater than him; in fact, I can safely predict that you'll always be second best.'

Playing second fiddle to one who'd lived a life of mediocrity wasn't much of an aspiration, and Paul realised the urgent need to radically alter his goals. His chat with Matt had started the ball rolling, but Mr Ammon's words were the catalyst. Paul wanted significance more than anything else in the whole world, and he was prepared to do anything to get it.

'So how do I escape my dad's shadow?' he found himself asking, almost subconsciously.

'Simple,' said Mr Ammon, smiling benevolently. 'You become an Apple Seed partner and learn to shut out your father's voice. The less you hear his voice, the less chance his life has of influencing yours.'

Paul nodded. That seemed to make a lot of sense. Albert was a negative influence and the more he toed the man's line, the greater the chance of remaining in his shadow. It wasn't going to be easy, but Paul was determined to make a clean break with the past and chart a new course to the future.

'Do I need to apply?' he asked timidly.

'As Nicole mentioned to you the other day, many apply but some are chosen; you've been chosen.'

Paul felt goosebumps and his pricked curiosity wanted to know why a sophisticated investor like Mr Ammon could ever find potential in an insignificant mechanic like him.

Mr Ammon took out his mobile phone and speed-dialled a number, and Paul listened as his host summoned Nicole.

Nicole arrived in under thirty seconds as if she'd been within earshot of them and seeing her again provoked a flurry of unhealthy thoughts deep within. She wore a modest white trouser suit that hugged her shapely form immodestly. She smiled at him briefly, but he read no meaning into it as it was a professional smile devoid of emotion.

'Has John Crane arrived yet?' asked Mr Ammon, without looking in her direction.

'Yes, Mr Ammon,' she answered in a subdued voice that bordered on subservience. Paul loved the way she said *Mr Ammon* in her delicate French accent and would gladly have sat listening to her say it all day.

'Good,' said Mr Ammon, glancing at the face of his wristwatch. 'Tell him to get his gear on; he's riding with Paul for the first race.'

*   *   *   *   *   *   *

John Crane was a young man with prematurely greying hair whose pale complexion betrayed his aversion to the great outdoors. His broad, toothy grin lent his features a weasel-like quality, especially as his moustache was a wiry affair with edges that resembled whiskers. What he lacked in physical charm, he made up for by being a motor mouth whose greatest difficulty was pausing to catch his breath between words. Within the first lap of Silverstone's international circuit, Paul had been informed that John Crane was both a financial adviser and a business analyst who had a retainer with a decent number of Fortune 100 PLCs and that his firm had masterminded more successful public-private finance initiatives than any other in the Southeast of England.

John Crane had an MBA from Cranfield, and his firm had an annual turnover of over fifty million, making him a very big fish indeed. John Crane was on the brink of his greatest coup yet, setting-up a hedge fund on Mr Ammon's behalf which was going to invest extensively in the Far East and pluck an inordinate number of lucrative government contracts from the Chinese and South Koreans. Paul, who had no idea what a hedge fund was, tried to appear interested, but couldn't wait for John to ask him about his particular case.

By lap two, John Crane was discussing the intricacies of investing in real estate in Spain and by lap three he was discussing his scheme for inner city gentrification, converting notorious council estates into gated estates for the privileged.

By lap four, John was analysing the benefits of setting up joint ventures with government-funded social enterprises and mutualized entities and then setting up ethical walls as a smoke screen for conducting ethically questionable commercial activity. By lap five, he was into supply chain restructuring and business process outsourcing as a means of stripping overheads and increasing profit margins. By lap six, he'd run out of steam much to Paul's relief. A high-speed drive in a German supercar with a fast-mouthed English man in the passenger seat was more speed than he could handle.

The race, which was currently being led by Mr Ammon in an Aston Martin, comprised ten expensive supercars, each being driven at breakneck pace by one of his middle-aged cronies, who each had an attractive young female in the passenger seat for inspiration. Paul wondered whether he was the only one on the circuit who thought it odd that the race leader didn't have a passenger in his car. Nicole was watching the race from the VIP area with the rest of Mr Ammon's guests, and hadn't even been invited to join her boss, something that Paul found odd considering he'd already written her off as the man's mistress.

Each time he rounded the corner before the paddock and grid area where she stood, he deliberately slowed his pace so that she wasn't a blur as he went by. The fact that he was trailing the pack by a full lap didn't bother him, as unlike the others he wasn't used to the circuit and had decided to spend the first race familiarising himself with it, suspending his competitive edge for the next stages.

'So, you're thinking of investing in Truman's business park, eh?' asked John Crane at the start of the seventh lap, his voice echoing through the earphone in Paul's crash helmet.

'Yes, that's right,' answered Paul, refraining from muttering, *It's about time too.* Instead, he said, 'and I hear you're the man to speak to.'

'I usually am,' answered John with an immodest thin-lipped smile. 'That's why in the City I'm known as the '*Oracle*.'

Paul felt like throwing up.

'I think it's an inspired vision,' went on John in the same smug tone. 'A motor city situated less than twenty miles from the capital, but easily accessible to those living in Hertfordshire, Bedfordshire, and Buckinghamshire. Having all the major motoring retailers and their service centres in one major location not only increases competition, but also attracts more customers, especially since there's going to be a motorsport-themed amusement park for kids and a shopping complex for their mums. As it's probably the first of its kind anywhere, it will prove to be a major draw.'

'So, you think it's a good investment then?' asked Paul, determined to get to the core reason for their being together.

'I think it's an epic investment opportunity,' said John enthusiastically, 'especially since the special entry rates are so attractive. Heck, if I was in the motoring trade, I'd throw my money in; it's too good to miss, unbelievable actually.

'I think the recession has had something to do with it, as the Americans who have survived the worst of it are investing aggressively in European and Asian real estate and trying to undercut each other.'

'So that accounts for the attractive rates then,' said Paul, trying to keep up with him.

'Yep,' John concurred, his head bobbing up and down. 'Truman's got competition and he's eager to get his project off the ground before the others rush in. By being the first in, at competitive rates, he becomes the market leader, making it more difficult for his rivals to gain any traction in the market, even with equally competitive products. Brand awareness favours the market leader and everyone else is an imitator.'

'I'm thinking of buying two units in the complex,' said Paul, as they steered onto the last lap, 'and my difficulty is how to go about funding them. Because I currently work on a debt-free site which I own I've never required financing.'

'You own debt-free industrial property?' asked John, perking up.

'Uh-huh,' said Paul hurriedly, 'and because I've got zero rental costs, my overheads are quite reasonable. It's a difficult decision because I've never invested in property before, and my accountant reckons I should stay right where I am.'

'Your accountant wants you to pass up on an offer like this?' John seemed genuinely bewildered. 'Have you provided him with a proposal?'

'Sort of,' said Paul, concentrating on steering around a tricky bend to avoid rear-ending a yellow Ferrari that was slithering around the track ahead of him.

'When you say *sort of,* what exactly do you mean?' asked John Crane, staring at him intently. 'Did you hire a business analyst to put together a workable business plan that incorporates several financial models?'

'Not really,' confessed Paul. 'I just wrote down what I wanted to do on a sheet of paper and asked him to okay it. However, he's taking too long to approve the investment.'

John Crane burst out laughing in a high-pitched, metallic tone that Paul found particularly irritating.

'That's not the way to do things, Paul,' said John, as his amusement waned. 'If you want him to take you seriously you need to present a properly thought-out business plan and tell him to select the most viable financial model for what you propose to do. It's not his job to okay your proposal. It's his job to find the most financially sound way of achieving your objective. After all, it's your money.'

'Right,' said Paul trying to absorb the radical approach.

'Your accountant isn't a business expert,' said John in a slightly condescending voice. 'He's a bean counter, someone who deals with figures, whose core skill is to assess the health of your business in light of what you're seeking to achieve and offer an opinion. It sounds to me like you've given your accountant too much power and he's capitalising on it.'

Paul restrained himself from openly blaming Albert for the arrangement. It was clear that Basil Mead had assumed a role by default that he ought not to have occupied. Albert had been content for Basil to take all the major business decisions and

Paul hadn't done anything to alter the status quo.

'Look, Paul,' said John, as they pulled into the grid at the end of the seventh lap, 'I'm sorry if I came across all gross, but I've seen this sort of situation more times than I care to recall, and each time I'm in disbelief. If you leave decisions like this to your accountant, he'll dissuade you from ever taking a business risk. Growth doesn't happen in your back garden or on your driveway, Paul. It happens when the rubber hits the highway. If all you're doing is playing it safe, don't ever expect to set the world alight. You'll forever be a small fish in a small pond.'

Paul pulled up the Porsche near the paddock and turned to John Crane who had taken off his helmet and was unbuckling himself.

'So, what can you do for me?' asked Paul.

'What do you *want* me to do for you?' asked John.

Paul was taken aback by the sudden servility and took a moment to comport himself. 'Well, I'm looking for advice on the best way of investing in the business park,' he said slowly, 'but I need a plan that'll enable me retain my current premises.'

'Does it have sentimental value?' asked John carefully.

'My dad left it to me in his will,' answered Paul.

'I understand,' said John sombrely. 'It's his legacy to you. Well, that's not a problem, because I can come up with a business model that enables you achieve that objective but still create room for your growth plan.'

John dug his hand into his overalls and took out a stylish business card which he handed to Paul. The card revealed that he was a business analyst with Eden Fruit Investments.

'As time is of the essence,' he said, 'I'll get my secretary to set up a meeting for some time next week and we'll take it from there.'

'Sounds good to me,' said Paul effusively.

'Good,' answered Crane, getting out of the car. 'In advance of our meeting I'll need to see your business accounts, an up-to-date property valuation and any documented advice your accountant has provided.'

'I'll send them off first thing on Monday,' called out Paul, as John strutted away. 'Thanks for your time.'

Paul remained seated for a while to let the adrenaline rush subside before taking off his helmet, getting out, and stretching to prevent cramp from setting in. He wasn't looking forward to another race.

'You're really privileged Paul.'

He spun round to find Nicole standing beside him with a smile that was anything but synthetic.

'Why do you say that?'

'Because if you knew how much it cost Mr Ammon to get John over here today,' she said caressingly, 'you'd realise how highly he regards you. John Crane was due to attend a meeting in Paris this afternoon, but he had to shift it to Sunday at the very last minute just so that he could accommodate you.'

Paul swallowed hard as he tried to do some quick mental arithmetic. He estimated that John's bill would include the costs of the postponed meeting and figuring that the man was probably paid by the hour, it meant an easy four figures.

'More than that,' said Nicole, before he could mouth a figure. 'John Crane is at the top of his game, and he doesn't come cheap. Now, if you'll excuse me, I need to go and change ahead of the next race.'

'Are you competing?'

'Yes!' she called out. 'And you're my passenger.'

*　*　*　*　*　*　*

The sight of Nicole in the spanking new overalls holding a crash helmet under her armpit did nothing to diminish Paul's excitement, if anything, it heightened it. As she approached, he went round to open the door for her and met her mocking stare. She sat down behind the wheel and by the time he'd buckled himself into the front passenger seat, she was already wearing her helmet and familiarising herself with all the controls and instruments.

'Whose idea was this?' he asked, slipping on his helmet.

'Mine,' she said simply. 'We've not seen all that this car has to give and, as long as you're at the wheel, we never will.'

'You think my driving's rubbish?'

'I'll let you answer that one after the race.'

As they drove up to the starting position on the circuit trailing behind the others, Paul took time to analyse her. Despite her docile appearance, she was no shy, retiring type. She looked like the sort of woman who enjoyed taking control when the mood caught her, and he imagined that Mr Ammon found it convenient to delegate a lot of the decision-making to her. It still wasn't clear if she was Mr Ammon's girl, but Paul convinced himself that if anything did exist between them, it couldn't be more than a casual affair.

'Are you a nervous passenger, Mr Munnelly?' asked Nicole as they trickled out onto the circuit in the convoy of supercars.

Before Paul could articulate an answer, they were thrusting forward on an enormous wave of torque that was both dizzying and addictive, with Nicole moving from tenth position to seventh before the first corner.

As they hurtled around the corners, aggressively tailgating slower moving vehicles, Paul realised that beneath her cool exterior Nicole was a psycho. The fact that she was driving like someone with a death wish was sufficient to silence him for the duration of the race. Corner after corner, lap after lap, Nicole pushed the Porsche to the limit, rocketing them into second position by the penultimate lap, right on the tail of Mr Ammon's Aston Martin which looked like it was working hard just to maintain pole position.

At one point, as they arrived at the start of the final lap, both vehicles drifted sideways through the corner leading to the longest straight. Paul saw Mr Ammon glance at them, but with visibility obscured by the helmets it was difficult to note his expression. Paul reckoned that if he were Mr Ammon, he would be pretty wound-up to see his female PA out-driving him in a less expensive car. Corner after corner Nicole maintained the pressure, revelling in the Porsche's techno-wizardry that kept the car on course even when the Aston appeared to be running out of traction. Finally, on the final corner of the last lap, the Aston broke away, spinning sideways in opposite lock, leaving Mr Ammon battling with the steering and creating a gap for Nicole to squeeze through.

As she whizzed past the chequered flag, she glanced sideways at Paul and the grin that radiated through the helmet's visor was one of unadulterated joy.

'All right, my driving's rubbish,' admitted Paul with upraised hands, 'but I could've told you that after the first lap if I wasn't too busy trying not to throw up. Now, as a goodwill gesture will you let me buy you dinner?'

He waited for the expected rejection, wondering where he'd found the guts to ask her out, but instead he was left in suspense as she maintained her silence all the way from the circuit to the grid.

He took a deep breath to steady himself in preparation for the polite refusal and thought about a suitable comment to show there were no hard feelings. But as the Porsche slowed to a halt at the paddock, he felt her hand on his right forearm and his composure crumpled in an embarrassing heap.

'This weekend's not good for me,' she said, sounding sincerely apologetic, 'but if you're free next weekend we could do lunch on the Thames. How about Sunday?'

Lunch on the River Thames? Now how romantic was that? Just what exactly did she have in mind for their date? Was he in for a picnic along the banks of the river to set the mood for something more romantic?

'Is that a yes, Mr Munnelly?' asked Nicole, taking off her helmet and treating him to one of her luscious grins.

'How can I refuse?' answered Paul weakly.

'Good,' she said. 'I'll sort out the arrangements.'

'But I'm supposed to be buying *you* lunch,' protested Paul, finding his full vocal range.

'I never said anything about paying, did I?' she asked, as she alighted from the vehicle and stretched. 'Relax, Paul, it's still your show. I'll be in touch.'

Paul's heartbeat became heavier, as she tossed her hair and

turned to wave at him on her way to the paddock where Mr Ammon was waiting. She'd just addressed him by his first name. For him, that was a sign of better things to come.

*　*　*　*　*　*　*

Paul was working on the brakes of Vijay's dad's Honda when the post-lady turned up with the day's mail and he immediately abandoned his task to receive the letters, one of which was sent by recorded delivery requiring his signature.

Scrubbing his hands clean, he headed to his office where he was able to open and read his mail in privacy. There was some junk mail containing special offers from part suppliers and a couple of customer warranty forms, but nothing from Nicole. The recorded delivery parcel was from Basil, and it had arrived a day before the official closing date for the sale of first-phase business park units.

He opened the package with a sense of foreboding and then carefully read through Basil's cover letter which summarised the bulky business plan contained within. Paul read the letter twice before diverting his attention to the business plan itself. The plan was well laid out with pages of detailed accounts and a lengthy explanation of the proposal complete with charts and graphs, but he found it inaccessible and so read the summary.

Basil's model was simple but controversial. The plan required Paul to take out a secured loan using his existing business premises as full collateral and then using two-thirds of the loan to purchase outright two units from the new business park. According to the plan, Paul would then occupy one of the new units and lease out the second one using the income from that to fund part of the loan repayments.

The second part of the loan repayments would be funded by rental income derived from letting-out his existing business premises. According to Basil's calculations even a modest rental income from both properties would cover the repayments in full, but if he were able to secure maximum value rent, then he would have a small profit which could be used to further reduce his loan repayments. The remaining one-third of the secured loan would be used to cover his set-up costs in his new premises, saving him the burden of taking out a further loan and increasing his indebtedness.

Basil made it clear that the aim of his plan was to ensure that, even if rental income fell below expectations or the rental properties failed to find business tenants, the very worst-case scenario would be that Paul would forfeit his old business premises which had been used as collateral for the secured loan. Paul would still be left with two debt free units in the business park which would eventually appreciate in value.

Paul tossed the report aside and fumed silently, recalling all the information he'd downloaded about Basil's professional negligence the previous year. How could Basil advise him to relinquish his existing business premises which had been bequeathed to him by Albert and was part of his legacy? Albert would turn in his grave if the property he'd worked hard to make debt-free was ever repossessed owing to Paul's failure to repay a loan taken out on the property. There had to be another way of raising the funds to purchase the business park units that didn't involve using his existing premises as full collateral for a loan. One mind urged him to go back to Basil Mead and request a further review but the other reminded him that Basil was already biased.

Paul was still lost in contemplation when the rapping of knuckles on his half open door broke his concentration. He looked up to see Giovanni standing there mopping his brow with a grease-stained handkerchief.

'Mr Pandya is outside,' said Giovanni, 'and he wants to know if his car will be ready before five o'clock, because he has an appointment in London.'

'Yes,' said Paul absentmindedly. 'I'm sure it'll be ready. Tell him to give us a call later.'

'What time should he call?'

'I don't know,' said Paul distantly. 'Tell him to call sometime this afternoon.'

'Si, boss, I'll tell him.'

Giovanni vanished from the doorway, leaving Paul to his thoughts. However, no sooner had Paul begun mulling over the matter, there was another interruption; this time it was the sound of someone noisily clearing their throat.

Paul looked up in frustration expecting to see Giovanni, but instead his unfriendly gaze encountered Arjun Pandya's stern one.

'Eh, good morning, Mr Pandya,' said Paul, sitting upright.

'Good morning, Paul,' answered Mr Pandya, after a brief pause. 'I've come to find out about my car, as no one seemed to be answering the phones.'

He was a short bespectacled Bangladeshi man with a balding scalp infested with grey wisps of hair, and he had a pointed nose that reminded Paul of an eagle's beak. Arjun Pandya was one of his oldest customers and was a stickler for efficiency. He hated being told to do anything without being given precise details and had complained in the past about being asked to phone back without being given a time. He had brought his Honda to Paul's garage on Saturday for the brakes to be fitted, but one of the other mechanics had ordered the wrong brake discs, meaning that the vehicle wasn't ready by close of play on that day.

'I'm sorry about that,' said Paul, forcing out a smile in an attempt to pacify him. 'We ordered the wrong rear brake discs, but we're expecting the correct ones this morning. I'm about to fit the new front discs, so the car should be ready by noon.'

'Good,' said Mr Pandya, brightening up, 'because I have a meeting in London at six pm and can't afford to be late.'

'The car will be ready before then,' assured Paul, 'and just to make sure I'll be working on it myself. I apologise for any inconvenience.'

'You don't need to apologise,' said Mr Pandya, looking uncomfortable. 'Your explanation was sufficient.'

Mr Pandya was a champion of punctuality, but he wasn't a troublemaker.

'Thanks,' said Paul, relieved at having successfully pacified one of his most valued customers who always paid his bills in full and on collection.

'By the way,' said Mr Pandya, lowering his voice, 'is it true what I'm hearing?'

'What are you hearing?'

'That you're investing in some business park outside town with a view to moving there?'

'Vijay told you?'

Mr Pandya nodded. 'I was taking him to task about his reckless investment schemes in the real estate market,' he said, gravely, 'and to convince me that his activities were all kosher, he mentioned that you were also investing.' He sighed deeply and took off his heavy framed spectacles so that his soft brown eyes were locked on Paul's face. 'He knows what high regard I hold you in and that if he mentioned you as one of the investors I'd back down. However, I realise that he's breached your confidentiality and apologise on his behalf for the indiscretion.'

Mr Pandya had two children, a daughter named Zula and the irrepressible Vijay. Zula Pandya shared her father's philosophy of hard work and integrity, whilst Vijay's philosophy was derived from the glamorous world of Bollywood and a wasted public school education. He might as well have been an astronomer, as his head was forever in the clouds stargazing and Mr Pandya was forever either complaining about him or apologising on his behalf.

'Forget about it, Mr Pandya,' said Paul, waving aside the apology. 'It's not a secret and besides, I've not even put down a deposit yet.'

'But will you?' The question was asked casually but carried a depth that unnerved Paul. He knew that the question was a precursor to a more forensic interrogation, and at this precise moment, the last thing he wanted was a grilling.

'I'm interested,' said Paul carefully, 'but everything's subject to my financial adviser.'

Mr Pandya said nothing, which Paul found even more unnerving. What was on his mind?

<hr>

114

'Come with me, Paul,' said Mr Pandya, after what seemed like an eternity. 'Let me show you something.'

Paul followed him without protest, driven by curiosity. As they stepped out of the workshop, Mr Pandya halted abruptly and spread his arms like a preacher at a crusade.

'Look around you,' said Mr Pandya, leading by example.

Paul looked around him at the rows of monotonous looking business units along the pot-holed road, till his expectant gaze settled back on Mr Pandya's face.

'What is now no more than a piece of history was once a new industrial estate that was the talk of the town,' said Mr Pandya, pensively. 'Thirty years ago, every small and medium-sized business wanted to lease a unit here and the developers had difficulty keeping up with the demand. Today, it's a little run down but still in demand. The real attraction is its location. Everyone knows where it is, so you don't need Satnav. There's a good bus network around here, so customers can avoid expensive cab fares and the healthy network of pedestrian bypasses and walkways means that it's walking distance from the town centre for those who fancy a bit of exercise.'

'Yes, it is a good location,' agreed Paul, still anxiously awaiting the rationale for the dreary sermon.

'So why do you want to move?' asked Mr Pandya.

Paul exhaled in disbelief. This had nothing to do with Vijay's investment strategy, but everything to do with Mr Pandya's personal agenda.

It was clear Mr Pandya wanted Munnelly and Sons to remain on its present site for his own convenience. After all, the site was only a short walking distance from his house and afforded him the opportunity of strolling over to check on his car whenever it was in for repairs instead of hoping on a bus or paying the cost of a cab. Mr Pandya was a practical man, just like Albert and Basil Mead.

'Every business goes through a season of change,' said Paul, studying Mr Pandya's face, 'and Munnelly and Sons is just going through a phase where it's trying to reinvent itself.'

'Why?' asked Mr Pandya adamantly. 'Why can't the

business undergo a change here?'

'Because we're trying to attract new business.'

'New business?' asked Mr Pandya, turning up his nose. 'What new business? As things are, you can barely keep up with demand in this place. Because of Albert's good reputation, you enjoy a high degree of customer loyalty.'

The focus on Albert's legacy hurt, but Paul was careful not to betray his feelings. It was customers like Mr Pandya who'd made Munnelly and Sons what it was. As much as Paul wanted to be recognised for his own impact, he couldn't afford to lose the loyalty of old customers – at least not yet.

'We're looking to expand,' said Paul, 'and we've sort of outgrown this place.'

'So why not expand within the estate?'

'We've considered that option but feel it's better for us to move to newer larger premises as part of our re-branding.'

'Have any of us complained about your image?'

'Not exactly,' admitted Paul, 'but like I said before, we're targeting new business; the sort of customers who wouldn't use us in our present location but would if the image was more appealing.'

'Listen to your *existing* customers,' said Mr Pandya sternly, 'and then think long and hard about this move.'

'We'll do that,' said Paul patronizingly.

Mr Pandya shrugged and then sauntered away, leaving Paul staring after him in dismay.

* * * * * * *

Paul watched as Mr Pandya's Honda was rolled off the ramp where it had been suspended all weekend, and then driven outside the workshop by Giovanni where it was handed over to Mr Pandya. As always, Mr Pandya paid the bill to the cashier without fuss and then to Paul's relief waved before getting into his car and driving away. Paul had been half expecting him to continue from where he'd stopped earlier that day but had been spared the dilemma of trying to think of a satisfactory response to the man's questions. In a way, he was grateful for Mr Pandya's interrogation because it revealed a major issue that needed to be tackled early - communication. He recognised the need for a communication strategy to handle the transition from his existing premises to the new site so that none of his customers were kept in the dark.

On the engine-tuning side of things, he had a dedicated following of young drivers who would remain loyal, and they were the ones who really counted because they spent the most money on their cars. The car-tuning arm was a money spinner and would always stay that way provided there were enough young drivers dissatisfied with the performance from their common-rail diesel engines.

For many of his older customers, eco-tuning was the in thing now, and many were seeking to extract more economy from their engines by having them 'chipped'. As for the traditional business for Japanese cars, that was unique enough to keep on attracting new customers. It was inevitable that some older customers would look elsewhere in protest at the move but, so long as the quality of his workmanship remained high, he was convinced they'd eventually come back, dragging their tails between their legs.

He spent the next half hour ignoring Violet's irritating humming whilst preparing a package for John Crane, comprising his most recent property valuation, his profit and loss accounts for the previous two years and Basil Mead's report. He then phoned the local courier company to send someone round to pick it up for same day delivery and sat back to watch the local news broadcast on his portable TV set, which he turned up to drown out Violet's voice.

A spokesperson for a large Japanese car manufacturer was speaking at a press briefing where he confirmed his company's pledge to invest in the business park over the long term, and Paul listened to the entire broadcast with a broad grin.

8

John Crane's office was just as Paul had imagined it, only more ostentatious. Situated in a towering office block within the city of London's financial district near Bank, it made a statement that both intrigued and intimidated Paul. The office's glass and aluminium architecture juxtaposed with marble flooring was a mecca for city-slick professionals. The sight of smartly dressed confident looking people made him regret his decision not to wear a suit. Judging by a couple of disdainful stares, he looked completely out of place in his trainers, denims, and leather jacket.

The receptionist, a posh-talking, wafer-thin woman, cast a disparaging eye all over him before reluctantly dialling John Crane's secretary to confirm whether the *'gentleman'* standing before her indeed had an appointment. Her red-faced expression at the end of the intercom discussion spoke volumes, and Paul watched in amusement as she altered her tone and politely offered him a seat whilst Mr Crane's PA came out to usher him in.

A Nicole Matisse look-alike appeared in the doorway leading into Eden Fruit Investments' administrative section and Paul couldn't help noticing how well she blended into the environment, with her pin stripe trouser suit and white blouse. She smiled at him politely and shook his hand curtly, before leading him through the power sliding double glass doors into the open plan administrative area where two dozen staff were seated behind desktop monitors. Most of them were either wearing call-centre style headsets or Bluetooth devices for their mobiles to facilitate multi-tasking.

Hardly anyone looked up as they walked through and Paul used the opportunity to note all the key features around him, such as the large widescreen computer monitors, each displaying the activities in the world's major stock exchanges, and the half a dozen clocks for different time zones.

Whilst it resembled a trading room, very few of those talking appeared to be buying or selling stock and the place lacked the frenzy commonly associated with such places. It was a harbinger of normality.

'Mr Crane is running a very tight schedule this afternoon,' said the PA as they exited the open-plan office and emerged on to a corridor at the other end, 'so he can only spare you half an hour, but he has asked me to book a follow-up appointment in a week's time. He hopes by then that you would've had time to read his financial recommendation.'

'He's prepared a report already?'

'I believe so.'

She led the way to the large glass-walled office at the end of the corridor and went in ahead of him, announcing his arrival, before standing aside to let him by. Paul found John Crane seated in a high-back swivelling leather armchair with a cordless handset in his hand and his legs resting on the surface of his expensive looking glass desk. John glanced up at him and winked whilst indicating with a tilt of his head that Paul should take a seat. The PA departed and Paul sat down across the desk, waiting for John Crane's call to finish. The view out of the windows behind John Crane was terrific and Paul could see right across the city without even standing up, thanks to the curved glass walls. The office itself adopted a minimalist approach to its interior design and décor that made it seem hi-tech but cold, a fact made stark by the tiles gracing the floor. The call lasted another two minutes, at the end of which John looked up apologetically.

'I have to be in Zurich this evening,' he said, by way of introduction, 'so I'm compressing all my appointments and trying to shave-off minutes and hours wherever I can. I hope you understand.'

Without waiting for a response, he reached across his desk and located a glossy looking laminated folder which he tossed over to Paul.

'That's my interim analysis,' said John, reclining backwards, 'but if you agree with my proposal, it should be enough for you to take a decision and start the financial conveyor belt rolling. It contains a concise cost-benefit analysis, and a series of cash-flow options.'

'You've got to help me out here, Mr Crane,' said Paul, without bothering to glance through the contents of the report in his hands, 'because a lot of this financial stuff goes right over my head.'

John Crane glanced at his watch before sitting slightly upright, swinging his legs off his desk, and swivelling around so that he was facing his client.

'Well, in summary,' he said breezily, 'I discarded your accountant's recommendations which would've meant wiping out all your equity in your existing business premises, making the property vulnerable in the event of an economic downturn or property devaluation. Instead, I opted for a financial model that would see you retain most of your equity in the existing business premises.'

'Terrific,' said Paul jubilantly. 'So, what does it involve?'

'Well, by examining your profit margins over the past three years,' explained John, in his accelerative style, 'and by projecting future increase in those margins, I've concluded that your best way forward is to take out a bridging loan to fund part of the deposit on three business units as opposed to two, and I'll explain why in a minute. You then take out a small, secured loan on your current business premises amounting to about twenty percent of your equity. This will pay back the bridging loan upon completion of the property transaction. In addition, you should take out an unsecured loan or business overdraft to cover the balance of the deposit. The rest of the purchase is funded by taking out secured loans on each of the three business units.'

'But how do I fund repayment of those loans?' asked Paul, leaning forward intently.

'By renting or leasing out two of your three new business units as well as your old business premises,' answered John Crane. 'By my estimates, you'll still be left with a profit from the rental income sufficient to cover the repayments on the new business unit that you're retaining for yourself, so you end up operating from rent-free premises.'

'Rent free?'

'That's right,' said Crane emphatically. 'As you're not making any loan repayments on your new premises from your business profits, you'll remain profitable, able to ride any storm that ravages the economy.'

'That sounds brilliant,' said Paul, looking impressed, 'but why have you gone for three new units instead of two?'

'Because I've spoken with Sam Truman and got him to offer you a further discount for acquiring the extra business unit,' said John Crane. 'So, for a little extra outlay you'll be the proud owner of four properties including your existing premises and be collecting rental income from three of them. The most important thing is that you'll still own eighty per cent equity in your existing business premises and not be at risk of losing it.'

'That's absolutely brilliant,' said Paul, equally impressed with what he was hearing and how it was being delivered. There was no doubt in his mind that John Crane was in a different league from Basil Mead. The small loan on the existing premises could be paid back from business profits eventually leaving that property debt-free again and there would be no risk of losing it. Basil on the other hand wanted him to take out a massive loan on his legacy and risk losing it irrespective of its sentimental value which was priceless. It was time to finally dispense with Basil Mead's services.

'I'm rolling with your plan, Mr Crane,' said Paul, without hesitation. 'How quickly can we start the paperwork?'

'It's all in the pack,' said John Crane, gesturing towards the laminated folder in Paul's hands, 'and, by the way, please call me John. I've marked all the places on the forms that you've got to sign. Once you've signed them, there's a self-addressed envelope for you to send them back in. The moment we receive the signed forms, we'll set the ball rolling.'

'Couldn't I sign them now?' asked Paul, eager to get it over and done with.

'I would suggest you take them away and read them,' said John firmly, 'and if necessary, get a good lawyer to review them with you before you sign, just to make sure that you're adequately protected.'

'I trust you Mr Crane,' said Paul, impressed by the man's level of integrity. 'So, is it essential for me to get a lawyer to review the documents?'

'Well, that's the recommendation of the Financial Services Authority, the body that regulates our activities for your protection,' said John soberly, 'but ultimately it's your choice and it really boils down to your level of trust.'

'I trust you Mr Crane, I mean John,' answered Paul, leaning across the table, and opening the folder. 'I'm determined to sort this matter out today and since I agree with your well-thought-out recommendation, just show me where to sign.'

'If that's what you wish,' said John Crane indifferently.

*　*　*　*　*　*　*

'This wasn't exactly what I had in mind,' said Paul, wrinkling his nose in disgust, before thrusting his hanky over the lower half of his face to filter out the odour of raw fish. Nicole stared at him across the table with an amused grin, but he failed to share her amusement. They were seated outside a Docklands seafood restaurant overlooking the Thames, but all around them was the nauseating smell of raw fish.

The root of the problem was that the restaurant owners bought their marine life directly from the nearby fish market. Overhead, the seagulls fluttered about looking for scraps and their squawking did nothing to improve his mood.

Nicole's invitation had merely given directions to a boatyard at the other side of the Embankment and Paul had turned up expecting to hire a boat to convey them to the venue of her choice. But when she'd said it was only a walking distance, the seafood restaurant was the last place on earth he would've expected to be spending his Sunday afternoon with Nicole; it was as romantic as sitting in a water-logged boat.

The menu before them was awash with oysters, shellfish, prawns, lobsters, and various species of fish. It was a wide selection but, for Paul, an unappealing one.

'You obviously don't appreciate seafood,' she said.

Paul was on the verge of shaking his head, but a quick assessment of the cost made him freeze. If the price for dating Nicole was eating boiled fish, then that was a price worth paying. He wasn't clinically allergic to seafood, but just couldn't stand the smell. It reminded him of his childhood, when stale bread and sardines had been the family's staple diet during the tough times. He also had vivid memories of the cod liver oil his mum thrust down his throat every Sunday as a preventative.

'Don't worry,' said Nicole perceptively. 'I'm not offended, although I *am* slightly curious.'

'Bad childhood memories,' he muttered, averting his gaze so that she couldn't register his embarrassment. He wasn't ashamed of his past; he just hated being reminded about it.

'Oh,' she said casually, 'you suffer from allergies.'

'No, I just can't stand the smell of raw fish.'

'Just stick to the oysters and lobster,' she said insensitively. 'This is the finest seafood restaurant in London, and I had to book our table a week in advance. So, I would appreciate it if you stopped making a scene.'

The harshness of her response momentarily threw him, making him wonder what he'd done to provoke the sudden mood swing. With a supreme effort, he quit wrinkling his nose and diverted his respiratory function to his mouth. This brought some relief but did nothing to alleviate the nausea churning away in the pits of his stomach. Without doubt, this was the most self-sacrificial date he'd ever been on.

'I'll order lobster,' said Nicole, lowering her sunglasses to get a better look at him, 'but I'd suggest a glass of dry white to deal with that tummy upset.'

Paul nodded his consent and kept swallowing hard to avoid throwing up. Nicole beckoned to a waitress and then reeled off their order, pausing to stab a finger in the direction of a large tank full of live lobsters. The girl jotted down the order and then beckoned to another waiter who headed towards the tank with plastic gloves. Paul watched as he fished a hand into the tank and retrieved a large lobster holding it up for Nicole to see. She nodded gently and the waiter transferred it to another tank which was empty, save for the water in it. He repeated the activity and withdrew another large lobster which he held up for approval. Nicole turned towards Paul, who nodded urgently to avoid breathing through his nose, and with a wicked grin she gave the waiter the thumbs up.

'They prepare an excellent lobster menu,' she said, following the waiter's departure with her eyes, as he conveyed the two death row lobsters in his hands to the kitchen. 'I've ordered their afternoon special.'

'Whatever,' spluttered Paul.

Nicole's amusement rippled across her face, so that her eyes appeared to join in the mirth.

'You're the most amusing man I've ever dated,' she said softly. 'To be honest, at the beginning, I thought that you were putting on an act by pretending to be uncomfortable here, because you thought it was too expensive and wanted an excuse to go somewhere else.'

'I genuinely despise fish,' said Paul, covering his nose and mouth with one hand as he spoke. 'Give me steak any day.

The waitress returned with two glasses of wine, white for Nicole and dry white for Paul. Paul gulped down the liquid in one mouthful and waved the glass at the bemused waitress indicating that he needed a refill. The lady went off to get another glass of dry, whilst Paul took deep breaths to speed-up digestion. By the time she returned with the fresh glass of wine, the nauseous sensation had already begun to subside, and Paul only needed a couple of sips to erase it.

'I've been very insensitive,' she said gently. 'I realise it was a mistake to bring you here.'

'I'll be fine,' he said, trying to inject as much reassurance as he could into his voice. 'I'm just glad to be with you.'

'And I with you,' she said shyly. 'I know it sounds, how do you English say it? Ludicrous?'

Paul nodded eagerly in confirmation and was rewarded with a bashful grin.

'From the moment we first met,' she went on, 'I visualised us sitting here sipping white wine and eating lobster *thermidor* but didn't think you would have the courage to ask me out.'

Paul reached for his glass and took a long sip to calm down, as he couldn't believe what his ears were conveying back to him. Had she really been attracted to him from the first day or was she merely being polite?

'I didn't realise you felt the same way,' he mumbled, staring down at his hands.

'Then you're not very observant Paul,' she said, pronouncing his first name in the exotic manner reserved by nature for French women. 'Even Mr Ammon noticed.'

'He *did?*' asked Paul, feeling sudden apprehension.

Nicole nodded slowly. 'I'm not off limits you know,' she said. 'I'm Mr Ammon's PA, not his mistress.'

Paul's shoulders rose and fell, as he heaved a deep sigh of relief. He valued his relationship with Mr Ammon, and despite his desire for Nicole, there had always been a niggling fear at the back of his mind that Mr Ammon might not approve.

'He's my boss, mentor and friend,' said Nicole morosely, 'but he's not my lover.'

The emphasis she placed on the last five words convinced Paul beyond all reasonable doubt that she was telling the truth. It, however, didn't stop him wondering why she was attracted to a mechanic from Waldon Town when she could have any man she wanted. He had no wealth or influence and Mr Ammon had hinted that she was high maintenance.

'I wasn't always this refined, Paul,' she said, rolling his name off the tip of her tongue, as if she enjoyed the effect her voice had on him. 'When Mr Ammon found me, I was desperate for success, having failed at everything I put my hands to. I had a failed marriage and was a struggling art college student pulling pints at a local pub in Waldon Town to pay my fees and the rent.'

'You live in Waldon Town?'

'I used to. Three years ago, I rented a room at the Horse and Canary and went to the local art college.'

'Well, I live and work in Waldon Town and I know the Horse and Canary. I'm surprised we never met.'

'It is a large town and I pretty much kept to myself.'

Paul tried to recall if he had ever seen her at the pub but couldn't remember.

'So, how did you meet Mr Ammon?'

'I applied for the Apple Seed Project, but my application was rejected. One day Mr Ammon showed up at the pub and asked me to paint a portrait of him. He said he had heard about my work from one of my lecturers and wanted to assist me in achieving my goal.'

'What is your goal?'

'To own an exclusive art gallery and auction house.'

'I'd love to see your artwork.'

'One day perhaps, when I'm feeling a bit more confident about my art.

'So, did you paint the portrait of Mr Ammon?'

'Yes, it wasn't very good, but he was very decent about it. He simply told me that he had come to rescue me and help me discover who I was truly meant to be, and for some weird reason I believed him. Since then, it has been an amazing experience.'

'It sounds like you owe him a great deal.'

'Yes,' she nodded. 'He has spent the last three years helping me adopt a healthy mindset and a more positive self-image. He helped me forget the trauma of my failed marriage and taught me to look after number one – me. Not even a psychiatrist could've done more for me.'

'You don't look like you ever needed a psychiatrist,' said Paul, staring at her in genuine awe. 'Come to think of it, you don't look like you were ever married.'

'I was very young,' she said wistfully, 'and he was very abusive, but that's another life.'

'I'm sorry,' he said awkwardly.

'What for?' she asked, brightening up again. 'I'm not. I've got used to not being a punch bag or the object of scorn for some man who's afraid to admit that he's a failure.'

'I would never hurt you,' said Paul, without thinking. As he realised the soppy implication of his words, his countenance dropped.

'That's very sweet,' she said, reaching across the table to touch his hands. 'I believe you because you're a gentleman, but Antoine was not gentle. He was frustrated because of all his missed opportunities in life. Contrary to what you may think, Antoine was hard working, and he never touched any drugs or alcohol. I also believe that he was faithful to me whilst we were married – his work was his passion.'

'What work did he do?' asked Paul, realising that she wished to unburden herself and talk about that 'other life'.

'He was an artist – a painter,' she clarified, 'probably one of the best in Paris at the time. Antoine was in demand, and he was making a lot of money. I was one of his models and because I wasn't shy to pose in…in the,' she struggled a bit; 'without my clothes on. Anyway, he started giving me work and that's how we became close and then we got married.'

She became silent and her eyes developed a crystalline quality, as she appeared to muse over a part of her life that was so detached from her present reality.

'So, what went wrong?'

'Antoine was small-minded,' said Nicole, looking past him even though her hands still gently caressed his. 'He was operating out of a studio in Paris bought for him by his grandfather, a famous artist, who'd raised Antoine after Antoine's father took his own life due to a failed business.

Antoine had watched his father struggle to pay his debts and his grandfather, who was a closet communist, began to lecture him on the dangers of capitalism. Even after his grandfather died, Antoine remained in the studio refusing to expand his business for fear of having to borrow money from the banks and then struggle to repay his debts like his father.

'About two years after his grandfather died, the French government commissioned Antoine to paint the portraits of all the presidents and prime ministers of the last century, as part of an exhibition celebrating French leadership. But the contract required Antoine to show evidence of having sufficient working capital to execute the project before it could be awarded to him. Antoine refused to borrow money by using the studio as collateral, but instead he used his savings and business profits to execute the contract.

Unfortunately, the contract was awarded too close to the general elections and a new government came in with a cost-cutting plan that resulted in the cancellation of the contract. No money was paid to Antoine who had used all of his savings, and this was the beginning of his depression. He lost his passion for art and began to paint buildings instead. It took him three years to battle the French government for his money and during that time the violence started.'

She paused to blink back the droplets gathering in her eyes and Paul squeezed her hands in solidarity, unable to think of any encouraging response.

'I'm all right,' she said with a calm smile.

'Look, you don't have to talk about this,' he said, realising that it was casting a cloud over what was supposed to be a happy occasion.

'I want to,' said Nicole fervently, 'because in many ways you remind me of Antoine, and I'm scared of my miserable past catching up with my bright future.'

She watched him placidly, letting her words sink in before continuing.

'Antoine was a verbally abusive person by nature,' she said, 'but when he lost his money, he started becoming physically abusive, blaming me for his misfortune. In the three years of hell, I miscarried twice because of the abuse and cannot count how many times I woke up in hospital after he'd beaten me unconscious.'

'I guess it was the frustration of the financial mess he was in,' cut in Paul, desiring to demonstrate his attentiveness.

'I don't know,' she said shaking her head sadly, 'because even after he eventually won his court case and was paid the money, the abuse kept on. During those three years, he was forced to take out a loan, his first ever, using the studio but because he refused to work on a regular basis, he fell behind on repayments and lost the studio. We had to move into rented accommodation and Antoine kept on saying that he regretted meeting me and accused me of being a witch who had cast an evil spell on him.'

'That's crazy,' said Paul. 'Why didn't you just leave him?'

'And go where?' she asked tiredly. 'Back home to my parents? They didn't want anything to do with me when I dropped out of school to pose as a model for Antoine. I had run away from home at seventeen and was living with Antoine in his studio.'

'What about friends?' he asked, trying to maintain the flow.

'I had no real friends and nowhere to go. When he got paid by the government Antoine bought another studio, but he never recovered the passion to paint again. He eventually threw me out without any money, and I began sleeping rough on the streets of Paris and in hostels run by charities. To survive I used to sketch tourists near the Eiffel Tower, but when I kept on having trouble with the *gendarmes,* I ran to Britain to try my luck and you know the rest.'

'That's an incredible story,' said Paul, unable to conceal his fascination, despite the gruesome nature of the account.

'It was a bitter lesson,' she said grimly, 'but one that I will never have to relive, because I never intend to end up with a man like Antoine ever again.'

Recalling that Nicole said he reminded her of Antoine, Paul felt the doors closing on his prospects and panic began to ravage his confidence. At this precise moment, the last man he wanted to be was an Antoine clone. The waiters arrived as if on cue, laden with platters containing their lobsters with a side dish of salad. Instinctively, he stopped breathing through his mouth and, as the food was laid out before them along with all the curious implements for tackling the lobster, he noticed that he'd acclimatised to the smell of raw fish.

As he pondered over the phenomenon, he wondered whether his adjustment had anything to do with the fact that, for the last half hour, all his senses had been trained on Nicole.

'Lobster *thermidor*?' he asked, switching topic in the hope of diffusing the tension.

'*Non M'sieu*,' said one of the waiters, '*Homard sauté à la crème*.'

Paul turned to Nicole in bewilderment.

'Lobster *newberg*,' she translated, relaxing visibly as she sniffed the aroma rising upwards from the dark red lobster on the platter before her. 'Lobster *thermidor* is usually on their dinner menu and it's by special order only.'

'Well, it sure looks good,' said Paul, leaning forward to inhale the various flavours. 'I only hope it tastes as good.'

'Better,' she said, reaching for an instrument that resembled a pair of pliers. 'I only hope you do too.'

Paul, who was slow on the uptake, had to replay her words in his mind twice before her subtle meaning hit him. She was still interested. He opened his mouth to respond, but she silenced him with a smile and a finger to her lips.

'Now you'll need the lobster cracker and the spatula,' she said softly, 'so you don't make a mess and advertise the fact that you're a lobster virgin.'

'I'm not Antoine,' he whispered, as she demonstrated how to dissect the lobster with the lobster cracker.

'I know,' she said quietly. 'Antoine was an expert at eating lobster.'

Paul studied her serious countenance and tried to figure out whether she was teasing, but she gave nothing away, leaving him more confused than ever.

* * * * * * *

'Have you thought this through?' asked Basil. His stiff tone betrayed his feeble effort at sounding unruffled.

Basil had just received a termination letter, the contents of which quite bluntly highlighted Paul's lack of confidence in his judgement. It was only natural that he'd want to know the basis for that damning assessment.

Paul looked at the pale-faced man in the tweed jacket and old school tie, whose lapel pin advertised the fact that he was an affiliate of a private cricket club and realised that he'd made the right decision. Basil was the epitome of a public school-bred English gentleman with a stiff upper lip and a sense of self-righteous indignation in the face of disapproval from those he considered his inferiors.

Paul and an apprentice had been recoupling a gearbox casing, when Basil had breezed in and strutted across the workshop, grimacing with every step as his handmade brogues made contact with the greasy, grimy floor. As a rule, Basil never left the *olde-worlde* confines of his office in Waldon Town's central business district, preferring to deal with his clients via phone or written correspondence. Any client who desired an audience with him made the trek up to his office where they were billed by the hour and subjected to his opinion, which usually erred on the side of caution.

Albert Munnelly was Basil's ideal client, a poorly educated, skilled workman who was wary of the new world and all the trends that accompanied it. Such men required accountants who thought like them and were opposed to even the gentlest rocking of the boat. But Paul wasn't Albert, and he was determined to get that message across.

'Look, I realise this must be tough on you...' began Paul.

'Tough on me?' asked Basil, looking at him with the unflappable expression that had become his trademark. 'Don't be silly, Paul; how can this be tough on me? You're the one I'm concerned about.'

Paul studied Basil's face for signs of strain but found none. Either the man was a very talented actor, or he was genuinely at ease. Was this anything to do with the old British reserve – that bulldog tenacity that never accepted defeat even in the face of overwhelming odds?

'You don't need to be concerned about me,' said Paul, deflecting his gaze to his apprentice who'd carried on working. 'Use the torque wrench, Harry, and tighten the last three bolts gently, as the thread in the housing is wearing thin.' He turned his attention back to Basil. 'Sorry about that, Mr Mead,' he said, wiping his brow with the back of one grease-stained hand. 'Look, I've thought this through, and I feel it's best if we call it a day.'

'Your letter indicated that you were dissatisfied with my professional competence,' said Basil bluntly.

'Yes,' said Paul, leaning back against a tool cabinet, 'I found your advice subjective.'

Basil's eyes narrowed to a squint. 'In what way?' he asked.

'I just found it subjective that's all,' said Paul, unwilling to spell out his real concerns.

Basil nodded and thrust both hands into the pockets of his jacket. 'If you're dispensing with my services,' he said gruffly, 'I deserve to know the reason why, and yet you've told me nothing. Why are you being so evasive, Paul?'

'I'm not being evasive,' answered Paul shiftily. 'I'm looking to do new things and I need an accountant who buys into my vision... not my father's.'

The period of silence that followed was deafening, as Paul felt the blood rush up to his head blocking out all sound. The pressure in his ears reminded him of the ear-blocking sensation that occurred anytime he was travelling in a train, as it went through a tunnel.

It wasn't his intention to break Basil's heart, but his mind was made up and there was no going back; not even if Basil relaxed his position on the business park investment and did a 180 degree turn around. To back down now and reinstate the man would be interpreted as a sign of weakness.

'I've always looked out for your best interests, Paul,' said Basil sombrely, 'just as I did for your father, but obviously that doesn't count for anything.'

'That's all in the past,' mumbled Paul obstinately. 'All that counts now is the future.' He stopped short of adding *'and you're not a part of it.'*

'Very well,' said Basil with a resigned sigh. 'I'll arrange for the client account to be closed and the books transferred to my successor in title, that is, your new accountant. What firm are you moving to, by the way?'

Paul was so surprised at the ease with which Basil had been made to cave in, that his response was delayed. The wily old fox had to be up to something.

'Unfortunately, I can't tell you that,' said Paul awkwardly, 'its professional privilege.'

'In other words, you don't trust me,' said Basil with a dejected shrug. 'This isn't like you, Paul, this isn't like you. I wonder who's behind the scenes advising you.'

'No one's been advising me!' protested Paul. 'I make my own decisions and I've decided to sever my links with you. Now I'll pay you what I owe you for the work you've done, but after that I'm moving my business elsewhere.'

'As you like it,' said Basil, taking his right hand out of his jacket pocket and extending it to Paul, with a wry grin on his face. 'It's been an honour and privilege to have served Munnelly and Sons for the last two decades and who knows what the future holds.'

Paul hesitated before shaking the outstretched hand, feeling uncomfortable with the content and tone of Basil's parting comments. He certainly had no intention of ever working with the old man again, but it would be unkind to say that. Best to let him depart with the illusion that Paul would be back on bended knee, seeking his services.

Paul watched Basil head for the exit, stepping gingerly around the grimier areas of the floor, until he reached his classic British racing green MK2 Jaguar which he'd reputedly owned from new. The vehicle was immaculate for its age and in many ways reflected the character of its owner – in good nick, but no match for a new one.

* * * * * * *

Paul took the long route to Mr Ammon's house, opting for the A5 dual carriageway, where he unleashed the revs and sent the Porsche hurtling northwards past Dunstable and Milton Keynes, before exiting in Buckingham and slowing down to a cruise. As the car was now fully run-in, he had reluctantly informed Mr Ammon that he would be returning it today. A part of him wanted to keep shut and wait for Mr Ammon to request for the awesome car's return, but his sense of integrity compelled him to make the first move. As he trickled along with the afternoon traffic through Buckingham, he reflected on the missed opportunities that he'd registered whilst the car was in his possession.

Out of the blue, his ex-girlfriend had ditched the butcher's son or vice versa and tried to make a comeback which he'd rebuffed. Then there was a gorgeous flight attendant, flying for a Middle Eastern airline, whose car had broken down near his workshop and he'd given a lift home. He'd fixed her car and returned it to her home address, but despite her offers to buy him dinner and her numerous texts, he'd not responded.

Ever since his date with Nicole, he'd had eyes for no one else. He found everything about her enigmatic personality alluring and wanted to spend a lifetime exploring her mysterious depths. She was undoubtedly high maintenance, judging from the eventual lunch bill he'd been hit with, but he wasn't dissuaded. He was determined to both love and be loved by her.

Driving up to the huge electric gates at the beginning of Mr Ammon's driveway, he wondered if she was in. Since their date a fortnight ago, he had left messages on her mobile phone, but received no response. It was as if she'd suddenly vanished into thin air. As the gates swung open, Paul drove sedately towards the art deco style mansion, keeping a sharp lookout for the ferocious dogs that he knew would be prowling around. This was his first time back since his initial visit and he sensed all the old fears resurfacing.

As he arrived at the porch, he noticed the jet black, late model Rolls Royce with a personalised number plate parked there but saw no sign of Nicole's BMW. Paul hoped she was in because it was for her sake that he'd worn one of his designer suits, the Hugo Boss, and had had an expensive manicure. To tackle the strong odour of engine oil, grease and petrol that often clung to him, even after a shower, he'd doused himself with *Jean Paul Gautier eau de' toilette.*

In anticipation of seeing her, he'd also taken the initiative to scribble down a note which he hoped to slip to her when he had the opportunity. The note simply stated that he was missing her and asked her to give him a call.

He alighted from the car, and cautiously left the door open, in case he needed to return to its safety in a hurry. He looked furtively around him for signs of vicious canine presence but saw nothing. Either the dogs had been given the day off or they were lying in wait, ready to attack from some invisible vantage point as soon as he stepped away from the car.

Realising that he couldn't stand by the car forever, he began to walk slowly towards the front door. Seeing none of the expected canine hostility, his strides became quicker and bolder till he found himself at the front door, where his quivering finger urgently pressed the doorbell. Less than a minute after he'd depressed the doorbell, the door was opened by a smallish white man in a butler's outfit.

'Good afternoon, sir,' said the man, standing to one side. 'Mr Ammon is expecting you.'

'It's a good thing you locked up the dogs,' said Paul, walking past him into the hallway.

'On the contrary, sir,' said the butler, nodding in the direction of the door, 'they've been behind you all the while.'

Paul spun around and his pulse raced at the sight of the four vicious Doberman dogs, sitting on their haunches on the spot he'd just vacated. They were real masters of subtlety.

'By the way, is Nicole about?' he asked in a hushed voice, as they headed to the venue of his meeting with Mr Ammon.

'No, sir,' answered the butler, halting at a ground floor door. 'She flew to Paris this morning to attend to some domestic situation.'

Paul's mind immediately zeroed in on Antoine, and apprehension set in as he wondered whether the man was staging a comeback. That obviously explained her silence and why none of his phone messages had been replied. He wanted to ask how long she would be away for, but caught himself, as the door ahead of them opened to reveal a smiling Mr Ammon. Behind the door was a home study, complete with wood panelling, an open fireplace, wooden floor, and a finely crafted oak desk with red leather topping. There were bookshelves stacked with books and a large charcoal-sketched portrait of the man himself. Paul wondered whether it was Nicole's handwork. Mr Ammon held a book in his hands, revealing that he'd been reading prior to the interruption. He looked relaxed in his stripy rugby shirt over plain khakis, and his laid-back demeanour instantly put Paul at ease.

'Nicole is not here, unfortunately,' said Mr Ammon presumptuously as the door shut behind his departing butler. 'She had to dash across to France to attend a funeral, but she should be back in a couple of days.'

'Oh, was it someone close? A family member perhaps?'

'Her ex-husband – Antoine.'

'Oh,' said Paul, as his heart began to pound inexplicably, and his muscles tensed up.

'Apparently, he'd been ill for quite some time,' said Mr Ammon, 'but she only found out a week ago when he contacted her to say he was dying and needed to see her. She flew out to see him for a few days and had only got back yesterday evening when she received a call informing her of his demise.'

'Thanks,' mumbled Paul, unsure of what else to say.

'So, the car's outside?'

'All waxed and vacuumed and it's even got a full tank of

petrol,' answered Paul.

'Good,' said Mr Ammon, handing him a bulky brown envelope. 'I knew I could rely on you to get the job done.'

Paul accepted the brown envelope without checking its contents. Every week since he'd been in possession of the Porsche, Paul had received a brown envelope from Mr Ammon via courier, containing a small bundle of crisp fifty-pound notes. It was a ritual he was going to miss.

'How's the investment progressing?' asked Mr Ammon, walking around his desk to occupy a leather swivel chair.

'It's going well,' said Paul, letting his eyes wander around the room. 'I've raised a loan to pay the deposit and now I'm just waiting for construction to be completed so I can take possession and start making some real money.'

'That's the spirit,' said Mr Ammon, nodding so vigorously that the leather chair beneath him started to creak in protest, 'and I note that you've finally parted ways with old Basil.'

'You know him?' asked Paul, mildly surprised at the revelation.

'Of course,' answered Mr Ammon. 'In assessing potential protégés, I always assess their social and professional acquaintances as part of my due diligence. You were right to dump Basil; he was weighing you down like baggage full of stuff you think you need, but don't. To make it in the 21st century, you need to run light.'

'Basil served my father well,' said Paul inexplicably, feeling slightly defensive.

'But you're not your father,' said Mr Ammon.

Paul nodded vigorously, but his mind had drifted. He needed to see Nicole and didn't feel able to wait for her return. He needed to know whether the memory of Antoine would cast a perpetual shadow over any future relationship. Several weeks ago, she'd painted the picture of an independent soul, free of any shackles to her ugly past. But her reaction to both Antoine's illness and his death proved otherwise.

It was possible that she was still in love with him and had not been able to expunge him completely from her system.

Would she return from Paris ready to face the future or would she remain enslaved to her unsavoury past? He needed answers before he lost his mind and the will to move on.

'You're in love with her, aren't you,' said Mr Ammon gently. The observation was delivered with a confidence that told Paul it was pointless lying to the man.

'Yes, I am,' he confirmed, 'but I'm also confused.'

'Then why don't you fly out to Paris and resolve the confusion?'

Paul considered Mr Ammon's warm smile and nodded. The man was right. Why pine away in the U.K speculating? Right now, he needed absolutes; he needed to know where he stood, and the best place to determine that was Paris.

'The funeral's tomorrow,' said Mr Ammon, with a disarming grin, 'and if you catch an evening flight you could be in Paris tonight and by her side tomorrow.'

'Yes,' began Paul awkwardly, 'but it all seems a bit rushed, maybe I ought to wait till she gets back.'

'If you love her, you'll go to Paris' said Mr Ammon.

Paul considered the suggestion and nodded slowly; after all, what did he have to lose?

'Good man,' said Mr Ammon, with a congenial wink. 'You know it makes sense.'

THE MUNNELLY AFFAIR
(The Hook)

9

Spring in Paris was a cooler affair than sunny Waldon Town and, as he emerged from the terminal building at Charles de Gaulle Airport, Paul regretted not bringing warmer clothes. The unwelcome crisp breeze that assaulted his exposed face and hands was a brutal reminder of the importance of checking the weather forecast before leaving home. Dressed only in a dark lounge suit with no tie, he looked out of place amidst fellow travellers all donning overcoats and scarves.

His plan to fly in the previous evening on the last flight and surprise Nicole was scuppered by heavy traffic into Luton Airport. Now he'd have to settle for surprising her at the cemetery but doubted it would have the same impact.

True to his word, Mr Ammon had provided the funeral details and also given an alternative mobile phone number that Nicole could be reached on. The funeral was taking place at the crematorium located within the cemetery complex at *Père Lachaise,* and the cremation ceremony was slated to start at nine thirty am. Paul had been advised by a fellow passenger, a lively American tourist who claimed to know Paris like the back of his hand, that the best way to get into the city at that time of day was by train to avoid the rush hour.

Paul had initially toyed with the idea of hiring an executive rental car in a bid to impress Nicole, but the prospect of turning up late for the funeral due to traffic made him cave in and catch the fast train to *Gare du Nord* station in Paris, from where he caught the metro line to *Stalingrad* station and then switched to another metro line which was heading in the direction of *Père Lachaise* station.

Almost two hours after boarding the train at Paris CDG Airport, Paul emerged at the station near *Père Lachaise* Cemetery, promising himself never to travel by rush hour metro ever again, and began the brisk hike towards the crematorium, glancing intermittently at his watch. The time was already quarter past ten and he was sure that the ceremony was already over.

As he approached the imposing building that housed the crematorium, he slowed down to admire the Roman influenced architecture. It looked nothing like a crematorium. He meandered his way through the tourists wandering up and down the complex, armed with cameras and camcorders and tried to get his bearings. The *columbarium* that surrounded the main building with its series of arched columns reminded him of a beehive and he wondered how on earth he was going to trace Nicole.

A brief chat with a *gendarme* secured directions to the ceremony chamber on the ground floor, and he arrived to find Nicole in the midst of a small gathering watching a casket slowly vanish into the furnace of the cremator.

As everyone's backs were to the door, no one saw him arrive. He stood behind them, impassively watching the spectacle until the door of the cremator slid shut. In all, there were five people, excluding Paul, observing Antoine's final moments indicating that he couldn't have been the most popular of people. Perhaps more telling was the emotionally cold atmosphere. Except for a stooped elderly woman with a cane, who was sobbing quietly, no one else made a sound. Like a speck of dust carried by the wind, Antoine evaporated.

Nicole looked nothing like the grieving widow. Her cream-coloured outfit and rakish hat painted the picture of a woman who was about to embark on a Caribbean cruise. Although her eyes were obscured by lightly tinted sunglasses, as she leaned towards the old lady, Paul could see no trace of tears streaking down her cheeks. If she was hurting, it was well-concealed.

The other mourners were a middle-aged woman dressed in plain unattractive woolly clothing, and two stocky men in coarse work clothes. The stench of poverty was almost as overpowering as the light fumes emanating from the cremator, and Nicole was like a potent deodorant struggling to suppress it. Paul wondered if they were her relatives. The old woman suddenly pulled back and thrust a crooked index finger at Nicole's face. What followed was a torrent of guttural French words from the older woman, accompanied by a shower of saliva and exaggerated gesticulations.

The verbal assault lasted a full thirty seconds, before the old woman turned to one of the men beside her and reached up to hold on to his upper arm. They turned around and headed for the door followed by the other woman and her male companion. As the quartet walked past Paul, they sized him up from head to toe, their faces wrinkled with hostility. They'd obviously written him off as being on the side of their enemy and therefore not worthy of their time. Paul wondered what Nicole had done to incur their wrath.

'Paul!' exclaimed Nicole, shattering the momentary silence.

Paul turned round to face Nicole's exuberant face and in that moment the trip seemed worth it. He'd never seen her look so excited in the brief period he'd known her. She walked briskly towards him with outstretched arms, and her dazzling smile was the warmest he'd seen. As she threw herself against his chest, he felt like one of the allied troops in 1945 after the liberation of Paris. He gingerly wrapped his arms around her expecting her to retreat, but she didn't.

'What are you doing here, darling?' she asked softly, making his knees go wobbly. She'd just called him 'darling' for the first time and that was worth a celebration in itself.

'Mr Ammon told me where to find you.'

'And you flew all this way to be with me?' Her shaded eyes stared at him in disbelief, making him realise that she was genuinely moved by his gesture.

He shrugged casually to downplay the whole thing, but the

fact that she was still nestling in his arms was poignant.

'This really means so much to me,' she said in a wavering voice. 'You can't imagine how lonely it's been, especially with all the hostility…' Her voice faltered, as they came apart.

'I'm sorry about your husband,' he said cagily.

'*Merçi*,' she said, taking off her sunglasses to appraise him with sultry eyes. 'And I'm sorry that I've not returned any of your calls …' Again, her voice faded.

'Forget about it,' he said chivalrously. 'Antoine was your ex, and it'd be crazy if there weren't still feelings for him.'

'Antoine has always been my husband,' she said, lowering her gaze slightly. 'At least he was until two days ago when death separated us.' She looked up again, but this time with tears sparkling in her eyes. 'We were never divorced … I'm sorry for the deception.'

Paul nodded gently. It made no difference. What mattered now was that she was free from any marital ties and legally available for a new relationship.

She looked over his shoulder and smiled with tears still welling in her eyes. 'I can only imagine what they're thinking,' she said quietly.

Paul glanced over his shoulder at the hostile-looking gathering, standing in the chamber's doorway.

'Members of Antoine's family?' he asked.

'Antoine's mother, sister, and cousins,' she answered, 'and right now they wish that I was the one in the cremator.'

'They blame you for the separation?'

'They blame me for the reunion,' she murmured bitterly. 'They're convinced that my showing up at Antoine's deathbed accelerated his demise, sending him to an early grave. Early grave – pah! They were the ones who killed him with their constant demands, and now they resent me.'

'They're just upset,' said Paul, running out of inspiration.

'They're always upset,' said Nicole, taking a handkerchief out of her bag to dab the corners of her eyes as the tears seemed to evaporate. 'Even when Antoine threw me out and they had him all to themselves, they were always upset. A bitter heart can never produce sweetness.'

Paul nodded, wondering why she was telling him all this.

'They've gone now,' she said, looking over his shoulder again, 'but believe me it's not over. Antoine's mother has already made it clear that she intends to claim his ashes and take them back to Lyon to scatter them over the family's ancestral land and she's warned me not to assert my right as the widow. She's also told me not to expect any portion of Antoine's estate because my name's not in his final will.'

'Antoine left a will?'

Nicole nodded and smiled blissfully. 'That's what this is all about,' she said. 'It's why I intend to attend the reading of that will and claim what is rightfully mine.'

'Are you a beneficiary?' he asked, even though he felt he already knew the answer.

She nodded again. 'Antoine was very generous,' she said, softly.

'He left you his canvas and paint brushes?' asked Paul in a flat attempt at humour.

'He left me his new mortgage-free studio along *Rue de Rivoli*,' she answered ecstatically, 'and a hundred thousand euros to furnish it.'

Despite the voices in his head alerting him to the fact that he was in love with a gold digger, he blanked them out, and focussed on her finer qualities such as her smouldering gaze which was, at that precise moment, trained on him.

*　*　*　*　*　*　*

As the taxi wound its way through the congested streets of central Paris, Paul pondered over everything Nicole had told him and struggled to put it in context. Just three weeks ago, Nicole was describing Antoine as the scum of the earth and promising never to be fooled by the likes of him again. Now, here she was, heading to the office of his lawyers for the reading of his will.

Before setting off from the crematorium, Nicole had

disclosed that the contents of the will were not yet known by Antoine's family. Before he died Antoine had confided in her what her share of his estate would be. He knew it would be controversial, as his mother and sister disliked her, and he'd warned her to expect a fight. For this reason, he'd advised her not to attend the reading of the will, but to wait for his lawyer to contact her at a later date. However, she was ignoring that advice – determined to get the keys to her new studio apartment that very day.

Antoine had had a crisis of conscience on his deathbed and was determined to make amends. He'd become a Christian and repented of the way he'd treated her. He sent for her through a mutual friend who revealed that Antoine was seriously ill and on the verge of dying. At first, she'd been reluctant to go, believing him to be broke and soliciting for her assistance. She also couldn't figure out how he'd traced her or why he'd gone to so much trouble. She'd initially feared that it was a ruse to get her to Paris so he could harm her.

However, Mr Ammon had convinced her to take the risk. He'd even offered to accompany her, but she opted to travel alone and found Antoine no longer living in squalor, but in a decent rented apartment in the suburbs. Antoine was being cared for by Marceline, his sister, and was battling a lung infection that turned out to be a malignant cancer, thanks to his chain-smoking habit. He'd lost a lot of weight and his complexion was pale.

She recounted how Antoine immediately got to the point explaining, with great difficulty owing to his respiratory problems, that he'd asked her to come because he wished to apologise to her in person for how he'd treated her.

Antoine had begun to weep as he recalled how harshly he'd dealt with her rather than face up to his own responsibility for his predicament. He begged for her forgiveness, and she'd reluctantly forgiven him, unable to forget the mental and physical torment she'd been subjected to in the slums of Paris when he threw her out. However, she had no desire to see him die in sorrow and so had shelved her bitterness. The prognosis was bleak, and he had only a matter of days left to live. She'd decided to spend several days with him and, it was on the second day of her visit that he confided in her that he'd changed his will to make provision for her and that he was leaving her a newly acquired studio and one hundred thousand Euros to decorate it.

He'd explained how the cancelled government project was reinstated, and he'd been paid for his paintings and permitted to exhibit them. His exhibition attracted new commissions and as his workload increased, he rediscovered the passion for painting. He'd begun to mint gold and his fame spread within art circles. Respiratory problems and a routine check-up revealed the onset of lung cancer, but he continued to paint knowing that he was living on borrowed time. It was at this time his discovery for the meaning of life led him to Jesus Christ and the peace that he'd been seeking for all his life. He'd drawn up a will and hired a private investigator to track Nicole down all over Paris and neighbouring suburbs. When there was no trace of her in Paris the search spread across France until immigration records showed that she'd obtained a passport and travelled to the U.K.

After hearing the good news, she'd extended her trip in Paris to a full week to shower him with care and attention, whilst she waited for him to die. When Antoine defied his medical prognosis, she'd returned back to the U.K only to learn that her husband had died that evening. Her sole purpose for being in Paris now was the cremation, the reading of the will and the possession of her inheritance.

As the studio was across the street from the law firm, Nicole aimed to kill two birds with one stone. Paul offered to catch up with her later, but she insisted on him accompanying her for the taxi ride to *Rue de Rivoli*.

At their destination, Nicole alighted from the taxi, leaving Paul to pay the fare. Walking towards the building, he noticed a rugged looking young Asian man in a leather jacket lurking around the entrance. Their eyes met and Paul shuddered at the other's steely, red-eyed glare. Nicole was waiting for him in the lobby, and they headed to the first floor, where Antoine's lawyers had their offices.

The office was an airy modern open-plan environment adopting a minimalist approach to maximise what little space was available. There were a number of individual glass-walled rooms around the perimeter, with adjustable drapes providing a degree of privacy.

Whilst Nicole had a quiet chat with the receptionist, Paul took a seat in the waiting area studying the simple but tasteful décor, trying to figure out whether the framed Monet gracing the wall was the genuine article. Albert had loved collecting prints of famous paintings and telling him all about the artists. When Nicole eventually joined him, she followed the direction of his gaze and grinned.

'It's a print,' she said breezily. 'The real painting's hanging in a Dutch art gallery.'

It was an authentic looking piece of art, far better than any of the prints Albert brought home. 'It's lovely,' he murmured appreciatively. 'I would never have guessed.'

'That's one good thing that came out of my marriage to Antoine,' she said in a low voice. 'I can always spot a fake.'

'So, what now?' he asked.

'We wait. The lawyer's still in another meeting.'

They waited in silence for another ten minutes till an athletic-looking sun-tanned man wearing a well-cut suit emerged from one of the offices and came up to them introducing himself as Alain Touzé, Antoine's lawyer. He kissed Nicole on both cheeks and shook Paul's hand firmly. He drew Nicole aside and they began to converse in French for about five minutes. Unable to follow the conversation, Paul instead studied their body language for clues.

Nicole gesticulated frequently and her expression conveyed distress as she spoke. It wasn't clear why she'd suddenly become upset, but Paul suspected it had everything to do with Antoine's family. Alain on the other hand appeared to do more listening, conveying empathy with a slow nod or a gentle hand on her shoulder. At one point, he raised two hands to halt her mid-sentence and then gestured towards his office, making the point that it was more discreet in there.

Without warning, Nicole broke down and started to weep bitterly, much to Alain's discomfort. As the lawyer stood looking at her helplessly, Paul hurried across the reception area to wrap an arm around her shoulders, drawing her close to him. It was an opportune moment unlikely to be repeated.

'Let us go into my office,' said Alain, in fluent English, with only a hint of his French accent; 'there's more privacy there.'

In the comfort of his office, Alain offered Nicole a handkerchief which she accepted and Paul a cigar which was declined, before asking if it was all right if he smoked. As he went through the motions of lighting and then puffing on his cigar, Alain's face retained the empathy, but there was also a hint of strain lurking behind his stare. Paul wondered whether the man was aware of the family wrangling and whether that would influence his decision regarding the reading of the will in the absence of other interested parties.

Sitting beside Paul, with her hand now resting limply in his, Nicole dabbed at the corners of her eyes with her head lowered so that her smudged makeup wasn't visible. From the heaving of her shoulders, and the occasional sniffle, she painted the picture of a grieving widow. Across the desk, Alain puffed away patiently, waiting for Nicole to visibly calm down before speaking again. He spoke to Nicole in French, occasionally looking in Paul's direction, and at the end of it she shook her head and whispered her response. She then slipped her hand out of his and began to rummage through the contents in her small handbag.

'She tells me you are a close friend,' said Alain, lowering his smouldering cigar, 'so I believe it is all right for me to speak with you present.'

Paul looked at Nicole who had raised her head and was looking in the opposite direction, as she reapplied her makeup.

He wasn't sure if Nicole would want him to sit in for something as private as the reading of Antoine's will and had to be sure. He caught her eye in the corner of her petite vanity mirror and she nodded softly.

'I'd really like you to stay,' she said, pausing in the act of lining her eyes with mascara. 'Right now, I'm feeling very vulnerable after all those threats made by Antoine's family. I would feel more comfortable if you stayed with me.'

Paul considered the request and nodded; it wasn't a difficult decision.

'Very good,' said Alain, temporarily stubbing out his cigar in the ashtray provided. 'We are still waiting for Antoine's mother and sister, and once they arrive, we will go to the conference room where I will read the will and deal with any immediate questions.'

Nicole began to speak in French, but mid-sentence remembering that Paul was in the room switched back to English. 'So, it's just the three of us?' she asked.

Alain shook his head.

'Who else?' she asked bluntly.

'The daughter,' answered Alain, 'she's waiting in the conference room.'

'Whose daughter?' asked Nicole, half rising from her seat in anxiety.

'Antoine's, of course,' replied Alain detachedly.

There was a period of silence, during which Paul studied each person's face in turn. Alain's casual demeanour contrasted very effectively with Nicole's apprehensive one.

'He had a daughter?' she asked at length, as if she hadn't heard him the first time.

'Yes,' Alain replied. 'Monique. She's just turned eighteen.'

'He had a previous marriage?' asked Nicole anxiously.

'No,' replied Alain. 'He never married Monique's mother and initially he denied paternity of the child, but recent DNA tests prove that he is the biological father, so under French law he must provide for the child in his will.'

Nicole absorbed the bombshell with remarkable aplomb and her body language relaxed as did her countenance. She calmly rose to her feet, but her crooked smile seemed to conceal her inner thoughts. 'I want to see her,' she said simply.

Alain also rose up but made no effort to move from behind his desk. Instead, he stood studying her face as if trying to elicit her real motive. He began to speak in French, but then translated for Paul's benefit. 'I don't want any trouble, Madame,' he said softly.

'There won't be,' assured Nicole grinning disarmingly; 'at least not from me, Alain.'

'Very well,' said Alain. 'I'll take you to her, but remember you've given me your word.'

They followed Alain out of the office and across the open-plan area to a larger glass-walled room at the opposite side. Alain opened the door and politely stood aside before following them in. The room was dominated by a long conference table and seated at one end of it was a large, faired-haired, teenage girl wearing a tight denim jacket over a faded T shirt. Her face was smothered in uneven makeup, and she had a couple of studs over her left eyebrow. Her most distinguishing features were the dark area around her right eye, the bruising to her nose, and her split upper lip, which looked like they had been inflicted by a person's fist.

As they walked in, she looked up and her eyes roved from one face to the other, finally settling on Paul's for some reason. Paul's eyes shifted around uneasily trying to avoid her blue ones in a cat and mouse game, but every time his gaze lowered to her face, he found her staring at him unnervingly.

'Monique Matisse,' announced Alain, 'meet Nicole Matisse – your father's widow.'

Neither woman said anything to the other but, whilst Monique blushed and shyly turned away, Nicole's stare was scornful. Maybe the sight of the opposition reassured her of her chances of claiming her inheritance without hassle.

'Where is your mother?' asked Nicole, in a tone that contrived to sound condescending, as she strolled over to where Monique sat.

'She speaks little English,' said Alain apologetically. 'She is eighteen but has the mental age of a child of thirteen, so I need to explain things to her in a way that she can understand.'

<hr>

Alain dovetailed back to his native dialect, speaking gently to the girl, and she began to smile shyly and nod in response to his explanation.

'Shouldn't she have a guardian?' asked Nicole.

'I am her guardian and the trustee of her share of the will,' said Alain. 'That is because her mother abandoned her many years ago and she has been in and out of foster homes ever since. Her story is a truly harrowing one.'

'Poor thing,' said Nicole disdainfully. 'I can see why Antoine wanted nothing to do with her. Presumably, her mother was just as backward.'

Paul blushed with embarrassment at her cruelty but convinced himself that Nicole was most probably feeling sorry for herself. By putting down Monique, it was a way of masking her own pain. A while ago, he'd heard a psychologist on the radio discuss the syndrome of transferred aggression.

The more Paul considered Monique, the more sorry he felt for her. She looked so vulnerable and confused. Her facial bruising was down to the crowd she was hanging out with. There was probably some boyfriend out there abusing her, waiting to squander her inheritance.

'Well, if you'll wait here with Monique,' said Alain, opening the door, 'I'll go and get the will and other documents. Hopefully, Antoine's mother and sister should soon be here.'

They sat opposite Monique, and for the first time Paul noticed the stale body odour that seemed to emanate from Monique's direction. She clearly had personal hygiene issues and he wondered about her ability to properly care for herself.

'Maybe we should open the window,' said Nicole, sniffing the atmosphere around her indiscreetly. 'I suspect Alain's cleaners have gone on strike.'

Monique blushed even more, and her gaze hit the table's surface, making Paul realise that she understood more English than Alain credited her with. Paul felt like nudging Nicole and suggesting that she be more sensitive, but held back, unsure of how his intrusion would be received.

'I can't believe he never told me about her all the time we

were together,' said Nicole in disgust, speaking more to herself than anyone else. 'Why didn't he mention that he already had a child instead of telling me he didn't want children because they would interfere with his creativity?'

'Maybe he was afraid of having another child like her,' said Paul, without thinking.

Nicole's expression froze as Paul finished speaking, and he felt like jumping out of the window as she recoiled in horror at the implication of his statement.

'I didn't mean that you would've given him a disabled child,' he said hurriedly, dreading the prospect of being alienated from her affections. 'What I meant to say was that he was probably afraid that he was incapable of fathering a child without disabilities.'

His explanation seemed to do the trick, as her expression softened, and she relaxed. She nodded in agreement.

'You are right Paul,' she said pensively. 'I mean, you only need to take one look at his mother and sister to know that the family is unbalanced. Maybe I should be grateful we never had children.'

Paul nodded, but his concurrence went no further than that. Deep within, he was noticing strains of Nicole's character flaws that were worrying. Her vulnerability was only surpassed by her cruelty. She was clearly incapable of making a kind remark about anyone less fortunate than herself and he wondered how long it would be before he too became the object of her scorn and derision.

Alain returned with a medium-sized folder and took his place at the table next to Monique. He glanced up at the wall clock and then consulted his wristwatch, as if he wanted to confirm the clock's accuracy. The slight frown on his face indicated that there was no discrepancy in the time, and it was clear that he was perplexed about the whereabouts of the other members of the Matisse clan.

'I have asked my secretary to try phoning Madame Matisse to find out if she is still coming,' said Alain, 'but I have decided that if she isn't here in the next ten minutes then I will press ahead and read out your individual entitlements. I may have to then arrange for a second reading of the will, which you're all welcome to attend again if you so wish.'

'Will their absence hold up disposal of the estate?' asked Nicole.

'Unfortunately, Madame,' said Alain, sounding sincerely apologetic, 'for the sake of transparency, I prefer not to dispose of any assets until every beneficiary is aware of the full contents of the will and has a chance to contest it.'

Nicole hissed and sucked in her breath.

They waited for an extra twenty minutes, at which point, Alain dialled his secretary on the intercom to confirm whether she'd tracked down the missing family members. From his frustrated expression and muttering at the end of the conversation, Paul figured that she hadn't.

'I suppose we have to press on then,' said Alain, opening the folder. 'I will first deal with your entitlement, Madame and after that I shall read out Monique's, but I will reserve the disclosure of the other entitlements until a later date when the relevant beneficiaries are present.'

'I guess we have no choice,' said Nicole, with a bored sigh.

'Very good,' said Alain. 'So now we can get down to business. Because you are English, Mr Munnelly, I will speak in that language, but may occasionally have to read out some documents to Mrs Matisse which are written in French, okay? I will then read out Monique's entitlement in French, okay?'

Paul nodded. It made no difference to him.

'Now, before I read the will,' said Alain, looking directly at Nicole, 'I need to briefly explain French succession law, as it applies under the *Code Napoleon,* so that you will understand why Antoine Matisse's family may decide to challenge your entitlement. My job as Antoine's *notaire* is to ensure that his wishes are carried out. That is what I am paid for and so that is what I have to do.'

He paused, to see if anyone wished to speak, but was met with a wall of silence and so continued.

'In many ways, I am grateful to Antoine for disclosing the

contents of the will to you when he was alive, because it means that what I am about to read out will not come as a surprise.'

'*Qui M'sieu*,' said Nicole sedately.

'Generally speaking,' went on Alain, 'under French law, a deceased person cannot leave his entire estate or even a significant portion of it to his surviving wife, where there are children or surviving parents involved. What this means is that Antoine would have to divide every part of his estate in proportions equal to the number of close family members who have outlived him. Now, as Antoine had a daughter from a previous relationship before he married you, she would ordinarily be entitled to at least a third of the entire estate as would his mother, leaving you with only a third of the portion allocated to you.'

'Well, as Monique is now eighteen,' said Alain, consulting the folder on the table before him, 'under French succession law, she is automatically entitled to a third of her late father's estate, which I will administer on her behalf as trustee.

'Anyway, six months ago, when Antoine discovered that he was dying, he was determined that you receive a generous portion of his estate after he died, so he appointed me as his *notaire* to advise him on what to do. To get around the succession law problem, I advised him to buy a new art studio in your joint names and include a *tontine* clause in the *acte de vente*.' He glanced at Paul, 'or what you British call *a deed of conveyance*,' he clarified.

'The clause meant that in the event of his death he could transfer the property to you without any of his family being able to stake a claim in it under French succession law. Now, Antoine chose not to inform his mother of what he'd done. Instead, he wrote her a letter which he authorised me to post on the day after he died.'

'Has she received it yet?' asked Nicole apprehensively.

'*Qui Madame*,' answered Alain, 'His mother received the letter by courier yesterday evening and immediately she came to see me, threatening to challenge the will in court, because she is convinced that you influenced her son to change his

---

154

original will.'

'That is nonsense!' shrieked Nicole, baring her crimson-tipped nails like a predator. 'I did no such thing! *Ils sont tous des menteurs*! They are all liars!'

'It doesn't really matter, *Madame*,' said Alain, fanning downwards with both hands to calm her down. '*La loi est de votre côté*, you have the law on your side, and I have explained this to them.'

'Their case is weak?' asked Nicole expectantly.

'Very weak,' affirmed Alain, 'because your late husband was acting on sound legal advice from a *notaire* when he purchased the property in your joint names. Your mother-in-law wrongly believes that the studio apartment was purchased *en indivision* which is the normal way most couples over here buy their homes where each person owns half of the property but is not automatically entitled to the other half upon the death of their partner. However, as Antoine purchased *en tontine*, when he died, you became the sole owner of that property, and the law recognises your right to take full possession.'

Paul heard Nicole's deep sigh of relief, and a quick glance confirmed that her demeanour had brightened considerably. It was difficult to figure out what was going through her mind at that precise moment, especially as she'd swung from tearful drama queen to snarling alley cat, but he remained convinced about the sincerity of her grief and the righteousness of her cause. She was in his view a misunderstood woman whose determination to flee her past and improve her future had been taken out of context by the covetous members of her late husband's clan.

He made up his mind to stand by her through her present ordeal, and be there for her, even if it meant having to contend with her mood swings.

'Your words reassure me, Mr Touzé,' said Nicole, smiling serenely. 'I am at peace now.'

'I am so glad,' said Alain, 'and now unless you have any questions, I will read the will.'

Alain reached for a pair of spectacles resting on his desk, adjusted them on the tip of his nose like a judge about to pass sentence, and then reached for the will. Paul felt Nicole's hand squeeze his tightly, and a sideways glance at her face revealed a measure of the euphoria bubbling within her. She was about to inherit a studio apartment in Paris, and he wondered if this would suffice to heal the pain of the past.

For the next ten minutes, Antoine Matisse's lawyer read out the terms and conditions of the will confirming that the testator was of sound mind at the time and that the will had been properly witnessed by two others. He then proceeded to read out the details of Nicole's inheritance, confirming that she was to receive a fully paid-up studio apartment along *Rue de Rivoli* in the *Le Marais* area within Paris's 4th *arrondissement* and all its contents.

She was also to receive a cash sum after tax of one hundred thousand euros to decorate the place and cover her legal expenses. Nicole's nails dug deeply into his flesh, inducing pain, as her inheritance was being read out, but he made no effort to extricate his hand from hers.

Sudden commotion outside the office broke Alain's concentration and, before Paul could figure out what was going on, the door crashed open, revealing Alain's flustered looking secretary. The poor woman was struggling to restrain the four people behind her, who were pressing forward like a wild herd. Paul recognised the members of Antoine's clan who'd attended the cremation ceremony earlier that morning and the looks on their faces were anything but friendly.

'Mr Touzé!' exclaimed the terrified woman, as she was shoved aside by one of Antoine's burly male cousins, '*Je ne sais pas qui sont ces gens! Dois-je appeler la police?*'

'*Il est bon; je sais qui' ls sont,*' replied Alain Touzé calmly, rising to his feet with his hands held up in a peace gesture. 'I know them — there's no need to call the police.'

The secretary's expression remained dubious as she gingerly pulled herself together and edged backwards toward the door, visibly shaken by the Matisse clan's violent intrusion.

Alain waited for her to depart and close the door behind her before turning towards Madame Matisse and Marceline who were still looking combative. For almost three minutes, there was an aggressive exchange between Antoine's lawyer and Madame Matisse, with lots of gesticulating.

'What are they saying?' asked Paul, leaning closer to the smug-looking widow beside him.

'He is telling her off for bursting in like that and making a scene,' Nicole quietly translated, 'and she is accusing him of foul play for starting the reading of the will without her. According to her, she had received a phone call earlier today informing her that the reading had been postponed till two pm and he is denying that his office made that call.'

Without warning, Madame Matisse suddenly turned towards Nicole, pointing one crooked finger at her, and speaking angrily in French, as if she were placing a hex on her.

Nicole's jaw line hardened as the older woman continued to hurl what Paul presumed were insults, but she wisely held her peace. The look of unadulterated hatred in the old woman's eyes was more effective than any subtitles and Paul couldn't help but feel that there was more to her diatribe than Nicole had told him. Nicole's silence seemed to incense Antoine's mother even more, and she began to shake her fists and weep uncontrollably, prompting Marceline to step in and calm her down with a caressing arm around her shoulders.

As Madame Matisse allowed herself to be steered to the nearest chair still sobbing, Alain, who looked absolutely drained, pointed at her two nephews and then at the door. Both men, however, stood their ground looking at Marceline for definitive instructions. Marceline's slight nod was sufficient to make them retreat from the conference room. But before Paul could relax, Marceline pointed at him and began to speak rapidly in French. This time, Nicole retorted, and a fresh shouting-match ensued, with each woman rising to her feet as they vied for honours. Paul didn't need an interpreter to figure out that he was the topic of discussion and that the dispute centred on his presence at what was after all a family affair. He realised that he had to do something to contain the situation. Without hint, he got up and headed for the door.

'Paul!' called out Nicole as he opened the door.

'It's all right,' said Paul, without pausing. 'I'll be in the waiting area.'

*   *   *   *   *   *   *

As he sipped the coffee provided by Alain Touzé's secretary, ignoring the malicious stares from Antoine's cousins who hadn't been offered any beverages, Paul recalled the events surrounding the reading of Albert's will.

The only hostility in the room had been between Matthew and himself, but even then, it had been veiled behind plastic grins and laughter that went no deeper than their throats. Even after Matthew discovered the full extent of Albert's disapproval of his chosen profession from the contents of the will, there was no angry outburst, just silence. What Paul had witnessed this morning was evidence that there were families out there more dysfunctional than his.

A quarter of an hour later, Nicole emerged beaming from ear to ear. Looking past her, he noticed the sullen stares on the faces of Madame Matisse and Marceline and guessed that they'd just been floored by his girlfriend-to-be.

'I'm in the mood to celebrate,' said Nicole as she came within a few metres. 'Where do you suggest we go?'

'This is your town,' said Paul, 'you choose.'

'Why don't we kill two birds and combine a sightseeing tour of the real Paris with lunch on the Seine afterwards?'

'Sounds good to me,' answered Paul indifferently, 'though I'm bursting to hear what happened in my absence.'

'Nothing much,' she said, perching on the armrest of the sofa he was seated on. 'Alain read through the whole will and explained that the studio apartment did not form part of Antoine's estate, as ownership automatically passed to me the day he died. Antoine's estate was made up of four hundred thousand euros after tax and some oil paintings which had been conservatively valued at fifty-five thousand euros. We each got a hundred thousand euros, but Antoine left the paintings to some art galleries that had patronised him during his lifetime.'

'Sounds fair to me,' said Paul. 'At least there weren't any surprises.'

'Madame Matisse's silence was a bit surprising though,' said Nicole, 'I expected her to put up a fight when Alain explained that the studio apartment was excluded from the will, but she didn't say a word…'

'Shameless whore!' said Marceline Matisse, cutting in unceremoniously. 'Do you really think this is over?'

Paul found the fluency of her English more stunning than her rude interruption or choice of words. Up until that moment, he'd wrongly presumed that she was restricted to her native dialect, but now he was impressed. It was clear, though that Marceline had spoken in English for his benefit.

Nicole sneered at her sister-in-law and looked the other way, obviously determined not to be drawn into a pointless rematch. The contents of the will had been disclosed and, as controversial as it appeared to be, the will constituted Antoine Matisse's intentions for his closest family members.

'You can pretend to ignore me,' continued Marceline in the same hurtful tone, 'but the truth cannot be buried forever. You never loved my brother, and everyone knows that, except those you blind with your promiscuity, like this poor fool.' She glanced at Paul's dumbfounded face and went on. 'I know you phoned mama and gave her the wrong time for the reading of the will because you were too ashamed to confront us, but mark my words, whore, one day you will reap the reward for your life of deceit.'

Unable to hold her peace any longer, Nicole sprang up like a cobra and began to rant in French with her arms defiantly planted on her hips. The thrust of her words hammered into Marceline like nails, and from the look on the other woman's face, Paul sensed that a brawl was about to kick off.

He watched helplessly as Marceline took two steps forward towards her adversary with a raised hand and was relieved when one of her cousins waded in to intercept her before the slap could be delivered. The man drew Marceline away with a firm grip on her upper arm and Paul watched as she was led out of the office with a weary-looking Madame Matisse following behind, aided by the other nephew.

After they'd gone, Alain Touzé emerged from the conference room with Monique walking behind him. Turning back to Nicole, Paul could see that her exertion and possibly the apprehension of being assaulted had taken its toll on her.

'Take no notice of her,' said Nicole breathlessly. 'She's a bitter and miserable woman who's frustrated because she cannot get a man. Maybe now that she's got a little bit of money, men might find her more attractive.'

The callous remark didn't go down well with Paul, but he absorbed it in silence refusing to pollute his mind with negative thoughts. Nicole was upset and the remark had to be considered in light of that.

'This has been a most interesting day, Madame,' said Alain, halting in front of them, 'but I would very much like to get back to my routine, so if you accompany me to my private office, I will conclude our business and get on with my life.'

'Yes, let's do that,' said Nicole soberly.

'I'll remain out here,' said Paul, unwilling to get further involved in her business affairs.

'I understand,' said Nicole, in the same placid tone, 'and I'm sorry for all the trouble.'

Paul nodded but felt that Alain was a more qualified recipient of the apology.

He watched them head towards the lawyer's office, but it wasn't until the door shut behind them that he remembered Monique. Looking around the waiting area, he couldn't find any trace of her and wondered if she'd left. He felt he owed her an apology for the way Nicole had spoken about her.

He wandered over to the window overlooking the street and sighted her on the pavement. He left the waiting area and ran down the stairs to street level. Stepping out onto the pavement, he paused as he saw Monique standing next to the wild-eyed Asian guy in the leather coat, who was in the process of mounting a large old motorbike.

'Monique,' said Paul, approaching her. 'Can I have a quick word?'

The Asian guy paused with one leg over his motorbike and his inquisitive glare made Paul freeze. Monique, who was holding a crash helmet in her hands, stared at him blankly.

'*Pardon, mademoiselle*,' said Paul, cautiously remaining where he was. 'I just wanted to say sorry – eh –*pardon*.'

Monique blushingly lowered her gaze to pavement level.

'Why?' she asked.

'Because my friend insulted you back there,' answered Paul quickly, 'and I know you must have been hurt.'

Monique nodded, but her gaze remained lowered.

'Are you all right?' he asked. 'Can I help in anyway?'

Monique shook her head vigorously and put on her crash helmet before getting on the motorbike behind the Asian guy and wrapping her arms around him. Seconds later the bike was whizzing away from the kerb blending with traffic.

'She's confused,' said a familiar female voice behind him.

He turned slowly to find Marceline Matisse standing near the entrance to the office with her hands lost in the deep pockets of her unattractive dark overcoat. Her grim smile and pale blue eyes conveyed an inner melancholy.

Staring at her more closely, Paul realised that Marceline was not unattractive. Her refined middle-aged features projected an austere charm, which had its own appeal.

'Who's the guy with her?' asked Paul. 'A boyfriend?'

'He's North African,' said Marceline, approaching him slowly; 'just one in a long line of men who've used and abused her. He will hang around as long as she's got money and she will do whatever he says, because she believes he loves her.'

Paul's heart bled for the shy teenager whose learning difficulties had exposed her to such a turbulent lifestyle.

'The world is full of girls like Monique,' said Marceline

bitterly, 'girls who have been denied love in their childhood and spend the rest of their lives searching.'

'But she's so vulnerable.'

'That's the attraction,' said Marceline. 'Men don't like women who talk back.'

In her remarks, Paul sensed a revelation about her own predicament.

'Look,' he said choosing his words carefully, 'Nicole will soon be out, so maybe it's best if you just left.'

'Don't worry,' she said calmly, 'I have nothing more to say to that whore. I came to warn you to stay away from her before she ruins you like she ruined my brother.'

Paul was offended at the intrusion into his privacy. It was clear that this was one bitter woman.

'I warned Antoine,' went on Marceline, 'I told him to beware of her, but he didn't listen and see how he ended up. Believe me *M'sieu*, she will only bring you bad luck.'

'Thanks for the advice,' said Paul quickly, concluding that it was time to part ways; 'but if that's all you have to say …'

'If you doubt me,' said Marceline sneeringly, 'just ask her about Samira Faruk and then make up your own mind?'

'Who is Samira Faruk?' asked Paul, as Marceline walked away with a long, cruel chuckle.

10

The studio apartment that Antoine bequeathed to Nicole was at the other end of *Rue de Rivoli* near the *Marais* neighbourhood and not exactly across the street from Antoine's lawyers as she'd insinuated earlier in the day.

The third-floor studio was a spacious airy affair furnished only with a sofa and a couple of paint-stained easels, and Nicole seemed to recover her former buoyancy as she paced up and down her new inheritance. The self-control was resurfacing, as was the sardonic humour, and Paul realised that she was slowly morphing into an astute businesswoman.

'It's beautiful,' she enthused from her position at one of the large windows overlooking the main avenue below. 'It presents all kinds of possibilities. For instance, I could partition it into a two-bedroom apartment or create an open plan living area. It's just so flexible.'

'I'm happy for you,' said Paul. 'I guess this is worth celebrating.'

'What did you have in mind?' she asked, grinning mischievously.

'Dinner in some fancy restaurant,' he answered, 'but preferably not one that specialises in seafood, and after that, if you're feeling up to it, we could go clubbing.'

'I don't feel like dancing,' she said, 'but I am famished.'

'Okay so we'll do an early dinner.'

'That's fine with me. By the way, what was Marceline saying to you earlier?'

'You saw us?'

'Yes, I was watching you from Alain's window.'

'She accused you of ruining Antoine's life and tried to warn me off you,' he answered.

Nicole chuckled. 'She would say so. She's still bitter about the will.'

'Who is Samira Faruk?' he asked boldly.

Nicole's expression deflated and the colour left her cheeks.

'Me,' she replied after a suspenseful pause. 'Samira was my middle name and Faruk was my maiden name. I suppose Marceline told you.'

'Not in so many words, but I don't understand.'

'What don't you understand? That I'm not pure one hundred percent Caucasian? Is that a problem for you?'

'No of course not, I was just wondering.'

'Well, wonder no more. I was born Nicole Samira Faruk,' she said, looking him straight in the eye. 'My father is Algerian. Surprised?'

Paul was silent, for what seemed like an eternity. She looked nothing like a North African, having features and a complexion which were distinctly Caucasian.

'I would never have guessed,' he said honestly.

'That's because my mother was white,' said Nicole. 'I'm half Algerian, half French, but I have my mother's eyes and complexion. And in case you're wondering what Marceline was getting at, she was just trying to tarnish my makeover. She and her family are racist. Antoine knew this; he knew his family wouldn't accept me, but he married me anyway.'

'I'm sorry if you think I was prying.'

'I have no secrets, Paul. I'm not ashamed of my past – I just don't want to go back there. I was born in a squalid estate located in a depressing neighbourhood called *Clichy-sous-Bois* where I became acquainted with the smell of poverty. I lived there until the age of fourteen when my mother died. Shortly afterwards I ran away. My devout Muslim father wanted to force me into a marriage with an older man from his Algerian community and I was having none of it. Because I used to

164

model for Antoine, I moved in with him, dropped my middle name, and never returned. So now you know all there is to know, do you have any more questions about my past?'

He shook his head. He hadn't come to Paris to take sides in a dispute that predated him, but to convey his love for a woman he found fascinating, despite her very obvious flaws.

'All you need to know about me is that I hate poverty because it stinks, and I'll do all within my power to never experience it again. I've come too far to look back and there's nothing Marceline and her pitiful clan can do about it.'

The ferocity of her words made Paul shudder.

'Look,' he said, with a sigh, 'I'd rather not get involved in your family business, so just leave me out of it, all right?'

'If we're going to be in a relationship,' she said brusquely, 'then my business must become your business, after all you didn't fly out here to mourn Antoine, did you?'

Paul admired her forthrightness, even though he found it slightly unnerving. She wasn't a woman who beat about the bush. In one statement, she'd dispelled any presumption on his part and conveyed her willingness to progress things to the next level. She had just bridged the gap and it was now his duty to walk over it.

*　*　*　*　*　*　*

The journey between Paris du Nord and London's St Pancras station had been a brisk but memorable one. At Nicole's request they had caught an express train to London, adding a couple of hours to the normal journey time, but affording them the opportunity of spending more time together.

Nicole insisted on travelling first class and Paul had obligingly covered the expense, still revelling in the afterglow of their Parisian romance. After an unforgettable candle lit dinner followed by an evening stroll along *La Rive Gauche* – the left bank of the Seine, he was willing to be her slave for life. If Nicole had asked him to fly her on a first-class trip around the world, it would've been a small price to pay for the inexorable pleasure of her company. Without a doubt, he knew he was in love with her.

At St Pancras, they'd clung to each other like star-struck lovers and shared a lingering kiss before reluctantly parting ways at the taxi rank. Nicole caught a black cab to the City, where she had a meeting with Mr Ammon and some of his clients, whilst Paul caught a train to Luton Airport where he'd parked his car. The trip was spent reminiscing about the mind shattering Parisian experience. Nicole's perfume still caressed his nostrils, the result of their protracted proximity, and he luxuriated in it all the way to Luton Airport.

As Paul turned into his street, the sight of his drab-looking maisonette depressed him. Now that he was dating a lady with class, he needed the right sort of accoutrements. The fact that his home and car were affordable was no longer a valid consideration. He needed to cultivate the right image.

As Vijay often said, Paul had to see himself as an engineer and not a mechanic. Vijay always introduced himself as an investment consultant specialising in real estate rather than an estate agent. He reckoned that that subtle distinction had opened doors that would otherwise have remained shut. Paul knew if he was going to successfully transition, he had to take a leaf out of Vijay's book.

He had just inserted his key in the front door lock when his blackberry rang, but he waited until he was in the narrow hallway before answering it. The caller ID screen indicated that it was his mother, and he had a very good idea of the reason for the call.

'What's going on, Paul?' asked Mrs Munnelly, dispensing with the pleasantries. 'Why have you fired Basil without consulting me?'

'I would have called, but I've been extremely busy.'

'Basil Mead is a trustworthy man,' went on Mrs Munnelly, as if she hadn't heard him, 'and his advice has always helped us make the right business decisions. You also seem to forget that he was your father's best friend.'

'I know all that, Mum,' said Paul tiredly, 'but Basil's out of touch with the marketplace. For Munnelly and Sons to grow, we need someone who is forward thinking.'

'What are you talking about?'

'I'm talking about growth, Mum,' said Paul. 'We need an accountant who can properly assess our future business needs and not keep us rooted in tradition. We need a business plan that recognises our growth potential and enables us to exploit every available opportunity in the marketplace.'

'You're still not making any sense, Paul.'

'I wasn't happy with Basil's advice,' said Paul sighing heavily, 'so I fired him and replaced him with an accountant who is more in touch with the 21st century.'

'So, what arrangements have you put in place for Basil?'

'I've paid him off and closed our client account with him.'

'You know that's not what I meant!' said Mrs Munnelly. 'I want to know what plans you have for reinstating him. I've already apologised on your behalf for the way you sacked him and assured him that you would review your position.'

Paul felt like his head was on the verge of exploding. What was she talking about? Why did she think she could dictate how he ran his business? He had no plans of reinstating Basil Mead, and he wasn't about to reverse that decision just so that he could be in her good books. Basil could remain a part of her life, but not his.

'I'm not taking him back, Mum,' said Paul heavily. 'I've moved on.'

'What?'

'You heard me, Mum.'

'Are you going to make me a liar?'

'You should've consulted me first,' he said numbly. 'If Basil thinks he can go reporting me to you in the hope that I'll reverse my decision, then he's in for a rude shock.'

'Basil didn't call me,' said Mrs Munnelly quickly. 'Rather, I called him to apologise after Violet informed me of...' Her voice faltered.

'I see,' he said, smiling to himself. 'So, Violet's your inside man. Thanks very much, Mum.'

'Now look here, Paul,' said Mrs Munnelly strenuously, 'you just leave her alone.'

'I won't lay a finger on her,' promised Paul.

'Stop playing with words, Paul Munnelly!' she barked.

'Goodbye, Mum,' he said, terminating the call.

*   *   *   *   *   *   *

Paul sat in the posh but minimalist waiting area of Eden Fruit Foundation, soaking up the ambience of the ivory and charcoal themed space. The Foundation's headquarters was situated in a glass and aluminium framed building at Canary Wharf and as Paul learnt upon arrival, it occupied the top three floors including the penthouse.

Paul had been invited over by Mr Ammon at short notice. Having just received the summons two hours earlier, he'd hurried over from Waldon Town, abandoning the head gasket he'd been repairing. He had no clue what his mentor wanted to see him about, but knew Mr Ammon wasn't a man who took kindly to being refused. To create the right impression, he'd showered, donned one of his designer suits – the Hugo Boss and doused himself with a strong after shave.

From discussions with Nicole, he learnt that Eden Fruit Foundation was the parent body of Eden Fruit Investments and that the EFF was also the custodian of the Apple Seed Project which developed community leaders. According to Nicole, Mr Ammon had minimal direct involvement with either the foundation or its investment arm and he was merely listed as a trainer and mentor in relation to Apple Seed Project.

In the week since his return from Paris, he'd neither seen nor heard from Mr Ammon until that morning. But he was on the phone with Nicole every day. Having taken their relationship to a new level of intimacy, Paul had been invited to her apartment in a plush development near Waldon Town and she'd cooked for him. She'd also let him stay the night to reinforce the fact that they were an item, so things were looking up for him.

After two hours of patient boredom, a smartly attired Chinese woman informed Paul that Mr Ammon was ready for him and escorted him in a private elevator to the penthouse. As the doors opened, another smartly dressed Chinese woman ushered him to the glass walled waiting area where there was an expensive coffee machine and assorted flavours of tea and coffee. The second lady left him there, assuring him that Mr Ammon would be with him shortly.

Standing in front of the tinted glass wall, sipping frothing cappuccino and nibbling a biscuit, he admired the uncluttered view over the River Thames. It was a view to die for and he found it strangely empowering scanning the great city from thirty floors up. When he was eventually ushered into Mr Ammon's sprawling office three hours had elapsed since his arrival and he was borderline restless. If it had been anyone else, he would've walked away at least an hour ago.

The office adopted the same minimalist theme, favouring open space over clutter with expensive tasteful fittings dotted all over the place. The floor retained the charcoal wood theme with ivory-coloured walls and there were several seating areas with chairs covered in soft fabrics. The rugs were thick and looked like authentic North African articles.

'Good to see you Paul,' said Mr Ammon meeting him halfway and gesturing to a comfortable seating area with plush plump sofas. As always, he was immaculately presented, wearing a Harris tweed suit and suede brogues. 'It's been a busy day and I've had a number of urgent video conferences.'

Paul nodded and tried to mask his disappointment with a grin on his otherwise dour face. Looking around he noted the two large Plasma TV screens on telescopic stands bordering Mr Ammon's mahogany desk, each projecting a different audience seated around conference tables in discussion. They looked like live video feeds.

'Yes, the meetings are still going on in New York and Singapore,' said Mr Ammon with a careless flick of the wrist, 'but they're not discussing anything that requires my involvement yet. I know you've had coffee, but if you're hungry we can go up to the roof garden and have lunch.'

Paul was tempted but declined with a gentle wave.

'Do you know why I asked you over?'

'Not really – you didn't say.'

'It's about our discussion the other day – at Silverstone.'

'The Apple Seed Partnership?'

'Have you given it any thought?'

'But I thought I was chosen?'

'You were, but it was an offer and I do not recall you accepting.'

'Yes, of course! Why would I refuse?'

Mr Ammon's lips cracked into a grin. 'We never impose,' he said. 'It is purely voluntary.' He pointed to the ornate coffee table between them where a leather-bound folder lay with the Apple Seed Project logo embossed in gold letters across it.

'You need to study the terms of partnership,' he continued. 'They set out the guidelines all partners must adhere to. These terms have been adapted to suit each partner's vision.'

Paul opened the folder and withdrew the document inside. It was seven pages of printed text set in numbered paragraphs and Paul read through it slowly ignoring the footnotes. It appeared relatively straightforward, and Paul skimmed through it only pausing as he got to the section dealing with the financials. He looked at the simple charts and graphs mapping out an investment strategy for him over a seven-year timeline. It included some simple projections based on Eden Fruit Investments investing up to one hundred thousand pounds a year on his behalf into a project they had approved. Over seven years, they would invest up to seven hundred thousand in his chosen project with fifty percent of profits going to the Apple Seed Project and the other fifty percent being split between Eden Fruit Investments and Munnelly and Sons. Paul was no accountant but even he could see the benefits of reaping twenty five percent of profits from a project that he wasn't even bankrolling.

'These returns are incredible,' he murmured, looking up from the folder. 'Are they for real?'

170

'If the economy holds up – yes.'

Munnelly shook his head in disbelief. Albert always said *if it looks too good to be true flush it down the loo* because that was all it was good for. The last page of the document required his signature, but he hesitated. A strange sense of foreboding enveloped his mind ushering in an inexplicable discomfort.

'Having second thoughts?' Mr Ammon's voice penetrated his tense thoughts. 'Need more time?'

Paul considered the offer but a pernicious voice in his head mocked him. It suggested that he exhume Albert's corpse to resume control of Munnelly and Sons because it had more guts in its small finger than he had in his whole body.

'No' he said with sudden decisiveness.

He fished inside his jacket for a pen, but Mr Ammon proffered a gold-coated Montblanc fountain pen.

*　*　*　*　*　*　*

Paul inspected the first of his three newly completed modular business units and, as he strolled around the open space, he suddenly felt good about life. Contrary to initial forecasts, the site had been finished ahead of schedule and the developers were putting the finishing touches to the leisure areas where the theme park and shopping mall would be located. The site manager had contacted all purchasers and allocated time slots for a personalised inspection of their units with a champagne reception thrown in for them and their guests. The grand opening was still at least two months away, but the business park was already generating a huge amount of interest within the local community and the motor industry at large and Paul was proud to be part of it.

In the six months following his trip to Paris, he'd embarked on a thorough revamp of his image in preparation for the transition of Munnelly and Sons from local mechanic's workshop to modern service centre.

He'd moved out of his humble maisonette into a new three-bedroom detached house in a gated residential estate on the outskirts of Waldon Town. He also traded-in his Toyota MR2 for a gleaming Porsche 911 which he'd paid a premium for to jump the waiting list. It wasn't a turbo, but still looked impressive. Along with new furniture and décor for the apartment, on Nicole's advice, he'd also overhauled his wardrobe and started having weekly manicures and facials.

On the staffing front, there'd been a development. Violet had turned up to work one morning looking suitably subdued. Initially he suspected it was a ploy to dissuade him from following up on the threat to suspend her for her treachery and breach of confidentiality. However, he soon found out that Violet had been attending a weekly Alpha Course event and become a Christian. From that moment she toed the line, being eager to please him no matter how demanding he got. She gradually ceased the cussing and snide remarks, but the only downside was her determination to convert him.

All staff had been informed that as part of the move to the new site they would be issued with new uniforms and tools and that they would undergo intensive training in the use of the new leased equipment that would be installed.

John Crane had been phenomenal, offering loads of useful tips for the image makeover which Paul found intriguing. John had suggested sending the staff for various client care courses to make them more professional in their jobs and had advocated team building events such as away-days and weekend retreats for all the staff in luxurious conference centres to ensure cohesion. On John's advice, Paul was in the process of recruiting a marketing and sales manager to engage in a creative advertising campaign for the rebranded Munnelly and Sons. Paul had also commissioned the design of a new logo, to erase the dowdy old logo designed by Albert, along with a new glossy website.

The cherry on the cake was a hot and intensive relationship with Nicole that showed no signs of abating.

11

One Year Later

Paul looked around the resplendent ballroom with its gold, marble and crystal fittings, and glittering chandeliers, struggling to control his euphoria. He was attending the Eden Fruit Foundation's annual gala dinner at a Park Lane venue in London, and it was his first black-tie event. Five hundred immaculately dressed guests had paid a thousand pounds a head to attend. In addition, there were seventy Apple Seed partners in attendance dotted strategically all around the glamourous venue mingling with the celebrities, entrepreneurs and sports personalities gracing the occasion.

At Paul's table were a couple of bankers and their wives, a popular female newscaster, a rugby player and his girlfriend, and a man named Gordon Pinsent and his wife. Paul had arrived with Nicole, but they parted at the venue as she was one of the event hosts. She was currently hovering around Mr Ammon coordinating the arrangements on his behalf. Paul knew Gordon from back when he used to service his Toyota at Munnelly and Sons. That had been a while ago. Nowadays Gordon drove a Bentley. A couple of times their eyes met briefly, and each time Gordon turned away. Like so many others in the hall, he was trying to bury his past.

Paul had bumped into Gordon previously at one of the Apple Seed partner wellbeing events which was part of their leadership development activities. Gordon had attended the same holism sessions and had looked surprised to see Paul there. Paul had tried to speak with him then, but Gordon had been evasive even during the breaks. Despite Gordon's condescending behaviour, Paul was encouraged to discover that he was part of the partnership because his success was a testament to its effectiveness. Paul was optimistic.

Also in attendance was Vijay Pandya with an attractive Indian girl named Aisha whom he introduced as his fiancé. She was probably the fifth girl Vijay had introduced to him as his fiancé. Vijay had found out that Paul was an Apple Seed partner when they met at an Eden Fruit Foundation leadership seminar. Vijay had congratulated him on his successful application and been generally enthusiastic, until he learnt that Paul hadn't applied but still been selected. From that point onwards Paul had noticed a difference in his attitude. He also sensed rivalry, especially when Vijay splashed out on a more expensive model of Porsche.

The most prolific Apple Seed partner in Hertfordshire was Amy McBride, his mother's ex-hairdresser, and his brother's mistress. Amy was being honoured this evening because of the number of international awards she'd won for her designs. For her success, she was being bestowed with the coveted Apple Seed partner of the Year award. Apart from a gold-plated trophy, she would also receive a hundred thousand pounds from Eden Fruit Investment.

Amy was present at the event with a prematurely greying middle-aged man whom he recognised as her husband. His name was Shaun, and he was a chef at one of the local Marriott hotels. The man kept gazing at her admiringly and when she was invited to accept her award, he applauded loudest and longest. He looked so proud, as she went up to the lectern to accept her trophy and give her acceptance speech. In giving her the award, Mr Ammon spoke about her virtue and integrity in business as well as her passionate drive to make a difference through her apprenticeship scheme for young women in Hertfordshire. He called her an inspiration and a born leader who set an example all women should emulate.

Paul struggled to reconcile the virtues being attributed to the woman he knew was in an adulterous relationship with his brother, yet he applauded along with others as she thanked her husband of fifteen years for his love, sacrifice, and support. She spent the next ten minutes sharing her vision for driving ethical standards in textile manufacture and ending the oppressive sweatshop regime in third world countries. She spoke about inspiring gifted women who wished to step into the fashion industry to pursue their dreams the same way Mr Ammon had helped her discover hers. At the end of her speech, she received a rousing round of applause.

Amy soaked up the adulation blowing kisses as the applause and whistles became a crescendo and confetti rained down from above. Paul wasn't surprised at Amy's reception; he'd overheard someone remark that half of the women in the room were either wearing her gowns or carrying one of her award-winning handbags. She was also the wealthiest and most prominent of the Apple Seed partners, with millions in the bank and a large social media following.

Paul's eyes followed her all the way to her table where Mr Ammon and her husband were waiting to receive her. However, his attention was deflected by the reflection in one of the mirrored walls of Mr Truman and Nicole huddling beside a pillar. Truman was whispering suggestively in her ear making her giggle and Paul was dying to know what she found so amusing. Their proximity made him uncomfortable.

* * * * * * *

Six months later

Paul bent his knees slightly, making sure that he'd got a firm hold on the grip of the eight iron before hitting the ball in a neat arc down the green. The ball landed over a hundred metres away and rolled along the ground till its momentum expired a few feet away from its intended destination, the hole.

'Good shot,' acknowledged Mr Ammon, who had been silently observing him. 'A bit more experience and you could've hit a hole-in-one.'

'Thanks,' said Paul, slotting the club back into his golf bag.

'Call it beginner's luck.'

'And a favourable wind direction,' added Mr Ammon with a light chuckle. 'But you're not out of the woods yet.'

'At least I've reduced your lead to three holes,' countered Paul, slinging his golf bag across his shoulder with difficulty.

'But it's a nine-hole course and we've only got three holes to go,' answered Mr Ammon, clearing his throat, 'but then I'm sure you'll only need three strokes to wrap this up.'

Paul grinned at the veiled sarcasm. Mr Ammon was what the Americans would dub a 'scratch golfer'. His handicap of 0 was on par with the very best professional golfers and he'd already comfortably won the first round of the match, playing flawlessly, hitting tee shots of over three hundred metres in a single stroke. For a man of his medium build and lean muscle structure, that was outstanding, and Paul had been riveted by the consummate ease with which the man repeated the feat again and again.

In the year since he'd taken up playing golf, Paul had developed a handicap over an eighteen-hole course that his instructor labelled phenomenal. However, in Mr Ammon's company he wasn't nearly good enough no matter how many hours a day he spent on the course. John Crane had hinted that the golf course was where all big deals were sealed, and Paul had promptly taken up golf.

Unable to join the more exclusive golf clubs because of his background, he'd contacted Mr Ammon who'd secured him honorary membership at the Waldon Town golf course frequented by many motoring industry executives. For Paul, the real thrill was dressing up in all the gear and then slinging his golf bag into the back seat of his Porsche every evening, whilst his envious neighbours observed.

'So how are the preparations for the move coming along?' asked Mr Ammon, as they strolled down the course in the direction of Paul's golf ball.

'Very smoothly,' answered Paul. 'The company supplying the new equipment we've leased is installing this weekend and the following week we'll be moving all our tools and work in progress to the new site.'

'I'm glad you opted to lease the equipment rather than carry over your old stuff,' said Mr Ammon. 'Putting old wine into new wine skins is never a sensible way to progress.'

'Well, it *is* rather unsettling,' said Paul, 'considering that we've always owned our own equipment, but John is convinced that we can buy it off the leasing company in a couple of years when annual depreciation would've reduced its net book value to scrap.'

'So, it's all happening then.'

'Yes, it's all coming together, and my staff are pretty excited, so that's encouraging.'

'It's probably all the booze they've been guzzling during your weekend retreats,' said Mr Ammon lightly. 'On the other hand, it may well be the anticipation of working for a higher profile employer and the exposure that comes with it.'

'I'm inclined to think it's the latter,' said Paul optimistically.

'I'm sure you're right,' said Mr Ammon, as they reached the spot where the ball lay. 'And how are things shaping up with Nicole?'

'We're still dating,' said Paul with a smirk, as he selected an arm lock putter from his bag and assumed the position, ready to putt the ball into the hole ahead.

'It's been over a year, hasn't it?'

'Almost two.'

Mr Ammon whistled. 'Well, you must be doing something right,' he said with a sly grin. 'I must admit that she has a certain glow about her these days. Maybe she's in love.'

'You reckon?'

'Well, I'm no expert,' said Mr Ammon, 'but I would say that she's softened considerably since you started dating her and that's always a good indication. When a woman's in love, everyone benefits.'

Paul concentrated on the ball, measuring the angle and distance to the hole with the shaft of his putter, before gently knocking the ball in a straight line towards the hole.

'What was she like when you first met her?' asked Paul, as

the ball slipped into the hole.

'Rough around the edges and raw on the inside,' said Mr Ammon bluntly. 'She's a far cry from what she was.'

'Was she always strong-willed?'

'Stronger. Nicole is a complex character.'

Paul was inclined to agree. He let her get away with murder despite his unease. With Nicole, he was always giving, and she was always taking. She was closed and didn't appreciate him trying to probe her silence on certain issues. She could be a passionate lover, but compassion was not her strongest suit. He was also discovering worrying narcissistic tendencies, but it never crossed his mind to call it quits even when she flared-up and cussed him out. She was always profusely apologetic afterwards and affectionate which partially made up for it.

'She's complex.' said Paul wistfully.

'That's why she needs a simple man like you in her life.'

'I wish I could believe that. At times she makes me feel like an accessory.'

'It's nothing to do with you,' said Mr Ammon, selecting an iron from his bag and examining its grip. 'She's battling insecurity and still trying to escape her past.'

'Sounds to me like she needs counselling.'

'What she needs is patience,' said Mr Ammon, moving into position for his next shot, 'so hang in there.'

Mr Ammon's slice sent the golf ball soaring, and Paul sensed the game slipping further outside his reach.

'So, what made you choose her?'

'Instinct,' replied Mr Ammon, standing back to admire his shot that had bagged him yet another hole-in-one. 'I realised she had something from the moment I first laid eyes on her — just like I know that you don't belong in Albert's shadow, it's a gift I have. I treat each of my protégés like a blank canvas and imagine the portrait I wish to paint on them and then paint. To me, you and Nicole are my portraits but when we first met, you were both blank canvasses.'

There was a hint of pride in Mr Ammon's voice as he spoke, and his thin-lipped smile conveyed a sense of self-satisfaction.

'I can honestly say that meeting you has been the best thing that ever happened to me,' said Paul, choking back the emotion that was threatening to overwhelm him, 'and I know that my life will never be the same again.'

'Do you really mean that?' asked Mr Ammon, staring at him intently.

'Yes, I do,' answered Paul, feeling the tears stinging the sides of his eyeballs.

'Then prove it by writing that cheque,' said Mr Ammon, grinning smugly, 'because believe it or not I'm now four shots ahead, and with only two holes to go, there's no way you can bridge that gap.'

'I know when I'm beaten,' admitted Paul, reaching for his cheque book.

*   *   *   *   *   *   *

Three Months Later

'Looking good, Mr M,' said Vijay, as Paul pulled up the gunmetal grey Porsche in his reserved parking spot outside Munnelly and Sons' new workshop. 'I like the private number plate – it's an excellent statement.'

'Thanks,' answered Paul, who had only recently acquired it at Nicole's suggestion. He alighted from the vehicle and shook hands with the shrewd property consultant.

Vijay, who had been waiting outside the workshop, leaning against his own low-slung Porsche, nodded slowly with respect, and then his eyes widened slightly as he saw the tanned brunette lounging on the front passenger seat.

'Well, well, well,' said Vijay, with a broadening smile, 'what have we here?'

'None of your business, mate,' said Paul, steering him by the elbow towards the workshop's entrance.

Vijay glanced over his shoulder at Nicole as they entered the workshop, and his grin acquired an unending elasticity. Paul guided the impressed hustler into his new office and shoved him in the direction of a spare seat.

'New house, new office, new girl,' said Vijay poetically. 'So, what else's new?'

'New life,' said Paul, plumping himself down on his high-back swivel chair. 'Now, what brings you to this part of town.'

'Isn't that Nicole – Mr Ammon's PA?'

Vijay had never seen Paul and Nicole together before because of Nicole's insistence that they keep the relationship discreet. She had proffered no reasons and he hadn't challenged. He was just grateful for being with her.

'How can I help you?' asked Paul evasively, as he stared out through the broad glass window at the workshop where his technicians were hard at work in their new overalls.

'I've found a new tenant for your old business premises,' said Vijay, 'and he's ready to pay a ten percent premium over what the current guy pays.'

'But my current tenant is reliable and has good references.'

'Reliable, but tighter than a gnat's armpit,' scoffed Vijay, 'and he isn't willing to match the prospective tenant's price.'

'Well, isn't it a bit late in the day?'

'You haven't signed the tenancy renewal yet,' said Vijay stroking his chin, 'so you can pull out at any time.'

Paul was uncomfortable, but the thought of getting more rental income was irresistible. It was also clear that Vijay wasn't being proficient for nothing. His commission would rise commensurately if he could pull it off.

'Are there any legal implications?'

Vijay shook his head. 'There's no contract until we sign,' he said, 'and with no signed contract it's open season. The lawyers only get interested when there's a signed contract, so we've got nothing to worry about.'

'Okay,' said Paul with a steep sigh. 'Do it but make up some sort of apology when you're handing back the deposit.'

'Why?' asked Vijay looking flabbergasted. 'We don't owe them jack!'

Paul shook his head and tried to focus. He still recalled the day Tanner, the proprietor of the local used car retail outlet, had turned up at Munnelly and Sons' old premises, seeking to take it over for a moderate rent. Tanner had been Albert's friend and over the years had brought all his vehicles there for servicing and routine repairs. Tanner also had excellent references from other local businesses, all well known to Paul. Paul had directed him to Vijay, who had instantly expressed dismay at the quantum of rent being proffered. The difficulty now was how to face Tanner and apologise.

'Do whatever you have to do,' said Paul quietly, 'but don't tell him I had anything to do with it, because we go way back.'

'Consider it done, Mr M,' said Vijay, springing up jubilantly, 'and don't feel too bad about it, after all, this is business, and in your position, he'd have done the same thing.'

'I feel better already,' said Paul, reaching for his office mobile phone. 'Thanks a bunch for cheering me up.'

'And I'm about to make you even happier.'

Paul's enquiring stare loosened Vijay's tongue.

'Has John Crane mentioned anything to you about Waldon Valley Leisure Park?'

'No, is that another new development?'

'Yes, the plan is to site it close to the new shopping mall.'

Paul had learnt about the shopping mall which Eden Fruit Investments was developing as part of a consortium. It had gathered a lot of support in the local press and with the town planners because it was located on the outskirts of town in an area that didn't interfere with country life.

'What's the plan for the leisure park?'

'It's a casino and hotel with an amusement arcade.'

'Will that work in a place like Waldon Town?'

'Are you serious? Of course! Do you have any idea how many avid gamblers travel from Hertfordshire, Bedfordshire, and Buckinghamshire to London just for a flutter?'

Paul pondered this. He never gambled – a legacy of a sensible upbringing but he had customers who did. Whilst there were casinos in Bedford, Luton, and Watford the big players always headed to London.

'This is going to be the biggest casino in the Southeast,'

went on Vijay, 'and we have an opportunity to be a part of it.'

'We?'

'Apple Seed partners. EFF is giving us the opportunity to invest in the development.'

Paul was intrigued. 'So how do I get involved?' he asked.

'Just speak with John Drake. He'll sort it out.'

'Thanks for the heads-up.'

'All part of the service, Mr M,' said Vijay smoothly, as he made his exit.

Paul remained where he was, dwelling on the situation. He desperately wanted to invest in the new development but didn't know how much he would require by way of capital. Given his current commitments, he wasn't sure if he could afford to. A knock on his door forced him out of his rumination and he looked up to see Violet neatly clad in a dark skirt suit that hugged her full figure uncomfortably.

'There are several messages for you, Mr Munnelly,' said Violet demurely. 'Do you want to hear them now or when you get back from your trip?'

Paul paused to ponder. He was going away for the weekend with Nicole to the Lake District and wouldn't be back to work until Tuesday. 'Read them out,' said Paul urgently, 'and make it quick because my lady's waiting.'

'The recruitment agency called to say that the new marketing manager will be starting work on Monday,' said Violet efficiently, 'and they've e-mailed the contract for you to sign. We're also expecting a batch of ten ex-demo cars from the retail outlet in unit 5 for repairs under warranty. The fleet manager says he's already discussed this with you.'

Paul nodded; he recalled the phone call. 'Finally,' she went on, 'the manager of the lease company in Dunstable has signed the retainer contract for the servicing and repairs of all their cars in the Bedfordshire area.'

'Is that all?' he asked, maintaining a business-like manner.

'Eh, your mother called,' mumbled Violet hoarsely, as if she didn't want to be understood.

'I'll get back to her next week,' said Paul nonchalantly, 'but if she calls again today, tell her I can't be reached.'

'Yes, Mr Munnelly,' said Violet, looking relieved.

Violet departed briskly and a grin lit up his face. Since her conversion, Violet had become subservient to the point where it was amusing. Gone also were the flirtations with Giovanni, and Paul was now starting to see her as an asset.

He walked over to the large window bordering the workshop and studied the activity in there, noting that all eight hydraulic lifts were occupied by customers' cars all hoisted up and undergoing various repairs. Smiling to himself as he noted the clean floor, his mind travelled back to his old workshop which was a health and safety disaster in comparison. The new site was a definite improvement, and the volume of new business he was attracting bore this out. Moreover, all the mechanics were working more efficiently with the aid of new equipment, enabling him to step back. These days, he rarely got his hands dirty. He spent most of his time in the office, leaving oversight to Giovanni.

The two other business units he'd purchased were already occupied, albeit on short leases, because Vijay wanted to make sure that they got the right sort of tenants – the sort who paid a premium without blinking. With business booming and his investment plans yielding dividends, Paul had never had it so good. He was sure that even Albert would've applauded his astute planning. With time, Paul was sure that his mother would appreciate his strategy as she witnessed the phenomenal growth that was just around the corner.

12

Matt stared at Nicole for the umptieth time, and then leant towards Paul, clearly bursting with curiosity.

'So how did you meet her?' he asked quietly.

Paul's cryptic grin preserved the aura of mystery surrounding the French beauty who was sunbathing on the deck nearby with Amy McBride.

Paul and Nicole were attending an Apple Seed partner retreat weekend in the Lake District and Amy McBride had shown up at the Swiss-influenced lodge with Matt. The shock of seeing Paul in the foyer the previous day rendered Matt speechless. But Paul was quick to react and reintroduce himself to Amy as Matt's old college mate. Paul and Nicole had been heading out for a spot of water skiing at the time and so there was no time for chitchat. Later that evening they had met again at dinner but with Amy and Nicole present, there had been no opportunity for a brotherly catch-up.

When Paul had suggested they meet up after breakfast, Matt showed up early with Amy in tow. For Paul, it was an opportunity to bring Matt up to speed. Whilst the ladies sunbathed and discussed fashion and art, Paul and Matt sat by the lake sipping Guinness.

'Why are you being so secretive?' asked Matt.

'It's not important,' answered Paul coolly. 'All that matters is that we're dating.'

'Is it serious?'

'We've been together over two years.'

'That long? It *is* serious.'

Paul's cryptic smile met his inquisitiveness.

'Well, she's a looker,' admitted Matt. 'Not bad looking at all and very classy.'

'On that we can both agree.'

'Too good looking for you though.'

'Well, mum was too good looking for dad, and it worked out for them.'

'Yes, but I'm the only attractive fruit of that union.'

They both erupted in laughter.

Over the course of the weekend, they spent more time together than they'd spent in a decade. They'd driven around Cumbria, using Paul's Porsche. Even though Matt had a brand-new Mercedes AMG coupe, a birthday gift from Amy, he'd been genuinely impressed with Paul's wheels, after ascertaining that it wasn't a customer's car. He'd even suggested that they attend a track day event together and asked Paul to teach him how to play golf. For the first time since they were kids, Matt had fussed over him, playing the role of a big brother. It felt good to be in the spotlight.

Amy, on the other hand, had been warm and chatty, having made Paul's acquaintance during some of the Apple Seed partner events. Unlike their first meeting when she treated him as something unpleasant stuck beneath her stylish shoe, these days she treated him with mutual respect. As far as he knew she was still married with no intention to divorce since she attended most public events with her husband. It made him query the status of her relationship with Matt which she had somehow kept out of the scrutiny of social media.

The weekend was not all fun and games but included themed group sessions, with psychologists and life coaches who emphasised wellbeing and empowerment. In one of the final day sessions, requiring them to share their visions, Paul was paired with Amy McBride. It was awkward for both of them because it was the first time they had spoken alone.

'You're not really Matt's old classmate, are you?'

Her forthrightness caught Paul off-guard. He slowly shook his head and averted his gaze.

'You're his brother.'

Paul nodded and lifted his eyes. 'How did you know?'

'Matt let slip during one of our conversations.'

'Does that bother you?'

'Not really, provided you're discreet. I like to keep my affairs private, after all I'm still married – at least for now.'

'It's really none of my business.'

'Great. I'm glad that's sorted. Now what are we supposed to be discussing in this session?'

'We're sharing our vision. What's yours?'

'That's easy. I want to be the most influential fashion designer in the world.'

Her bold statement stunned Paul to silence.

'That's quite some ambition,' he said as soon as he found his voice. 'But aren't you afraid of not making it?'

Amy stared at him strangely. 'Not making it is not an option,' she said haughtily. 'The Apple Seed Partnership has given me the platform I need to succeed.'

'I admire your confidence.'

'I wasn't always this confident but having spent most of my adult life in a dead-end career struggling to breathe, I now have the opportunity to build the most influential fashion empire in the world. What about you?'

Paul thought for a moment. 'I want to build the most successful vehicle service centre franchise in the country.'

'Impressive,' said Amy, 'but you need to think bigger.'

As she got up and headed to the coffee shop, Paul stared after her in disbelief. Like Nicole, the intensity of her convictions was unearthly.

* * * * * * *

On the last evening of their stay at the Lake District, Matt cornered Paul and invited him for a drink. They went to a pub in a quiet street near the Beatrix Potter House where they ordered pints of Guinness and Matt got straight to the point.

'Tell me about Apple Seed Partnership.'

'What do you want to know?'

'Everything.'

'But surely Amy has discussed it with you.'

Matt shook his head. 'I never asked, and she never offered. We never discuss business.'

'Are you looking to apply?'

'Don't be daft,' said Matt sniggering scornfully. 'I just want to know that's all.'

Paul was uneasy with the sudden interest, but he explained to the best of his understanding what the Apple Seed Partnership offered in terms of investment opportunities, networking, mentoring, and leadership development. He also mentioned how Mr Ammon had chosen and supported him.

'That explains a lot,' murmured Matt, as he finished.

'A lot about what?'

'About how you've been able to achieve this level of success and escape Albert's shadow.'

Paul could almost read his brother's thoughts. Matt was struggling to accept his transformation. The last time they met Paul was a greasy skilled worker stuck in a local garage. Now here he was driving a Porsche and dating a goddess whom Matt had been ogling all weekend. He sensed the dreaded rivalry creeping in again.

'I don't get it,' said Matt, shaking his head emphatically. 'I mean, I just don't get it.'

'Take your time,' murmured Paul unkindly.

'Why would Mr Ammon invest in you?'

Paul shrugged. 'He sees my potential.'

'What potential? You're just a mechanic.'

Paul was hurt. 'Correction, I'm an engineer and the proprietor of an upmarket service centre.'

Matt nodded and sat back sizing his younger brother up.

'I've been checking out Nicole's gear,' said Matt, after a silent, contemplative interval, 'and she's into designer stuff in a big way. Any woman who invests in Prada, Moschino, and

Gucci like she does, is high maintenance, and from where I'm sitting, it looks like you're in over your head, mate.'

'I can handle it,' muttered Paul, resisting the temptation to give into his rising temper.

'Albert will turn in his grave,' said Matt chuckling cruelly.

Paul tut-tutted. 'You're clearly having difficulty admitting to yourself that I've got the better girl.'

'You're having a laugh, aren't you,' said Matt staring at Paul incredulously. 'Do you think I'm going out with Amy because I can't get anyone younger or more attractive?'

'Well, you always had a thing for older married women, which tells me all I need to know.'

'No, Paul,' said Matt, answering his own question. 'I date women like Amy because they're generous and attend to my every need. Has your girl bought anything for you lately?'

'I'm not a gigolo,' said Paul, sidestepping the issue.

'Neither am I,' answered Matt, 'but I select my girlfriends very carefully.'

'And ditch them when you get too bored, right?'

'Nothing lasts forever.'

'So, you're still selfish and insecure then.'

Paul's words had a stinging effect that successfully erased the smug grin that was evolving around Matt's lips.

'I'm not using Amy,' grunted Matt, 'I'm saving her from a loveless marriage and an abusive husband who won't grant her a divorce.'

Paul grinned and shook his head slowly in disbelief at Matt's attempt to whitewash his despicable activity with a tale of chivalry. His older brother was clearly using her for his own selfish ends and biding his time until a more lucrative opportunity presented itself. Amy wasn't the first and she definitely wouldn't be the last.

* * * * * * *

The longer John Crane stared at Melvyn Bragg's documented marketing strategy, the broader his smile became till his lips threatened to split at either end.

'Brilliant, Mel!' he exclaimed, looking up after a long interval. 'Absolutely top notch!'

Melvyn Bragg kept his cool, betraying no signs of euphoria, though Paul noted the twinkle in his eye. Melvyn wasn't known for his displays of enthusiasm, but Paul could tell that he was well chuffed with the unexpected praise.

Seated in John Crane's office in London's financial district, Melvyn had tendered Paul's marketing strategy for John's assessment. Just as he had done under Basil's tenure, Paul was content for all non-administrative matters pertaining to the business to be handled by the accountant. Though Melvyn had explained the strategy to him several times already, Paul wasn't willing to bankroll it until John had endorsed it. It wasn't that he didn't trust Melvyn, but rather that he had no confidence in his own judgment.

In the six months of his tenure as sales manager for Munnelly and Sons, Melvyn had embarked on an aggressive publicity drive, aimed at turning the service centre into one of Hertfordshire's most visible and prestigious motoring outlets. Phase one of his plan was already in full swing.

Fresh out of university, Melvyn — Mel to his friends — was an Australian on a mission to establish himself as the U.K motoring industry's answer to the iconic American Lee Iacocca. His plan was simple but effective: start big — grow bigger. His core assets were a high IQ, youthful but roguish good looks and a wardrobe of sharp suits that hugged his thin frame like a membrane. He also had the gift of the gab, speaking so rapidly that many times Paul found himself nodding without understanding a single word he'd said.

The recruitment agency that located him had supplied a long list of references and one of those had been from Sam Truman, the property developer with whom Mel had served an internship. On the strength of that endorsement, John Crane had advised Paul to hire Melvyn without an interview or risk losing him to a rival business. As always, Paul left the arrangements to John Crane.

'What do you think, Mr Munnelly?' asked Mel, who refused to address Paul by his first name, preferring to keep things business-like.

'It sounds impressive,' said Paul, who was still struggling to understand why he needed a glossy TV ad in addition to a radio slot, 'but maybe you could explain why I need to run a publicity campaign across Hertfordshire, Bedfordshire, and Buckinghamshire.'

'Because those counties border each other,' said Mel testily, 'and we expect your new customers to come from there. With my plan to arrange a pick-up and drop-off shuttle service as well as complimentary courtesy cars for executives, distance will no longer be a factor.'

'And we're mainly targeting Japanese cars, right?'

'Paul, we've gone through this before,' interjected John, unable to mask the exasperation in his voice. 'Japanese cars perform too well in the JD Power car owners' survey to make them a viable proposition for growth.'

'That's right,' said Mel, concurring with a nod. 'European cars are better than they used to be, but still require more repairs in between scheduled servicing than equivalent Japanese and Korean cars. The greater majority of Japanese car specialists concentrate on servicing imports and sourcing parts for niche products, but their growth potential is capped for this very reason. Your way forward is to diversify and focus on high-end European cars, where the labour costs are traditionally high at main dealers. You should be targeting owners of high-end German cars over three years old, just out of warranty. My research shows that owners of these cars are on the lookout for a reputable alternative service centre that offers lower labour costs.'

'Listen to the man,' said John excitedly. 'He's making a lot of sense. Think about it Paul. For every three Japanese cars you repair, you could on average be earning the same amount of money for repairing one German car.'

'I know we've discussed this before,' said Paul weakly, 'but I specialise in Japanese cars, and all my mechanics are Japanese car experts. It's our passion…'

'Passion doesn't pay the bills,' muttered John, burying his face in the palms of his hands.

'It's all about the money, Mr Munnelly,' said Mel, reclining with his hands clasped behind his head. 'Think about it.'

Paul pondered over the detail, and for the first time in a while, he wished Albert Munnelly was around to provide a steer. The sales plan was ambitious, as was the marketing strategy, and he could certainly see some of the benefits. He'd developed a passion for Japanese cars, but their reliability didn't make them such a viable proposition. He had to let his head rule his heart.

Melvyn Bragg's plan was financially profitable but would ultimately snuff out any job satisfaction from the equation. What should he do? He couldn't call his mum as she didn't know the first thing about the business; and Basil Mead was out of the question. It was a straight choice between passion and profitability, but it wasn't an easy one. Then it hit him. Mr Ammon! Yes, he could phone Mr Ammon and seek his wise counsel. Whatever Mr Ammon advised would be final.

'I need to make a quick phone call,' he said whipping out his mobile phone; 'a quick private call.'

* * * * * * *

Mr Ammon was, as always, the patient listener, allowing Paul to unwind at his own pace and at the end of Paul's narrative, there was silence whilst the capitalist mulled over the situation.

'You can have both, you know,' said Mr Ammon at last.

'Pardon?' said Paul, on the brink of confusion.

'You can have your cake and eat it,' clarified Mr Ammon. 'You want passion, but you also want profitability and with careful planning you can enjoy both.'

'Tell me how?' implored Paul.

'By opening a dedicated service centre for Japanese cars and keeping your operations separate,' said Mr Ammon. 'It will inevitably mean opening a new business unit, but will keep your existing customers happy, allowing you to open the doors to new ones. Both operations can be governed by the same management guidelines which John Crane could draw up for you. How does that sound?'

'Terrific!' exclaimed Paul. 'It's the best of both worlds.'

'My sentiments exactly,' said Mr Ammon.

'What would I do without you?' asked Paul, gazing out of the reception window at the neighbouring glass walled building nicknamed *The Gherkin*, admiring its futuristic design.

'Live in Albert's shadow,' answered Mr Ammon with a dry chuckle.

*   *   *   *   *   *   *

Paul spent the rest of his allotted time finalising the revised business strategy proposed by Mr Ammon with John Crane and Melvyn Bragg and as the meeting was wrapping up, he recalled his discussion with Vijay. He asked John for a few minutes of his time to discuss something private but waited until Melvyn had departed before disclosing his subject.

'I'd like to invest in Waldon Valley Leisure Park.'

John Crane's raised eyebrows conveyed his surprise.

'How did you find out about that project?' he asked. 'It's still at the planning permission stage.'

'Vijay mentioned something about it.'

'Vijay's got a big mouth – Mr Ammon didn't want us to share it with the Apple Seed partners until we'd secured planning permission.'

'Oops, I wasn't aware it was confidential.'

'It's not your fault, who can blame you for wanting to get in early. Do you know anything about the project?'

'He said you plan to build a casino, an amusement arcade and a hotel.'

'Well, that's the plan. We're teaming up with Sam Truman to build the largest leisure complex of its kind in the Southeast – one that'll appeal to the high rollers.'

'You said something about planning permission.'

'Yes, it's a brownfield site so securing approval from the county council should be relatively straightforward, but you never know. The proposed site is strategic because of its access to all the major motorways and A roads in the area. We hope to adopt the Vegas model and attract out-of-towners who'll sleep over after losing all their money.' He chuckled at his own wit.

'And how can I invest in it?'

'How much were you thinking of?'

Paul shrugged. 'I don't know – ten thousand maybe.'

John Drake stifled a snigger.

'Maybe I could stretch to fifteen,' said Paul making a mental calculation of how much he had in savings.

'Entry for early birds is six figures Paul.'

Paul paused. A hundred thousand was way out of his league. 'I don't think I could stretch to that much without taking out a loan.'

'You don't need a loan Paul,' said John soothingly. 'Have you forgotten your annual apple seed allowance?'

Paul stared at him curiously and then it hit him. He'd forgotten his annual allowance of one hundred thousand pounds over seven years. His eyes brightened. He'd thought he could only use it for his business.

'Can I access it for this project?'

'Of course. It's been granted for anything you wish to invest in, provided I approve.'

'And what sort of returns can I expect?'

'Better than a typical long term Private Finance Initiative deal – you can expect to earn an estimated annual return of over thirty percent if you buy in early. That's more than double the returns expected over the life of most PFI deals. Our deal with Truman is for us to buy the land, build the project and then manage it for ten years before passing it to his American consortium of Wall Street investors.'

Paul nodded even though he didn't understand the mechanics. He knew that he had an interest free investment grant of one hundred thousand pounds per annum over seven years known as the apple seed allowance. At the end of seven years he had to repay the aggregate amount of whatever he had drawn down over each of the seven years. He was not obliged to draw down the entire amount. He did some mental calculations and worked out the returns and his heartbeat raced. He would be able to repay his allowance and still have a healthy profit at the end.

'Count me in,' he said boisterously.

*　*　*　*　*　*　*

Paul studied the screen of his diagnostic computer that was plugged in at one end to the massive engine of a Mercedes SUV, noting all the fault codes that were registering themselves one by one. Thanks to the electronic wizardry installed in twenty first century cars, identifying faults was no longer the sweaty, nail breaking, ritual that it used to be.

In the three months that he'd begun servicing high end German cars, he'd been impressed with not only the level of engineering that went into their manufacture, but the fact that he didn't need to get a college degree to figure out how to repair them. Following John Crane's advice, he'd occupied a new business unit dedicated to the repairs of German cars and taken on some new mechanics – all BMW, Mercedes, and Audi specialists.

In roughly a year since he moved to the business park, his business had tripled and profits quadrupled, resulting in a pay-rise for all mechanics and a hefty bonus for him. Melvyn's campaign was yielding fruit and the response to the TV ad in particular had been astronomical. The glossy ad had been shot over one weekend using amateur actors and a handful of Paul's staff showcasing the level of expertise and proficiency on offer as well as the incomparable degree of client care.

Giovanni had been spruced up for the ad and his Italian accent put to maximum use for most of the narrative. Paul, who had been granted a private viewing of the ad with Nicole, couldn't believe that it had been shot at his business premises.

194

Every week since it had first aired on local TV networks across Bedfordshire, Hertfordshire, and Buckinghamshire, Paul's phones had been ringing off the hook from potential new customers making enquiries.

Violet had surpassed herself, collating information from the callers with the help of a temp and then sending them glossy welcome packs designed by Melvyn. Almost half of all those contacted eventually became customers.

Melvyn had also been the brains behind a client database which for the first time collated the names and contact details of all of Munnelly and Sons' customers.

By monitoring the volume of each customer's repeat business, Melvyn came up with a strategy for sending out special offers to the most valuable customers and incentives to those who hadn't been in for a while. The strategy was paying off, and right now Paul's head was in the clouds.

His mum had phoned from Northern Ireland upon hearing about the extent of his success, but rather than celebrate, she'd spent half an hour cautioning him against growing too fast too quickly. Whilst he could never conceive of his mother being an enemy of progress, her restraint was nevertheless very worrying. Why couldn't she just be happy for him?

'Paul!'

Paul's neck snapped around and his eyes latched on to the stern-faced Mr Pandya, Vijay's dad, who was standing in the doorway of the customer reception area. He hadn't seen Mr Pandya in months, the last time being a brief encounter during the opening ceremony of the new business premises.

Because of the business expansion and the high volume of new customers, Paul no longer had time to meet customers on a one-to-one basis, leaving that task to Giovanni, who had been promoted to workshop manager. The look on Mr Pandya's face indicated that all wasn't well.

'Good afternoon, Mr Pandya,' said Paul, with a quizzical grin. 'Are you booked in for a service?'

'I was,' said Mr Pandya blinking rapidly, as he did

whenever he was angry, 'but I've just been given my invoice...' he waved the sheet about, 'and it's crazy!'

Paul took the invoice from the elderly Asian man and scrutinised it carefully. The bill covered the cost of a replacement exhaust and catalytic converter for the man's ageing Honda Accord and had been embellished by the addition of the dreaded VAT. Paul had never itemised VAT separately on Mr Pandya's invoices before because, even though the man had been with the Inland Revenue for most of his working life, he hated the sight of what he liked to term '*Vague Addition to the Total*'. Mr Pandya always paid cash in hand and didn't see why a local garage should charge VAT.

'I see,' said Paul, looking up from the sheet of paper. 'You're worried about the VAT.'

'VAT?' asked Mr Pandya, looking aghast. 'No, I'm concerned about the balance on the invoice *before* VAT. Your labour costs are at least ten percent higher than I expected.'

'Oh,' said Paul, who hadn't seen that one coming, 'I think I can explain...'

'I don't want an explanation,' said Mr Pandya, 'I want a reduction. I thought pensioners were entitled to ten percent discount on all labour costs.'

'They are,' said Paul patiently, 'but we've revised all our gross labour costs upwards by ten percent, so, whilst you still get a discount, from now on your invoices will reflect an increase over the old price.'

'Why wasn't I told about this in advance?'

'We sent out a letter notifying all the customers on our database about a month ago,' said Paul softly, whilst furiously thinking about how to pacify him.

'Well, I didn't receive one,' said Mr Pandya gruffly, 'so the increase shouldn't apply to me until my next visit.'

Ordinarily, Paul wouldn't have minded, but John Crane had advised against any discounts apart from those offered in the publicity material and Paul had already turned down two of Munnelly and Sons' oldest customers who were pushing for the same discount. To offer Mr Pandya a discount would make nonsense of the invoicing regime that Melvyn and John had so painstakingly established.

'Mr Pandya,' he said quietly. 'If it was down to me…'

'It *is* down to you,' cut in Mr Pandya. 'You're the boss.'

Paul searched around him, trying to think of an appropriate response, whilst Mr Pandya stood studying him like a hawk.

'I'm really sorry…,' began Paul.

'So am I,' said Mr Pandya, taking out his wallet with a grave expression. 'Albert was never this inflexible, especially with loyal customers.'

'All right, all right,' said Paul with a heavy sigh. 'I'll give you a five percent discount, but just this once.'

'Forget it,' said Mr Pandya, snatching his invoice out of Paul's fingers and heading to the cashier slowly. 'I'll pay the full price like everyone else. I keep forgetting Albert's dead.'

The import of the old man's last statement wasn't lost on Paul, and it rattled him. His reluctance to exercise his discretion was about to cost him a valued customer.

He hurried towards the cashier's cubicle, arriving at the same time as the irate Asian man, and waved at Karen the cashier, who was in the process of receiving Mr Pandya's cash.

'Mr Pandya gets a ten percent discount,' said Paul breathlessly, 'and that's ten percent over the usual pensioner price…he's a valued customer.'

Mr Pandya hesitated as Karen efficiently deducted ten percent from the cash he'd handed her and passed it back to him through the payment slot. He turned to look Paul in the eye, before shaking his head slowly.

'I don't want to coerce you into doing anything you don't want to,' he said dryly.

'It's a pleasure,' said Paul grinning sheepishly. 'After all, you are a valued customer.'

Mr Pandya nodded and reached for the refund unenthusiastically.

'You have a great legacy Paul,' said Mr Pandya, returning the money to his wallet, 'and never forget that.'

Paul watched the old man saunter away with the slight swagger of a man who'd just won a major wager and realised that the man had just played him. Mr Pandya knew that the last thing Paul could afford to do now was lose paying customers who gave cash up-front, unlike the corporate clients who settled their account in arrears through electronic bank transfers. Cash in hand was more valuable to a service centre than a credit line from the banks, and with his vastly increased overheads, Paul needed all the cash he could lay his hands on. It was something Melvyn's brilliant marketing strategy hadn't factored in.

13

Six Months Later

Melvyn's glum expression was unsettling, and Paul braced himself for the unexpected. Although Melvyn was the sort of person who appeared incapable of smiling on the best of days, Paul knew all wasn't well.

'We have a problem, Mr Munnelly,' said Melvyn, itching the side of his unshaven cheek with a nervous finger.

'Yes?' invited Paul impatiently.

'There's an anomaly that's proving difficult to resolve.'

'What anomaly?' Paul wished he would just get to the point.

'Well, the accounts don't seem to balance out,' answered Melvyn, looking everywhere, but at Paul's face, 'and I'm struggling to reconcile the budget overspend.'

'Budget overspend?' asked Paul, half rising from his swivel chair. 'How much are we talking about here?'

'About twenty five percent.'

'In layman's terms?'

'About twenty thousand pounds.'

Paul sucked in his breath deeply, and his feet started twitching beneath his desk as he absorbed the negative feedback. For a man in his position, twenty thousand pounds was astronomical. The marketing budget had been drawn up by Melvyn and approved by John Crane, who had even provided a generous allowance over and above what was requested. His justification for this gesture was that there would be a significant reduction in the budget in the next financial year when the advertisements would have attracted new business and increased revenues.

However, Paul was worried that the overspend would cancel out the value of projected budget reductions for the next financial year. Munnelly and Sons was stretched enough already and there was nothing left in the kitty to make up the loss. All profits were being ploughed into meeting the increased overheads, and the only other way of raising cash was through the traditional routes of securing a further bank loan or an increased overdraft.

'What does John Crane say?' he asked, after an agonising moment of erratic meditation.

'He's checking the figures again,' mumbled Melvyn, 'but I doubt if he'll arrive at a different outcome. I went over my calculations several times with Karen and cross-checked with the bank statements for the period.'

'This isn't good,' said Paul, on the verge of going ballistic. 'For a business our size, a twenty thousand pound overspend is catastrophic. How did you let it happen? Haven't you managed a budget before?'

'I can't accept all the blame here, Mr Munnelly,' said Melvyn stubbornly. 'I believe that Karen and John should also get the stick for failing to cap my budgetary allocation.'

Paul stared in disbelief at the young Australian who was still avoiding eye contact.

'You're the budget holder, Melvyn,' said Paul, rising to his feet, 'and it's *your* job to ensure that you keep within budget allocation. We're stretched enough as it is, and we can't just go taking out further loans any time there's an overspend!'

'Well, that's no excuse for having a go at me,' Melvyn muttered moodily, 'after all, hasn't my strategy paid off?'

'I wasn't having a go at you,' said Paul lowering his voice, realising that the matter was about to blow out of proportion.

'Well, it came across that way,' said Melvyn sulkily.

'I didn't mean to raise my tone,' said Paul wearily, 'and I'm sorry if you think I was having a go at you.'

Melvyn shrugged and rose to his feet, avoiding eye contact

as usual. 'I've got to shoot off now, Mr Munnelly,' he said distantly, 'but if you want to talk about this thing again when you've cooled down…'

'It never happened,' said Paul dismissively. 'I'll sort out the accounts with John and resolve the overspend.'

Melvyn shrugged again indifferently and left the office, taking out his bag of tobacco leaves as he went. Smoking filter-free, rolled-up cigarettes was his way of combatting stress, and when the heat was on, he could get through as many as twenty of the filthy things in a single afternoon.

Paul wasn't happy about the discrepancy in the marketing budget, but there was little he could do. For now, it was important to maintain cordiality and not send off the wrong signals. The last thing he needed right now was for Melvyn to sense his edginess and jump ship. Paul hadn't spoken to John Crane yet and it was possible that after a further review, the overspend might not be as drastic as Melvyn was predicting.

*　*　*　*　*　*　*

'It's actually just over twenty-five thousand,' said John Crane, sounding anything but sombre, 'but as we haven't got all the receipts and invoices in yet, it may well end up nearer the thirty thousand mark.'

Paul reeled, as if the man had just punched him full in the face. The situation was worse than expected. He pondered for a moment, frantically scrabbling around in his mind for a solution and then a light bulb flickered.

'What about my annual apple seed allowance? Could I drawdown from it to offset my overspend?'

John cleared his throat, and his expression became uneasy.

'The allowance is specifically for capital investment and your overspend doesn't fall within the class of activities that qualify for financial support.'

'But I thought you said the allowance has been granted for anything I wish to invest in, provided you approve?'

'Yes, but I can't approve your request in this instance.

Covering your overspend is an accounting matter because you're balancing your books. Your agreement clearly states that this is an excluded financial activity. You also can't use the allowance to repay debts or as collateral for loans.'

'The agreement said that?'

John Drake nodded sombrely.

With the new financial year still at least three months away, it was shaping up to be a Siberian Winter at Munnelly and Sons. The company needed a survival strategy to see it through to the end of the general accounting period, and Paul believed that he already knew what had to be done.

'So, I suppose the best way forward then is to cancel all ads until the new financial year,' said Paul presumptuously.

'Well, that's not viable, I'm afraid,' said John, lowering his tone a shade, whilst studying his well-manicured fingernails.

'And why not?' asked Paul, slowly losing the enthusiasm that had begun to build-up.

'Because of outstanding contractual commitments,' explained John, sounding apologetic as he spoke. 'We are contractually bound to continue running ads in the local papers and certain car magazines for the next quarter, not to mention endorsement and sponsorship arrangements with a touring car rally team and a formula three team. If we fail to pay, they sue us; it's that simple.'

'We can't just pull out?' asked Paul incredulously.

John shook his head firmly. 'Pulling out isn't an option,' he said soberly. 'It'll cost you more in the long run.'

Paul sighed deeper than he'd ever done before. Without warning he struck the glass desk with one reddening clenched fist, making the wine in his glass spill slightly over the rim.

'Then we'll just have to slash next year's marketing budget to make up for the loss,' said Paul defiantly. 'I'm pretty sure that by scrutinising Melvyn's figures, you'll be able to identify areas where potential savings can be made.'

'Possibly,' said John, reclining backwards, 'but the knock-on effect of a move like that might impact growth and market share in a climate where it's imperative that we don't stagnate.

We've got a growth strategy to deliver, lest you forget.'

Paul hadn't forgotten, but he was desperate. In the interval between his last conversation with Melvyn and his visit to John Crane, Paul had gone over the budget statements himself and identified a leasing arrangement for a Lexus SUV that he hadn't noticed before. This was in addition to bills for hotel accommodation and lunch appointments that Paul couldn't recall being informed about. Whilst John Crane was contractually obliged to authorise all expenses, the agreement had included a clause that Paul be notified about large bills. A leasing arrangement for a Lexus was a large bill.

'The Lexus will have to go,' said Paul decisively.

'What Lexus?' asked John, looking stumped.

'The one you authorised on Melvyn's behalf,' answered Paul. 'The one you failed to tell me about.'

'Oh, but that's just his company car,' said John with a relaxed chuckle. 'After all, he's contractually entitled to a company car, isn't he?'

'Yes,' agreed Paul, 'but I was expecting you'd get him a Ford or a Toyota or something.'

'Not good for the image of your business,' said John waving both hands casually. 'Think about it Paul. You're in the process of re-branding. We've already registered a new logo as well as a limited liability company, both of which are vital tools in our strategy to take Munnelly and Sons to the next level. Melvyn's going to be busier in the next financial year than he's ever been, as his bonus depends on results. He'll be going to places, meeting people and for that he needs the right car to project the right image.'

'But it's costing us,' moaned Paul.

'Image makeovers cost money,' answered John Crane gravely, 'and I'm simply acting on instructions. After all, wasn't it you who emphatically said you wanted us to do everything possible to bury the local garage image?'

Paul recalled the conversation and held his peace.

'Relax, Paul,' said John brightening up. 'What you need is a positive outlook. You're expanding rapidly, and in twelve months you'll have driven out some of the local competition. All that matters is that you're earning enough profit to justify your expenses and I'm here to tell you that you are.'

Paul nodded numbly and forced out a smile.

'Good man,' said John. 'You know I'm making sense. Now if you've got a moment, there are some cheques and other documents I need you to sign.'

* * * * * * *

Paul slowly pushed his trolley down the aisle of the local supermarket, lost in thought. Christmas was fast approaching, and this was the first time he'd used a credit card to do his shopping in a long while. It was a sign of the times that, even though Munnelly and Sons was turning over a tidy profit, very little of it was finding its way into his pocket.

As he paused to study some buy-one-get-one-free special offers, he was jolted by someone's trolley smashing into his. He looked up at Tommy Denny's grim face and groaned. Tommy was the owner of a rival garage specialising in German cars. Tommy's dad, Nigel, had been Albert's friend and drinking partner. Both men had shot pool and played darts at their local pub every Sunday, after a large booze-up.

Both men had an unwritten understanding that neither would stray into the other's area of specialisation. Nigel would stick to German motors and Albert to Japanese. It was a distinction that had been upheld by both businesses, even after Albert's passing and Nigel's retirement.

Tommy and Paul didn't get on, having once been bitter rivals for the affections of a pub landlord's daughter, who eventually married someone else and emigrated to Australia. Despite this, they maintained cordial relations. Because Tommy had failed to build upon his father's achievements, remaining on the same site, serving the same customers. Each time their paths crossed Paul sensed growing resentment.

'Tommy,' said Paul, acknowledging the other's existence.

'Paul,' answered Tommy dourly.

'How's it going?' asked Paul, backing up his trolley for a hasty departure.

'It's going well,' said Tommy, 'and you?'

'You read the local papers, don't you?'

'Oh yes,' said Tommy scathingly. 'Your *father's* business recently won a local award for excellence or something.'

'Yes, *my* business won the coveted award,' said Paul, brushing aside the deliberate slight.

'Albert would've been proud of you,' said Tommy, intent on belittling Paul's contribution to the motoring industry. 'How much did it cost you by the way?'

Paul smiled to himself and reached for the special offer yogurts in preparation for his retreat. It was clear that the unwritten truce was now broken.

'Have a nice one,' said Paul, steering his loaded trolley around Tommy's sparsely laden one.

'Not so fast, Munnelly,' grunted Tommy, blocking Paul's exit. 'I want to have a word with you, and now is as good a time as any.'

'For you, perhaps,' said Paul, looking up at the taller man's thunderous expression, 'but some of us actually have a business to run.'

'That's right, Munnelly,' said Tommy, ramming his trolley into Paul's again, oblivious to the attention that his raised voice was generating. 'Your subversive manoeuvres have finally succeeded in putting me out of business!'

Paul stared at him strangely, trying to get his head around what he was saying. Tommy had a very short fuse and the towering physique to back it up, so a snide response was probably not the smartest approach.

'I don't know what you're talking about,' said Paul softly.

'You put me out of business, Munnelly,' reiterated Tommy, leaning forward menacingly.

'But how?' asked Paul, averting his face as he smelt the alcohol in Tommy's breath.

'We had an understanding,' said Tommy gruffly, 'and you trampled all over it.'

'You're not making any sense,' said Paul becoming slightly bewildered.

'You had to go and open a dedicated German motor garage, didn't you,' said Tommy vehemently. 'It wasn't enough that you'd already monopolised the servicing and repair of Japanese motors, but you also had to extend your empire to the German motors as well to compete with me – and ruin me!'

'Is that what this is all about?'

'Yes, Munnelly,' said Tommy, sticking out his chest like a silver-back gorilla. 'It's about me having to close the business that's been in my family for two generations!'

'Tommy!' said a high-pitched female voice, intruding before Paul could respond.

They turned in her direction and Paul recognised the short, curvy girl in a chunky roll-neck sweater over tight-fitting jeans striding purposefully toward them with a box of store brand soap powder in her hands. She tossed the box into Tommy's trolley and positioned herself between them like a referee.

Her name was Doris, and she was Tommy's long-term girlfriend, having dated him from the day she walked into his workshop seeking an apprenticeship. She was acknowledged to be the best BMW engine specialist in Hertfordshire.

Her presence had an abrupt calming influence on Tommy.

'How's it going, Paul?' she asked coolly.

'It's going well,' he answered. 'And you?'

'It's been better,' she said pensively. 'By the way, congratulations on that award thing.'

'Thanks,' he said soberly. 'Tommy was just telling me…'

'Forget about it,' she cut in; 'it's not your fault.'

'What do you mean, it's not his fault?' asked Tommy momentarily forgetting himself.

'Leave it out, Tommy,' said Doris, raising her left hand and revealing the sparkling diamond ring on the second finger from the left.

'Why should I?' asked Tommy desperately. 'You know it was his tactics that drove us out of business. He targeted our customers with cut-price offers and lured away our mechanics with aggressive wages.'

'We agreed to let it go, remember?' said Doris, lowering the hand. 'What's done is done. We've got to move on. It's not the end of the world.'

'But it is for me,' said Tommy weakly.

Doris hugged her man, to the delight of some female onlookers and Paul's discomfort. It was clear that Tommy's bankruptcy would have a knock-on effect on their marriage plans, but Paul wasn't prepared to concede that he was in anyway responsible for their misfortune.

Melvyn Bragg had run a brilliant marketing campaign and the customers had voted with their feet. It didn't help that Tommy lacked his father's diplomacy, being inflexible, and short-tempered. He had had more than his fair share of scraps with customers and was reaping what he'd sown.

'Congratulations on your engagement,' said Paul, unsure of what else to say in the absence of the grovelling apology that he wasn't inclined to give.

'Thank you,' said Doris, turning to him with a brave but grim smile. 'We're getting married in two weeks.'

'I'm happy for you,' said Paul quickly, as he got a brainwave, 'and if after the ceremony you're looking for work, I'd be glad to give you a job…'

'Are you bonkers?' asked Tommy, breaking free from Doris' embrace. 'Are you having a laugh or what?'

'I was just trying to help,' said Paul inexorably.

'Well shove your help,' snarled Tommy, 'and get out of here before I kick your teeth in!'

'No, Tommy,' cut in Doris, seizing hold of his fist. 'Not like this. You promised me.'

Tommy calmed down, but his chest was still heaving from the adrenaline rush, and Paul counted himself lucky.

'See you around, Paul,' said Doris, hugging her man tightly, 'and thanks for the offer, but no thanks. We'll work this one out on our own.'

Paul nodded and speedily navigated his way around them

before Tommy snapped again.

*   *   *   *   *   *   *

Paul covered the journey between the superstore in Waldon Town and Nicole's apartment in Stanmore in less than ten minutes, a journey that usually took him twice as long. All the way there, he'd gripped the steering wheel as if testing its integrity, but the palms of his hands were all clammy with perspiration. The encounter with Tommy had been too close a call for him to settle back into a relaxed routine so quickly. Tommy's proclivity for committing random acts of violence was legendary and Paul knew that, but for Doris's intervention, a near fatality might've been on the cards.

He had no sympathy for Tommy's plight, because everyone in the business had seen it coming. Tommy's people skills were abysmal, even if his ability as a mechanic was first rate. It was ludicrous of Tommy to expect him to maintain the understanding that existed between their dads. Albert and Nigel had been drinking pals, but Tommy and Paul were love rivals who couldn't stand each other. Paul hadn't gone out of his way to put Tommy out of business. After all, there were several other German motor specialists still thriving in the neighbourhood. Tommy wouldn't see that, of course, because he'd already made up his mind at whose door to lay the blame.

Driving up to the front porch outside Nicole's apartment, he could still hear the thumping of his heart above the Porsche's throbbing engine. After switching off the ignition, he remained in the car, still gripping the steering wheel trying to compose himself before confronting the love of his life.

Quite why he'd driven to her home was a mystery, but after his encounter he'd instinctively set his trajectory for the London Borough of Barnet even though his own home was just a stone's throw from the superstore. Maybe he just needed Nicole's comfort to restore his lost manhood.

After ten minutes of sitting at the wheel of his car, he felt stable enough to emerge and make his way to the front door.

It was customary for him to alert her that he was coming over, but tonight he was bypassing protocol.

He buzzed the door phone a couple of times and waited till Nicole's exotic tone answered the summons.

'Paul,' she said, sounding surprised to hear his voice as he announced himself. 'Why didn't you phone first? What are you doing over here so late?'

'I had to see you,' he said hurriedly, 'and I was too hyped-up to phone.'

'What's the matter, Paul?' she asked, sensing his agitation. 'You don't sound yourself.'

'I'm fine,' he said, in the same urgent voice. 'Just let me in, will you? I nearly got into a fight tonight and the experience has just left me a little worked up.'

'Oh my goodness!' she exclaimed, and seconds later he heard the buzzing sound of the front door unlocking. 'Come right up.'

Paul pushed the door open as forcefully as he could and bounded up the stairs to her first-floor apartment, taking two stairs at a time.

He found her door partially open as he arrived, and he strode into the hallway with his chest thrust out in keeping with the image of a man who'd almost murdered another. Nicole was waiting in the hallway, clad in a pair of loose-fitting silk pyjamas with her chestnut brown hair cascading over her shoulders. Her smile was welcoming enough, but he detected a slight hesitance in her body language as he embraced her.

'I have a visitor, Paul,' she said, looking him straight in the eye, 'and I was just about to cook him a meal. You're welcome to stay of course, but I'd prefer it if you didn't.'

Paul felt as if a powerful suction pump had just sucked all the breath out of his lungs and he struggled to maintain a placid expression.

'Any particular reason?' he asked, amazed that he could still find his voice in the circumstances.

'It's a business engagement,' she said calmly, 'and it just happens that we chose to have it here. I promised to cook him a meal one day and he's taking me up on my offer, that's all.'

Paul wasn't convinced but didn't have the guts to say it. What sort of business dinner involved the hostess wearing a pair of pyjamas?

'It's obviously not a good time,' he said uncomfortably. 'So, I'll leave you guys to continue doing whatever it was you were doing before I got here.'

'Are you accusing me of lying?'

The question was asked in a docile tone with no hint of anger, but it rattled Paul, nevertheless. She looked him straight in the eye and he shrank back from the challenge.

'I didn't mean it like that,' he stuttered. 'It just came out wrong. I really meant that I'd leave you to continue your business affairs…'

'Honey, who's there?' asked a familiar American drawl.

Before Paul could match a name to the voice, Sam Truman showed up in the hallway from the adjoining living room, clad in shirtsleeves over cotton chinos. From his bare feet and relaxed demeanour, it was clear that this was not a formal visit. It would be morning before Sam hit the road.

'Don't I know you?' asked Sam, squinting at him with recognition. 'Haven't we met?'

'Yes, it's been a while,' said Paul making no effort to extend his hand. 'Enjoy your meal.'

He turned on his heel, and headed for the front door, with a weight in his chest. He sensed Nicole walking beside him and wanted to tell her to go to hell but was too drained.

'Going so soon?' called out Truman, as Paul vanished out of the apartment.

'I'll give you a call tomorrow,' said Nicole, as they reached the front door.

Paul nodded but didn't have the courage to stare in her direction. The sickening, gut-wrenching sensation in his stomach was making him nauseous and he needed fresh air.

* * * * * * *

Paul stared blankly at the TV screen, watching the coverage of the opening ceremony for London's Fashion Week without actually registering anything. Matt had phoned up a couple of days ago urging him to watch the opening event because Amy's new fashion line would be on display, and Paul had numbly given his word that he would. In the week that followed his memorable visit to Nicole's apartment, he'd spent more days at home than at either of his two workshops.

Getting out of bed had become a major chore, as had shaving, and eating. Content to guzzle his favourite Guinness several times a day, he'd abstained from food and developed untidy stubble that was on the verge of becoming a beard. Showering was also off the cards and so he'd worn the same tracksuit to bed – bed being the comfiest sofa in his living room. On his handful of brief visits to the workshops he'd turned up in his tracksuit, scowling to put his staff off. It worked. No one approached him or enquired after his welfare.

Nicole had tried getting through to him, but he'd refused to take her calls. There were too many unresolved questions revolving around inside his head, but he didn't have the guts to confront her about them.

For the first time in his life, Paul wished he'd had the courage to put himself out of his misery. He'd built up his hopes on a long-term relationship with Nicole, believing that they both wanted the same thing, but like a fly in her soup, she'd evicted him. What was she phoning to tell him? That she still cared about him? That Truman was nothing to her and that there was nothing between them?

He felt like the grandest of fools for becoming putty in her hands. He'd received enough warnings from his Parisian trip to realise that he was putting his bare hands into a furnace. She was a flirtatious vulture who preyed on the carcasses of love-blind novices. Her pretence at being vulnerable was the bait that ensnared him, and her enticing charms the hook that reeled him in. He wanted nothing more to do with the schizophrenic witch. There were cheaper ways to die.

But Nicole was only part of his troubles. In fact, she was the least part of his troubles. His financial situation was becoming a nightmare. The weight of his overheads was harrowing. His wage bill alone was worth almost thirty eight percent of his net income and it showed no signs of reducing anytime soon.

With two fully manned sites catering for different vehicle brands and consultants who were forever getting him entangled in all sorts of contractual obligations, it was clear that the bubble was about to burst. To crown it all, one of his tenants at the new business park had indicated their intention to relocate owing to falling revenue, which meant that in a month's time he would have a vacant business unit for let and an additional mortgage to fund from his own profits.

Contrary to original forecasts, tenants weren't exactly queuing up to rent business units on the site, thanks to the construction of a rival site less than a quarter of a mile outside Waldon Town. The new site offered similar facilities, bar the shopping complex, but had the advantage of being near a major overground train station. Most motor retailers were moving their operations there with supersonic velocity, leaving only very basic operations behind. Paul wondered how long it would be before they were looking to renegotiate their retainer with him. So much for John Crane's brilliant strategy! John had already given strong hints that further re-mortgaging was essential to raise funds, and Paul knew that that meant reducing his equity in his old premises to next to nothing as that was the only asset he had left.

Following the rejection of six previous loan applications, he'd put in a seventh loan application through John Crane to the Sloane Bank for a five-figure sum in addition to an application for an increase in his overdraft facility, and just thinking about it gave him a migraine.

He recalled with a wry smile what Albert used to say about The Sloane bank. Albert was fond of saying that, *'a loan from Sloane never leaves you alone,'* referring to the bank's aggressive debt recovery policy that had hounded one of Albert's

Pakistani mechanics, Ash, till the impoverished man hung himself on the eve of his daughter's wedding.

Ash had maxed out his credit cards and taken out a secured loan with The Sloane Bank to cover his daughter's dowry and wedding but defaulting on the repayments had unleashed the bank's enforcers, who stayed on his back till he could take no more. Suffice to say, his daughter's wedding was cancelled by the groom, who had no desire to marry into an accursed family, leaving the jilted bride in hysterics. Albert had footed the bill for Ash's funeral, where he'd uttered the immortal lines, '*a loan from Sloane never leaves you alone*'. Five months after the funeral, the Sloane Bank forced the sale of Ash's house forcing the widow and her two daughters to move up to Bradford, where housing was more affordable. Albert hated The Sloane Bank and so did Basil Mead, but Paul was willing to take a liberal view. In his present predicament, any bank that could advance him the required finance was reputable.

Hopefully if the loans were granted, he could cover his overheads and finalise payments on Melvyn's marketing campaign. Though they were still running ads on radio and television, they weren't really attracting sufficient new business to cover for the business they were losing. Every other day, an old customer would call in to complain about the invoicing and then never bother to call back again, even when he seized the initiative to phone them back, contrary to Melvyn Bragg's advice.

Melvyn had advised that it wasn't savvy to call back departing customers lest they get the impression that he was desperate. Melvyn was convinced that the ones who appreciated quality would be back, but the ones who haggled over price were a good riddance. Paul failed to appreciate the logic, but as always went along with it, unwilling to confront the combined intellectual superiority of Melvyn and John. They were the business experts telling him to hold his nerve even in the face of an impending financial quagmire, and in their eyes, he never had anything strategic to offer. Their management information showed that Munnelly and Sons was in good health and operating like a well-oiled machine.

Paul knew all about well-oiled machines and didn't accept the analogy. He'd tried to contact Mr Ammon, but when Nicole had answered the man's mobile phone, he'd hung up. The last thing he wanted was Nicole finding out about his financial difficulties.

His one safety net was the investment in the Waldon Valley Leisure Park which he had funded from his Apple Seed Partnership allowance. He had staked two hundred thousand over two years to join a consortium of Apple Seed partners which included Vijay Pandya, Amy McBride, and Gordon Pinsent. The consortium was investing as a collective in the leisure park and from all indications that deal was on track to make a killing. He was also counting on future annual Apple Seed allowances to invest in his business despite the strict stipulation that the funds couldn't be used to pay off debts.

The ringing of his mobile phone thrust him out of his rumination, and he was about to answer it when he recognised the number of one of his creditors and resisted.

He had taken to using credit cards to finance his domestics and he had already maxed two of them, each for a four-figure sum. The credit card companies were on his case because he had fallen behind with his payment of the minimum monthly charge, and one was even threatening to sell the debt to third sector debt collectors for enforcement.

Paul had become adept at recognising the phone numbers used by his creditors and deliberately avoided answering them. His phone started ringing again and he reluctantly glanced at the caller ID, noting that it was an unfamiliar landline. He reached for his handset and took the call, hoping that he wasn't playing into his creditor's hands. He recognised Matt's voice, but the panic-stricken tone that assaulted his ears denied him the luxury of relief.

'What's the matter, Matt?' asked Paul, as his brother babbled breathlessly at the other end.

'It's Amy!' Matt blurted out.

'Is she all right?' asked Paul cautiously.

'I-I don't know!' screeched Matt. 'I think she's overdosed … I think she's dead.'

The information took a while to register in Paul's mind, during which time Matt babbled on about how he'd returned home to find her.

'You better call for an ambulance,' said Paul.

'I-I can't,' said Matt hysterically. 'I just need to get away from here. The sight of her is freaking me out, man!'

'Get an ambulance, Matt!' urged Paul, struggling to remain even-tempered. 'If she's still breathing, they might be able to save her life.'

'No, man, I can't do it,' said Matt nervously. 'I don't really want to get involved.'

'But she's your girlfriend,' said Paul, still unsure of what was going on, 'and she's lying in your apartment, so I guess that means you're already involved.'

'Look, Paul … can you come over?' asked Matt awkwardly. 'It's just that I'd feel more confident if you were here. I think she's already dead because she's not moving, so I guess the police might get involved …'

'All right,' said Paul, emitting a deep sigh. 'I'm on my way.'

* * * * * * *

Matt's rented apartment was in a quiet street near Marylebone Tube Station overlooking a gated communal garden, and as Paul emerged from the black cab that had literally raced him over from Euston Station, he shivered. Sure, temperatures had dropped as they did every night in the capital, but he knew that his reaction had nothing to do with the climatic conditions. There was a sense of foreboding of what lay ahead. His journey from Waldon Town had taken him just under forty minutes, door to door, but every one of those minutes had been nerve racking.

He paid off the cabbie and then advanced towards the building with heavy reluctant strides, feeling more foolish the closer he got. Why hadn't he insisted that Matt call an ambulance? What if Amy died from her drug overdose, would the police accuse him of being an accomplice? Stupid! Stupid! Stupid! Why did he let Matt talk him out of doing the most logical thing in a situation like this? Yet it wasn't too late to make the call and redeem himself. He could phone for an ambulance and pretend that his brother had just called him. That might work…yes, that might just do the trick!

Paul reached for his phone as he arrived at the front door to the apartment block but bottled out after his finger depressed the number nine key twice. What was he doing? What if Amy wasn't as bad as Matt had claimed? What if she'd recovered? What if Matt had somehow revived her? He had to be sure that there was an emergency before he made the crucial call. Yes, he had to ascertain whether the situation had changed before making the call.

Paul depressed the door buzzer, and the concierge on duty released the door lock from the safety of the reception desk. As Paul approached him, the elderly man in the ridiculously grandiose uniform eyed him up and down.

'Good evening, sir,' said the concierge stiffly. 'How can I help you?'

'Matthew Munnelly's apartment please,' said Paul abruptly. 'I'm here to see him.'

'Then you've just missed him, sir,' said the concierge. 'He left about ten minutes ago as if his tail was on fire.'

Paul groaned inwardly. What had he let himself in for? What about Amy? The curiosity was killing him.

'What number's his apartment?' he asked.

'Twenty-one on the first floor,' said the concierge brightly, before catching himself, as Paul strode past in the direction of the quaint cage-like lift. 'Hang on you can't go up if Mr Munnelly's not at home.'

'I'm here to see Amy McBride and she's in Matt's apartment!' called out Paul, abandoning the elevator in favour of the stairs.

He bounded up the stairs, taking two at a time and arriving at the first floor in seconds. He hurried down the deserted carpeted corridor scanning the doors until he located apartment twenty-one. Though the front door was wide open, giving a clear view down the hallway to the living room at the other end, Paul paused for a moment to psych himself up for what he was about to see. Whatever had made Matt bolt out of his apartment, without waiting for him, had to be pretty gruesome, and Paul wasn't sure if he was ready to confront it.

He walked mechanically into the apartment's hallway, barely seeing the tasteful décor around him. The lights were on in almost every room and, from the clothes strewn on the floor here and there, it was clear that Matt had packed and then left in a hurry. Paul ventured further into the apartment, but, finding it vacant, made his way to an adjoining bedroom, and then he saw her. She was lying across the bed half-dressed, with her eyes shut. Next to her, were several empty sachets. From the residue of whitish powder in the bags, it was clear that they were the source of her predicament.

He considered checking her pulse the way he'd seen it done in the movies, but his nerves failed him. Instead, he did what he should have done in the first place. He dialled the number nine on his mobile phone three times.

* * * * * * *

Paul sat numbly on Matt's exquisite chesterfield and stared blankly at the paramedics and uniformed police officers who wandered past him, going about their business, almost oblivious to his presence. An ambulance had arrived roughly ten minutes after his call and Amy had been rushed out on a stretcher by two paramedics after they failed to resuscitate her. The police turned up seconds after the paramedics and had immediately engaged him in a rigorous line of questioning that made it clear they'd already spoken to the concierge.

They wanted to know about Matt's whereabouts, but he could tell them nothing. Matt had a proclivity for walking away from anything too challenging and tonight merely showcased that trait. When Matt walked, he never looked back and Paul was confident that even if Amy survived this, things were over between them. Paul's ID was checked and once validated, the police pretty much left him alone, except for instructing him to attend his local station to supply a written statement.

*　*　*　*　*　*　*

All bleary-eyed and dishevelled, Paul strolled into the female wing of the Royal Free hospital, where Amy McBride was recovering from her close shave with death. Whilst providing a written statement at the local police station, he'd been informed that Amy McBride had regained consciousness after hours of emergency procedures by medical staff. The inspector who took his written statement casually remarked about how lucky he was, that it wasn't a murder enquiry. This prompted Paul to ask whether he was ever a suspect. Paul's story was simple. He'd come to see his brother but arrived there to find his brother's girlfriend unconscious.

Though the police had told him he was free to go, he felt duty bound to pop in and see Amy before returning to Waldon Town to face his own challenges. He was also half-hoping that Matt had the same idea, since his older brother hadn't been answering his calls.

Amy was sleeping when he arrived at her ward. Staring at her from the doorway, he realised that without make-up she was really a very plain-looking woman. In some ways, she looked just like their mum did in her younger days and it was easy to see where the attraction lay for Matt.

'Where is he?' a hard-edged male voice hollered out, slashing through the silence. 'Is that him?'

Paul swung around to see the burly white middle-aged, man in a chef's livery, who was tearing down the corridor towards him. On closer inspection, Paul recognised the man who had attended the Eden Fruit Foundation's annual gala dinner. It was Amy's husband and Paul noted his glistening bloodshot eyes and the meat cleaver he was drawing out from under his tunic. Panic took over from curiosity.

'Are you Matt Munnelly?' asked Mr McBride, halting in front of Paul breathlessly.

Paul shook his head. 'No, I'm his brother,' he answered.

There was silence as the chef chewed on it for a moment, his face hardened with grief. Then he slowly lowering his meat cleaver, much to Paul's relief.

'What has he done to her?' asked the chef, in a subdued but tremulous voice, tears glistening in his eyes.

'I'm really sorry about this,' Paul said uncomfortably. 'Is there anything I can do to help?'

'Yes,' said the chef, in a bloodcurdling voice, without taking his eyes off Amy. 'You can warn your brother to stay away from my wife, right?'

Paul heaved a sigh and nodded gently, before turning around and heading for the exit. In the circumstances, he considered it quite a reasonable request.

*   *   *   *   *   *   *

Three Months later

'Not good news I'm afraid,' muttered John Crane, in his matter-of-fact manner.

'What now?' asked Paul who had only answered the call when he recognised the business analyst's number. He was so used to receiving bad news that it no longer fazed him.

'It's the leisure park.'

'What about it?'

'It's on ice.'

'On ice? What does that mean?'

'It's been suspended.'

Paul absorbed the information slowly and then chuckled gently. He had two years' worth of Apple Seed allowance tied-up in that project and it represented his cushion against the storm brewing over his legacy.

'What happened?' The calmness of his tone surprised him.

'Planning permission screwed us. They've discovered

ancient Roman ruins beneath the brownfield site.'

'What does that mean? I thought we already had planning permission to build on that site.'

'We did, until the Chief Planning Officer at Waldon Town Borough Council threw a spanner in the works. The only complaints received during the public consultation was from a pressure group led by the vicar of St Joseph's Anglican Church protesting against the building of a casino in the borough. That protest fizzled out because of the greater cost benefit of having a perennial income generating business within the borough. No one mentioned anything about historical Roman ruins submerged beneath a site which was previously occupied by an old Second World War factory.

'Three months after the council granted us planning permission, it received a notification pointing to an earlier request for the site to be designated one of national historic and archaeological interest that was suitable for conservation. The nosey Chief Planning Officer suspended our planning permission because the notification preceded our application. There's every likelihood that our application will be terminated but Mr Ammon's instructions are not to fight the council's decision because of all the negative publicity.'

Paul exhaled trying to ease the pressure building up in his head. 'So that's it?'

'Unfortunately.'

'And our investments?'

John Crane's silence worried him.

'Are you saying my investment can't be recovered?'

'We're looking into that, but I wouldn't hold my breath.'

'I don't understand. If construction hasn't started yet, how can I lose my investment?'

'It's complicated, but I'll send you something via email which should help clarify how the investment scheme works and how risk was allocated amongst the different consortia under that scheme.'

'That'll be pointless. You know I never understand the technicalities of these sorts of matters. All I need to understand is whether I'll still be liable to repay any lost investment at the end of my time with the Apple Seed Partnership. Because you advised me on the investment, and I've kept to the terms of the arrangement, I shouldn't have to repay that money.'

'Unfortunately, it's not that simple.'

'Why not?'

'Because you were part of a consortium, there is collective liability…'

'What collective liability? I didn't go into partnership with anyone on this deal.'

'Unfortunately, you did. The scheme required you to be part of a consortium which had rules governing risks and liabilities. The consortium was set up with collective liability as well as a pain and gain share mechanism.'

'Pain and gain share? What's that?'

'A means by which parties share any gains or losses in relation to the investment.'

'But I didn't sign up to that!'

'I'm afraid you did.'

Paul glanced at his trembling hands and fear flooded his soul draining out any optimism. With his mind plagued by conflicting thoughts, he said the only lucid thing he could think of. 'I need to speak with Mr Ammon.'

14

Three Months Later

Paul stared at his reflection in the mirror, and was startled by the mask that stared back at him. The pale, unshaven, sunken-eyed face in the mirror looked at least a decade older and the excessive weight loss was all the more apparent by the sharpness of his cheekbones. The fact that he had hardly slept more than two hours a night in the past fortnight obviously had something to do with it, as did his loss of appetite and sole reliance on alcoholic beverages.

He had also refused to take any phone calls or open the mail, as they were most likely from creditors calling in his bad debts. The loan advance and extended overdraft facility had long since evaporated, lost in a sea of business expenses that were threatening to ruin him. In response to the frequent bad news, he'd buried his head in the sand and stayed clear of his two workshops. He had very little equity left in Munnelly and Sons' original business premises, but even that was beyond his reach because of the secured loan attaching to the property.

To make matters worse, several days earlier he'd woken up in the early hours to find that his car had vanished from his front driveway. Someone had accessed the gated estate and surreptitiously removed the car. Paul was not amused. Several frantic phone calls to the police subsequently confirmed that the car had been repossessed. His beloved Porsche was going to be auctioned off to some lucky punter at less than its sale sticker, all because several repayments had been missed.

He'd barely acclimatised to being without his chariot of fire, when he received a hefty five-figure invoice from John Crane for his consultancy services. Coming at a time when cash was tight, the bill was a blow beneath the belt, especially from one who had orchestrated Munnelly and Sons' failure. He'd ignored the bill and all subsequent ones from the same source and refused to take the man's phone calls.

Insult was added to injury when Melvyn Bragg announced that he was resigning to set up his own practice and demanded all his commission entitlement in one large pay-out. Unlike John, however, Melvyn had stalked Paul, bombarding him with demands for the payment of the unpaid income plus bonus payments. Unwilling to get the police involved, Paul had paid him off with a cheque which subsequently bounced higher than a slam-dunked basketball. There was currently an ongoing police investigation into the matter, with Melvyn keen on pressing charges against his former employer.

Fortunately, so far, Paul had been able to keep up with the payments of workshop staff salaries, paying them from the business proceeds, but had reached a decision to close the workshop specialising in German cars by the end of the month and to scale down operations at the surviving workshop in a bid to reduce overheads. He reckoned that the emergency measures would enable him to retain all the old loyal mechanics.

He'd not yet spoken to Mr Ammon about the failed leisure park investment scheme, and it had been three months since his chat with John Crane. Crane had sent him an email setting out the obligations of each consortium in relation to the investment scheme. He'd placed particular emphasis on the small print which Paul had glossed over, pointing out matters such as the pain and gain share mechanism as well as the joint and several liability each consortium member faced in relation to the scheme. The email also highlighted the section that recommended each consortium member to take out insurance cover. On seeing that, Paul reckoned that it was pointless speaking with Mr Ammon who would more than likely parrot

Crane's position.

In the aftermath of the failed investment scheme, the Apple Seed partners in his consortium had arranged a meeting to assess the risk and John Crane had been invited to clarify the Pain and Gain share mechanism. Paul had attended the event held in a ritzy Park Lane hotel where partners were served a sumptuous three course meal. He learnt that Apple Seed partners were contractually obliged to share the pain – in respect of any lost or missed projections up to fifty percent of the gross value of that loss. There was no get-out clause for Acts of God – events occurring outside the control of the investment scheme managers. What it meant for Munnelly was that he remained liable for an as yet undisclosed sum over and above his two hundred-thousand-pound investment.

Then, there was the Matt Munnelly affair, which was still a cause for concern. Matt hadn't been seen since fleeing his apartment six months ago. Paul no longer answered his mum's frantic calls, as lately she'd begun blaming him for not doing enough to dissuade his older brother from fleeing the scene.

Even though the wimp was now officially on the police's missing persons register, Mrs Munnelly believed that Paul should be out there searching for him before he did something foolish. The way Paul figured it, Matt should've at least contacted their mum to assure her.

Amy McBride was on the mend, but her mental breakdown and subsequent drug overdose had affected her sales and reputation badly, resulting in her pulling out of a number of fashion shows. For a while, she had been a regular feature in the news, where rivals gloated over her fall from grace and rumours about the state of her personal health and financial difficulties were bandied about. However, she'd not featured for a while, a clear sign that the media was losing interest in her. The last rumour that surfaced on the internet claimed that she was in the process of closing down her business. There was no talk, however, of whether she'd reconciled with her husband.

Paul recalled the man's anguish. Mr McBride was still in

love with his wife, despite everything she'd done, and Paul couldn't connect with that. Amy had ditched him for a younger man and invested a small fortune lavishing gifts on her new lover, yet her clearly distraught husband felt duty-bound to intervene at one of the lowest points in her life. That was a level of commitment that Paul hadn't come across in a long while.

The banging on his front door jerked him back to reality, and he hurried over to the nearest window, as fast as his lethargic body could manage. Being a gated estate, nobody could access his home without first alerting him from the gate. As he wasn't expecting any visitors, his curiosity was aroused.

A quick glance at the wall-mounted clock confirmed that the time was almost ten am, which meant that his white-collar neighbours had already left for work. So, who was at the door?

He peered out through the window nearest the front door, and his heart rate accelerated as he recognised the police patrol car parked outside. His mind instantly went to the bounced cheque he'd handed to Melvyn, and the threat of criminal proceedings that was still hovering over him like a guillotine's blade. Had they come to arrest him?

The lawyer he'd consulted prior to providing a witness statement, had assured him that unless the prosecution could prove he intended to give the cheque knowing that he had insufficient funds, they had no case. The lawyer had, however, advised Paul to make Melvyn a cash settlement, adding a self-imposed ten percent penalty to discourage him from pressing criminal charges. That had been a fortnight ago, but Paul had procrastinated and now he was about to pay the penalty – unless of course he made the offer.

He gingerly made his way to the front door, knowing that it was futile to pretend he wasn't at home. If they had a search warrant, they would gain access to his premises anyway, damaging his front door lock in the process. He unlocked the door and stood aside as he saw the two police constables standing at either side of the front door porch. One was a middle-aged white male and the other a cute looking Asian female. The female constable looked familiar.

'Hi Paul,' she said gently. 'How are you keeping?'

'Not so good,' he replied, squinting at her, as his brain struggled to recall who she was. 'Do I know you?'

'Zula Pandya,' she answered. 'I'm Vijay's sister.'

Paul's heartbeat decelerated abruptly. They had attended the same school, and, for a brief while, he'd been infatuated with her. He hadn't seen her in a while.

'Hi Zula,' he said, trying to inject some enthusiasm into his tone. 'It's been a while, but I must say you're looking good.'

'Thanks,' she answered, smiling wistfully. 'Sorry I can't say the same about you. You look like you could do with a shave and a good night's sleep.'

'I've got a lot on my mind right now,' he confessed, 'and seeing you in that uniform isn't helping matters. I suppose they assigned you to the case because you know me, right?'

She nodded in confirmation and gestured to her colleague, unable to hide the discomfort discolouring her smile.

'Neil's been working on this,' she said slowly, 'but the inspector thought it would help if I came along…you know…to soften the blow.'

Paul nodded. He understood. He, however, wondered whether there was any way they could refrain from handcuffing him until he was out of the estate. The last thing he wanted was for any of the *stay-at-home* wives, whose husbands envied him, to see him being led off in chains. The gossip across the estate would kill him faster than any bullet.

'Look, Zula,' he said heavily. 'I've already promised my lawyer that I'll do all within my power to find him and make amends. Doesn't that count for anything?'

'Well, I'm afraid it's too late for that now,' said Zula biting her lower lip, and taking a deep breath. 'I'm really very sorry.'

'Can I get changed first?' he asked, swallowing hard to suppress the lump in his throat.

'There's no real urgency,' said Neil, stepping forward. 'If you're not feeling up to it, we can always come back later in the day. Obviously the sooner the better, so we can wrap this whole thing up.'

'No, I'd rather get it over and done with,' said Paul. 'Which police station are we heading to?'

'No, we're going to a morgue in North London,' said Neil, looking aghast.

Paul froze as a paralyzing thought engulfed his mind. Melvyn was dead!

'When? How?' he asked, covering his mouth with his hand.

'His body was found yesterday on the bank of the Thames in Richmond,' said Zula, stepping back into the conversation. 'Forensics reveal that he drowned, and whilst it's still too early to confirm, we believe he either jumped or was pushed off a bridge into the river and got washed up in Richmond.'

Paul didn't know whether to mourn or rejoice. Melvyn didn't come across as the suicidal sort. He was far too ambitious to throw in the towel, but then again, his arrogance could've pushed him beyond the edge of reason. It was also possible that he'd been a victim of a random mugging and knowing him, he would've fought his attacker rather than relinquish his wallet. With Melvyn dead, would the police drop their investigation into the bounced cheque?

'I can see you're clearly upset,' said Zula, reaching forward to pat his upper arm. 'So maybe this isn't a good time, but we really do need you to ID the body as soon as possible so the forensic guys can do their thing.'

'How long will this take?' asked Paul.

'A couple of hours,' answered Neil impatiently.

Paul contemplated the situation for a moment. Melvyn Bragg was an Australian with no family in the U.K, and as Paul was his last employer it explained why the police had approached him to ID the body. Paul hated morgues but, in the current circumstances, he was compelled to go on acting the role of the distraught ex-employer. His cooperation might even influence the outcome of the bounced cheque saga.

'Give me five minutes to get changed,' he said quietly.

*　*　*　*　*　*　*

The last place on earth Paul desired to be in right now was the morgue. As he followed Constable Zula Pandya into the bowels of the modern underground mortuary in Haringey North London, he couldn't help but reflect on how much time he'd been spending around the dead lately. The memories of his morbid Parisian excursion were still too fresh in his mind, and he wondered whether it was a foreboding of what lay ahead for him in the not-too-distant future.

Albert had often said that hanging around the dead was like queuing up at an airport departure gate. Though Albert had been referring to those with an unhealthy obsession for cemeteries, Paul felt that the statement was still apt.

Zula left him in the reception area whilst she went ahead to sort out the administrative details with the mortuary attendants, and Paul took the time to inspect his surroundings. Despite the clear effort that had gone into making the place less sinister than traditional hospital morgues, Paul was uncomfortable and couldn't wait to have it all over and done with. Once Zula was through with all the paperwork, the mortuary attendant on duty led them to the cold storage where the pull-out refrigerator trays were and, after consulting his list, pulled out one of the trays, revealing the lifeless body of a male Caucasian.

Paul looked away and steeled himself for the ordeal ahead. Up until that moment he'd been indifferent about the task, but now reality was gradually beginning to set in. He was about to view the corpse of someone he knew well and had last seen about a fortnight ago. It wasn't going to be as easy as he'd envisaged. He felt Zula's hand gently touch his upper arm and instinctively flinched. He clenched his fists till his fingernails dug deeply into his palms, inflicting pain. He took a deep breath and turned around slowly.

His eyes latched onto the unkempt brown hair crowning the head of a man that was instantly familiar. Leaning forward for a closer look, his eyes and mouth gradually widened till they reached their full elasticity. The chiselled cheekbones and closed deep-set eyes of the strikingly attractive man on the cold tray beneath him didn't belong to Melvyn Bragg. Paul was staring down at the face of Matt Munnelly! Suddenly, it all began to make sense, in the coldest possible way.

* * * * * * *

As the rain pelted down relentlessly on the small gathering of mourners, Paul struggled with his flimsy umbrella, wondering why funerals always seemed to attract rainfall. It had been a clear morning, with not a hint of a cloud, until Matt's corpse had arrived at the cemetery. As if on cue the heavens unleashed their fury, instantly drenching the stone-faced pall bearers, who did their best to stick to the script.

Mrs Munnelly, dressed in black and wearing large dark sunglasses, had hardly said a word to him since he'd broken the news to her a fortnight ago. She was clutching onto Basil Mead's arm with one hand whilst holding an umbrella in the other. Several times he'd tried to catch her attention, but she studiously ignored him.

Of the remaining mourners, Paul recognised familiar faces. Vijay and Zula had turned up with their dad Mr Pandya, and a handful of bone-thin female models had made a late appearance in a gaudy white limousine, escorted by a silver-haired man whom Paul recognised facially, but couldn't put a name to. All he knew was that the man was the head of some fashion house that had hired Matt's services. A number of staff from Munnelly and Sons had turned up, including Violet and Giovanni, which was comforting. Violet was running the business in his absence and from what he'd heard she was doing an amazing job.

In all, there were about thirty people, not impressive for someone who was once one of the country's highest paid male models.

As expected, Amy McBride hadn't shown up. Even though he hadn't invited her, he was sure she knew about the ceremony through her sources in the industry. Right now, she had her own problems. The papers had taken a renewed interest in her affairs ever since it leaked out that she'd not filed accurate tax returns. He'd read in the papers that the HMRC were on her case for hundreds of thousands of pounds in unpaid taxes.

As the shivering, soaking-wet reverend finished his Bible reading and stepped back for the coffin to be lowered into the ground, Paul sensed someone's presence to his right and swung round to see Mr Ammon, impeccably clad in a black handmade Nehru suit with glossy black shoes. Mr Ammon's disarming grin met Paul's surprised expression.

'I invited myself,' said Mr Ammon quietly. 'I felt it important enough to put everything else aside to be here.'

Paul nodded and his heart was heavy with gratitude. He hadn't even notified Mr Ammon about Matt's death and felt humbled by the man's gesture.

'Thank you,' he whispered.

'My pleasure,' said Mr Ammon.

It had been over seven months since he last saw Mr Ammon. But seeing him now, he felt like taking the man to one side and unburdening himself.

As Paul joined his mother to throw a handful of earth on Matt's coffin, he sighted Melvyn Bragg and John Crane standing together observing him silently and his heart sank. What were they doing here? Had they come to remind him of his indebtedness? Paul avoided eye contact and fulfilled his last rites to Matt, before sauntering back to where Mr Ammon stood. If they had come for a confrontation, then he would rather that Mr Ammon was present to referee the bout.

At the end of the graveside ceremony, Mrs Munnelly was briskly escorted away by Basil to the waiting undertaker's limousine whilst the rest of the people dispersed after commiserating briefly with Paul. John and Melvyn were the last to pay their respects, and to Paul's relief neither man mentioned anything about their unpaid income. He wondered whether it had anything to do with Mr Ammon's presence.

'They'll be back,' said Mr Ammon softly after they'd gone.

'But even sharks honour the dead before tearing the carcasses to shreds.'

'I guess John Crane's been updating you.'

Mr Ammon shook his head. 'I have my sources,' he said, 'and when you stopped keeping in touch, I figured out that things weren't going too well for you. I'm told you have amassed quite a sizeable debt over the past year which you're struggling to repay.'

'Yep, and I'm three stone lighter, thanks to all those sleepless nights.'

'Why didn't you come to me?' asked Mr Ammon, leading the way to the car park where his black Rolls Royce Phantom was parked. 'We could have worked something out.'

'I considered calling but thought it would be pointless.'

'Why? I'm here to help.'

'Would you have approved my application to use my apple seed allowance to address my cash flow issues?'

Mr Ammon cleared his throat gently. 'Ah, now that's outside my control. Do you know the terms and conditions of your partnership? John should have explained them to you.'

'He did, but surely there's room for discretion?'

Mr Ammon shook his head gently. 'No exceptions I'm afraid,' he said ruefully. 'The FSA wouldn't take kindly to us straying outside our remit. The Apple Seed Fund is for capital investment only.'

'And you've never given assistance to any of the partners to restructure their businesses?'

'Where the restructuring is part of their business plan – yes. But you're asking for a loan.'

'I thought the allowance was a repayable loan.'

'No, it's not. You really should have spent more time with John for him to explain how it all works.'

Paul exhaled deeply, watching his cold breath slowly dissipate. It had been worth a try.

'So Paul, how are things between you and Nicole?'

'She's the last person I want to see right now.'

'Then you don't have anything to worry about,' said Mr

Ammon, as they arrived at his car. 'She's been busy opening a new art gallery and even I haven't seen her in a while.'

Paul absorbed the news in silence. So, she was now an art lover again.

'Nicole's a restless soul,' said Mr Ammon, as his chauffeur stepped out to open the rear passenger door nearest them. 'Women like her never settle down because they're chasing after something they'll never find.'

'Money?' asked Paul absentmindedly.

'Peace,' said Mr Ammon, stepping into the rear of the imposing vehicle.

Paul nodded. He could relate to that.

'Where's your car, by the way?' asked Mr Ammon, looking around him, as his chauffeur prepared to close the door.

'Repossessed,' answered Paul, 'and I haven't got round to replacing it.'

'Then can I offer you a lift?'

'No,' said Paul, shaking his head, 'I'll walk. The underground station's two minutes away. Thanks anyway.'

'We should get together sometime and play a round of golf,' said Mr Ammon; 'it's been quite a while.'

'My golf clubs were in my car when it was repossessed,' said Paul wearily, 'and I couldn't be bothered to retrieve them. I've got a lot on my mind right now and golf isn't in my top ten. Sorry.'

'I understand. You want to put your house in order.'

Mr Ammon nodded curtly, and the chauffeur shut the door before going around to the front. Mr Ammon lowered the window on his side and his genial smile betrayed no sign of offence at the diplomatic snub Paul had just dished out.

'Goodbye, Paul,' he said, with an air of finality that was unsettling.

Paul acknowledged him with a slight wave and then stepped back as the huge vehicle pulled away. As he watched the behemoth vanish out of sight, he sensed that he wouldn't be seeing Mr Ammon again.

The voices in his head began their deafening cacophony, and Paul clutched both ears in a vain attempt to silence them, making his car swerve towards the kerb. He quickly regained control of the steering wheel, wrestling with it whilst doing his best to ignore the jeering voices. The ancient Nissan Bluebird eventually veered back on course amidst the erratic horning and hand signs from other motorists.

Though he was getting more sleep at night, thanks to the sleeping pills prescribed by his doctor, he'd started hearing voices in his head. There were mocking voices, angry voices, cruel voices, persuasive voices, and he was finding it increasingly difficult to think straight. Day and night, they argued amongst themselves debating his value to humanity. Some of the voices called him a failure destined to die in ignominy like Antoine Matisse and Matt Munnelly, others urged him to end his life.

Coupled with the voices was the memory of Matt's face as he lay in the refrigerator at the Haringey mortuary. The sight of his brother's corpse was something he was sure would live with him for the rest of his life. More worrying was the fact that he'd never really mourned Matt, at least not in the conventional sense. From the first sight of the corpse in the morgue, till the time the coffin was lowered into the grave, Paul had not shed a single tear and it worried him. He worried that the conflict in his mind was Matt's way of getting back at him from beyond the grave.

Paul consulted his doctor who referred him to a private psychotherapist named Kirsten Thorpe who ran counselling sessions from her office in St Albans. Kirsten was a fan of the philosophy of holism, and ancient Chinese meditation, as a route to achieving inner peace and endeavoured to combine this with regular counselling sessions. As Paul couldn't stump up the cost of her one-to-one sessions, he joined her weekly group therapy sessions, which attracted the weirdest bunch of participants in the British Isles. At the sessions, Kirsten taught them how to make contact with the inner man, using eerie humming sounds to ward-off negative environmental influences. The inner man, according to Kirsten, had the ability to achieve peace amid chaos, and meditation was the key to creating a cocoon of tranquillity. At one of those sessions, he'd met Gordon Pinsent who looked as fed up as him with Kirsten's antics and was refusing to participate. After five futile sessions, with him no closer to achieving peace, Kirsten concluded that he was a *special case*.

John Crane and Melvyn Bragg waited a week after Matt's funeral before simultaneously launching county court legal actions to recover their unpaid fees which ran into tens of thousands of pounds. Both were using the same city law firm and had indicated their willingness to settle out of court for half of what they were owed, but Paul knew that even if he sold all his worldly assets, there was no way he could settle their claims. At present, his most viable option was bankruptcy, but that didn't even bear thinking about.

He had already taken the drastic course of putting his house on the market to avoid the bank foreclosing but Vijay, who was acting on his behalf in the sale, was forecasting a much lower profit margin than earlier envisaged. On the plus side, the Sloane Bank had contacted him with respect to his loan application and invited him to a meeting to discuss it. His appointment was in three hours' time, and for the occasion he was decked out in his sharpest suit. He'd also taken the pains to shave, have a haircut and a manicure.

A loan from Sloane would sort out two-thirds of all his present financial difficulties and provide him an escape route from bankruptcy's waiting room.

Before his meeting with the Sloane Bank, he had an appointment to see Basil Mead, who'd phoned the previous day, requesting to see him urgently. When pressed for details, the old accountant had refused to talk on the phone, insisting that he had some confidential documents to show Paul which would be of benefit to him.

The suspense had kept Paul awake all night, wondering

234

what new misfortune was about to drift his way. He was mentally weary from worrying about issues that seemed to be escalating daily and for which he had no solution. For him, Sloane was the last bus stop.

Driven by a mixture of apprehension and curiosity, he made his way to Basil's.

*   *   *   *   *   *   *

Paul studied the pile of documents spread out on the table in Basil Mead's conference room, with a furrowed brow, struggling to comprehend their content. Across the table, Basil Mead looked on dispassionately. Upon Paul's arrival at the office, Basil had quickly ushered him into the conference room where the documents were already spread out on the long table and asked him to read through each one carefully. Paul had obeyed without hesitation, despite the dozens of questions spiralling around in his mind. The documents were comprised assorted letters and statements of account, all marked 'confidential', and either addressed to or compiled by John Crane.

'I'm lost,' admitted Paul, after half an hour of browsing. 'What's this all about?'

'Your accountant and business adviser,' said Basil pointedly. 'He's a crook and I'm out to expose him.'

'So,' said Paul gently, 'you dragged me all the way out here to complain about your rival John Crane, but what makes you think I give two hoots?'

'Because John Crane has been fleecing certain Apple Seed partners for the past three years and you're one of them!' said Basil Mead angrily.

The news took almost a minute of silent meditation to sink in, and when it did, Paul's curiosity index went stratospheric.

'You mean John Crane has been conning me?' asked Paul, with the eagerness of a dog awaiting a juicy bone.

'Yes, you and others,' answered Basil more evenly, 'about twelve others, to be precise.'

'But how?' asked Paul.

'By issuing some of you with different contracts containing small print that allows him to exploit your naivety.'

Basil's comments were below the belt and Paul restrained himself from an angry reaction.

'All the risks that you should have been advised about were captured in very wordy small print. John knew you wouldn't seek independent investment advice and that enabled him to create loopholes to exploit.' Basil picked up one of the documents on his desk and waved it in front of Paul's face. 'John Crane included all kinds of benefits and entitlements into your contract to enable him charge you for what was being provided free of charge to others.'

'I don't understand,' said Paul, desperately seeking clarification.

'You were targeted. John Crane took advantage of you. For instance, there's a discrepancy in the billable hours he charges each Apple Seed partner who seeks his opinion. He charges his more gullible clients higher hourly rates and misrepresents the time allocated to their listed tasks.'

'I see,' said Paul, slowly grasping the concept. 'So, he's been over-charging me.'

'Exactly,' said Basil. 'He's been doing that to small and medium sized businesses and raking in a fortune over the years, but now it's time to expose him.'

'So, is that what these are all about?' asked Paul, looking down at the documents spread out before him. 'Is this the evidence that proves he's a fraud?'

'Some of it.'

'Where's the rest?'

'That all depends on the level of cooperation I get from his victims.'

'You want us to testify against him?'

Basil Mead nodded. 'If I can get most of his victims to testify, I'll turn the evidence over to the Financial Services Authority, who will then carry out their own investigation and prosecute him, if they believe they've got a good case.'

Paul stared at Basil in disbelief. 'What if the FSA doesn't prosecute?' he asked.

'Oh, I'm confident they will,' said Basil. 'I have a contact working inside John Crane's firm, who is ready to turn whistle-blower if I act on her behalf in negotiations with the police. She's afraid of testifying without assurances.'

'But why did she come to you?'

'Because she knows that John Crane used to work with me,' answered Basil, 'and felt I ought to know in case he'd done the same thing whilst he worked here.'

'John Crane worked with you?' asked Paul, feeling the blood drain out of his face.

'Yes,' confirmed Basil. 'I thought you knew. Didn't he tell you? He was a junior partner here for three years... the worst years of my professional career.'

'Why didn't you tell me this earlier?' asked Paul.

'Because you never told me you'd engaged him,' replied Basil. 'I only found out through your mother, who had tasked Violet with finding out who my replacement was.'

Paul shook his head in frustration and wrung his hands under the table.

'John joined this firm five years ago,' said Basil heavily, 'but it wasn't a happy relationship because he had his own ideas about how to attract new business, which conflicted with mine. I'm not into smearing the partners in other accountancy firms or spreading malicious gossip that tarnishes their reputation, but that was John's way of getting ahead.

'He was, rather is, a maverick – a risk taker who sees collateral damage as inevitable in the hustle to the top. His recklessness cost me a very lucrative retainer with a large public company and tarnished my reputation…I'm sure he's told you about the incident five years ago.'

'I heard about it,' said Paul, unwilling to disclose his source, 'but the corporation sued you for negligence.'

'That's because I genuinely believed at the time that I had signed off the investment strategy that cost the corporation the million-pound loss,' said Basil ponderously. 'It wasn't until sometime later that I found out that John had given the green light for the financial disaster. At the time, I was going through personal difficulties. Isabella, my wife, was undergoing chemotherapy. As I was caring for her, regrettably, I left most business decisions to John.'

'But why didn't you try to clear your name?'

'As the partnership wasn't a limited liability partnership at the time, both of us would've still been jointly liable for John's actions, so I didn't bother. Looking back now, I could've tried warning you about him, but I didn't think you'd believe me.'

Paul swallowed hard, as he recalled his first meeting with John Crane and wondered how he'd been so gullible to be taken in by such a smooth-talking crook.

'So, you called me here because you want me to testify against him, right?'

Basil nodded. 'I can guarantee that, if you do, John Crane's civil lawsuit against you will evaporate.' he said. 'I'll even assist you in preparing an air-tight counter-claim.'

Paul considered the enticing offer but, deep down inside, had some misgivings.

'It's a gamble,' muttered Paul.

'Yes, but one I'm confident you'll win because I've got an ace up my sleeve. My insider informs me that you lost a packet as part of a consortium set up by John to invest in the Waldon Valley Leisure Park.'

Paul heaved a sigh and nodded.

Basil smiled knowingly. 'What you don't know is that John recovered the consortium's funds and reinvested them in an internet gambling site which has started raking in a fortune.'

Paul perked up. 'So my investment wasn't lost?'

'Technically no, but John will deny that of course. He'll also make sure there's no audit of the transaction, which I'm told was funded via offshore accounts.'

Paul considered reaching out to Mr Ammon, but quickly scrapped the idea. Mr Ammon was John Crane's boss, and it was inconceivable that he didn't know what his employee was up to. There was, however, another niggling concern.

'What about the other investors?'

'Only two of you took a hit. The others all reinvested their recovered funds in the online gambling business.'

Paul felt drained and his focus became blurry. 'Who is the other investor?'

Basil shrugged. 'I understand he's deceased.'

A sense of loneliness engulfed Paul. 'Why me?'

'Because you are honest and naïve.'

Paul processed Basil's brutally candid assessment soberly.

'With your consent,' went on Basil, 'I plan to initiate an investigation into the scam via the Office of Fair Trading.'

'And what will that achieve?'

'It'll overwhelm him and put him under the spotlight. Once he's exposed, his backers will ditch him and leave him to face the heat. Without their support he'll be vulnerable and I'm confident he'll seek to settle the claim out of court.'

Paul was initially intrigued by the prospect but as he pondered the situation, his confidence started to ebb. He couldn't help feeling that Basil's supposedly honourable intentions were a smokescreen for a personal vendetta. John Crane was no fool and it would be foolish to underestimate his resourcefulness. Paul's fear was that if the police were ultimately unable to prosecute owing to lack of evidence, then John Crane would most likely press ahead with a separate claim for slander against Basil and all those who had given witness statements against him.

'Let me think about it,' said Paul quietly.

'There's nothing to think about, Paul,' said Basil wearily. 'This man has been conning you out of tens of thousands and now he's got the nerve to sue you for unpaid fees. You should be mad at him.'

'I am,' said Paul with a tired grin, 'but I think he's far too clever for either of us.'

*　*　*　*　*　*　*

As Paul sat down, Abigail Jones, the smartly dressed, black

female banker, appraised him with smiling hazel eyes, and he took that as a good sign. If she was smiling, then it meant that he was but two steps away from securing financial liberty. His business plan was simple. He would downsize his operations and retain only his original mechanics. When business picked up, he would resume his expansion plans, but move at a more moderate pace.

The lady had a folder on the desk in front of her but, from the moment he sat down, her eyes remained glued to her computer's flat panel monitor. Leaning forward, he could see his name inscribed on the folder and reckoned that his proposal was inside. The fact that she wasn't looking at it meant that she'd already read it. He found this reassuring. The meeting was probably just a formality to iron out the final details of the loan arrangements and the documents he had to sign for the money to be transferred to his account.

He smiled to himself, as he remembered Albert's saying, *'A loan from Sloane never leaves you alone.'* Well, Albert was wrong. Paul Munnelly was about to not only secure the loan, but ultimately pay it back in less than half the time. That was the plan, at least.

'Mr Munnelly,' said Miss Jones, intruding upon his thoughts. 'I've read your proposal which sets out the reason why you need the loan and your repayment plan, and I must say that we found it quite impressive.'

'Thank you very much,' said Paul modestly.

'You're clearly the sort of small business that the bank is keen to invest in,' she went on in the same positive voice, 'because you deliver an invaluable service to the community.'

'Well, it's a generational thing,' said Paul, struggling to remain modest. 'I'm just carrying on my father's vision, really.'

'Quite commendable,' she continued, without taking her eyes off her computer. 'However, there is one glitch which presents us with a problem and that is your risk profile.'

'My risk profile?' asked Paul quizzically.

'Your ability to repay the loan,' she explained.

'My proposal includes details of the collateral I'm putting

up with respect to the loan,' said Paul nervously, 'and as you would have seen I'm putting up two properties.'

'Yes, we've seen that,' she said calmly, 'and that all seems to be in order, but we're more concerned about your liabilities, which may have a knock-on effect on your ability to repay, and to be honest, your risk profile gives us cause for concern.'

'What liabilities?'

'Well,' she said, curling her lips distastefully, 'for instance, you're facing legal claims filed by your accountant, and your marketing manager for unpaid fees, and then there's all that irregularity with your tax returns.'

'What irregularity?' asked Paul, half rising from his seat.

'That's for you to sort out with HMRC,' she answered evasively. 'We are more than a little concerned about it and, for as long as it remains unresolved, we must factor it in when scoring you to determine your eligibility.'

'So, what are you saying in effect?' asked Paul, even though he knew the answer.

'You scored too low on the credit rating to be eligible,' said Miss Jones, fixing him with a sad smile. 'Even if the lawsuits against you were dropped and the tax irregularity resolved, we would still factor you as a borderline case for bankruptcy in the next six to twelve months and that's why, unfortunately, I have to inform you that your application for a loan has been refused – I am sorry.'

Paul sat still, almost frozen, and contemplated the situation. In a nutshell, he was finished. Without the much-needed injection of funds, his business would fold in a month, and he would have to file for personal bankruptcy.

'A loan from Sloane can sometimes leave you alone,' he murmured.

'I beg your pardon?' asked confused Miss Jones.

'Nothing,' he said as he rose heavily to his feet. 'It's just a variation on something my father used to say.'

'I really am sorry,' said Miss Jones, looking pained.

'This was my last hope,' he said quietly, 'and now I've come to the end of the road.'

He strolled away from Miss Jones' desk, staring blankly at the window across the second floor open-plan office space, as the voices inside his head began their evil dialogue. One voice that was more prominent than the others and sounded strangely familiar urged him to exit life with dignity, by diving out of the window. However, another voice reminded him of the agony his mother had suffered when Matt died and asked whether he wanted to send her to an early grave. Then without warning, the voices began to argue, debating the issue of life and death. At one point, the voice urging him to jump drowned out all the other voices, and Paul knew that in his hopeless state it was the easiest way out of his predicament.

Oblivious to the people milling around him, he broke into a short run and hurled himself at the window with so much force that the glass shattered on impact. As he plunged into the next phase, he closed his eyes waiting for the end. It came suddenly. He hit something hard and explosive pain jarred every nerve in his body forcing his eyes open before the darkness and silence took over.

DOWNEY'S PROGRESSION

15

Downey stared morosely at Kirsten Thorpe, not really absorbing anything she was saying. With her voice in the background, and Paul Munnelly's image in the foreground, he was struggling to focus.

It had been five days since his first trip to see Paul, but it felt like yesterday. So vivid had Paul's account been that Downey was sucked into the unfolding events, forming a psychological relationship with the main cast in the depressing saga. Over the course of several long afternoons, Downey had spent time with Paul acquiring in-depth understanding of the dangers of bad financial advice and the unscrupulous individuals who offered it to gullible punters.

Paul Munnelly was no different from thousands, probably millions, of other simple-minded souls who merely wanted to improve their circumstances and earn an honest living. Many weren't out to make their mark in the world. Ambition wasn't the problem; rather, it was the lack of wisdom. Although he'd survived the physical fall, the prospects of Paul surviving the financial decline were abysmal.

At the end of his last visit, the previous day, Downey located the surgeon who'd operated on Paul's spine, and he listened, with a heavy heart, as the Chinese lady confirmed the irreversible damage that would confine Paul to a wheelchair for the rest of his life. In effect, his days as a mechanic were most likely over for good.

'Are you getting enough sleep, Roger?' asked Kirsten

barging in on his thoughts.

'Six hours a night,' answered Downey, flinching at the use of his first name, 'and I'm not even taking pills.'

'Any nightmares?'

Downey restrained himself from saying that he had nightmares of visiting her clinic and instead shrugged.

'Everyone has nightmares,' he muttered.

'Any voices in your head?'

'Yours,' he answered, keeping a straight face.

'I don't mean actual voices,' she said hastily. 'I mean imaginary voices.'

Downey shook his head.

'What sort of man was your father?' she asked.

The unexpected question rattled Downey and, for the next thirty seconds, he struggled unsuccessfully to comport himself. What was she getting at?

'Have I touched a raw nerve?' she asked, making no effort to mask the smugness that filtered out through her voice.

Downey studied her straight-faced countenance, trying to figure out an appropriate response. It wasn't a question he'd asked himself at any time during his adult life. What sort of man was his father?

'I haven't got a current image in my head,' he said softly, 'so I'll pass for now.'

'Difficult relationship?'

She was clearly determined to get beneath the skin of his complex psyche.

He stared her straight in the eye. 'I apologise,' he said, 'but it's hard to answer a question about someone you never knew.'

The answer clipped Kirsten beneath the chin, like the upper cut from a boxer's glove, and she glanced away probably to give herself time to consider her follow through.

'You never knew him?' she asked carefully.

Downey shook his head and his thin-lipped smile conveyed angelic sincerity.

'Do you want to talk about it?' she asked half-expectantly.

'I don't remember him,' said Downey point-blank. 'He

died a long time ago.'

'How long ago if you don't mind me asking.'

Before my tenth birthday.'

Downey's father had died in a house fire, and he had no vivid memories of the man, not even photos of them together which had perished in the blaze.

Kirsten lowered her head, gazing pensively at the open file on her desk. Downey suspected that from her perspective, the absence of a male role model or villain in his childhood made further interrogation unprofitable.

'What about your mother?'

'Is there a point to this?' asked Downey lethargically.

'Yes, I'm trying to build up a picture. Is she still alive?'

'Yes, but that information should be in my file.'

'Has she ever shared anything about your father with you?'

He shook his head. 'It's a difficult subject for both of us.'

'Did you ever have a father figure?' she asked, looking up with a well-rehearsed, benevolent smile.

He pondered the question and then shook his head. His mother had remarried but his stepfather wasn't a role model.

Kirsten closed his file, even though the session still had ten minutes to run.

'This is a good place to stop for today don't you think?' she said rising up and glancing at the door.

'I agree,' said Downey, getting up with mildly veiled relief.

'Next time we'll explore other aspects of your childhood.'

Downey wasn't looking forward to it, but he realised how crucial the sessions were to his fitness for work report. He headed for the door pausing as he reached it. He'd just remembered something out of the final chapter of Paul Munnelly's narrative that he was hoping Kirsten could clarify.

'I believe Paul Munnelly was your client, wasn't he?'

'My clients' list is confidential,' she said flatly.

'I have been speaking with Paul. You've probably heard he recently attempted suicide,' said Downey gravely.

'Yes, that was sad to hear.'

'Paul mentioned attending your group therapy sessions.'

'I hope you're not accusing me of professional negligence,' she said frostily.

'Why are you being so defensive?' he asked.

'You're not on official duty, Roger Downey,' said Kirsten smiling sweetly, 'and you're unlikely to be unless I clear you, so quit running around playing detective.'

'I just need to know if he ever mentioned being defrauded.'

'Did he tell you he was being defrauded by anyone?'

'Not exactly, but I'm curious about his involvement with something called the Apple Seed Partnership.'

Kirsten flinched. She clearly knew something.

Downey pressed. 'I also understand that the late Gordon Pinsent, was another of your clients.'

Kirsten knew all about his brief encounter with Gordon Pinsent and the impact it had had on his life.

'I don't know what you're getting at,' she said opening his file and starting to scribble something inside it, 'but you're clearly barking up the wrong tree. I don't have to answer any of your questions but I'm making a note of this obsession as something we need to explore further.'

'Obsession?'

'Yes, an unhealthy obsession with suicide.'

'Are you trying to blackmail me into backing down?'

'Blackmail you?' She chuckled icily. 'Look Sergeant, even if you were back on duty, I wouldn't breach my duty of confidentiality to my clients unless you were involved in an active criminal investigation – and you're not.'

Her answer, cold as it was, reminded Downey of Kirsten's role and the level of influence she wielded in the ultimate decision as to his future in the force. A negative report from her would seal the coffin that contained the fragments of his fragile career. As far as the Hertfordshire Constabulary was concerned, he was a mentally unfit police officer on the verge of early retirement, unless Kirsten marked him fit for active duty. With his ego well and truly deflated, he strolled out of her office wilting beneath the glimmer of her mocking grin.

Two days after his therapy session, Downey drove into Waldon Town centre. He parked in a multistorey carpark and made his way on foot to the business district. He was looking for an accountant named Basil Mead who despite various phone calls had not bothered to get back to him.

Paul Munnelly had mentioned that Basil Mead was gathering information to expose John Crane's fraudulent activities and Downey needed to speak with him.

Basil Mead's office was as Downey expected. A neat but functional small office with nondescript furniture and staffed by six staff of varying ages all dressed staidly as if *boring* was the office's motif.

Basil's PA, a haughty silver haired white lady, told him that Mr Mead was away on business and asked him to make an appointment. Downey tried explaining the reason for his visit, but she brushed his words away and made him book a diary appointment. The appointment was three weeks away and all his efforts to get a closer booking fell on deaf ears. Getting fed up with her lack of cooperation, he reluctantly flashed his warrant card and demanded a review of his appointment. Basil's PA was unmoved and insisted that it was still a three-week appointment because her boss was in Spain.

One week later

Downey went for a lengthy walk along his favourite forest path that wound its way through Waldon Valley. It was a ten-mile round trip and the longest trek he had undertaken in several months. He usually walked this route whenever he needed to pray, meditate, or just think. The forest pathways with their idyllic greenery and the hedgerow-bordered country lanes provided a perfect setting for decluttering his mind.

248

The Paul Munnelly affair had injected some much-needed vitality into Downey's schedule, but things had been quiet as of late, partly due to Inspector Wajid Hussain being on leave. A week ago, he'd given Wajid a list of names to check up on. All were people acquainted with Paul Munnelly via the Apple Seed Partnership and he was waiting for Wajid's clearance to speak with them. As he was officially on sick leave, Downey couldn't interview anyone without clearance. Though he still had his warrant card, he wasn't authorised to act in that capacity. He often found it amusing how on TV, and in the movies, cops on sick leave conducted private investigations without clearance. In the real world, they would be suspended or sacked, and that wasn't a risk Downey was willing to take.

On the plus side, he didn't need to make further enquiries regarding the failed Waldon Valley Leisure Park investment scheme. His wife, Sally-Ann, had been the Chief Planning Officer in the borough council when planning permission was sought. It was Sally-Ann who had flagged the anomaly in the planning application after stumbling across a prior historical area assessment for the brownfield site. Someone in the council had failed to register the brownfield site as one potentially containing an archaeological site beneath the foundations of the old factory that had previously occupied it. Given the level of corruption within the borough council, Sally-Ann believed that the omission to register was deliberate.

As Paul narrated the events surrounding the collapse of the investment scheme, Downey held back from mentioning that his wife had been the whistle blower.

Having failed to gain the support of either the Chief Executive or Principal Planning Enforcement Officer to interrogate further, she had turned whistle blower and notified English Heritage – the custodians of historical buildings and monuments. From that point, an investigation had been launched and despite her role in bringing the anomalies to light, Sally-Ann became the fall guy. She was still battling her unfair dismissal by the council.

Downey was particularly interested in Apple Seed Project.

There had been one suicide and two attempted suicides by former partners – Gordon Pinsent, Amy McBride, and Paul Munnelly. John Crane, Vijay Pandya, and Mr Ammon were the primary protagonists of interest, but he also wanted to speak with Basil Mead, Nicole Matisse, Amy McBride, and Melvyn Bragg, to build up a picture of the kind of influences that had tipped Paul over the edge.

It was doubtful whether any criminal charges would ever be brought but he was determined nevertheless to expose the Apple Seed Project and all those associated with Eden Fruit Investments. The leisure park investment scheme highlighted a torrent of corruption that they were involved in. He also held them responsible for Sally-Ann losing her job and for his current predicament. Their actions had directly and indirectly affected his family and he wanted justice.

Allied to his desire for justice, was his ongoing health challenges which were impacting his return to duty. Though he still had occasional night-time recollections of Gordon Pinsent's tortured face and the sound of the gun going off, the episodes were becoming fewer. Most nights he slept right through. However, even he admitted that his fixation with debt-driven suicide was disturbing.

* * * * * * *

Inspector Hussain observed in silence as Downey thumbed his way through the pages of the folder in front of him. Earlier on, Downey had provided an update of the Paul Munnelly affair but gone into unnecessary detail. His report devoted an inordinate amount of content to the subject's state of mind and the roles of the major protagonists who had, allegedly, in one way or the other, contributed to his downfall. As fascinating as the tale was, Wajid could find no evidence of substance to justify pursuing further enquiries into the lives of Munnelly's detractors.

Wajid was therefore upset when Downey requested that he flout data protection guidelines to obtain personal data about six subjects with links to Apple Seed Project and the Eden Fruit Foundation.

Against his screaming conscience, Wajid had obtained the data, but there was a proviso; Downey could only review the documents within the confines of Wajid's office. The other proviso was that he couldn't make notes but had to rely on his memory to retain relevant detail. Although, technically, Wajid was still guilty of flouting the data protection rules, the risk of exposure was low because there would be no documentary evidence of the violation.

Downey memorised phones numbers and postcodes as he waded through the documents, reciting them to himself to be sure that he wouldn't mix them up. He wasn't blessed with a photographic memory, but years in the force had taught him various little tricks like using abbreviations and police mnemonic codes to aid recollection. Wajid had been able to compile a reasonable amount of data regarding John Crane, Melvyn Bragg, Vijay Pandya, and Nicole Matisse, but had absolutely nothing on Mr Ammon.

Downey found this lack of data puzzling because there ought to have been some information from the Land Registry, DVLA and Companies House registers. In his book, to draw a blank was grounds for suspicion.

'His name didn't come up in any of our searches,' explained Wajid, 'and there is no social security number allocated to him. It might have been easier if we had his first and middle names. We exhausted all the male first names starting with M but found no record of a Mr Ammon with the initial M residing in Buckingham.'

'What about public utilities, voters register, and local authority records?' asked Downey. 'Surely the man owned or leased some real estate?'

'An absolute blank,' said Wajid. 'We even tried deed poll records, but as you know they're notoriously unreliable. Perhaps Nicole Matisse and John Crane can shed more light on the real identity of this Mr Ammon character, but I'm afraid I've come to a dead end with him.'

'Apple Seed Project is the link,' murmured Downey pensively; 'and Matisse, Crane, Bragg and Pandya are part of some devious scheme cooked up by this Mr Ammon, but they're not just going to roll over and incriminate themselves.'

'Maybe I can assist there,' said Wajid, noting his friend's frustration. 'If you're looking for leverage, you'll probably find it in their financial affairs.'

'They're linked?'

'At the hip,' answered Wajid. 'In the folder before you are financial records compiled by corporate credit reference agencies, which indicate that McBride, Matisse, and Pandya were part of the consortium that participated in the investment scheme, but they lost no money on it. They all took out insurance to cover their investments but the premiums on that policy were covered by Eden Fruit Investments. Now why would they not extend the cover to Gordon Pinsent and Paul Munnelly?'

Downey hurriedly rummaged through the folder's contents, wondering how he could have missed such vital information, until he eventually found the financial report listing McBride's, Matisse's, and Pandya's indebtedness to Eden Fruit Investments. There was arguably evidence of professional negligence on the part of John Crane in relation to Gordon Pinsent and Paul Munnelly.

'But is there any way of linking Mr Ammon to John Crane's activities?' said Downey breathlessly.

Wajid shook his head slowly, noting the deflation in Downey's expression. 'Companies House lists the CEO as one John Crane, but Mr Ammon doesn't feature anywhere. He's not even mentioned in the registration for Eden House Foundation – the charitable arm of the arrangement.'

'So, John Crane is the front,' said Downey, processing the information slowly, trying to make sense of it.

Wajid heaved a sigh. He was concerned about the potential reputational risk of having a maverick on the loose. But, from the intensity in his friend's eye, it was clear that he wouldn't be easily dissuaded from his chosen course.

'Try one Mark Pierce,' said Wajid heavily.

'Who's he?' asked Downey.

'Companies House lists him as the Chairman of the Eden Fruit Foundation board which is the parent body of Eden Fruit Investments.'

'So that's the link,' said Downey slowly. 'What do we know about this Mark Pierce?'

'He's quite a discreet character,' answered Wajid, trying to recall the scanty bits of information he'd come across. 'We didn't focus our enquiries on him, but from what we know he's John Crane's boss.'

'Please tell me he lives in Buckingham,' said Downey, becoming excited again.

'The voters register indicates that he *resides* there,' said Wajid cautiously, 'but that's not to say he's your man.'

'Thanks,' said Downey, closing the folder and sliding it back across the table to Wajid. 'I've got enough to initiate private enquiries.'

'Is that wise?' asked Inspector Hussain, visualising the spate of complaints that were bound to spurt forth.

'Probably not,' admitted Downey, 'but I believe that Paul Munnelly was the victim of an elaborate scam and I intend to prove it.'

Inspector Hussain sat back and exhaled. He had made up his mind to close the Munnelly file. But rather than accepting the investigation's objective conclusions, Downey was looking for an alternative angle to warrant keeping the case open. Paul Munnelly had clearly attempted to kill himself; did it really matter why? The surrounding circumstances in this case were unimportant facts, more relevant for statistical purposes than a police investigation. How could he persuade Downey to see it that way?

'This is where I've got to draw the line, Downey,' said Wajid, sitting upright and placing his fingertips together. 'I'm closing the Munnelly case and re-allocating my resources elsewhere. It's an attempted suicide and we've got sufficient eyewitness evidence to support that finding. A man falls on hard times due to some bad financial decisions, and in desperation tries to take his life, period. Your discussions with Munnelly haven't yielded any new or useful information to convince me that it's a case worth investigating any further.'

'But what about his last discussion with Basil Mead regarding Crane's professional negligence and the fraudulent activity involving the Apple Seed partners?'

'It's a gamble – an expensive one.'

'I understand,' said Downey.

'From here on you're on your own,' said Wajid.

'I understand,' reiterated Downey.

'I'm not going to stick my neck out for you - all right?' stressed Wajid.

'I don't need you to,' answered Downey, smiling vaguely.

Wajid sighed at his friend's stubbornness. 'Give it up, Downey,' he said wearily.

Downey shook his head emphatically. 'I can't do that, Wajid,' he said calmly. 'There's still so much I don't know, and I haven't hit my saturation point yet.'

'You will, my friend,' assured Wajid knowingly. 'You most certainly will.'

* * * * * * *

Downey slowed his classic Saab 9000 to a crawl as he arrived at the narrow, gravelled private road that led all the way up to the gates of the palatial Art Deco style gated mansion named *Paradise Villa*. Though it was tucked away behind a farm on the outskirts of a small village near Buckingham, it hadn't been hard to locate because Paul Munnelly's directions had been precise. Wajid's enquiries revealed the owner of the freehold property to be a shell company registered in the Cayman Islands that was affiliated with Eden Fruit Investments. Unhelpfully, all bills on the property were paid for by the corporation and there was no documentary evidence linking it to Mark Pierce. However, the address matched the one Munnelly claimed he had met with the enigmatic Mr Ammon on a number of occasions, further convincing Downey that Mark Pierce and Mr Ammon were either one and the same or very close associates. All he needed was some direct evidence to corroborate his hunch.

He pulled up at the ornamental gates and disembarked, looking around him for signs of human activity. Peering through the gate's bars, he saw a black Rolls Royce parked under the front porch. Hoping to get lucky, he strolled over to the intercom unit mounted on one of the gate pillars. As he reached out to depress the call button, the creaky sound of wheels trundling over gravel prompted him to swing round in the direction of the intrusion.

The sound belonged to the rickety wheel of a wheelbarrow, stacked high with freshly chopped logs, that was being pushed by an elderly white man, in a quilted coat over corduroys tucked into muddy wellingtons.

'Can I help you sir?' he asked, as he drew near.

'I'm here to see Mr Ammon,' said Downey flashing his warrant card to bypass formalities. 'Is he in?'

'Sorry officer,' said the man, halting in front of Downey, 'but the property's vacant.'

'Oh,' said Downey, glancing at the Rolls Royce, 'and so whose car is that?'

The old man shrugged. 'I'm told it's for sale,' he said, looking clueless. 'I was just employed as the caretaker last week by Mr Vijay Pandya, a local property consultant.'

'Right,' said Downey, guessing the answer to his next question. 'So, is the property on the market?'

'As far as I know,' said the caretaker.

Downey gritted his teeth in frustration and nodded slowly. It looked like Mark Pierce was ten steps ahead.

16

According to the information Downey gleaned from Inspector Hussain's folder, Nicole Matisse had opened an art gallery in the heart of London's West End simply named *Madame Matisse*.

Downey had gone online to obtain further information from some social gossip web pages and noted that the gallery opening had attracted some of the richest and most influential people in the British Isles.

He found the web page for *Madame Matisse* that showcased some of the paintings on display, and the photo gallery provided up-to-date photos of Nicole.

She was undeniably beautiful, with a tinge of innocence in her green eyes that was instantly disarming. Her bronze complexion, visible from her face and through the multiple slits in her flamboyant dress, lent her an exotic look, and he could see what the attraction was for an ordinary-looking bloke like Paul Munnelly. In Munnelly's shoes, he would've fallen for her in a big way.

Armed with her image firmly embossed at the front of his mind, he sallied forth to London, catching a fast train into Euston Station and then choosing to walk the rest of the way to the gallery near Green Park; he needed the exercise.

Whilst the gallery looked less glamorous than in the photos, it was still a posh affair. The fittings and furnishings reeked of money – lots of it. Large paintings, hung on chalk white walls under modern light units, and the airy feel of the place was accentuated by the large windows overlooking the street outside. The gallery's central atrium was crowned with a perspex skylight, providing a conduit through which natural light flooded in. He was indifferent to paintings of any sort, being unable to tell the difference between a Picasso and a Rembrandt but sensed that the portraits he was strolling past were priceless. His difficulty was pretending that he was even remotely interested.

'Can I help you, *M'sieu*?' asked a gentle voice behind him.

Hearing the unmistakable French accent, Downey swung round full of anticipation, but, instead of Nicole Matisse, he found himself staring at a petite brunette in a stylish trouser suit, whose piercing hazel-brown eyes and flawless makeup lent her a porcelain doll-like quality

'I'm here to see Madame Matisse,' he said, 'but I'm afraid I don't have an appointment.'

'Ah, pardon, *M'sieu*,' answered the girl apologetically, 'but Madame will not see anyone without an appointment.'

Downey sighed, as he fished out his official warrant card. He was flouting the rules, but he needed to see Nicole Matisse, and in the circumstances, this was the only way.

'Tell her the police wish to see her,' said Downey, discreetly flashing his warrant card so that no one else could see. 'My name is Sergeant Downey.'

The girl looked slightly alarmed, but she recovered quickly with a nervous smile.

'One moment *M'sieu*,' she said, walking away briskly.

His eyes followed her as she exited the main part of the gallery through a door at the far end of the atrium, and for the first time, he noticed the security guards on duty observing him through a window near the door. Downey was contemplating whether to help himself to the complimentary champagne on offer when he noticed the girl returning with her complexion now bright crimson. She'd obviously been on the receiving end of a dressing down, and Downey steeled himself for the inevitable response telling him that Madame Matisse was unavailable.

'Madame will see you now *M'sieu*,' announced the girl.

Downey inwardly sighed with relief and nodded. His tactic had paid off.

'But she says she can only spare a few minutes.'

'I only need a few minutes.'

The girl led him back the way she'd come, and through an open-plan office to a door at the far end. The girl knocked on the door and opened it in response to the summons from the other end, standing aside to give Downey access.

The office was outfitted like a luxurious lounge, with a single desk and chair flanked on either side by inviting leather couches. At one end was a wine bar constructed of stainless steel that snaked its way around two walls. Nicole Matisse was seated behind the desk with her long, bronzed legs propped up on the desk's surface, leaving him staring at the soles of her delicate-looking bare feet. Her head was thrown back against the backrest of her chair and, as he drew nearer, he noticed she was on the phone with a cordless handset pressed to her left ear. With her free right hand, she waved him to a seat without looking at him.

The phone call which was being conducted in French lasted a further five minutes before Nicole finally put down the handset and uncoiled her legs from the desk's surface. As she sat forward, her intelligent eyes latched on to his, teasing him as they gazed unwaveringly at his sombre face.

'You have come to arrest me?' she asked mockingly.

Downey shuddered, and in that moment, he appreciated Paul Munnelly's predicament. She was a temptress.

'No, Madame,' said Downey, embarrassed by his reaction to her charms. 'I'm just here on eh what you might call a routine visit to ask some questions.'

'Have I done something wrong?' she asked, treating him to a smile that conveyed both innocence and seduction.

'No, Madam,' he said, frantically waving his hands; 'not at all. It's just a routine visit.'

'Call me Nicole,' she purred, placing both elbows on the desk and resting her hands against the sides of her cheeks.

'When you call me Madame, it makes me feel so old.'

'Can I call you Mrs Matisse?' he asked, unwilling to stray into the arena of familiarity.

'You can call me Nicole,' she insisted, 'and what do I call you?'

'Eh, Downey,' he answered.

'Is that your first name?' she asked.

Downey shook his head.

'So, what is it?' she asked, smiling expectantly.

'Roger,' he said, in a low voice.

'I like that name – Roger,' she said, pronouncing it *'Rowgee'*. Downey didn't protest. He rather liked it.

'Now how can I help you?' she asked.

'I'm here about the Paul Munnelly incident.'

'Yes!' she exclaimed, throwing her hands in the air, as her face became tinged with sadness that was genuinely moving. 'I read in the papers that he tried to kill himself. Poor Paul. How is he?'

'Paralysed from the waist down,' answered Downey, 'and the chances are that he may never walk again.'

'Poor Paul,' she said, sounding distraught. 'I should've been there for him, but he didn't want anything to do with me. I left many messages on his phone and tried to visit him. Oh, if only I had tried harder.' She buried her face in her hands. 'I feel so guilty *Rowgee*,' she continued, 'as if it was I that pushed him out of that window.'

'Did you have some sort of a quarrel?' asked Downey, not wishing to let on that he knew the whole story.

Nicole nodded and looked up sadly. 'He accused me of having an affair,' she said huskily, 'and he never spoke to me again after that.' Her voice caressed his ears.

'Were you having an affair?'

Nicole looked away and for about thirty seconds there was silence. Then she turned back to him with a cool stare that signalled the start of hostilities.

'My private life is my private life, officer,' she said sedately, 'and it's not your affair.'

'Sorry if I appear to be intruding,' said Downey. 'I'm only trying to piece together events leading up to Paul's attempted suicide, and it seems to me that he was pretty broken up about the way things turned out between both of you.'

'If he was really that broken up, he could've returned my calls,' said Nicole, glancing at her slender, diamond encrusted wristwatch. 'Now is that all, officer?'

'No, Madame Matisse,' he said, jettisoning all efforts to remain affable. 'I have one last question and it concerns your former employer.'

Nicole looked at him quizzically.

'Mr Ammon,' clarified Downey. 'Where is he?'

Nicole shrugged and rose to her feet. 'In your imagination, officer,' she replied. 'I know no one of that name – now, if you don't mind, I have a busy schedule and I'm due to be at an auction in the next half hour.'

'Are you saying Mr Ammon doesn't exist?'

'He exists in your imagination,' she replied, reaching forward to press a button on her desk-top intercom, 'so maybe that's where you should direct your enquiries.'

'What do you know about Mark Pierce?' asked Downey, determined not to leave without something substantial.

'Who?' she asked with a blank expression, accentuated by her furrowed brow.

'Mark Pierce, the chairman of Eden Fruit Foundation, which is the parent company of Eden Fruit Investments, the company that funded your start-up,' he clarified.

'I know nobody by that name,' she said flatly, meeting his gaze unflinchingly.

'Are you sure?' he asked, trying hard to mask his desperation, 'because I'm convinced, he *is* Mr Ammon.'

'It is clear that you have taken leave of your senses,' replied Nicole coldly. She pointed one shapely, well varnished finger towards her door. 'Now if you don't mind?'

Her cruel smile made it clear that his time was up, and he got up without hesitation.

'One last question – do you know why Paul Munnelly and

Gordon Pinsent were excluded from the insurance policy that Eden Fruit Investments took out on behalf of certain members of the Apple Seed consortium in respect of the Waldon Valley Leisure Park?'

'Why would I know that?' she asked aggressively.

'Because I understand you were Mr Ammon's PA.'

'You are making no sense! Now leave!'

'Thank you for your time, Madame.'

'May I see your warrant card officer?' she asked, as he turned to leave.

Downey inhaled deeply and slowly held up his warrant card for her to see, before returning it to his pocket.

'Thanks, Sergeant Downey,' she said sweetly. 'I look forward to never seeing you again.'

'As long as you weren't part of a conspiracy to fleece Paul Munnelly,' said Downey, heading towards the door, 'your wish might just come true.'

* * * * * * *

Vijay Pandya's firm of property developers was located above a small parade of modernised shops, in the town centre, and Downey found it without much difficulty. It was a posh, open-plan space with half a dozen desks, all occupied by sharply dressed young men and women, all Asian. At the far end, in a glass walled cubicle, was a greasy-haired Asian man, whose face Downey instantly recognised from the photo Wajid had shown him. The man was nattering away on the phone, oblivious to activities in the open-plan office space, so Downey seized the opportunity to look around him at the display boards advertising high end properties for sale.

All the properties advertised were commercial and in the steep six to seven figure price range. There was, however, no ad for an art deco style mansion in Buckingham. Downey wasn't surprised as he'd already run a fruitless online search for it before coming over. He stared at the commercial ads absentmindedly until his eyes stumbled upon a workshop for sale in the Waldon Town industrial area. He didn't recognise the property, but the signboard above the entrance provoked his curiosity: it read, '*Munnelly and Sons*'. It was being advertised at just over a quarter of a million pounds for outright sale or lease, and the brief property description below indicated that it was a large fully equipped mechanic's workshop in a sought-after industrial estate.

Downey stared at the photo of the workshop, and a sudden inexplicable wave of sadness washed over him as he visualised Paul Munnelly lying paralysed in a hospital bed less than ten miles away. Munnelly had been naïve and slightly impetuous but didn't deserve the hand that life had dealt him. Fast-talking, flamboyant parasites like Vijay Pandya had spun him a lie and stepped out of the way as he plummeted down the financial and social ladder into a wheelchair.

'Can I help you?' asked a young Asian lady, with a pleasant smile, seated at the desk nearest him.

'I have an appointment to see Vijay Pandya, he answered, 'Could you tell him that Sergeant Downey is here to see him once he gets off the phone?'

'Certainly,' she said, glancing at her boss's open doorway. 'Can I get you anything while you wait? Tea? Coffee?'

'A glass of water would be appreciated,' he answered.

He sat in the waiting area whilst the lady went off to get him a plastic cup of water from the cold-water dispenser. As he patiently sipped his water, his mind travelled to Sally-Ann and her sad smile loomed up large in his mind. Over the past week, she'd been quieter than usual and that worried him. While she wasn't talkative, her body language was loquacious.

He wondered whether her withdrawn manner had anything to do with his mother-in-law's visit to the house two weekends ago. He knew that Elsie was fond of him, but her maternal instincts meant that Sally-Ann was her priority. He had no idea what they'd spoken about, but Sally-Ann's mood dipped soon afterwards. He'd mentioned it in passing to Joe Baker who mumbled something unhelpful about troubled mothers giving birth to troubled children.

'Mr Pandya will see you now,' said the young Asian lady, intruding upon his thoughts.

Downey made his way across to Vijay's office and found the smug-looking man sprawled out on his leather swivel armchair, with his expensive-looking, black boots resting on the surface of his desk. The price tag was still glued to the sole of one boot and Downey's eyes widened involuntarily as he saw the three-figure amount.

Vijay looked pleasant enough, though Downey now knew that behind the genial grin lay a ruthless streak that only respected anything that had a quick lucrative deal tagged to it. He hoped, however, that Vijay wasn't bullish enough to demand to see some ID. As he wasn't on official business, he was becoming uncomfortable with flashing his warrant card.

'Sorry to have kept you, officer,' said Vijay languidly gesturing to a seat, 'but as you can see, I'm a very busy man. Now how can I help?'

Downey sat down, and his soft brown eyes drilled holes in Vijay's vibrant hazel-coloured ones. Paul had given a detailed description of his relationship with Vijay, but Downey was convinced that Paul was too naïve to see all the neon-lighted warning signs hovering over Vijay. Paul was a division three player who'd been trying for the premiership.

On his part, Vijay found the whole staring down game amusing, but not once did his gaze waver from the police sergeant's face. Like everyone else in Waldon Town, he knew about Paul's failed suicide bid, but hadn't visited him as Paul was no longer a member of the fold.

He suspected that the black police sergeant was on a fact-finding mission in connection with Paul Munnelly but was surprised that Zula hadn't forewarned him.

The benefit of having a sister in the Force meant that he got useful tips and was always able to stay one step ahead of the cops. Even though he was wholly unprepared for the police sergeant's interrogation, he was smart enough to know that being evasive was as good as an admission.

'You know one Paul Munnelly?'

Vijay nodded. It was pointless lying. He'd reserve lies for matters outside the scope of the sergeant's knowledge.

'You heard about his attempted suicide?'

'Yes,' said Vijay, soberly. 'Rather sad, isn't it.'

Downey found Vijay's demeanour unconvincing.

'You had business dealings with him, didn't you,' said Downey forging ahead.

'Yes, I did,' answered Vijay, relaxing into his chosen role of innocent bystander. 'I helped him spot property deals and received a commission for every introduction or sale I made. Everything's documented. Would you like to see my records?'

'That won't be necessary at this time,' replied Downey, determined not to be distracted.

'Are you sure?' asked Vijay accommodatingly. 'I could arrange for my accountants to show them to you.'

'Would your accountant by any chance happen to be a man named John Crane?' asked Downey, going for the jugular.

Vijay's grin broadened and he nodded gently without hesitation. The sergeant had probably done some checking up, so lying was pointless; besides, the information was harmless, and he was in no danger of incriminating himself.

Downey furiously plotted the next question. Earlier that day he'd run a search through HMRC and Companies House in respect of Vijay's company and noted that a subsidiary of Eden Fruit Investments, chaired by John Crane, was handling Vijay's accounts, a coincidence that didn't surprise him.

'I believe John Crane also acted for Paul Munnelly,' said Downey casually.

The question threw Vijay and he hesitated. If he answered, '*yes*,' the sergeant would probably want to know how he knew and open up a whole new line of questioning into his business affairs. On the other hand, if he said, '*no idea*', it could possibly indicate that he had something to hide.

'Maybe you should ask John Crane,' said Vijay carefully.

'Did you introduce Paul to John Crane?' asked Downey quickly. He'd anticipated Vijay's response and had already prepared the follow-up.

'No,' said Vijay becoming slightly irritable. 'I believe Mr Ammon did…'

His voice faltered, as he realised his unwitting admission. The sergeant was smart.

Downey raced to the next question. 'Who is Mr Ammon?'

'You should be asking John Crane,' said Vijay as his grin lost some of its original sparkle. It was a bit too late in the day to kick himself for his blunder, but he could still attempt to neutralise the damage.

'Why?' asked Downey, leaning forward. 'After all, you're the one who hired the caretaker to look after Mr Ammon's house, so you're obviously someone he knows and trusts.'

'Not all of my business is conducted face to face,' blurted out Vijay, 'I suspect it may have been a referral that one of my staff dealt with. I believe John Crane made the referral,'

Downey decided not to press, as Vijay would only clam up. Besides, he had some other questions.

'Do you know of any reason why Paul would want to kill himself?' he asked.

'I can think of at least three,' said Vijay, with the verbal ease of a batsman who'd just knocked a six and completed a crucial series of runs.

'Yes?' ventured Downey, leaning backwards.

'Lost his girl, lost his cash, and lost his business,' replied Vijay laconically. 'Can you think of any better reasons?'

'Would this girl happen to be Nicole Matisse?'

Vijay nodded and his grin regained some of its shine. 'I hear she's a real classy babe,' he added.

'You've never met her?' asked Downey.

Vijay shrugged to mask his frustration at slipping up once again. 'I might've,' he said ponderously, 'but then again I meet so many girls in my line of work.'

'But Nicole Matisse is an Apple Seed partner just like you.'

Vijay knew there was no way out.

'Oh! *that Nicole Matisse.* Yes, I do know her.'

'And presumably she knew John Crane?'

Vijay realised that, from here on end, he would have to

dole out a litany of lies if he was going to extricate himself with any modicum of dignity.

'I suppose so officer,' answered Vijay, 'but I'm sure either John or Nicole could answer that one.'

'I hear Nicole worked for Mr Ammon.'

'Mr *who*?'

'The man you claimed introduced Paul to John Crane, and whose home you hired a caretaker to look after,' said Downey patiently; 'or maybe he's better known to you as Mark Pierce.'

'Have you considered speaking with John Crane?' asked Vijay, glancing at his watch suggestively. 'I'm sure he would be better placed to answer all these questions.'

'You're all just one big happy family, aren't you,' said Downey grinning for the first time.

'I'm not quite sure I follow you,' said Vijay uneasily.

'I'm referring to the Apple Seed Partnership.'

'Oh, that – yes we are.'

'Are you aware that Paul was being sued by John Crane and a man named Melvyn Bragg?' asked Downey.

'This is the first time I've heard of it,' said Vijay, pretending to be concerned. 'What are they suing him for?'

'You can ask them at your next family gathering,' said Downey eyeing Vijay's mournful countenance with disgust. 'But just for the record, I know that Melvyn Bragg recently ran a newspaper advertising campaign for you.'

'I never said that I didn't know Melvyn,' said Vijay, wriggling through the perceived escape route. 'I merely indicated that I didn't know anything about the lawsuit.'

'I'll take that with a pinch of salt,' said Downey, rising to his feet slowly.

'Are you questioning my integrity officer?' asked Vijay, pretending to look aghast.

'No, Mr Pandya,' replied Downey, 'far from it. I'm merely wondering why a man who's had dealings with both Paul Munnelly and Melvyn Bragg has no idea about a lawsuit in which he's cited as a witness for the plaintiff.'

Vijay lowered his head and cursed under his breath.

Extricating himself would be awkward. He'd provided Melvyn with a witness statement in which he'd supplied the details of a meeting that took place between himself, Paul, and Melvyn to discuss commercial rental income in the Waldon Town area. At that meeting, they'd also discussed the success of Melvyn's marketing campaign and Paul had showered praise on Melvyn, calling him an 'invaluable asset'.

'An oversight,' said Vijay weakly.

'I'm sure it was,' said Downey, stretching out a firm right hand in Vijay's direction. 'At this point, I have no further questions.'

Vijay shook the hand, but his expression remained quizzical. Sergeant Downey knew a lot more than he was revealing and Vijay was worried that there was incriminating stuff still under wraps which might be revealed at any moment. He hated surprises. He urgently needed to speak with Zula to find out what she knew.

Downey left Vijay's office and headed for the main entrance. His visit confirmed what he already suspected; Vijay, Melvyn, Nicole, John, and Mr Ammon were part of some sophisticated scheme to enrich some folk at the expense of others. Gordon Pinsent knew Mr Ammon and that relationship had driven him to commit murder and suicide. Paul Munnelly had also tried to take his own life, so it was not mere coincidence. Whilst he didn't know how the scam worked, and who the other key players were, he was convinced that Gordon and Paul weren't the only victims. If he could prove there was a conspiracy, Paul Munnelly might get justice after all.

* * * * * * *

Melvyn Bragg alighted from his shiny grey Maserati coupe and stepped back to admire it before shutting the driver's door and blipping the remote electronic central locking system on his key fob. In the months following his resignation from Munnelly and Sons, he'd set up his own company to market his skills and talents.

Thanks to the success of his marketing campaign for Munnelly and Sons, he'd achieved recognition which translated into more lucrative work and, the Maserati was his gift to himself for a job well done. From his early days in Melbourne, he'd dreamt of a day like this when he would take delivery of his own brand-new sports car.

Things were definitely on the up. He'd even begun a new relationship with an attractive Spanish girl, Camilla, who'd been enticed by the smell of success. Suddenly, Melvyn was cured of his homesickness and his life smelt of roses. For one acquainted with rejection, it was thrilling to discover prosperity and romance all at the same time.

He walked across the car park towards the entrance to his apartment in the trendy gated estate, and a wistful smile tugged at the corners of his mouth, recalling that his former employer had once lived in this very estate on the very same street. What an irony.

'Mr Bragg!' called out an unfamiliar male voice, bursting the tranquillity. 'Can I have a word with you, please?'

Melvyn spun around in the direction of the intrusion and saw a tall, black man, dressed simply in a navy-blue suit with a sky-blue open-neck shirt, running towards him from the slowly closing gates to the estate. Melvyn swore under his breath and kept on walking. The guy was probably one of the many advertising agents who bombarded him daily with all manner of propositions. This wasn't the first time that they'd located his residence and tried to ambush him with an 'offer he couldn't refuse'.

'Hello, Mr Bragg!' The man's voice sounded closer – a lot closer.

Melvyn increased his strides, regretting that he'd opted to park in the open rather than avail himself of the underground car park, where he had another allocated space. If he could get to the front door quickly enough, he stood a good chance of losing the guy. Once inside, he could alert the estate's security personnel about the intruder.

'Just a minute of your time Mr Bragg,' said the voice that was so close now that Melvyn could sense the man's hot breath on the nape of his neck.

Melvyn sighed and turned around, uttering a string of four-letter obscenities under his breath.

'What?' he asked out loud.

'I'm Sergeant Downey,' said the man, holding up a warrant card whilst simultaneously trying to catch his breath. 'Could you spare me a moment to answer a few questions?'

'About what?' asked Melvyn, maintaining the hostility in his tone as he noted the copper's name. Right now, his mind was on Camilla, who was waiting for him in the apartment. What did the cops want with him anyway? As far as he knew, he hadn't committed any prosecutable offence – well at least not in the U.K.

'Paul Munnelly,' answered Sergeant Downey.

'He owes me money, officer,' said Melvyn, opening the front door, 'and unless he's sent you with a cheque for the full sum, I have nothing to say.'

'I believe you heard about his accident,' persisted Downey.

'You mean his failed suicide bid,' clarified Melvyn, proceeding into the building with a snigger. 'Yeah, I heard – I'm glad he survived.'

'Yes,' observed Downey dryly. 'Saves you having to chase his estate for payment especially if he didn't leave a will.'

'Look, officer,' said Melvyn, with undisguised contempt, 'I have nothing to say about him that you don't already know.'

'Do you know an accountant named John Crane?' asked Downey, getting to the point.

'What if I do?' countered Melvyn.

'Have you ever worked for him?' asked Downey, putting one foot in the door jamb.

'Why are you asking?'

'Why are you being so evasive?'

'My relationship with John Crane is none of your business,' said Melvyn nastily. 'Now, unless you have a warrant to arrest me or search my residence, I suggest that you leave this estate before I have you escorted out – forcibly, if necessary.'

'From the records of the recruitment consultants that sourced you,' went on Downey, sounding undeterred, 'until recently, you were contracted to John Crane's accounting firm – at a time when you were also working for Munnelly and Sons. Did Crane recruit you to swindle Paul Munnelly?'

'Are you calling me a crook?' asked Melvyn striving to look shocked.

'Yes, I am,' answered Downey, going all the way into the building till he was standing eyeball to eyeball with the arrogant Australian, planting both hands on his hips.

'That's defamatory!' cried Melvyn stepping backwards dramatically. 'I can sue you for that, you know!'

'Not without a third-party present, you can't,' clarified Downey, 'and even if you did have a third-party present, I know enough about your life Down Under to justify my remarks.'

'That was a long time ago!' snapped Melvyn.

'Try telling that to all those folks you duped in that timeshare scam back in Sydney.'

'I have nothing to say to you,' said Melvyn, heading in indignation toward the lifts. 'From now on you can reserve what you have to say for my lawyers.'

'Lawyers will represent anyone, even scum like you,' muttered Downey, making no effort to follow him.

Melvyn ignored the remark, but once inside the safety of the lift he whipped out his mobile phone and waited until the lift halted at his floor before speed dialling John Crane. As the phone rang at the other end, Melvyn could only think about all the business and cash he stood to lose if his past became public knowledge.

*　*　*　*　*　*　*

John Crane read the letter presented by his visitor who was seated across the table from him. The tall, black Police officer in the plain, navy blue suit wore a serene smile, but Crane wasn't fooled. Vijay and Melvyn had already forewarned him, so he was on the alert. The letter Downey had handed over was from Paul Munnelly instructing Crane to hand over his client records to Downey. The permission granted by Paul meant that Crane didn't have to invoke the data protection rules relating to the security of personal data. However, there was an overriding factor in Crane's favour that he believed would frustrate the sergeant's investigation.

'Ordinarily, I would be glad to oblige,' said Crane, with an apologetic grin, 'but, as Mr Munnelly owes me a considerable sum of money in unpaid fees, I am within my rights to refuse his request. It's called a *right of lien*, officer.'

Downey nodded and his serene smile broadened. Before visiting Paul Munnelly to get his written authorisation, he'd considered the possibility of Crane claiming a right of lien to get out of his duty of compliance, and so double-checked the legal position.

'The Data Protection Act provides certain exceptions, I believe,' said Downey, 'and one of those relates to the investigation of a criminal offence.'

John Crane recalled the legal position. A criminal matter always trumped a civil one. He reluctantly slid the plastic wallet containing Munnelly's records across to Downey.

'Thank you,' said Downey sweetly, as he picked up the wallet and dunked it into his worn-out leather attaché case.

He wasn't sure about the value of the information contained within the accounts and knew that Crane wouldn't be so naïve as to hand over any self-incriminating evidence. The client account records wouldn't expose Crane, or anyone within his organisation, as being guilty of malpractice. However, Downey hoped that the records would give some indication as to when Paul Munnelly's affairs started to nosedive. Even if John Crane had given Munnelly risky financial advice, he hadn't forced Munnelly to act on it. Professional negligence was a civil offence and therefore not a matter for the police.

'I hope you find what you're looking for,' said Crane

forcing a grin.

'I always do,' answered Downey, with a disdainful stare.

'I can tell you don't like me,' observed Crane, leaning back on his swivel chair and, eyeing Downey through a squint.

'Very observant,' said Downey bluntly.

'Why?' asked Crane. 'Because of Paul Munnelly?'

Downey nodded. 'Yes, in part,' he answered, 'but mainly because of your liberal interpretation of your duty of care.'

'Everyone makes a bad investment every now and then,' said Crane with an indifferent shrug.

'Yes,' agreed Downey. 'But your duty is to protect your clients' interests by providing sound financial advice; instead, you exploit them and then cover your tracks.'

'Hmm,' said Crane, grinning slyly, 'that sounds very much like slander to me.'

'There's no third-party present,' said Downey looking around the office.

Crane stared at Downey placidly, but inside he was raging. From the moment Vijay Pandya had phoned to warn him about a potential visit from the police, John Crane had put his house in order. He had arranged for Munnelly's accounts to be tidied up and then prepared an edited copy just in case it was requested. For this reason, he wasn't surprised when the cop had phoned to say he was coming for Paul Munnelly's client records and that he had a letter of authorisation from Munnelly. However, despite his precautions, John Crane was starting to feel uneasy. Something in the officer's expression convinced Crane that this was only the beginning.

'Well, you've got what you came for,' said Crane with barely disguised restraint, 'and as I need to get back to the business of making money, I guess it's time for you to leave.'

'On the contrary,' said Downey, registering the flicker of fear in Crane's eyes, 'once I've read these neatly edited records which you've compiled for me, I'll be back.'

'What are you suggesting?' asked Crane, feigning offence.

'I'm not suggesting anything,' answered Downey. 'I'm merely clarifying how things will be from now on.'

'Are you trying to intimidate me, officer?' asked Crane, getting to his feet slowly.

'Now, why would I want to do that?' asked Downey, staring at Crane straight-faced.

'I don't know,' said Crane awkwardly, searching around with his eyes as if he'd lost something. 'Maybe you're doing this because you've got a personal interest in what happened to Munnelly and feel I'm somehow responsible.'

'You're innocent until proven guilty,' replied Downey, deriving internal satisfaction from seeing Crane squirm uncomfortably in his handmade suit. 'That's the law and as an officer of the law, it's my duty to uphold it.'

John Crane knew that the officer was toying with him, possibly even watching to see his reactions but he couldn't shroud his unease. He hadn't bargained for this. Why were the police so interested in a spineless gullible mechanic from Waldon Town? Munnelly wasn't the first person to attempt to end his life in desperation due to a personal financial crisis.

'I only made suggestions,' said John Crane quietly. 'I never forced him to do anything. He was free to seek a second opinion at any time.'

'But he went along with your advice,' pointed out Downey, 'and it brought him to the place of financial ruin.'

'Well, at worst that makes me negligent, not fraudulent,' answered Crane. 'So, I'm not about to guilt trip just to satisfy your hatred for financial advisers.'

'If you're feeling the heat and wish to unburden your soul,' said Downey, sensing that it was time to make his exit, 'just give me a call, okay.'

'If you *do* decide to return,' said John Crane, recognising the importance of having the final say, 'please note that I will have my lawyer present. I had hoped that we could deal with this amicably, but your hostility leaves me no choice.'

'My hostility?' asked Downey staring at him in awe.

'Yes, officer,' concurred Crane. 'Now please go. Your presence annoys me.'

'The feeling is mutual, Mr Crane,' said Downey, strolling

towards the door.

'Oh, by the way,' said Downey, pausing by the door, 'you can tell your employer, Mark Pierce aka Mr Ammon that I'm scrutinising his affairs and that I intend to unmask him and expose him to the light.'

'Mark Pierce, I know,' said Crane, meeting Downey's gaze steadily, 'but who is this Mr Ammon you're talking about?'

'Mark Pierce's alter ego,' answered Downey, studying Crane's face for tell-tale signs.

He registered the flicker in Crane's otherwise steady gaze and acknowledged its evidential value.

'I have absolutely no idea what you're talking about,' said Crane, sensing himself palpitate. 'Mr Pierce has nothing to do with your enquiries.'

'Says who?'

'The matter's beneath him,' said Crane, taking a deep breath to compose himself, 'and you drag him in at your peril.'

'Out of curiosity,' said Downey, 'do you happen to know where he is? I've been trying to contact him.'

'You've been warned,' answered Crane flatly.

'Yes, I have, but in case you see him tell him we need to have a chat,' murmured Downey, opening the door and exiting the office.

The battle line had been drawn.

17

Superintendent Steven Metcalfe had a reputation across Hertfordshire Constabulary as being the angriest police officer behind a desk. A bullet in the knee, fired from a gun in the hands of a teenager, whose sentence was lighter than a paper kite, had frustrated his ambition as a field officer. On returning to work, he'd been assigned a desk job in a station, in Welwyn Garden City which he loved to hate. If he'd been angry before the incident, being confined to a desk job amplified his bitterness, making him extremely volatile. All the officers under his command knew that Metcalfe's face always glowed bright crimson when he was on the fringe of exploding. Downey, who'd steeled himself for the eruption that he could sense was coming, was surprised when Metcalfe's rage appeared to dissipate through some invisible outlet. This was more worrying.

'What was going on in that thick head of yours?' asked Metcalfe, still in the grip of superhuman self-restraint.

Downey shrugged. His answer had to be measured so as not to upset the artificial calm. Humility was the only way.

'I guess I wasn't thinking, sir,' he said in a tone that was barely above a whisper.

'Is that all you've got to say?' asked Metcalfe, staring at him in disbelief.

Downey lowered his head and nodded. This wasn't the time for justification or mitigation. If he kept to his game plan, the storm would blow over in a matter of minutes.

'Do you know who John Crane's lawyer is?' asked Metcalfe, leaning close to Downey so that the odour of his recently consumed garlic and mayonnaise embellished beef sandwich assaulted Downey's nostrils.

Downey averted his face and shook his head.

'Have you ever heard of Betty Madison?' asked Metcalfe, drawing even closer, much to Downey's discomfort.

Downey nodded, but subtly drew back from the overpowering odour emanating from his superior officer's breath. Everyone in the Force knew Dame Betty Madison QC. Betty was a Queen's Counsel and one of the highest paid barristers in Inner Temple. She was also one of the most influential women in the country, having been knighted for her services to the development of criminal law.

'Betty Madison is the architect of that damning report on the quality of Hertfordshire Constabulary's investigations,' said Metcalfe, glowering at Downey's blank expression.

It was no secret that Metcalfe and every other senior officer in the constabulary hated her guts with a passion and dreamt of the day when they could book her for the most minor offence, and then interrogate her in the most abusive manner, to show her just what they thought of her report. For a couple of months after the release of the report, Metcalfe had hung up a photo of Betty on the dartboard and then proceeded to improve his accuracy by aiming darts at her forehead. Unsurprisingly, his game had improved.

'Betty was over here yesterday with her client,' said Metcalfe trembling, 'and could you believe that she demanded that I either charge her client or lay off him before she slaps us with a lawsuit! Can you imagine that, huh? She walked in here and threatened me, and it's all because of you!'

Downey had been forewarned by a colleague of the reason for Metcalfe's impromptu summons and, for the first time since his sick leave commenced, he was seriously bothered. He couldn't afford to attract any disciplinary action which could result in his instant dismissal whilst still on sick leave.

Having been assessed as unfit for active duty, how could

he explain his current actions? Metcalfe could use that as evidence of his fitness for active duty and even suggest that he'd been faking his mental health problems.

'I'm sorry, sir,' he said quietly. 'It was stupid.'

'Stupid is an understatement,' bellowed Metcalfe.

'Yes, sir,' said Downey unnecessarily.

'What right had you to go questioning John Crane anyway?' asked Metcalfe, appearing to calm down. 'You're off duty and, besides, it's not even your territory. According to Madison's written complaint which she's threatening to copy to the commissioner, you were insinuating that Crane had something to do with Paul Munnelly's attempted suicide. What's your business with that, huh? You're a rapid response officer. The Munnelly case is Hussain's territory.'

'I guess I got carried away after what happened and something inside me sort of snapped. I took it personally.'

'Is there a connection between Gordon Pinsent and Paul Munnelly?' asked Metcalfe, genuinely calming down.

'They were both Apple Seed partners and had recently invested in a failed investment scheme for the Waldon Valley Leisure Park, as part of a consortium.'

'So what?'

'They both lost large sums of money.'

'That happens every day.'

'They were both treated disproportionately by Eden Fruit Investments and excluded from an insurance policy that could have covered their losses.'

'That's professional negligence; it's not a crime.'

Downey was about to nod, but Metcalfe's comment sparked off a brainwave which made him freeze. It was a long shot, a very long shot, but one worth exploring.

'I learnt from Paul Munnelly that John Crane the CEO of Eden Fruit Investments was defrauding him and other select Apple Seed partners including Gordon Pinsent by issuing them contracts with technical terms that provided a loophole for over-charging them and issuing deceptive invoices.'

'So why didn't Munnelly and Pinsent seek independent

advice before signing up?'

'Because they were commercially naïve,' answered Downey, 'which is all the more reason why John Crane should have ensured that they were making informed decisions. He didn't because it suited his purpose.'

'This is all speculation.'

I believe that the disproportionate treatment Pinsent and Munnelly received in relation to the insurance policy was because of their naivety.'

'And what was the motive?'

'To ensure that in the event of anything going wrong with the project they would lose their investment and be forced to sell off their assets to cover their losses. John Crane planned to purchase these assets for peanuts and resell at a profit.'

'And you can prove this?'

'I am working on it. But there's more to the Eden Fruit's activities than meets the eye.'

'Such as?'

'Eden Fruit Investments put in a potentially fraudulent planning application for a brownfield site in Waldon Valley where the leisure park was to be constructed. There was a prior historical area assessment regarding that site indicating that there was a Roman historical site beneath the foundations of the old factory that had previously occupied it. But someone within the borough council failed to have it registered. I believe this was deliberate so that planning permission for the site would be granted.'

'And you know this because?'

'My wife was the chief planning officer turned whistle blower who discovered the anomaly.'

There was silence as Metcalfe fixed him in his glare.

'You've just admitted to being conflicted,' said Metcalfe.

Downey met the observation with silence.

'So, correct me if I'm wrong,' went on Metcalfe, 'your only interest in this is clearing your' wife's name, right?'

'No, sir,' mumbled Downey. 'Following Gordon Pinsent's suicide, I developed a fixation with suicide cases linked to personal financial crisis; that's how this all started. I wanted answers to help me understand my problem. But now I just want to see that Munnelly receives justice.'

'You've completely lost the plot, Downey,' said Metcalfe with a weary groan. 'You can't just go around investigating every suicide or attempted suicide in the hope of somehow finding a cure for your problems. And for clarity, it's not the duty of an off-duty Police officer to seek justice for those who were too naïve to take precautions. Investigating financial services fraud isn't our territory – you know that.'

Downey nodded but maintained subdued silence.

Metcalfe sighed again and thumped one brick size fist down onto his desk. He liked Downey even though he'd never come out to say it. In his book, Downey was a dependable officer who, until his unfortunate mental breakdown, had had a brilliant record. Metcalfe hated throwing the book at good officers but, with a cretin like Betty Madison breathing down his superiors' necks, the pressure would soon escalate the matter out of his grasp. How could he convey that to a man who was still psychologically unbalanced?

'Stay away from John Crane,' said Metcalfe quietly.

Downey nodded soberly, but inside he was grinning. The coast was clear.

'Is that all, sir?' he asked in his most subdued voice.

'For now,' grunted Metcalfe. 'It's still possible that Madison's complaint has gone all the way up to the commissioner and if it has…well, you understand where I'm coming from. I have no leverage at that level.'

'I understand that sir,' said Downey meekly, 'and I'm sorry for all the hassle.'

'Forget about it,' said Metcalfe waving one hand. 'I just don't want to see you end up like Baker. I can't afford to lose any more dependable men.'

'Baker?' asked Downey, his heartbeat racing. 'Joe Baker? What's wrong with him?'

'It's a sorry mess,' said Metcalfe, looking genuinely pained, 'but he only has himself to blame. How could someone be so daft as to screw up on the doorstep of retirement?'

'What's happened to him?' asked Downey urgently, fearing the worst.

'He's been officially dismissed for soliciting and accepting backhanders from offenders,' answered Metcalfe morosely.

* * * * * * *

Joe Baker's Ford Capri was parked in its usual pride of place on Joe's driveway but, as Downey drew closer, he noticed the large handwritten 'For Sale' notice pasted to the vehicle's rear window. Downey groaned inwardly and took a deep breath. Joe loved that car; it was his pride and joy. But it looked like he'd begun to offload his assets to raise capital.

As he pressed the doorbell, he wondered whether it was Joe's desire for a fresh start that had prompted the sale.

Joe answered the door in person and his buoyant grin confronted Downey's gloomy countenance.

'Downey!' he exclaimed, reaching forward exuberantly to seize both of Downey's forearms in his boxing glove-size hands and then dragging him into the hallway. 'Mate, am I glad to see you!'

Joe knew his friend well. Downey was a discerning fellow who could detect an act by merely measuring the tone of a voice or uncharacteristic body language, so Joe knew he had to be on his guard. He hated self-pity and didn't want Downey smothering him with a bucket-load of empathy; it was bad enough finishing off a brilliant career in such an abysmal fashion, and he didn't want emotion clouding the issue.

'Can I get you a beer?' asked Joe, steering Downey to the comfiest armchair in his small living room. 'I've got Budweiser on ice or, if you prefer cider, I've got some Bulmers lying around somewhere.'

'Cut it out, Joe,' said Downey, yanking his forearms free from Joe's grip. 'This isn't a social call.'

Downey's quiet but stern rebuke seemed to have the desired effect on Joe, who halted in the middle of the living room and began studying the pattern on his carpet.

Downey knew that Joe was hurting and that being the strong silent type, he was doing his best to shroud the pain he felt inside. Joe had been in the force a long time and he'd been looking forward to his retirement for a while. He'd even laid out his plans regarding the sort of wild retirement bash he was looking forward to, with lots of booze and girls young enough to be his daughters, but all that was on the back burner now. His dark secret had been thrust unceremoniously into the spotlight. Downey was sensitive to Joe's pain, but he was also angry at his friend for wrecking the dream.

'I screwed up,' said Joe quietly. 'Twenty-five years of dedication with less than a year to go, and I screwed up.'

'You did,' said Downey, refusing to patronise him. 'You screwed up badly, Joe, and I want to know why.'

'Greed,' said Joe flatly. 'I just got greedy, and I guess a little bit careless.'

'How long have you been on the take?' asked Downey, scrutinising Joe's features.

'A long time,' said Joe, sitting down on the sofa behind him. 'Longer than I care to recollect, but I got complacent.'

The lack of remorse in his voice was stunning, and Downey marvelled at the man's indifference. How long had he been taking bribes in exchange for getting offenders off the hook? Was he alone? Or was he part of an internal cartel that specialised in misplacing vital prosecution evidence? Then another thought occurred to him: what if *he* was also under suspicion? What if *he* was secretly being investigated as an accomplice? What if *his* movements were being watched?

'We've been partners for five years,' said Downey, unable to restrain his curiosity. 'Don't tell me you've been doing it that long.'

'Way before then,' answered Joe, examining his fingernails, 'but in those days I was more careful, especially around coppers like you.'

'I don't believe this,' said Downey pensively. 'But why?'

'Let's not go into all that now,' said Joe. 'The stuff's all out in the open and, to be honest with you, the only thing I regret about the whole mess is my carelessness.'

Downey stared at his ex-partner, searching for any signs that would indicate he was putting on an act, but worryingly he found none. For five years, he'd been riding shot gun with Joe Baker chasing after criminals, and all the while Joe had been lining his pockets. It was all the more baffling, because both men worked tonnes of overtime, typically putting in an 80-hour week and doubling their take-home pay.

'And what did Gillian think about it?' asked Downey. 'Or didn't you tell her?'

'Why do you think she left me?' asked Joe.

Gillian was Joe's ex-wife, who was well known for her stingy ways. She hated spending money and shied away from shopping malls, preferring instead to furnish her wardrobe from charity shops and street markets. As whacky as she was, Gillian was one of the most trustworthy people he knew. She'd once found a diamond bracelet in a ladies' toilet and had handed it in at her local police station. When valued, the bracelet was found to be worth over a hundred thousand pounds. The grateful owner sent Gillian a thousand pounds as a reward which, according to Joe, was buried away in her steep savings account.

'So, she didn't approve of your crooked ways.'

'She was naïve,' spat out Joe.

'So, was it worth it?' asked Downey as anger welled up on the inside. 'Was it worth chucking your career away at the doorstep of retirement? Did you really think you could get away with it?'

'If you had my addiction, you'd probably do the same,' muttered Joe, biting his nails.

'What sort of addiction?' asked Downey, suspecting that he already knew what it was.

'I love the occasional flutter,' said Joe unwaveringly.

'Flutter?' asked Downey ponderously. 'You mean you've got a gambling problem?'

Joe nodded heavily and grinned wryly. 'You'd never have

guessed, would you?'

Downey shook his head. He wouldn't have. 'How long?' he asked, trying to quell his anguish.

'Too long,' answered Joe gravely, 'and I don't need to tell you what an expensive habit it is when you're on a losing streak several times a week.' His eyes appeared to glaze over, but then quickly regain their focus. 'Grafting was the only way I could keep up the lifestyle without Gillian ever catching on.'

'So have you told her?'

Joe shook his head and chuckled. 'Forget it,' he said. 'You know her love affair with money; she hates seeing it thrown anywhere but a savings account. Besides, what does it matter now? She's moved on, thank God.'

'You should've told her, Joe,' said Downey softly. 'Gillian's a reasonable woman and I'm pretty sure she'd have recognised the need to hang around and help you out.'

'I don't want her back!' snapped Joe defiantly. 'I'm tired of fighting over money all the time; at least gambling gave me *some* control – I wasn't always losing, you know.'

Downey reached a conclusion. Joe was clearly in denial.

'It wasn't supposed to end this way,' said Joe becoming red-faced. 'I wasn't supposed to leave the force this way!'

'You should count your lucky stars,' said Downey unsympathetically, 'because if they'd found out about your gambling habit, you'd have been kicked out a long time ago.'

'Is that supposed to console me?'

'No,' said Downey determined to needle him till he snapped. 'I thought dating girls young enough to be your daughters was supposed to cover that angle, or is that just another addiction?'

Joe's countenance crumpled as he digested Downey's cruel jibe, and for a moment he looked like he was about to break down and bawl his eyes out.

'I think you better go, mate,' said Joe in a low but menacing tone, 'otherwise I'm likely to do something I'll regret.'

Downey recognised the ferocious intensity in Joe's eyes and realised that it wasn't wise to hang around any longer.

He'd clearly outstayed his welcome. He headed slowly for the front door, conscious of the fact that Joe's eyes were probably following him all the way, and as he twisted the door handle, he turned to look at his ex-partner. Joe was still seated on the settee, with his head now buried in the palms of his hands. Downey wanted to go over to him, but common sense prevailed, and he opened the front door, leaving his embattled friend in solitude. Right now, Joe needed to be alone.

*　*　*　*　*　*　*

Sally-Ann stared at her husband, who'd been walking around the living room aimlessly, and tried to figure out the root of his bizarre behaviour. He'd not said a word to her since he walked in earlier that afternoon, and all her enquiries had been brusquely rebuffed. She'd made tea, which he declined, and, for the first time in years, he'd snapped at her when she walked into his study without knocking. It was clear that something had happened to him that morning to trigger the negative behaviour, and she was dying to know what it was. Just when she was convinced that he was improving, he appeared to have relapsed. She didn't know how much more she could handle before she suffered a major breakdown of her own.

On his part, all that Downey could think about was Joe Baker's fall from grace, and his heart bled for his ex-partner. Joe was a good man. He wasn't a crook, but clearly he'd picked up a habit that had become an addiction. Just like anyone battling with drugs or alcohol, Joe was a victim and all victims needed help. All the way back from Joe's house, Downey had felt increasingly guilty about abandoning his friend in his hour of need and wished he'd stayed on to keep him company.

Joe wasn't the suicidal type, but he was vulnerable right now and, in that mode, an act of aggression wasn't out of the question. Though Downey had never divulged the information to anyone, in a fit of rage, Joe had once damaged the radio communication equipment in his patrol cruiser because it had malfunctioned during a high-speed pursuit. Joe had logged a report that the vehicle had been vandalised, whilst parked in a car park in Hatfield, and Downey had privately suggested that Joe seek anger management therapy. As far as he knew, Joe had not sought any sort of therapy and, for a man who was pushing retirement, there didn't seem to be any point. After all, what could therapy have done for him other than to make him a more restrained old age pensioner with arthritic hands and knees?

He was still pacing around the living room when his mobile phone rang and he initially ignored it, letting the call go to voicemail. However, when it rang a further two times, he decided to answer it and recognised Joe Baker's personal mobile number in the caller ID screen.

Downey briskly answered the call, but the caller sounded nothing like Joe Baker.

'Who's this?' asked Downey carefully.

'Mr Downey, it's Happy Larry,' answered the caller anxiously. 'You know who I am.'

Downey did. Happy Larry was Joe Baker's favourite snitch, a slippery character whose nickname was derived from his facial expression which was permanently buoyant due to a damaged nerve. He always looked like he was smiling even on the rare occasions when he was being convicted for some offence. Larry was a bookie who freelanced for several betting agents, when he wasn't inventing or executing some scam.

'Larry is everything okay?' asked Downey. 'Why are you using Joe's phone?'

'You've got to get over here!' said Larry, ignoring the question. 'Mr Baker's in trouble!'

'What sort of trouble?' asked Downey, his heart fluttering.

'Just get over here,' said Larry. 'I don't want to get involved, Mr Downey; that's why I'm calling you – I'm outside his house. Hurry!'

The line went dead, and Downey's heart almost flatlined. Happy Larry was usually a cool customer who never flew off the handle, so it had to be something pretty gruesome to make him get all jittery. What sort of trouble was Joe in? Why didn't

Larry want to get involved?

Downey headed for the front door, pausing to grab his tweed jacket off the cloak rack on the way out.

'Is everything okay?' asked Sally-Ann.

'I'll see you later,' he said distantly, before slamming the door shut behind him.

* * * * * * *

As the minicab pulled up outside Joe's driveway, Downey sighted Happy Larry standing beside Joe's Ford Capri. Downey quickly paid the driver and alighted without checking the actual amount, though from the driver's raised eyebrows he suspected he'd given a fair bit more. As Downey hurried over to the house, Happy Larry met him halfway, looking as pleasant as always, but Downey knew that all wasn't well. Why hadn't Joe made the phone call himself?

'Thanks for coming, Mr Downey,' said Happy Larry nervously. 'I didn't know who else to call and I didn't think Mr Baker would want me to call the police.'

'Where is he?' asked Downey, without slowing his pace.

'In the sitting room,' answered Larry morosely.

Downey found Joe on the floor of the sitting room lying on his back, and, as he dropped to his knees beside his ex-partner, he noticed that Joe's eyes were closed and that his complexion was extremely pale.

A quick examination revealed that Joe was unconscious and that his pulse was very faint, but there was no sign of bruising. From all the signs, it appeared that Joe had just had a heart attack, though it wasn't yet clear how serious it was, and Downey was too distraught to recall how to administer CPR. He quickly unbuttoned Joe's shirt and then dialled the emergency services on his mobile phone.

'It's all my fault, Mr Downey,' moaned Happy Larry, sounding more distressed than his expression indicated. 'If only I'd kept my big mouth shut!'

Ignoring him, Downey spoke hurriedly to the emergency

services, identifying himself and then asking for an ambulance and police assistance. He supplied the address and described Joe's condition as best as he could, and then listened as a paramedic issued instructions regarding the administration of CPR whilst waiting for the ambulance.

*　*　*　*　*　*　*

Downey sat staring blankly at Metcalfe who had not stopped talking about the whole sordid affair from the moment he'd arrived at the Downey residence. Downey, who wasn't taking in a word that Metcalfe was saying, couldn't erase the image of Joe lying unconscious on the living room floor. It had been almost a week since the incident, but for Downey it felt as if it had happened that morning.

He'd administered CPR in two stages, first pinching Joe's nose and blowing oxygen into his lungs, mouth to mouth, and when that elicited no reaction, had begun to pump his chest at over a hundred compressions a minute. He'd alternated between mouth to mouth and chest compressions, but his frustration grew as Joe remained unresponsive.

To their credit, the paramedics had arrived in record time and attended to Joe whilst Downey watched in silence. Before their arrival, Happy Larry had narrated how he'd turned up at Joe's residence to take Joe's bets for the week. Apparently, Larry had been placing bets on Joe's behalf for the past seven years, paying out when he won and commiserating with him when he lost. On this particular occasion, Joe had lost a four-figure sum, betting on horses at the Grand National. As usual, Larry had turned up to commiserate with him over the traditional brandy that Joe always provided and to take new bets on the Premiership football matches.

Upon hearing about the extent of his loss, Joe had become distressed and then without warning had clutched at his heart and collapsed backwards on the floor. All Larry could think of was protecting Joe's reputation so, rather than phone the emergency services, he'd called Downey, thinking that he was still on active duty. He'd found Downey's number on Joe's mobile. Downey had no reason to doubt Larry, who had never been associated with any form of violence.

Besides, Larry owed Joe for all the bets he placed with him, and in return Larry supplied Joe with tips about local criminal activities. As Larry was a valuable grass whose identity had to be protected, Downey had allowed him to depart before the first police car arrived.

The ride in the ambulance with Joe would forever remain indelibly imprinted upon the canvas of Downey's memory, as several times Joe had almost given up the ghost, but each time he somehow miraculously revived. The paramedics had placed Joe on life support because apparently when his head hit the floor, he'd suffered a massive brain haemorrhage. Gillian had been contacted and she consented for the life support machine to be switched off when it was made clear that Joe was clinically dead.

Joe Baker was pronounced dead within two hours of arrival at the Accident and Emergency ward, and Downey had wept continuously for several hours. Sally-Ann heard the news through a mutual acquaintance who was a male nurse at the hospital, and she'd rushed over to be with her husband.

Sally-Ann had sat silently next to him on a cold bench, allowing him to grieve, and when his energy to cry appeared to have dissipated, she'd gently steered him to the car park and driven him home. That night, Downey had lain on her chest, and slept like a baby, whilst she stayed awake and softly stroked his head. In the days that followed he never cried again, but neither did he speak with her or anyone else for that matter. On his part, Downey was struggling to come to terms with the fresh tragedy.

Now, as he sat in his living room facing Superintendent Metcalfe, Downey tried to reflect on the situation dispassionately. Joe's heart attack was the corollary of hard drinking and womanising. Joe was also getting on in age and, a couple of months before his death, had confided in Downey that he'd recently been prescribed medication for high blood pressure. But it wasn't unusual for a middle-aged man in a stressful job to be on medication for high blood pressure.

He'd most likely placed his large bet with Larry hoping that it would net him enough for a comfortable retirement and, for this reason, he'd taken the news of his loss more badly than he otherwise would have done. His addiction had killed him prematurely, but sudden death was always a real possibility when a proud man like Joe was stripped of his dignity.

What options did Joe have anyway? His marriage was on the rocks, he'd suffered loss of reputation, he'd been ostracised by his fellow police officers, and to crown it all he'd lost a lucrative means of fuelling his gambling addiction. What was there to live for? Dating girls young enough to be his daughters wasn't a panacea for emptiness; if anything, that lifestyle merely publicised the void. A disreputable discharge from the police force meant that all the usual lucrative career options were closed to him, such as working as a security consultant in a city corporation or as an investigator in one of the government's many investigative agencies.

Downey had confided in Metcalfe that Happy Larry had been present when Joe had the heart attack, and Metcalfe had gone ballistic. Even after Downey gave the details of Joe's gambling addiction, Metcalfe refused to be pacified. He had Happy Larry arrested, and then interrogated the betting agent till he was reduced to a whimpering, nervous wreck. Metcalfe's bone of contention was that Joe's life might have been saved if Larry had called for an ambulance sooner. Metcalfe was also mad at Downey for not calling the emergency services after getting Happy Larry's call. It was blame season and someone's head other than Metcalfe's, of course, had to roll.

'…if only you'd called the emergency services,' Metcalfe was saying, 'who knows?'

'Sir, I refuse to live with the guilt,' said Downey stoically. 'The paramedics said that there wasn't much that could have been done for Joe once he'd had that brain haemorrhage.'

Metcalfe immediately became defensive and averted his eyes from Downey's keen gaze.

'I didn't mean it like that,' he said hurriedly, as his eyes darted around the place in search of refuge. 'Joe's death was clearly a direct consequence of his financial loss, but one likes to think that more could've been done for him if I'd been informed about his problems earlier – well, at least before his suspension.'

'I only found out about his gambling on the day,' said Downey, determined not to accept the role of sacrificial lamb.

'Well, maybe you could've been a bit more observant...'

'I guess that goes for all of us,' remarked Downey coldly.

'Well, that's all history now,' said Metcalfe, realising the need to move on. 'Joe's dead and his funeral's in five days. As a favour to his widow, we've decided to quash his pending dismissal and pay her all his entitlements as if he'd died in active duty.'

'Very magnanimous,' muttered Downey, 'but isn't that medicine after death?'

Metcalfe considered the question and shrugged. Downey was probably right; instead of a dismissal, Joe could've been offered early retirement with all entitlements and maybe he wouldn't have tried to sort out his retirement through gambling – maybe.

'Look,' said Metcalfe, raising both hands imploringly, 'I only came over to offer my condolences, knowing how close you and Joe were.'

'Thanks,' said Downey curtly, 'and now if you don't mind, sir, I'd rather be alone.'

Metcalfe recognised his cue and rose from the armchair he'd been perching on. It was obvious that any progress Downey had made with the clinical psychologist had been wiped out by Joe Baker's death. Metcalfe could only imagine how traumatising the sight must've been for Downey, and his heart genuinely went out to him. However, right now, he felt duty-bound to take concrete steps to ensure that Downey's private investigations ground to a halt before he embarrassed the constabulary any further.

'I'm leaving,' said Metcalfe heavily, 'but before I go, I need your ID.'

Downey looked up at Metcalfe's serene expression which was at odds with the hard-edged tone that had issued the instruction, knowing that a refusal to comply was tantamount to disciplinary action. Reluctantly, he dipped one hand into his pocket, drew out the warrant card and handed it to the superintendent.

As if on cue, Sally-Ann appeared out of nowhere to escort a grave Metcalfe to the front door and as she opened it and stood aside for him to get by, he paused to study her countenance. She had visibly aged since he'd last seen her, but her smile was still warm.

'He doesn't mean to be rude,' she explained softly. 'It just comes out.'

Metcalfe nodded. 'I understand,' he said, 'but I'm more concerned about his recovery.'

'Don't be,' said Sally-Ann confidently. 'Downey's a fighter and what happened last week will only make him stronger.'

Metcalfe nodded again and walked towards his patrol cruiser, unwilling to challenge her optimism. He'd been in the force a long time and he'd very rarely seen a man as traumatised as Downey return to active duty in the field. At best, Metcalfe figured that Downey was only good for a desk job if he ever recovered and to that effect, he'd already put his recommendation in writing.

* * * * * * *

Sally-Ann stuffed a pair of cotton khakis into her cabin bag, and then tried to zip it up carefully so that the khakis didn't foul the zip. After several attempts, she succeeded in lifting the bag off the bed, instantly feeling its weight drag down her right arm, leaving an ache in her shoulder.

'Emily are you packed yet?' she called out.

'Not yet!' replied Emily from her room across the landing. 'I still can't figure out what to take along!'

'Just take all your jeans and trainers!' said Sally-Ann,

groaning inwardly. 'Lest you forget, we aren't going to a five-star hotel, young lady.'

'I'll try!' Emily replied wearily.

Sally-Ann sighed. They were only going away for a week, but Emily made it sound as if they were moving house. Following Superintendent Metcalfe's visit a fortnight ago, Sally-Ann had made up her mind to get some respite from her husband's mood swings and called a family friend who owned a farm in Wales. When she'd mentioned it to Downey, he had initially appeared indifferent until he discovered that Emily was going along too, then it dawned on him that he was going to be alone for the week. Emily was on half-term break, and hanging out on a farm was for her, far more attractive than putting up with her dad's grumpy countenance.

Sally-Ann decided to use the opportunity afforded by Emily's delay to touch-up her make-up. She was halfway through the process when Downey appeared in the doorway and leant against one of the posts.

'All set to go?' he asked, unable to think of anything more appropriate to say.

'I am,' said Sally-Ann, turning back to the mirror to finish off her make-up, 'but your daughter's going through one of those indecisive phases again. I think she takes that from your side of the family tree.'

'I've just checked the weather forecast,' said Downey morosely, 'and they reckon there's likely to be fog patches – maybe you should postpone the trip till tomorrow.'

'We're leaving this evening, Downey,' said Sally-Ann rigidly, 'even if Emily has to travel in her birthday suit!'

'I see,' said Downey, almost to himself. He knew that when her mind was made up nothing dissuaded her.

'Do you really?' she asked, abandoning her activity to spin around on the dressing table stool so that she could stare him in the eye. 'Do you really see what's going on here?'

'What do you mean, honey?' he asked jerkily. He wasn't ready for a showdown, and right now he was praying for some sort of divine intervention to arrest the eruption.

'Roger Downey,' said Sally-Ann, struggling to contain her confused emotions, 'I can't do this anymore, you hear? I can't. What gives you the right to subject this family to months of emotional trauma? Why must I always tiptoe around you on eggshells just because you refuse to move on?'

Downey opened his mouth to respond, but her raised hand silenced him.

'And before you call me insensitive and remind me of all the love and care you showered on me during my time of depression,' she went on, 'remember that I've never laid claim to being the strong one in this relationship – I always left that role to you but now you're quitting when I need you the most.'

Unable to bottle up her heaviness any longer, she let the tears gush out and buried her face in her hands to stem their flow. Downey remained where he was, staring at her dumbly, unable to move his limbs to respond to her need for comfort.

Her words had in a sense contributed to his paralysis. He'd never realised that she saw him as the strong one when, all the while, he'd seen her in that role.

As her hands parted, the sight of her smudged make-up gave her a comical look, but there was no laughter in Downey; only anger – anger at himself for being so insensitive and self-centred, anger at Gordon Pinsent and Joe Baker for choosing him as their audience. The problem was that he didn't know how to reverse the situation.

'I'm ready, mum!' called out Emily from her room. 'I'm taking my stuff out to the car!'

'All right, honey,' replied Sally-Ann in a deceptively cheerful tone. 'I'll be down in a minute!' She turned back to her mirror and began to diligently re-apply her make-up.

'I'm really sorry…,' began Downey.

'Don't be,' said Sally-Ann, surveying the results of her facial rectification, 'because I'm still travelling. I need a week away from you and all the baggage you're carrying and then maybe, just maybe, I might find the strength to continue to put up with your unreasonable behaviour.'

'I understand,' said Downey delicately.

'No, Downey,' said Sally-Ann, rising from the stool, '*you don't* understand, but maybe a week alone will give you time to reflect on the situation and decide the way forward.'

'What do you mean?' asked Downey, panicking slightly as his imagination ran wild.

'I'm giving you time to decide the future of this family,' said Sally-Ann, reaching for her bag, 'and in a week's time, Downey, I need you to tell me what the future holds for us.'

'I can tell you that now,' said Downey excitedly. 'I want us to be…'

'Tell me in a fortnight, when you've given it some more thought,' said Sally-Ann, cutting him short as she picked up her bag and brushed past him on her way out of the room.

Downey tried to reach out to touch her, but she shrugged his hand off her shoulder and hurried away down the corridor in the direction of the stairs.

'A fortnight?' asked Downey, almost in despair. 'I thought you said a week!'

'You need more time to sort yourself out,' said Sally-Ann, as she disappeared down the stairs. 'I'll be spending a week on the farm and another week with Elsie.'

Downey heard the front door slam shut seconds later, and the echo reverberated in his ears for at least five minutes after she'd gone, conferring an aura of finality.

18

Downey stared at his half-full pint of cider, trying to draw inspiration from the golden fluid as if it held the answers he was searching for, but it was an exercise in futility.

Downey desperately needed to know why he'd suffered such a protracted negative reaction to the sight of Gordon Pinsent's suicide; without an answer, his full recovery wasn't guaranteed. Sally-Ann was due back in a week's time, and she was expecting to see tangible signs of recovery. Though she hadn't mentioned it, what if she was planning to divorce him? A fresh wave of pressure engulfed him, and he began to panic. He couldn't afford to lose Sally-Ann.

Across the table, Simon Fay sat studying his friend's face over his pint of lager, trying to figure out what was going on in the man's mind. From the moment Downey phoned to invite him out for a drink, Simon knew that a crisis had arisen. In a way he was glad that Downey had made the overture, even if the motive ultimately proved to be selfish. Simon had headed for the rendezvous at the Horse and Canary Pub without bothering to tell Diane. Knowing his wife, she would've branded him a fool for responding to the summons of one who'd treated him so shoddily but, after all was said and done, this was his friend.

Simon had found Downey seated in his usual corner, sipping a cider, and was surprised at the warm hug he received before he'd even had a chance to sit down.

Downey had ordered a lager for him and then proceeded

to talk about everything from Manchester United Football Club to the latest scandal at No.10, until Simon casually interjected by asking after Sally-Ann.

Initially, Downey pretended not to hear the question. However, when Simon gently persisted, he just shook his head broke down, sobbing for at least five minutes, during which all Simon could do was pat his back reassuringly.

The reaction was completely out of character, and the first sign that all wasn't well in the Downey household, something that Simon had suspected for some time.

Downey recovered his composure after the initial breakdown and proceeded to recount all the events that had transpired since he'd last seen Simon at church, and by the end of it, the tears had begun to flow again. Guilt began to seep into Simon's mind, as he considered how petulant he'd been in relation to his friend. Downey was clearly messed-up and in need of better-quality specialist treatment than he was currently receiving, administered by someone who actually knew what they were doing.

On the home front, Simon didn't see any problem. He knew Sally-Ann was the reasonable sort who would eventually come round to seeing things Downey's way. All that was needed in the union was a little more effort on Downey's part to reignite the smouldering embers. Like any woman, Sally-Ann was yearning for a break in transmission, something out of the ordinary like a romantic weekend break in Venice. Then again, how could a man offer what he was incapable of delivering? The reality was that the weekend in Venice would be anything but romantic. It was an epic conundrum in desperate need of a solution.

'Have you considered a career change?' asked Simon.

'Quitting the force isn't an option,' said Downey rigidly. 'It's my life.'

'But what if you're not fit to return to active duty?' asked Simon, determined to make his friend see reason. 'What if you're retired on health grounds - then what?'

'I've not thought that far,' answered Downey grimly, 'and

that's my biggest fear. All I've ever wanted to be is a traffic cop, and for me being in the RPU is living the dream.'

Simon smiled at his friend's stubbornness. He could relate to the situation having been there himself a couple of years ago. For ten years, like his father and grandfather before him, Simon had been a firefighter. In his case there had been no career options, not because none existed in rural Lancashire where he grew up, but, because it was the only profession that fascinated him. His first ride in the cab of a fire engine had been an unforgettable experience; it paved the way for a career that had absorbed him for a decade of his life, until he'd panicked and failed to save a five-year-old girl from a raging fire that also claimed the lives of two other firefighters.

But that had been over ten years ago, and since then he'd retrained as a carpenter and turned his hand to the less risky business of designing and making furniture. These days, he had a medium-size factory that churned out bespoke fittings for discerning customers, earning ten times what he'd taken home as a firefighter. Looking back, he missed the thrill of sliding down a pole at short notice and leaping into a fire engine, though the financial rewards more than compensated for that lost pleasure.

He still recalled the face of the five-year-old girl as the bedroom ceiling collapsed on her whilst he watched in a daze. But after years of counselling, he no longer felt any guilt and had written it off as one of the hazards of a dangerous occupation. Downey had to do the same if he was ever going to make a full recovery.

'Have you considered travelling?' asked Simon, digging out a fresh option. 'A change of scenery can often accelerate a person's recovery rate, especially if you went somewhere adventurous like Australia.'

'What?' asked Downey. 'Are you a psychologist now?'

'No, but every carpenter knows you often have to travel far to find the very best wood.'

'Meaning?'

'Your future might lie elsewhere, but you'll never know

until you venture out.'

Downey pondered this point even though he felt no instant burning desire to pack it all in and emigrate. A protracted holiday abroad sounded sensible and might even help to bridge the yawning void in his marriage. Although realistically it was only a short-term solution. He could see them getting bored at some point and yearning for a return to the status quo in England.

'Thanks, but no thanks,' said Downey, smiling for the first time that afternoon.

'One tries,' said Simon with a mock sigh. He was glad the gloom was shifting.

'I've been a bit of a jerk, haven't I?' said Downey, raising his glass to imbibe the honey-coloured liquid within.

'That's an understatement,' answered Simon. 'For a more accurate analysis, ask Diane.'

They burst out laughing spontaneously and, for the first time in several months, Simon was happy to be in his friend's company. It felt just like old times.

'I bet you felt that her hatred for me was justified,' said Downey, lowering his glass.

'I must admit she almost persuaded me,' said Simon chuckling. 'That's Diane for you. I'll only start worrying about her when she starts liking you.'

'Now, that's a harrowing thought,' agreed Downey.

'Downey, you're hurting,' said Simon, seizing the opportunity to download his real concerns, 'and it has nothing to do with the Gordon Pinsent incident. I think it's something out of your past that's crept back into your life to haunt you.'

Downey digested Simon's analysis. He remembered one of his sessions with Kirsten when she'd tried to hypnotise him with a view to plunging into his childhood experiences and how he'd actively resisted her 'New Age' methodology.

However, as far as he knew, he hadn't suffered any trauma in the past that had any direct bearing on why he'd reacted so negatively to Gordon Pinsent's suicide.

'I can't think of anything,' he said softly.

'But there has to be a link,' said Simon anxiously. 'I remember watching a movie where this chap witnessed a murder and kept on having nightmares and stuff until ... hang on a minute, isn't that Basil?' His eyes latched on to the well-dressed elderly man who had just walked into the pub at a casual gait. 'Excuse me one moment. Hey! Basil!'

Downey followed the direction of Simon's gaze and saw the object of his attention; a silver-haired Caucasian man possibly in his mid-sixties, dressed impeccably in a tweed suit with white shirt and bow tie. The man was now staring in their direction, and his puzzled expression morphed into a pleasant surprise as he saw Simon.

'Simon!' he called out, half waving.

The man named Basil walked over jauntily to their table. As he arrived, Simon rose up and firmly shook his hand.

'Good to see you,' said Basil. 'Speaking on the phone isn't the same thing, is it?'

'Well, we're all very busy,' said Simon, 'but I must say it's a bit of a surprise seeing you out this way. Business?'

Basil shook his head. 'No, pleasure,' he said with a grin. 'I'm taking the missus out for the evening, and we just stopped by for a quick drink.' He nodded in the direction of an elegant-looking lady, in her late fifties, who was seated at the other end of the pub. 'How about you?'

'Just catching up with an old friend,' said Simon. 'Oh, where are my manners?' He turned to Downey with a flourish. 'Downey, meet Basil my financial adviser.'

As both men shook hands, Simon turned towards Basil. 'Roger Downey and I go way back but, as he's a police officer, I avoid him now in case he scares off my customers.'

They all laughed, but Downey knew there was a modicum of truth behind Simon Fay's words. Most of Simon's customers were millionaires with police records.

'I knew a Roger Downey,' said Basil, studying Downey's countenance strangely. 'This must be going back thirty years or so – he used to be a client. He was a Barbadian used car salesman who also ran a driving school. Are you related by any chance?'

'That was my dad,' said Downey excitedly.

'Roger!' said Basil, staring at him, obviously overcome with emotion. 'You probably don't remember me, but I knew you when you were very young – I also knew your mother, Gladys, quite well. After your father passed away, she appointed me as trustee of his estate for the first couple of years till she was able to get back on her feet. How is she, by the way?'

'She retired and moved to Devon,' answered Downey in a subdued voice.

He had not seen his mother in a while but stayed in touch with her by phone. They were effectively estranged as she did not approve of his marriage to Sally-Ann – a white woman. Because of all the discrimination she had faced, from patients and colleagues, whilst working as a nurse, she had refused to attend the wedding.

'It's been a while, but I'm so happy to see you,' said Basil, blinking back the tears.

'And it's a really small world,' chipped in Simon, staring from person to person in amazement.

'Yes, it is,' agreed Basil, fishing into his pocket and taking out a business card which he handed to Downey. 'Please, keep in touch.'

'I sure will,' promised Downey, taking the card, and transferring it to his breast pocket.

'Simon, I'll see you around,' said Basil, turning to leave.

'Cheers, Basil,' said Simon, sitting down again.

Downey watched the man as he sauntered back to his wife and felt a warm glow on the inside. Basil was a nice bloke and Downey was confident that he'd be seeing him again.

He took out Basil's business card to make a mental note of the address, before returning it to his pocket again.

'That's a man of integrity, if there ever was one,' said Simon, cutting into Downey's thoughts unceremoniously. 'Basil has kept me and quite a few other small businesses out of long-term debt with his thrifty approach. He's quite blunt but honest, and I respect that. I'd trust him with my life if I could put a price on it…'

A light bulb lit up, shattering Downey's inner darkness, and he smacked one fist noisily into the palm of the other hand interrupting Simon's flow. The name on the card! Basil Mead! Paul Munnelly's accountant!

'Is everything okay?' asked Simon, staring at his friend's stunned expression.

'Excuse me,' said Downey, getting up abruptly.

Simon watched, slightly bemused, as his friend hurried over to Basil Mead's table brushing past a female pub assistant and almost knocking the tray of drinks out of her hands.

Downey halted at Basil's table and dropped down onto the spare seat next to Mrs Mead, who was startled by the sudden intrusion. Basil, however, maintained his calm and his wise eyes benevolently appraised the younger man expectantly.

'You were Paul Munnelly's accountant, weren't you?' said Downey, taking out Basil's business card.

Basil paused before answering, and in that brief moment Downey registered the moisture that instantly clouded the man's eyes.

'Yes – I was,' said Basil, as his wife leant across to squeeze his hand reassuringly.

She was an elegant looking woman, not strikingly gorgeous but, with a patina of class – a throwback to an era when women went extra lengths to be meticulously groomed.

'Paul was like a son to my husband,' said Mrs Mead, smiling at Basil. 'In fact, he still is – where are my manners?' she turned to Downey with an apologetic smile. 'I'm Isabella, but my close friends call me Bella.'

'Roger Downey,' he said, shaking her proffered hand, 'but my mates just call me Downey.'

Downey turned to Basil. 'I've been trying to get an appointment with you but was told you were away on business – do you have a minute?'

Basil's countenance fell. 'I got back last night,' he said, 'but I never mix business and pleasure.'

'I understand,' said Downey gravely, 'but this is about what happened to Paul Munnelly.'

'The attempted suicide?'

'And the matters preceding it – in particular, the activities of John Crane and his associates.'

Basil perked up. 'Are you investigating that?'

Downey nodded. 'It's more of a private investigation.'

'Then I would be happy to assist in any way I can, but why the interest?'

Downey briefly narrated the incident with Gordon Pinsent and his reaction to what he had seen. He spoke about his struggles and the circumstances that led him to Paul Munnelly. He summarised Paul's tale of woe and clarified why he was determined to secure justice for him if possible. At the end of his narrative there were fresh tears in Basil's eyes.

'You've not forgotten,' said Basil, so quietly that Downey had to strain his ears to hear him, 'but then, how could you? After all, the subconscious is a bottomless repository.'

'Are you speaking to me?' asked Downey.

'Yes, I am,' said Basil. 'You've got a myriad of questions burning a hole in your mind, which is why you need to speak with Gladys.'

'Speak with my mother? Why?'

'Because she has all the answers.'

19

Gladys Downey's address was in a quiet prestigious cul-de-sac not far from the local train station in Torquay a seaside resort town in Devon, South West England. As Downey steered his Saab into the road, he slowed to a crawl that enabled him to read the house names as he drove by. There were no numbers on this road, only names, and the name of the house Downey was searching for was, *'Liberty'*.

Liberty was a detached cottage at the end of the cul-de-sac, set on a large plot with a neatly landscaped lawn bordering it on both sides. The building itself was unremarkable, but the ambience of the cul-de-sac elevated it. Downey pulled up at the start of the driveway and got out self-consciously. As he strolled up the driveway to the front door of Liberty, he felt himself becoming progressively light-headed. The mental heaviness that had been inundating his thought pattern over the past week since Sally-Ann's ultimatum was gradually evaporating, and Downey found this encouraging.

He rang the ornate doorbell and stood back from the front door so that he could be seen through the peep hole. Seconds later, the door opened, revealing a balding, middle-aged white man wearing a casual sports shirt and denims. For a moment they stood eyeing each other suspiciously. Downey glanced up at the plaque above the door to make sure that he was at the right address.

'Roger?'

Downey responded warily. 'Yes?'

'Roger Downey?'

Roger nodded slowly. 'I'm looking for Gladys Downey – my mother. I presume this is the right address.'

'Yes, it is.' The man thrust out a large hand. 'My name is Tony Robard.'

The handshake was flaccid and brief. As their hands parted, Downey noted the limp wrist and sweaty palm that accompanied Tony's handshake as classic signs of stress-related fatigue.

'It's so good to make your acquaintance at last,' said Tony. 'Please come in.'

Downey walked into the hallway and waited for his host to close the door and lead the way to the living room. The interior of the house was pleasant, with bright pastels gracing the walls and pale coloured drapes blending in nicely with the unassuming furnishings and décor.

It portrayed the home of a well-heeled retired couple whose children had flown the nest. Everything was neat but unremarkable and Downey instantly felt at home.

Sitting down on a floral-patterned chesterfield at Tony's invitation, Downey wondered who he was. Knowing his mother's prejudices, Tony had to either be her physician or physiotherapist. As Downey had phoned ahead, his mother had most likely mentioned that her son was visiting today.

'Can I get you some tea?'

Downey was about to decline, when he heard footsteps on the wooden floorboards and turned around to see his mother approaching. A smallish dark-skinned lady, with large brown eyes and short curly hair, she had barely aged.

'Roger,' she said softly.

He rose to his feet awkwardly unsure of what to do. Given their differences, he didn't know how she would react. But her open arms disarmed him, and they hugged warmly, clinging to each other as if their lives depended on it. As they came apart, she gestured to Tony with a fond smile.

'I'd like you to meet Tony Robard – my fiancée.'

Downey gawped and a thousand questions jostled for

prominence within the narrow confines of his mind. What was going on with his mother? He was tempted to ask what happened but knew she could read his mind.

'I grew up,' she said smiling placidly. 'Becoming a Christian does that to a person.'

He said nothing. It was such a seismic shift in perspective.

'I'm happy for you,' he mumbled when he recovered.

'Thank you. I was going to tell you when I felt the time was right.'

'Like after the wedding,' he quipped.

She chuckled and gestured for him to sit.

'I must be off,' said Tony stretching out his hand to Downey. ''I just came by to meet you – I'm sure we'll be seeing more of each other from now on.'

They shook hands again and Gladys went to see him off. When she returned, Downey's smile invited her to share the details and so the next half hour was devoted to her double love affair, firstly with Jesus and then Tony whom she met at an Alpha course run in a local church. It was one of those relationships that just happened, and she credited her revamped faith with helping her step over the racial divide and see people for who they were. Tony was a widower with a married daughter and a grandchild. They were planning a quiet wedding in a couple of months.

As the discussion progressed, she tearfully asked his forgiveness for how she had treated Sally-Ann and he had freely given it. The transformation in her was obvious and refreshing. He never thought he'd see this day and it was a bonus. He however kept silent about his marital challenges.

His mother mentioned that she had prepared lunch which he would ordinarily have skipped but, in Sally-Ann's absence, he'd been surviving on cereal twice a day and he was famished.

They had lunch outside on the patio overlooking her vast garden, and as they chomped their way through a delectable steak and kidney pie with assorted fresh vegetables, they chatted about the incident with Gordon Pinsent and how it had affected him. This was the first time his mother knew about it, but she listened with a sympathetic ear only interjecting to clarify the details.

After lunch, he helped her with the washing-up, and they returned to the living room for tea and her special recipe ginger cake. Downey waited for her to finish pouring out the tea and then mentioned his chance meeting with Basil Mead. Her countenance fell as he mentioned Basil's suggestion to speak with her, and she sighed heavily.

'Something told me that's why you are here,' she said smiling wistfully. 'I guess it was always a matter of when rather than if. There's never a right time in my experience.'

She appeared to be speaking in riddles, so he probed. 'I don't follow you mum. What are you talking about?'

'I am talking about the reason for your reaction to that poor man's suicide. You want to know why it affected you so badly, and that's why Mr Mead suggested you speak with me.'

Downey knew that his mother was a perceptive woman but even he was impressed. 'Yes, it's been bothering me.'

'What do you remember about your childhood before the age of seven?' she asked, staring at him intently.

Downey racked his brains, but nothing really came to mind. It was as if he had amnesia regarding any events that far back, which surprised him, even though he'd never really attempted to think back to his early years.

'It's a blank,' he confessed.

'You don't remember anything?'

Downey began to shake his head slowly, but then he recalled one detail she'd shared with him when he sought photographic evidence from his early childhood.

'Except that our house burnt down on my seventh birthday,' he said quickly. 'When I first met Sally-Ann, I remember asking you for copies of old family photos, and you saying they'd all been burnt in the fire that destroyed our house. You also said that Dad died in that fire.'

'But I never told you about the circumstances surrounding the fire, did I?'

Downey shook his head. He'd never asked, and she'd

never said.

His mother composed herself and slowly leant forward, alerting Downey to the fact that she had something momentous to say.

The expression on her face was a mixture of discomfort and sympathy that Downey found confusing. What could she say that hadn't been said before? What grand revelation did she have up her sleeve?

'Roger Downey,' she said, clearing her throat, 'I am not your biological mother.'

Downey stared at her for signs of mischief or mockery, but there were none. Her face betrayed nothing save for the confusing hybrid of emotions, and Downey became worried; seriously worried. The deafening sound of his thumping heartbeat paled into oblivion in comparison to the intensity of his laboured breathing.

'Can you run that by me again, please?' he asked croakily.

'I'm sorry, Roger,' she said blinking back the gathering tears. 'I was hoping that I would never have to do this. I have been living with this secret for so long.'

'Was I adopted?' asked Downey, trying to come to terms with the shocking broadcast.

'In a sense – yes,' said Gladys, 'but it's not that straightforward. You see, I was your father's younger sister, and being a spinster, I retained the family name.'

Downey absorbed this quietly. The woman he'd related to as his mother all these years was in fact not his real mother. She was his aunty. Even though everyone who saw them together remarked on their striking resemblance, she *wasn't* his mother. This was too much to swallow.

'I realise this must be quite confusing for you,' said Gladys awkwardly, 'but believe me it's the truth.'

She picked up a manilla folder that had been resting unobtrusively on a coffee table.

'Do you remember some years ago when you asked for a copy of your birth certificate?'

'Yes, it was when I applied to join the police force.'

'And do you remember the names of your parents as recorded on it?'

Downey nodded. 'Roger and Anita Downey,' he answered. 'But at the time you said you changed your first name to Gladys by deed poll after dad died in that fire.'

'But I never showed you a copy of the deed because I knew that you would never ask to see it; after all you had no reason to doubt me. There never was any deed poll because my birth name is Gladys.'

Gladys handed him the manilla folder, which Downey prised open and then began to study the documents within, one by one, starting off with her birth certificate and then working his way through her National Insurance records, records of social security benefits applied for and received, and her slim credit file. At the end of his inspection, he had to fight hard not to cry out in anguish from the pits of his stomach, as he confronted the truth.

Gladys Downey was not his biological mother. The most compelling evidence had been the adoption papers completed by Gladys and a social worker, which detailed the names of his real parents. The papers also gave the date of their deaths, which was the same date as his seventh birthday.

One of the documents contained a youthful photo of Gladys and a brief bio in which she described her career, daily routine, and hobbies. She stated in the application that she was the younger sister of the child's deceased father.

What Downey couldn't fathom was why she hadn't ever mentioned that he was adopted? Why had she pretended to be the widow of Roger Downey Senior? For years, she'd faithfully run Roger Downey Driving School and never bothered to change the business name, claiming that she was cherishing his father's memory, and all the while Downey believed that she was being a dutiful widow.

'But why?' he asked. 'What happened to my biological mother?' he prayed it was nothing sinister.

'It's a long story Roger,' she murmured, 'and to be honest I don't know where to start. I stepped into a situation I wasn't adequately equipped to handle which is why I approached your father's accountant Basil Mead to assist.'

'Does Basil know that you're not my biological mother?'

Gladys nodded. 'He had to know all the facts to advise me on the strategy for managing your father's affairs.'

'Is there a short version?'

Gladys stared across the living room at nothing in particular, 'Basil Mead was your father's accountant, until he was fired and had to transfer your father's investment portfolio to a financial investor named Stanley Budman. Your father believed that Basil wasn't taking enough risks with his portfolio and hence not making as much profit for him as he would have liked. He therefore took the view that Stanley Budman was a better bet.'

'Who was this Stanley Budman?'

'From what I learnt, Stanley Budman was a slick crook who specialised in fleecing people out of their savings or inheritance,' said Gladys, shaking her head gently. 'Basil knows more about his affairs. All I know is that he was a con artist and that your father was one of his victims.'

'And where is this Budman now?' asked Downey, feeling his blood boil.

'According to Basil he died in tax exile in Spain ten years ago,' replied Gladys. 'I don't know the exact circumstances surrounding his death.'

'Hmm, a cold trail,' murmured Downey. He sighed and lowered his head, sensing what was about to follow.

'Unfortunately, even if Budman had been found alive, I understand he was officially bankrupt.'

'So, my father killed himself, right?'

Gladys lowered her head and hesitated. 'That bit's unclear,' she said softly.

'I need to know!' snapped Downey, losing his cool and smashing one fist onto the armrest of the chesterfield, making Gladys jump involuntarily.

'The police report indicates that he set fire to the family residence,' said Gladys, recovering her composure, 'but not before he'd shot your mother in the head. According to the forensic report, he turned his gun on himself as the fire burnt down the house…'

'No!' roared Downey, collapsing back against his chair with his mind in turmoil. 'No! No! No! Why?'

In that moment of explosive enlightenment, memories began flooding back in and Downey shut his eyes as tightly as he could, trying to prevent them from invading his mind. He heard his voice in the background, screaming out in anguish like a wild cat in captivity, and he lashed out at the air, kicking out with both legs as if fighting some invisible foe. In his mind's eyes, he saw himself being transported to the day that he'd mentally blocked out of his memory – a day he would rather forget.

*   *   *   *   *   *   *

Thirty-Two Years Earlier

Roger Downey Junior was tinkering about with his Meccano set when he heard the crunch of tyres on the gravel driveway. Looking out of the window overlooking the front of the house, he saw the outline of his dad's Jaguar XJS rolling into view and raced over to the front door, gripped with excitement. Dad had hinted that they'd be moving to a new house soon, in a better neighbourhood. Roger was looking forward to the move because, as nice as their current house was, he was getting slightly bored with it. He opened the door, still gripped with euphoria, and ran out onto the front porch just in time to see dad alight from the low-slung sports car. Dad grinned as their eyes met, though his face looked weary. He'd never seen dad looking this tired before.

'Hello, son,' said his dad, shutting the driver's door, and then trudging to the house, as if his legs were too heavy to carry his weight. 'I hope you've left me some birthday cake.'

'Hi, Dad,' said Roger, waving to the stocky black man in the grey wide-lapel suit and black turtleneck who had forgotten to switch off his vehicle's headlights. 'Don't worry, we've not cut the cake yet so you're just in time. Oh, Dad, look your lights are still on.'

'You put them off, son,' said his dad, patting his head gently as he walked past.

Roger froze as he heard his dad's casual instruction. His dad never let anyone touch any of the switches in the car, because, as he'd said on many occasions, *'This car is very, very expensive.'*

Roger walked towards the glorious white beast with trepidation, wondering whether to ignore his father's instructions in case he touched the wrong switch and ruined the car. However, his legs were propelled by the fascination of having the beast all to himself and the fantasy of being like that action hero on TV who drove a similar car. This was without a doubt, the coolest car on the planet, and that made his dad the coolest dad on earth. Even Ms Marshall, his teacher, seemed to think his dad was cool. On one occasion he'd seen them driving around in the car together. Later that day, dad had given him a crisp pound note to buy his silence. As dad had said afterwards, mum didn't need to know their little secret.

Roger opened the heavy driver's door and pulled it towards him, releasing the aroma of leather from the cabin. His heart beat in anticipation of the thrill that lay ahead. Slipping behind the steering wheel, he gripped its thin rim and settled down comfortably on the driver's seat. He couldn't see much from where he was, but what he saw he liked. He closed his eyes and imagined himself in a TV show speeding down the motorway as baddies pursued him in a clapped-out Ford Cortina. He tried to reproduce the sound made by the car's twelve cylinders with his mouth, as the gap between him and the baddies widened. This was glorious – he couldn't wait to tell all his classmates about how he'd driven dad's Jag.

In the heat of the pursuit, he heard a gunshot, and the realistic nature of the sound startled him. As his eyes flew open, he remembered his original assignment and began to test all the stalks and switches one by one until he located the right one and turned the headlamps off.

He closed his eyes again and drifted off into his private dream world, where he was an action hero who didn't have to do his homework and go to bed before eight pm. He didn't know how long he'd been inside the car when he heard his dad's voice calling out for him.

Roger leapt out of the car and raced towards the house, forgetting to close the car's door. The last thing he wanted was six of the best, courtesy of his dad's belt, for disobeying his instruction regarding the car. Arriving in the hallway, the first thing Roger noticed was the smell of smoke. He wandered towards the staircase, and his eyes widened as he saw the plumes of smoke coming down from upstairs.

'Dad! Mum!' cried out Roger. 'There's fire in the house!'

Without thinking he ran upstairs, but as he reached the top landing the thick smoke drove him back almost suffocating him. Retreating downstairs, he covered his mouth and nose with one sleeve and headed towards the kitchen where he'd last seen his mum. Mum had been icing the cake and it was possible she knew nothing about the fire. He ran into the kitchen breathlessly and halted as he saw his mum lying face down on the floor.

'Mum!' he shrieked. 'Are you all right?'

His mum made no attempt to move, and he wondered whether she was badly hurt. Had she slipped and fallen? He walked over to her gingerly and knelt down next to her.

'Mum?' he said, reaching across to touch her shoulder. Then he saw the blood and froze. Her head was matted with blood from a wound beneath her black afro, but he couldn't tell how deep the wound was because of the thickness of her hair. He shook her shoulder gently at first, but when she didn't respond he began to shake her more frantically.

'Mum! Speak to me!' he cried out repeatedly, but she didn't utter a word.

In a panic, he got to his feet and ran out of the kitchen yelling 'Dad!' all the way to the living room, where he reckoned his dad was.

<hr>

Arriving in the living room, he saw his dad pacing around pouring out what looked like paraffin from a white plastic keg onto the curtains and carpets. What was dad doing? Didn't he know that paraffin was highly inflammable?

'Dad, there's a fire upstairs!' he cried, as smoke began to fill the room from the ceiling.

To his surprise, his dad ignored him and kept on dousing the furniture with paraffin until the place reeked of the stuff. Roger ran over to him and clutched at his arm but found himself flying backwards as his dad flung him away effortlessly. Fortunately, Roger landed on the sofa behind them and lay there to catch his breath as the fumes and smoke from above began to pour into the living room mixing, with the pungent paraffin.

He watched with tears streaming down his cheeks as his dad poured the remaining paraffin over a rolled-up newspaper and then set it ablaze with the aid of his gold-plated Dunhill lighter. His dad tossed the paper torch across the room, and it landed at the foot of one of the curtains covering a window overlooking the front of the house. The drapes immediately ignited, sending flames racing up the material to the ceiling and spreading to the other curtains.

As Roger struggled to his feet, feeling weaker by the second from the fumes that had penetrated his lungs, strangling his respiratory organs, he sighted the pistol lying on the floor next to the doorway leading to the hallway. Roger suspected the gun belonged to his dad. He recalled his dad boasting to some of his friends at the local pub about how he'd bought the gun from a Hungarian trucker for less than fifty pounds, but Roger had never actually seen it until today.

'I worked for all of this!' his dad roared suddenly, 'and nobody's going to take it away from me! Nobody!'

Roger fell to his knees and started crawling slowly towards the hallway choking with every movement, but intent on getting out of the house. Chunks of the ceiling above began to crumble and topple down, raining debris around him, and he flinched as some burning fragments hit him. He had to get to the door and get help.

He managed to reach the hallway and paused in the doorway to catch his breath. To his right, just outside his reach, lay the black pistol looking menacing, and Roger wondered if it had been used to hurt his mum. It looked dangerous and he had to get it out of the house. He reached for it, stretching as far as he could, till his fingers wrapped around the gun's butt.

'Put…that…down!' barked his dad, appearing beside him in a flash, spluttering as he spoke. 'Don't you… ever…touch that again!'

Roger felt his hand being crushed in his dad's larger one and winced in pain, unable to cry out, due to the overpowering fumes swirling round the room. He tried twisting his hand out of his dad's grip, still clutching the pistol, and felt his index finger slip around the trigger. He yanked his hand backwards instinctively as he rolled onto his back and found himself staring up into his dad's crazed eyes.

'Do it!' grunted his dad, staring at him crazily. 'Pull the trigger!'

Roger hesitated and, in that instant, felt the gun being prised from his grip. He watched helplessly as his dad got on his knees and pointed the gun at him. But then inexplicably his dad began to cry, with his shoulders heaving as his sobs racked his body.

'What am I doing?' his dad asked between sobs. 'What the hell am I doing?' Very slowly, he turned the barrel of the pistol away from Roger's head and aimed it instead at his own, just beneath the chin, with tears streaming down his cheeks.

'Happy birthday, Roger,' he whispered, and then pulled the trigger.

As Roger Downey Senior's body flopped forward on to the floor, the living room ceiling caved in and some of the furniture in the room above began to topple down. Roger steeled himself for the impact, when a strong pair of arms gripped him around the shoulders and began dragging him backwards.

'I've got one!' said a male voice above his head, as he drifted in and out of consciousness.

Seconds later, he was inhaling fresh air as the pair of arms gripping him dragged him out onto the driveway. Roger was gently placed down at a safe distance from the house and, as he drifted out of consciousness for the last time, all he could remember was the sight of the white Jaguar XJS and the uniformed policeman hovering over him.

*   *   *   *   *   *   *

'Take it easy son,' he heard Gladys say close to his ear. 'It's all right now.'

Downey opened his eyes and was surprised to find himself curled up on the ground in a ball sobbing uncontrollably. Gladys was kneeling beside him, embracing him gently. Downey couldn't recall how he'd ended up on the floor, but he had no desire to ever get up again. He felt safe here.

'Dad shot himself,' he said through trembling lips, 'and I watched him do it.'

'Yes, son, I know,' said Gladys soothingly, 'but it wasn't your fault. Your father was a sick man and he needed help.'

'I think he killed my mum – his wife,' said Downey shivering as he recalled the Gordon Pinsent episode.

'Yes, son,' said Gladys in the same caressing tone, 'but he was not in his right mind.'

Downey felt sick just recalling the gruesome incident. The sight of his father pointing the gun at him had been scary enough but turning it on himself had been worse. Why had he done it? Why had he quit?

'Why dad, why?' asked Downey quietly, as Gladys rocked him gently in her arms. 'Surely there was another way.'

'There's always another way, but sadly some, like your father – my brother, ignore it. He was always the ambitious one in our family, but he was also impatient.'

'You mean he was greedy.'

Gladys didn't respond, but her tears spoke volumes.

'Thank you,' whispered Downey.

'For what?'

'For protecting me.'

More tears flowed from her sad eyes and Downey sensed himself tearing up also.

'I should have shared this with you a long time ago, but I was afraid of how it might affect you.'

'You did the right thing mum.'

'Mum?'

'You will always be my mother.'

*　*　*　*　*　*　*

Two Days Later

Downey sat in Basil Mead's office staring morosely at the veteran accountant. Following his trip to Devon to see the woman, he now knew to be his aunty, he had phoned Basil to make an appointment.

Basil confirmed everything Gladys had shared with Downey and added some more details.

'All I know is that Stanley Budman was a con artist who ran all manner of Ponzi schemes across Europe,' said Basil, puffing intermittently on his pipe. 'He fled to the U.K when things got too hot for him on the continent. In those days, he targeted small and medium-sized businesses encouraging them to invest part of their profits in high risk, but high yield ventures and investments. It was all a con and many like your father lost money.'

'Initially, Budman paid your father fantastic returns on his original investments to encourage him to invest more, and your father took the plunge. Budman filed for bankruptcy three months later and your father and dozens of other gullible investors never recovered their money. 'Thanks to Budman, your father's business ran into trouble, and he had to borrow heavily to keep it afloat. Unfortunately, that meant having to mortgage the debt-free family house.'

'That should have been enough to get him out of the hole

he'd dug himself into.'

'Ordinarily, but he defaulted on the repayments, and in those days mortgage companies were less patient than they are now, so they foreclosed and gave him three weeks to vacate the property. Your father came to see me, and I tried to use what little influence I had to secure a bridging loan for him, but the mortgage company refused the offer.'

'Budman broke him,' said Downey bitterly.

'Your father was a strong man,' said Basil, 'but the combined effect of being defrauded of all his life savings and business profits, as well as the impending eviction notice, took its toll and I guess the strain was too much for him.'

'Well, thanks to you, it's a lot clearer now.'

'There's a man you should see,' said Basil, handing Downey a glass of brandy. 'He has most of the answers you are searching for regarding the Apple Seed Partnership.'

Downey accepted the drink, but deep within, he was sceptical. 'How come he knows so much?'

'He is a survivor.'

'A survivor of what?'

'You can ask him when you see him,' answered Basil, reaching for a notepad.

'What's his name?' asked Downey.

'Jay Cross,' replied Basil, as he wrote a name and address on the notepad's top sheet, ripped it off and passed it to Downey. 'That's not his real name, but the one he adopted at the start of his new life. Promise me you'll at least see him and hear what he has to say.'

Downey nodded heavily. 'I promise,' he said, studying the details on the notepaper.

20

Jay Cross lived on the outskirts of Leighton Buzzard in a cottage surrounded by trees and with a front garden overgrown with wild flowers. As Downey rang the doorbell, he had a sudden change of heart and felt like making a U- turn. However, he braved it and waited till the front door was opened by a tall, wiry, pale complexioned man with thinning white hair, clad in a casual patterned sweater over corduroys. There was something familiar about the man, though Downey could not recall ever meeting him.

'Sergeant Downey?' The man's smile was affable.

Downey nodded. Basil had obviously phoned ahead.

'Do come in,' said Jay Cross, stepping aside.

Downey walked into the entrance hall of the cottage noting the wooden beams in the ceiling, the stone walls and the wood flooring, trying to estimate the building's age. He heard the door slam behind him and turned to his host.

'This way,' said Jay, strolling past him towards the kitchen at the rear of the house, where there was a boiling pan on top of the stove. Jay waved to a chair at the dining table. 'I'll be with you in a minute,' he said, going over to the stove.

The stew's aroma was rich with diverse ingredients and, as he sat down at the circular oak dining table, Downey tried to guess what was in it. Jay lowered the stove's settings and joined him at the table with a bottle of puree and two mugs.

'Carrot juice?' asked Jay, plonking the bottle down on to the table and sliding one of the mugs across to Downey.

'Don't worry, it's organic. All my products are made from homegrown vegetables.'

Downey nodded and raised the mug expectantly, watching intently as Jay poured out the reddish juice till he'd brimmed the mug. Downey sipped the juice, and the creamy fluid left a tangy flavour in his mouth. It was delicious.

'Lovely,' he said, lowering the mug. 'What's brewing?'

'My secret recipe for turnip stew,' said Jay, tapping the side of his nose knowingly. 'You're welcome to join me.'

'No, thanks,' said Downey, waving aside the offer, 'I've just had breakfast. I presume you know why I'm here.'

'You want answers,' said Jay, pausing to sip his juice.

'So, what's so special about you?' asked Downey.

'Maybe it's because I'm self-sufficient,' said Jay musingly, 'or maybe it's because of my green credentials and low carbon footprint or maybe it's because I used to be one of the most highly paid financial consultants in the Square Mile.'

'I didn't come for financial advice.' Downey was struggling to join the dots.

'Yes, I know,' said Jay, glancing at the stove where his stew was gently simmering on low heat. 'Basil said you needed to access certain information in my possession – information I acquired as a partner in one of the largest investment firms in the City of London,'

'Information about Apple Seed?'

'Much more than that. It's information about a world hiding in plain sight,' answered Jay, unhurriedly. 'Information that's publicly available, but only privately decipherable.'

'I'm listening,' said Downey instinctively reaching for his notepad before remembering that he didn't have one.

'An excursion into the darkness I've witnessed only profits those who desire to see beyond their five senses.'

Jay's ominous tone put Downey on his guard, and he felt an urge to rise up and leave, but something more powerful kept him rooted to his seat – his curiosity.

Jay got up to check on his stew, giving Downey time to dwell on the cryptic nonsense he had just heard and wonder about the state of Jay's mental health. Jay lifted the lid of the pot to inspect the broth within, before partially resealing the pot and switching off the stove, signifying the stew was ready. Downey looked around the basic kitchen with the hard wooden furniture and *olde worlde* kitchen appliances and smiled at the quaintness of the environment.

Jay dished out a large serving of stew into one of his earthen bowls and then returned to the dining table.

'Are you sure you won't join me?' asked Jay, raising his eyebrows invitingly.

'No, thanks,' answered Downey, holding his ground. 'All I want are answers.'

'But what are the questions?' asked Jay, raising his spoon to his lips with a dreamy smile.

'This was clearly a mistake,' said Downey, rising to his feet in frustration.

'Be patient,' said Jay quietly, but authoritatively.

Downey paused and then slowly sat back down.

'It all starts with Mammon,' said Jay, lowering his spoon.

'Mammon?'

'Yes,' said Jay, with focused sobriety. 'Mammon is the sole reason why a discipleship programme like Apple Seed Partnership exists. Eden Fruit Investments is just one of many financial tools that promote Mammon and for over twenty years I was one of its most effective disciples.'

For the first time that morning, Jay Cross captured Downey's undivided attention.

* * * * * * *

'Mammon is a philosophy that governs this world's financial systems,' said Jay, between mouthfuls of soup. 'It's also a strategy for economic empowerment, enriching its disciples – capitalists, and impoverishing its subjects – consumers.'

Downey nodded even though it still seemed so abstract.

'Mammon's specific purpose is the exploitation of one of nature's inviolable principles – compound interest.'

'Compound interest?'

'Yes, this is the instrument at the heart of Mammon,' said Jay eruditely, 'and to ensure that it is effectively deployed, Mammon empowers select individuals. These are the gifted disciples who ensure that financial wealth remains in select hands. They achieve this by creating generations of financially dependent slaves. Are you following me?'

Downey nodded intently. 'Consumers are slaves to these capitalists.'

'Exactly,' answered Jay. 'However, no system can operate without controllers and that's where Mr M Ammon comes in. On the surface, he's no different from any other unscrupulous capitalist, fleecing investors, and entrepreneurs. But there's a spiritual dimension to what he does.'

'A spiritual dimension?'

'Yes, that's why he adopts the name Mr M Ammon – it's hiding in plain sight. There is no Mr M Ammon – it's a title.'

Downey recalled all his efforts to track down Mr Ammon and it began to make sense. It was a pseudonym.

'You know him.' It wasn't a question.

'Mr Ammon was my mentor and I worked with him for twenty years,' said Jay, uncomfortably. 'He's the reason I stay below radar these days, because I am one of the few people in the country outside his circle who can unmask him.'

'*Twenty years?*' asked Downey, mulling it over. 'Are you sure we are speaking about the same person?'

'Are you doubting me?'

'No, but one of Mr Ammon's victims, described him as being in his thirties,' answered Downey with a pensive frown. 'If he was your mentor, he should be older – a lot older.'

Jay took a deep breath, and his expression conveyed a sense of ominous occasion. 'That's because Mr M. Ammon is an *inherited* title.'

'Run that by me again,' said Downey, leaning forward.

'Mr M. Ammon is a title that has been held by different men over the years. Each generation produces a new candidate for the title, and during my twenty years in Eden

Fruit Investments I served with two different title holders. The previous title holder passes it on to his chosen successor as well as detailed data on all the protégés who have passed through the programme as part of succession planning.'

Downey's gaping mouth betrayed his thoughts. Emboldened by the revelation, he decided to probe further.

'My theory is that the present Mr M. Ammon is the alter ego for one Mark Pierce, the Chair of Eden Fruit Foundation,' said Downey, studying Jay's face for signs of capitulation.

Downey's remark was met with a wall of silence which confirmed what he already believed to be true. He persisted.

'So, I suppose the initial in the title stands for Mark.'

'It stands for Milcom.'

'Milcom Ammon.'

'Yes, Milcom is an ancient pagan god. It's all in plain sight. Now this is important, who else have you discussed the title M Ammon with?'

'I believe I've mentioned it to several Apple Seed partners including John Crane, the CEO of Eden Fruit Investments.'

'I know John,' said Jay softly. 'He was recruited just before I abdicated. He was assigned to ruin Basil's reputation.'

'Basil? But why?'

Jay exhaled heavily. 'They wanted to take over his portfolio of clients. People like Basil are a threat because they preach a contrary message to the philosophy of Mammon.'

The brief pause that followed felt like an eternity.

'So, Eden Fruit Investments is one of the corporate tools that Mammon uses to deploy its agenda on unwary local communities,' said Downey, trying to kickstart the discussion.

'Yes,' said Jay. 'Eden Fruit Investments is its British hub. On the surface, it operates as a discreet boutique investment bank working with assorted hedge funds to finance diverse public–private partnerships. But there's a lot more going on. In my opinion, the worst arm of Eden Fruit Investments is the one delivering leadership programmes like Apple Seed Project offering local partnerships to aspiring entrepreneurs. This arm provides coaching and mentoring along with free investment advice on new ventures. It also sources financing for those gullible souls who accept the bait and advises them on modernisation strategies. However, the funding scheme gives with one hand and claws back even more with both hands. The cyanide is always in the small print – hence the name Apple Seed.

'Because most Apple Seed partners operate through start-ups or small and medium sized enterprises, Eden Fruit Investments gets them to source their financial services from various Eden Fruit Investment subsidiaries like Sloane Bank, at rates that initially look attractive.'

'Sloane Bank is owned by Eden Fruit Investments?'

Jay nodded. 'It's the majority shareholder. As I was saying, the loan rates look attractive initially, but most start-ups buckle under the strain, crippled by credit facilities that bite hard in the medium to long term. Failing businesses are then bought cheaply, asset stripped, and their viable bits sold-off at a profit. And Eden Fruit Investments always targets their intellectual property, which is a portable, recyclable asset.'

'But isn't that how many big businesses operate?' observed Downey, looking unimpressed.

'Yes,' agreed Jay, 'but Eden Fruit Investments is the market leader in exploitation.'

Downey considered how Paul Munnelly had been lured away from the safety of a pragmatic strategy into the jaws of risky investments that crippled him.

'Have you heard of an American investor named Sam Truman?' he asked.

Jay nodded. 'He's a property developer who collaborates with Eden Fruit Investments to source funding from Wall Street on various UK construction projects, why?'

'He was part of a scheme that ruined a friend of mine,'

'That's what Mammon does,' said Jay reflectively, 'it sets the scene for a game in which the loser takes all the risks.' The loser is a player with a consumer's instincts who wishes to become a disciple. Apple Seed Partnership has accepted many losers over the years with a view to exploiting them. It seems your friend was never really a disciple – he was targeted.'

*   *   *   *   *   *   *

Downey knew some of what Jay Cross had been speaking about from reading the financial newspapers or browsing the internet, but the fact that Jay had been an integral part of such a widespread phenomenon and had played a pivotal role in its subversive strategies was truly eye-opening.

'Tell me more about how Apple Seed Partnership targets its victims,' said Downey, determined to maximise his visit.

'Simple, it promises something appealing but once the targets swallow the bait they're hooked. It's how casinos work, you win a bit and lose a lot.'

'It's a game?'

'That's it. Think about it from Mr Ammon's perspective. This is a game with few winners and multiple losers. Sadly, your friend was a loser. When you think you're a winner in this game, you're actually a loser because its rigged. The deck is stacked against you even before you roll the dice, and sadly its common knowledge. It doesn't matter how much you win – you'll ultimately lose something of greater value and when you open your eyes it's usually too late. Only then do you realise that in this game the loser takes all.'

'All the pain?'

'Absolutely. The loser is promised gain but takes the pain. For the unwitting, the bind is the prospect of greater wealth than they ever imagined and the flipside once they've swallowed the hook is the fear of falling back into poverty. Ever since Adam and Eve fell for the original deception, the same game has been performed in different guises. Apple Seed is just a modern interpretation, but the rules are the same. Have you ever played snakes and ladders?'

'Not really, but I know it's just another game where at the role of a dice you either win or lose.'

'Yes, but do you know the origin of the game?'

'Not really.'

———

'It's rooted in Eastern mysticism and is purportedly about morality with the snakes symbolizing evil and the ladders symbolizing virtue. But in actual fact, it accurately describes Mammon's agenda. At a roll of the dice, you either ascend or descend the board and the numbers on the dice determine your rate of ascent or descent.'

'It's hiding in plain sight,' muttered Downey.

'Yes, it's everywhere,' agreed Jay. 'As children, we played the game oblivious to the fact that we were dabbling in a realm of darkness where the losers suffer eternal pain and anguish. What unites the winners and losers is a shared ambition for the same destination. The difference is that the winners are more ruthless. They would rather commit murder than suicide. The losers on the other hand would rather commit suicide and that's what seals their fate. There is an emotional edge within the losers that makes them vulnerable. Each roll of the dice deepens their crisis.'

During the pregnant pause that followed, Downey thought about Gordon Pinsent and Paul Munnelly. Whatever void existed in their hearts before joining Apple Seed Partnership merely enlarged in tandem with their material gain. The more they acquired the emptier they became. Peace, contentment, security, and joy were replaced with distress, dissatisfaction, insecurity, and misery. It was clear to see how they were losers. Even when they thought they were winning they were losing.

'Thank you for the clarity,' murmured Downey. 'You've filled in the gaps and given me valuable building blocks.'

'Glad to have been of service,' said Jay with a slight bow. 'Contrary to what Eden Fruit Investment's glossy brochures may say, there is no shared pain. For capitalism to thrive there must be winners and losers.'

'Capitalism is no more than a bunch of ruthless people dividing up the world's wealth amongst themselves and then enslaving the rest of us,' growled Downey.

'You've got it in one,' said Jay. 'Mammon believes that failure is the key to success.'

'You've lost me,' confessed Downey.

'Simply put, the failure of its victims equals success.'

'You're talking about my bank manager there,' said Downey, with a brief chuckle.

'Not all bank managers,' said Jay, also chuckling, 'but I accept that there are some who operate according to that motto. Those that do, rely on one particular mechanism for achieving their objectives.'

'Compound interest?' ventured Downey.

'Exactly,' confirmed Jay. 'It is the single most potent tool for wealth maximisation and the most cost effective because it continues to earn money for your average capitalist long after the expiration of the contract it applies to. It's why the Third World remains the Third World.'

'It should be illegal.'

'It's not immoral from an existential perspective but is merely a perversion of the whole essence of wealth creation.'

'You're losing me again,' said Downey.

'At the beginning of creation, compound interest was put in place for the multiplication of the earth's resources,' said Jay, warming to his subject. 'Let me give you a simple example; take an apple tree. It carries branches loaded with apples, and each of those apples carries enough seeds for half a dozen trees. Plant those seeds and you increase your trees. That's the theory, but it was never supposed to impose burdens.'

'You could've fooled me,' Downey muttered.

'But it's true,' said Jay calmly, 'it was merely a wealth creation tool to ensure sufficiency upon the earth without the need to exploit the vulnerable. Today, however, it is embedded in all sorts of complex algorithms designed to create wealth for a handful. When you enter into a simple credit agreement, you begin to accrue interest which is punitively compounded every time you miss repayments. This is a perversion of compound interest.'

'I couldn't agree more,' said Downey nodding.

'You should take time to explore the world of City trading,' said Jay musingly. 'When I worked in the Square Mile, my business objective was simply to make the acquisition of money an end in itself rather than a means to an end. This is what Mammon preaches. It utilises a clever bunch of often unscrupulous people who work overtime to exploit loopholes within financial regulation.

'To show how much influence Mammon exerts in this sector, financial analysts even use the letter M on their graphs for what they call the 'double top pattern' or 'Classic M' when analysing share price movement. The M shape on their graphs indicates a steep slump in share prices after two periods of peak growth which usually results in a recession. It doesn't matter how many credit crunches or recessions hit a country; after all is said and done, Mammon is always back in business like nothing happened. Why do you think this is?'

'Because people are gullible?' asked Downey hesitantly.

'Yes, and also because they're greedy.'

'Mammon sounds so sinister,' said Downey slowly.

'That's because it is,' replied Jay. 'The most successful capitalists belong to secret societies created to protect their shared interests. They are an exclusive group who engage in dark rituals and pledge allegiance to their god – Mammon.'

'You mean like the Freemasons?' asked Downey.

'Yes and no,' replied Jay heaving a sigh. 'Every secret society has levels of secrecy which many of its members are oblivious to. I used to belong to a secret society which catered for an exclusive bunch of City traders, hedge fund managers, and investment bankers, guaranteeing us outstanding success regardless of the financial climate. Each year, the society's priest initiated a handful of ruthless but bright disciples into the inner caucus. I was part of an inner caucus.'

'And I suppose Mr Ammon was your society's priest,' said Downey, absorbing the information with rapt attention.

'Yes,' replied Jay, briefly lowering his gaze. 'Have you ever wondered why some smart, talented, and highly educated people dabble with secret societies and the occult?'

Downey shook his head slowly, ignoring the chill he felt.

'It's because their curiosity drives them to discover the limits of their abilities. And when they reach these limits, they have a burning desire to know what lies beyond them.'

Jay paused and his narrowed gaze swept past Downey's quizzical face.

Without prompt, he continued. 'One question propels them. Is there anything beyond the feasible limits of human intelligence? Because if there is then they have discovered their god and will willingly serve that god.'

'Mammon?'

Jay nodded musingly. 'However, to be accepted, that god must endorse their values and reinforce their beliefs. If that god fulfils that brief, they will owe it allegiance and promote its cause even if they don't fully understand what they're selling.' He heaved a sigh. 'This is how it is with Mammon. It reinforces the greed in men and promotes it as a virtue, but all the while its agenda is to steal, kill, and destroy anything and anyone that opposes its existence. Those who oppose it belong to a different camp and are targeted.'

'Targeted?'

'Yes, these are its adversaries – people like Basil Mead who eschew greed and covetousness. In Mammon's economy, moderation and contentment are the diseases of the timid and indolent – those who are averse to taking risks. In life there are certain decisions that have to be taken with a level of risk otherwise nothing happens. But Mammon perverts that truth by encouraging inordinate ambition for material gain.'

'You mentioned the occult.'

'That is Mammon's spiritual channel for empowering its agents. The accoutrements entice them, but the spiritual darkness enslaves them. On the outside they appear respectable but on the inside, there is a pervasive darkness that is revealed through their ruthlessness. Only those who take the oath of allegiance attain the highest heights.'

'And can anyone take the oath?'

Jay shook his head. 'No, only the chosen ones. People like me.' He fell into silence.

'What did the oath involve?'

Jay shook his head. Clearly there were things he was not

willing to divulge even though that life was now behind him.

Downey changed tact. 'As one of the chosen, you must've received loads of benefits.'

'Yes, but there is a trade-off. To get what you want from Mammon you lose something even more valuable – your soul. Mammon enslaves the souls of its disciples. There is a price to pay. Many who swear the oath and later try to quit the society don't survive.'

'But you got out,' said Downey. 'How did you manage it?'

'I put my trust in Jesus,' said Jay with a grin.

'You became a Christian?' asked Downey hesitantly.

Jay nodded and his smile became wistful. 'I was at my wits end and borderline suicidal, when a street preacher engaged me in a lengthy discussion about the condition of my soul.'

'And are you happier?'

'Happiness is circumstantial my friend, but I am joyful – that's eternal. Some days are better than others, but I have never lost my joy or the peace my faith gives.'

'Any regrets?'

'About the old life? None. I sold my assets and gave the proceeds to different charities. Less is more now.'

'So, what do you do for a living these days?'

'I'm a tree surgeon,' said Jay, brightening up. 'Whereas, I once contributed to society's denigration, I'm now rebuilding it through a valuable contribution to the environment.'

'And I also understand your name's changed.'

'Part cowardice and part strategy,' said Jay. 'It was my way of parting with the old life, but also the only way of remaining beneath radar. I'll go public one day when the time's right. For now, I'm undercover.'

'Don't worry,' said Downey, 'your secret's safe with me.'

21

As Downey steered the classic Saab onto the short driveway leading up to his residence, the sight of the mud-splattered BMW SUV outside the house made his heart leap within him. Sally-Ann was back! He hadn't expected to see the car for at least another four days or so and to see it now was cause for celebration. He hastily unbuckled his seatbelt and dashed out of the car without bothering to shut the door behind him.

He hurriedly inserted his key into the front door lock, before realising that it was the wrong one and then started fumbling about with the bunch of keys until he found the right one. The sight of Emily's backpack lying carelessly in the hallway would ordinarily have irritated him, but today it was heart-warming to behold. He walked briskly into the living room, and, seeing no one there, proceeded towards the kitchen and dining area, panting from the mild exertion. Emily was perched on a stool in the kitchen diner, fixing a sandwich with ham and cheese, and her expression was anything but welcoming, as she looked up at his broad grin.

'Oh, it's you, dad,' she muttered, refocusing on her chore. 'Mum's upstairs having a shower. Do you want a sandwich?'

'No,' said Downey, hurrying over to her, 'but I'm just so happy to see you!'

He crushed her in a one-sided embrace that elicited no reaction from her, and then hurried away to look for the love of his life. He stumbled as he ran up the stairs, but quickly grabbed hold of the banister to steady himself and continued upwards at the same pace. Walking into the master bedroom, he heard the sound of the shower pumping out jets of water and became even more excited, as he imagined what lay ahead. Rather than joining her in the shower, he chose to wait by the bathroom door rehearsing his lines. He would tell her how much he loved her and how sorry he was for all the pain he'd caused her. He would also assure her that he had discovered the root of his problem and now considered himself healed.

Then a wave of apprehension hit him. What if she was cold and unreceptive? What if she'd come back early to tell him she was thinking of a divorce? What if she'd confided in Emily about the marital problems? Could that explain Emily's indifferent attitude to him a moment ago? What if Sally-Ann had just come back for her stuff and was planning to move in with her mum? Was that why Emily hadn't bothered to unpack her bag? He was still wrestling with the negativity when the bathroom door opened without warning.

'Downey!' exclaimed Sally-Ann, pushing back her damp fringe from her face to get a better look at him.

Before he could respond, she treaded the short distance across the room to embrace him warmly, kissing his lips with an intensity that silenced his doubts.

'Honey, I missed you,' he said, pulling back slightly, so that he could stare into her eyes.

'I missed you too,' she said softly. 'I just couldn't stay with Elsie for the whole week when my heart was right here. I'm sorry for my outburst honey.'

'No, I'm the one who's sorry for all the stress I've caused you,' he said, kissing her again just to satisfy himself that it was really happening. 'A lot has happened since you've been gone, and I can't wait to tell you what I've found out.'

'It'll have to wait,' said Sally-Ann, slowly unbuttoning his shirt. 'Right now, I just want to make up for lost time.'

* * * * * * *

Downney stared at Sally-Ann, whose face was snugly resting against his chest, and bent to kiss her forehead eliciting a satisfied groan from her. She was actually smiling in her sleep, and he knew that it had more to do with how she felt on the inside. He'd spent an hour after their exciting reunion recounting all that had happened and, as he spoke, she'd cried. She'd then expressed her sympathy because he'd had to live so long with self-induced amnesia to block out the horror of his parents' tragic deaths. She'd suggested he go for specialised counselling, but he'd declined on the grounds that just knowing the truth was liberating enough and that he'd take each day as it came.

At one stage, Emily had come upstairs to see where everyone was, but finding their bedroom door locked and no response to her questions, she'd retreated to her room where she played loud music for an hour, taking advantage of her parents' preoccupation. He'd smiled as he heard the racket and made no move to rebuke her. He ordinarily couldn't stand loud heavy metal rock, but this afternoon it was music to his ears. All that mattered now was that he was on the road to recovery with his family all around him.

* * * * * * *

John Asker made Downey narrate the details of the discussion with Jay Cross twice, and each time he made notes. In all his years of teaching about Mammon, he'd never received such vivid proof of the accuracy of his theories, until that afternoon.

Downey cornered him earlier that Sunday, at the close of the second service, looking more exuberant than normal. Downey had begun babbling animatedly about Mammon's hidden agenda and its spiritual implications for the unwary, and this grabbed John's attention. However, when Downey's raised voice started attracting the attention of other congregants pouring out of the building, John had suggested that Downey see him at home for tea. Downey turned up earlier than the scheduled time, still bubbling with enthusiasm, and, having turned down Elsie's offer of tea, launched straight into the reason for his visit, speaking so rapidly that John had to make him repeat himself a couple of times.

Nothing that Downey shared was earth shattering. John had brooded over the financial sector's greed for years but like so many clergymen, he felt powerless. Society's approval of Mammon's ambition meant that people like him would always be in the minority. But Downey's revelations gave him renewed vigour to pick up the gauntlet once more.

'Most enlightening,' said the vicar, reaching for a chunky slice of the home-made fruit cake that Downey had politely rejected earlier. 'It confirms what I've always known but hearing it confirmed by such a reliable source is gratifying.'

'The bit that concerns me is the membership of secret societies by these disciples of Mammon.'

'But that's an open secret. Many of the world's most prominent financiers seek refuge in darkness. Greed will drive people to any lengths even at the expense of their souls.'

'So where does one draw the line with all this stuff?'

'For the average man on the street, it all comes down to moderation.'

'Moderation?'

'Living within our means and learning to be content.'

'Is this about the love of money again?'

'Yes. Part of the problem is people seeking money as an end in itself and doing whatever it takes to get it. The other part is people borrowing beyond what they can afford to repay to acquire stuff they don't need.'

'But surely there's a difference.'

'Is there? Those who pursue money as an end in itself often fall prey to those who exploit them, whilst those who borrow recklessly end up becoming servants to their creditors. Both become slaves to Mammon.'

'And what about those who have fallen on hard times but in an effort to survive end up in a similar place?'

'Unfortunately, compound interest makes no distinction

between its victims,' said John Asker with a sad smile. 'We all have to live with the choices we make.'

'That sounds so cold.'

'Yes,' agreed the vicar, 'but it's the truth. Moderation is the key to escaping Mammon's jaws and claws. I believe this is something I should start addressing on a wider platform.'

'Will anyone take you seriously?'

The vicar considered Downey's dubious expression and shrugged. 'It's a risk worth taking,' he said.

'Good luck with that,' said Downey. 'I doubt it'll be one of your more popular sermons.'

'Agreed, but it still needs to be addressed. I believe it was Charles Spurgeon who observed that contentment in all circumstances of life is not the natural tendency of man.'

'So why bother?'

John Asker pointed to an empty teacup on the tray between them. 'Look at that cup,' he said. 'What do you notice about it?'

Downey shrugged. 'It's empty,' he answered.

'That's right,' said the vicar. 'Anything I put in it will define it.' He then poured hot water from a kettle into it. 'So now we have a cup of hot water.'

He dropped a teabag into the cup, and they watched it disperse its contents until the water was transformed into a dark brown liquid.

'Did you notice what happened?' asked the vicar.

'You just made a cup of tea,' answered Downey resisting the temptation to mutter an even more sarcastic remark.

'Precisely! The cup now has a lower concentration of water molecules because of the tea leaves. Now imagine that that cup originally contained cooking oil and I poured water into it. What would happen?'

'I suppose you'll end up with an emulsion.'

'Exactly!'

Downey pondered the illustration for a moment and then he got it. 'So, it all depends on what's inside us.'

'That's right,' said the vicar exuberantly. 'The quality of our spiritual content is important. Light always resists darkness, just as oil and water don't mix.'

'Likewise, truth and lies.'

The vicar nodded. 'Mammon's lie is that one who doesn't achieve financial prosperity is a loser. And for those who adopt its false philosophy and hit hard times, it labels them failures and urges them to throw in the towel. However, the truth of the matter is that financial prosperity is not the A to Z of success. Sadly, for some people, the lie sounds more believable than the truth.'

Downey cast his mind back to the tragic circumstances surrounding his father's death.

'And how can a person in that predicament learn moderation?' he pondered. 'They're often at their wits end and all they can think about in that moment is their helplessness.'

'I'm not trivialising the very real trauma that many people face when confronted with the suggestion that jumping off the sinking ship of life is the way out,' answered the vicar. 'I am merely emphasising the importance of us dwelling on the truth long enough for it to provide us with a line of defence when the lies try to worm their way into our minds.'

'But those voices can be persuasive.'

'And so can the truth. But unless that truth cultivates in us a powerful conviction to embrace life, it means we unfortunately don't know it as well as we, or others around us, may think we do. Truth is like oil.'

'I can relate to that,' said Downey, nodding to himself. 'So, I guess the contents of my father's cup were too weak. Right?'

The vicar shrugged. 'Ours not to judge,' he replied softly, 'but with what you now know there's absolutely no reason why you should end up the same way.'

* * * * * * *

Downey spent the next fortnight working closely with Basil Mead on gathering evidence from a handful of former Apple Seed Partners who had chosen to testify against John Crane.

The evidence pouring in from these victims who had refused to cave in under the intimidation of legal action from Eden Fruit Investments was corroborative of the whistle blower's testimony. The whistle blower was John Crane's PA – a young lady whose conscience was ruptured by the blatant fraudulent practices being perpetuated by her boss.

The evidence gathered which included documentary records was pulled together into a report and Downey sought permission from Paul Munnelly to provide a detailed narrative about his experience – naming names, places, and events. The final report was sent by Basil Mead to the Financial Services Authority for determination. Even before the report landed on their desk, John Crane was sacked as CEO of Eden Fruit Investment, but with a very handsome payoff.

* * * * * * *

Downey withdrew some papers from a medium-sized box containing documents relating to his father that Gladys had sent him. He spread them out on the dining table and began to go through them one by one, sifting out anything that looked remotely interesting. In the background, he could hear the TV but barely looked at it.

He'd set himself a task to see if his father's documents contained anything worth keeping. But most contained little of substance, having been overtaken by events. As he came to the end of his sift, a small black diary caught his eye, and he isolated it. Flicking through its pages, he discovered that it contained the names and phone numbers of people who'd registered for driving lessons over thirty years ago.

He was in the process of closing the diary when something slipped out from between the pages and fluttered to the table. Reaching for it, he noted that it was a business card and as he picked it up, he instantly recognised the details. Apart from the phone number, it was a facsimile of the card Gordon Pinsent had had on him the day he shot himself.

M. Ammon

Venture Capitalist

Phone No: 01666-0666

As he studied the card's detail, his heart became heavy. The card confirmed his worst fears. His dad had been a disciple.

He was packing all the paperwork back into the box when the late morning news programme began on TV. As he finished his task, his ear picked up a familiar name – Nicole Matisse – being broadcast over the airwaves, and he quickly abandoned his task to join Sally-Ann in the kitchen diner where the TV was. He arrived just in time to see the last few seconds of the news report.

In the brief scene, the police had cordoned-off an art gallery in London's West End, and the news reporter was stating that the police claimed they had arrested a fifty-two-year-old woman in connection with the incident but had not yet charged her or anyone else. Downey recognised the art gallery. Some weeks ago, it had been the venue for his meeting with Nicole Matisse, but from the look of things it was now a crime scene. The news switched to coverage of the ongoing G20 conference, but his curiosity was aroused.

'What happened?' he asked, pecking Sally-Ann dutifully on the cheek as he sat down.

'The owner of that art gallery was stabbed to death by the wife of a man she was allegedly having an affair with,' said Sally-Ann absentmindedly.

'Oh no!' exclaimed Downey, rising in disbelief. 'Don't tell me she's dead!'

'That's what I just said,' said Sally-Ann glancing at him in surprise. 'Did you know her?'

Downey hesitated before slowly sitting down. He would've fibbed but his conscience berated him.

'I met her once in the course of an investigation,' he

replied. 'Her name was Nicole Matisse and it's so tragic.'

'It is,' she agreed, shaking her head in empathy, 'and she is so good looking too.'

'She *was*,' murmured Downey. 'What a waste.'

Sally Ann returned to her chores and Downey flicked to a different news channel where he could listen to the murder report in full. As he watched the broadcast Downey bit his lower lip recalling all Paul had shared with him about the deceased. In her bid to escape poverty, Nicole had played fast and loose with life but couldn't escape the ominous destiny that awaited Mammon's disciples. Reflecting on Paul's trip to Paris, he wondered whether she died intestate or had left a will, and if she had left a will, who her beneficiaries would be.

*　*　*　*　*　*　*

Paul Munnelly had been in exceptionally high spirits when Downey arrived at the ward, and had introduced Downey to his mother, Irene, who was on her way out with a tearful but joyful expression on her face. Downey guessed that she was probably just grateful that she wouldn't be burying two sons. After she'd departed, Downey informed Paul of all that he'd learnt since his previous visit, detailing his meetings with Basil Mead, and Jay Cross.

Throughout Downey's account, Paul had listened with rapt attention, not once interjecting, or disrupting, and at the end of it a slight frown had worked its way across his face.

'This is quite hard for me, officer,' he confessed, 'because I've never really believed in conspiracy theories.'

'But this one's true,' said Downey quietly. 'I guess by now you've heard what happened to Nicole.'

Paul nodded and his countenance dipped. 'I saw it on the news,' he answered, angling his head in the direction of the wall-mounted TV at the other end of his bed. 'Do you believe it's related to all this business about Mammon?'

'It's hard to say,' said Downey who had since learnt that the accused was Sam Truman's wife. 'I believe that it all comes down to the choices she made.'

Paul's pained expression gradually brightened, but he remained subdued. 'I guess I should be grateful my plans were frustrated,' he said, after a brief silent interval. 'Mum believes my life was spared, because God has a greater purpose for me and, somehow, I'm beginning to sense that.'

'I could use some help in that department,' said Downey, chuckling gently, 'because it seems I've come to the end of my quest, and now I don't know what else to do.'

'What about your job in the police force?'

'I don't know if it's what I want,' said Downey, fixing his eyes on two white doves that had perched on Paul's window sill. 'I'm still scheduled to attend more counselling sessions before I can be given the all-clear, but deep within I reckon I'm already healed.'

'So, what else would you like to do?'

Downey pondered for a moment. 'Depending on how I feel, I might decide to pack it in and join my friend's furniture making business,' he said. 'I just don't fancy returning to the job without Joe Baker as a partner.'

As if responding to his conundrum, one of the doves fluttered away from the sill, soaring upwards and out of view, but seconds later the vacated space was taken up by a larger dove that appeared to have just dropped out of the sky. Downey considered the seemingly innocuous activity and the more he analysed the sequence of events the more it became clear what course of action he had to take.

'What about you?' asked Downey averting his gaze back to Paul. 'Have you given any thought as to what life will be like after you're discharged? Life must go on, you know.'

Paul nodded. 'Yes, it must, officer,' he said, with a broadening grin, 'but I've got that angle all covered. I've taken my mum's advice and rented new business premises for Munnelly and Sons in a less pretentious business park. I've also spoken to Basil Mead this morning about his firm taking back our accounts and guess what – he's agreed. Basil is confident that John Crane and Melvyn Bragg will drop their lawsuits once they become aware of the FSA investigation into their activities, so it's looking good.'

'That's really good news,' said Downey uncomfortably. He didn't know how to clarify that the question actually related to the issue of what adjustments Paul proposed to make after he was discharged, bearing in mind his spinal injury.

'That's not the really good news,' said Paul excitedly. 'No, the really good news is that since last week I've regained some feeling in my feet and can now move my toes – look!' He pointed at his feet and Downey noticed the faint movement of the big toes.

'That's terrific!' exclaimed Downey in awe. 'So, you're not paralysed after all!'

'Well, its early days,' said Paul in a slightly more subdued voice, 'and there are still many more tests to run and a fair bit of physiotherapy, but it's looking a lot more positive.'

'Well, you hang in there, Paul,' said Downey, getting to his feet, 'and just remember that you've been granted a second chance, so don't make the same mistake twice.'

'From now on, its steady growth for me, officer,' said Paul. 'No more rapid expansion plans; I've learnt my lesson – thanks very much for caring, though.'

'You're very welcome,' said Downey, gently patting Paul's nearest hand.

He headed for the door but paused halfway and turned as he remembered something. He fished out the business card from his breast pocket and held it up for Paul to see.

'I found this amongst some of my late dad's documents,' said Downey, 'and the name on it caught my eye.'

Downey handed the card to Paul and watched intently as the young mechanic glanced at it and then flinched. He looked up at Downey with a troubled frown and nodded.

'Thanks,' said Downey, taking the card back from him. 'That's all I needed to know.'

EPILOGUE

The weather report had predicted high temperatures and clear skies but, from where he was sitting in the front passenger seat of the RPU Volvo estate, Downey figured that there had to be some kind of a mix-up. The grey clouds overhead and the temperature reading, at less than ten degrees Celsius, were opposite to what had been forecast.

Today was officially his first day back in Hertfordshire Constabulary Road Policing Unit, after a six-month hiatus, and Downey was glad to be back to general road policing duties, even if it was in the company of a new driver. At the wheel was a veteran driver named Tom Brubaker, who'd transferred over from Thames Valley and was reckoned by Superintendent Metcalfe to be as proficient as Joe. Tom was pleasant enough with a firm handshake and an infectious laugh, and they'd hit it off from the first introduction.

To ease him back in, Metcalfe had suggested that Downey only worked three-hour shifts for the first fortnight or so to see how he acclimatised before reviewing the situation. Tom had obviously been given some background to the situation because he was bending over backwards to make Downey feel at ease, something Downey was determined to put an end to. He found the treatment patronising.

As the Volvo rolled along on the slow lane, acting more as a visible deterrent than a bird of prey, Downey cast his mind back over the weeks building-up to his return to active duty.

After his visit to Paul Munnelly, he had called by to see

Amy McBride and her husband, sharing with them all that Jay Cross had told him as well as the details of his prior enquiries. His candour prompted Mr McBride to open up about their marital difficulties, triggered by his wife's lust for fame and fortune. He also confirmed that Amy had, also been a protégé of Mr Ammon, who had filled her head with a lot of nonsense.

At one point, Amy excused herself from the discussion, leaving the talking to her husband. Upon her return, her puffy eyes told their own story. Slightly more composed, whilst she staunchly refused to discuss her financial affairs, she hinted that she was toying with the idea of working in a less glamorous designing role with a large clothes retailer. She'd, however, betrayed her scepticism regarding Jay Cross's tale, making it clear that her more modest plans had more to do with rebuilding her home than giving up on her dream. Downey wasn't, therefore, surprised when, a month later, he heard that she'd walked out of her marriage on the eve of her brand relaunch.

Downey's decision to return to the RPU was largely influenced by the activity of the doves perching on the window sill of Paul Munnelly's ward. In the aftermath of that event, he had humbly returned to his counselling sessions and co-operated with Kirsten. He'd shared with her the details of the pivotal incident on his seventh birthday and the link between that and his negative reaction to Gordon Pinsent's suicide. Kirsten became more empathetic and used their remaining sessions to carry out a general assessment of his personality, which she then used to prepare a report for Metcalfe which gave Downey the all clear and recommended his reinstatement to active field duty.

'We're almost coming to the end of your shift,' remarked Tom. 'Would you like me to drive you home or do you fancy heading back to the station?'

'Let's go to the station,' answered Downey. 'I need to see Metcalfe about…'

Downey faltered as a huge metallic black Rolls Royce Phantom thundered past on the fast lane, sending smaller vehicles hurtling out of its fierce path, like people fleeing Godzilla. He instantly activated the VASCAR unit and digital video recording device to gather the evidence necessary for successful prosecution, and, as Tom pulled out from the slow lane to commence pursuit, it took Downey back to a similar episode six months before.

Tom activated the siren as he accelerated onto the fast lane in pursuit of the behemoth and Downey got on the airwave radio communications system to summon air support. The RPU Volvo was soon snapping at the Rolls Royce's heels, siren blaring and lights flashing. Realising that there was no way of outrunning the patrol car, the driver of the Phantom pulled over to the slow lane, and ultimately the hard shoulder, with the Volvo right behind it all the way.

According to the VASCAR unit, the Rolls had been doing an average speed of over ninety miles per hour, but Downey suspected that there had been peaks where the speed topped a hundred. The mobile unit manning the ANPR system had relayed that the vehicle belonged to an online executive car hire agency and hadn't been reported stolen. Downey alighted from the Volvo and strolled over to the Rolls.

A large Caucasian man in a chauffeur's livery got out of the Rolls and walked over to the other side of the car, meeting Downey almost adjacent to the rear door of the vehicle. The man's face was crimson, and he was perspiring profusely.

'I admit I was speeding, officer,' said the man tremulously, 'but my boss is running late for his flight.'

'That's no excuse, sir,' said Downey, taking out his charge book and scribbling down some details. 'Now, let's have a look at the evidence.'

Downey led the chauffeur to the Volvo and sat with him in the rear, making him watch a video of the pursuit recorded by the digital video recorder. The chauffeur accepted the evidence, and, after being issued with a form requiring him to produce his driving licence and other vehicle particulars to his local police station, he was allowed to go.

'Officer!'

Downey who was getting back into the patrol car, paused to look in the direction of the voice. It had come from a man whose head was poking out of the Rolls' rear window. With a sigh, he headed towards the car and paused near the open window. The passenger looked a few years younger than him, with fair hair and a tanned complexion, but his eyes were hidden behind trendy, dark sunglasses.

'Is there any way I can persuade you to let my chauffeur off with a caution?' asked the man smiling affably.

'No, sir,' said Downey, shaking his head slowly. 'Your chauffeur was doing in excess of ninety-five miles per hour and at that speed we usually recommend prosecution.'

'But he was only acting on my instructions.'

'As the driver he was responsible for obeying the law.'

'Don't be too hasty officer,' said the man doggedly, 'I'm sure we can come to an arrangement.'

'Are you trying to bribe a police officer, sir?'

'No, officer,' said the man, retreating; 'far from it. I was only seeking an amicable solution.'

'An amicable solution will be found in court sir.'

'I see,' the man, sounded resigned. 'Anyway, it was worth a try. Here's my card in case you have a change of heart.'

The man casually handed him a pasteboard business card and Downey jolted, as he recognised the details printed on it.

M. Ammon

Venture Capitalist

Cell Phone: 01 666.666

'Take off the glasses, sir,' said Downey harshly.

The man obliged with a charming grin, and, as the glasses came off, a pair of soft brown eyes fastened onto Downey's face with hypnotic intensity. As Downey stared at the eyes, a veil was slowly lifted, and he began to see the real creature lurking behind them. There was another personality there – one steeped in a darkness that chilled Downey's soul.

'Mr Ammon?' asked Downey ignoring his palpitations.

'In person,' said Mr Ammon elaborately, 'and you must be Sergeant Roger Downey.'

'Have we met?'

'No,' answered Mr Ammon gently, 'but I've had my eye on you for a while. Your father was an old acquaintance.'

His response riled Downey more than his smug grin.

'You never knew my father,' said Downey quietly, struggling to keep his tone in check.

'Oh, but I did,' said Mr Ammon chuckling gently. 'Despite his shortcomings he was one of my favourite protégés.'

Downey recalled Jay Cross's revelation about Mr Ammon but played along. 'I doubt that. You look younger than me and my father died a long time ago, when I was still a child.'

'You were seven years old I believe. But thanks for the compliment. I try to keep in shape and live a stress-free life.'

'Whilst tormenting those vulnerable enough to buy into your deception.'

'I don't follow you, Sergeant.'

Downey had a fleeting flashback of his grisly encounter with Gordon Pinsent.

'You peddle fantasies that appeal to the greedy and the morally weak, aiming to destroy them and their families.'

'Ah, childhood trauma,' Mr Ammon chuckled. 'You're still searching for answers about the tragedy that shaped you.'

'This isn't about my father; he made his choice.'

'And scarred you for life from the look of things.'

Downey ignored the taunt. 'I get why men like Gordon Pinsent attract your attention, but why target a simple blue-collar worker like Paul Munnelly?'

A whimsical grin danced across Mr Ammon's lips. 'I'll indulge you,' he said after a reflective pause. 'Paul's father was a thorn in my side. His business model conflicted with mine.'

Downey chewed on that. He recalled Paul mentioning Albert's business strategy which was built on honesty, humility and hardiness, and a light bulb went off in his head.

'You were targeting Albert's values – the three Hs!'

A shadow crossed Mr Ammon's face.

Downey chuckled. 'I bet his success hurt you.'

'Success?' sneered Mr Ammon. 'He was a small-minded fellow who snubbed my offer of investment.'

'And no doubt you never forget a slight.'

'It wasn't personal. It was just business.'

'Ah, yes. A business built on the three Es of exploitation, extortion, and egomania.'

'A business committed to wealth creation!'

Downey studied him for a moment. 'I know you don't believe that lie. You know what I think? I think you targeted Paul because his father was one of the wealthiest men you had ever met. Albert was content and immune to your enticements. You resented that and were determined to prevent Paul from preserving his father's legacy.'

'And I succeeded, didn't I?'

Downey found the conceit in his tone revolting.

'You almost destroyed him in the process.'

'Oh no, that was self-inflicted. I merely paved the way, just like I did with your father.'

Downey was about to react, but an enlightening thought prompted him along a different route.

'Don't worry Mark Pierce, I'm not my father.'

The startled look in Mr Ammon's eyes was palpable. Visibly shaken by the disclosure, he thrust the dark glasses back over his frenzied eyes and screamed at his chauffeur to drive on. Downey stepped back as the Rolls Royce pulled away from the hard shoulder, with scrabbling tyres, rapidly picking up speed as it re-joined the motorway.

Tom ran up to his side. 'Shouldn't we be going after them?' he asked breathlessly.

'No need,' said Downey with a crooked grin. 'He's got nowhere to hide now.'